SMEARED
LAVENDER

Wolf's Gliss

Smeared Lavender Wolf's Gliss is a work of fiction. Names, characters, places, and incidents are products of the author's imagination or are used fictitiously and are not to be construed as real. Any resemblance to actual events, locales, organizations, or persons, living or dead, is entirely coincidental.

All brand names and product names used in this book are trademarks, registered trademarks, or trade names of their representative holders. Natalie Rucando, Smeared Vampire, LLC., is not associated with any product or vendor in this book.

Smeared Lavender Wolf's Gliss. Copyright © 2025 by Natalie Rucando of Smeared Vampire, LLC. All rights reserved. Printed in the United States of America. No part of this book may be reproduced, distributed, or transmitted in any form or by any means, including photocopying, recording, or other electronic or mechanical means, including information storage and retrieval systems—except in the case of brief quotations embodied in critical articles or reviews—without permission in writing from its publisher, Smeared Vampire, LLC., except as permitted by U.S. copyright law.

For permission requests, contact Natalie Rucando at

smearedvampire.com

First Edition

ISBN 9798990869042 (print)
ISBN 9798990869059 (ebook)

the love of my characters grows each year

Smeared Lavender Wolf's Gliss

The second novel in the
Smeared Lavender series
by the writing brand

Smeared Vampire

RED SQUARE | 1

MOSCOW — 2014

With a gulp, Sergei finished a bottle of red wine and slammed his glass down. His jeans felt tighter—Where is she? He was waiting in the same suite in the Ararat Park Hotel where he first had Nexxa. His mobile buzzed; he looked away from the view of Moscow toward his phone. He lifted the suite's phone, called room service; a new bottle of wine was brought up.

    Another glass, two, thoughts of her fucking Mikhail in the back of his Jaguar on the way from the airport. Fireworks blasted off in the distance, belated New Year's celebrations. Neighboring towns had budget cuts and delays, so people celebrated way into the end of January this year. The news, his restaurant, even being Carlos Finch on Bloomberg—all of it meant nothing. None of it could change his new normal, his unchanged state of being. Nexxa.

Nexxa wore her Wolford thigh highs under her leggings on the plane from Rome. She imagined slipping off her leggings in the back of the Jaguar, freshening up her private parts with a baby wipe. Mikhail was watching the heavy traffic weaving in and out, catching a rearview mirror glimpse. No, she kept her leggings on, feeling sweat, a tingle or two of excitement between her thighs. In his trying English, Mikhail offered to walk her in—have a drink in the bar and bring her to Sergei after. Nexxa smiled as she shut the car door. No way.

He practically leapt to her. Nexxa felt his enthusiasm. She released her luggage; he pulled it along for her. "This way, I will take you to Mr. Sergei," he told her. He handed Nexxa the room key; she thanked him, offering a tip which he waved off since Sergei had already taken care of it. Nexxa opened the door. Sergei was stretched across the bed half asleep.

Nexxa removed her leggings, pulled her strappy tank off. She dashed to the bathroom, brushed her teeth. She contemplated washing between her thighs.

"*Nexxa.*" Sergei opened his eyes.

Nexxa turned off the bathroom light and opened the door. Sergei stood before her and pulled her into him and onto the bed. One arm pushed her back as he kissed her neck, tore away her bra, his mouth sucking a breast. With an extra-strong core, courtesy of her Pilates, Nexxa found her way atop Sergei. He reached out; one hand ran along a sheer black thigh high, and the other ran along a thigh high with a lace print. His smirk was fuckable. Nexxa ran a spread hand down her abdomen, pulling at her crotchless Le Mystere panties. Sergei leaned into her labia. "Mmm, my Nexxa." Nexxa held the back of his head between her thighs. When his tongue touched her, she forgot whether she felt dirty. He licked away the past few months. Her hand on his forehead, she was strong enough to push him back, but his lips had a hard time letting go. Sergei's penis smelled of his cologne, never disappointing. Sergei slurred. Nexxa was more turned on. He wasn't any weaker, though, practically throwing her down, mounting her—Nexxa's thighs were spread.

Nexxa parted the curtains; the outside was bleak, which lent happiness to her *Smeared* soul. She examined the landscape before her: bits of red, some slow-paced clouds, and some passersby. She carried with her pieces of her past: of Mr. Albert, her mentor who had encouraged her to believe in the white glow, of Iliada, her sister who was growing into a mature woman studying with Flash, their Gargowl, and something from Rome. Turning back, she looked upon a Russian. Nexxa had it all. If she wanted to go forward, she could, or she could go back.

Sergei awoke; he always looked ready. Moscow always looked ready. Nexxa could smell him, and she eyed him, knowing that she could smell him from countries away at this point. Sergei could smell her too. She was always under his nose, his "upper lip," as his babushka would explain to Sergei when he was a child complaining of strange smells… This was a wanted scent.

Nexxa kissed Sergei on his forehead as she walked by to the bathroom. In the shower, she thought about the extra bag she had brought with her. Catching a glimpse of herself in the mirror through the shower glass, she hoped the steam would soon prevent her view. Why did it seem hard to look at herself in the mirror? She knew why. She still had the money Quinn had left for her back in New York. She contemplated giving it to Iliada or mailing it back to Quinn, but the time had slipped away. There was so much she needed to figure out. The money was just one more task. She also had her ex-husband's ashes in a bag in their hotel suite. They were fresh; his death was still so new to her. Nexxa wiped the mirror with a towel, and seeing herself, she let out a silent scream.

  Sergei showered. While dressing, pulling on his shirt, he made a call speaking in Croatian. Nexxa knew he was speaking to Hoolihane since he had said "Hooli" a few times, but she would have known from the dialogue had he not spoken the name. Why was he speaking in Croatian? Did it mean anything? She understood he referred to a building then to something that should have been his or will be his. As he ended his call, Sergei motioned for Nexxa to come to him. Nexxa removed the clip she had holding her hair up. Moving into his grasp, she closed her eyes. He might have felt better than he did last night. He told her their plans for the day.

Saint Basil's Cathedral was surreal with its nine domes each shaped like the flame of a bonfire. Nexxa removed her Saint Laurent sunglasses. Standing in the Red Square, she understood the origin of the red: something beautiful but also associated with the communist movement, so something wicked. Nexxa spun around as Sergei spoke to her. Her eyes moved from a group of tourists to some *politsiya* on patrol and back to the adjacent department store. There were too many people to take count of, keep watch over. At least on a fundamental level. Sergei grasped Nexxa's hand. She looked at him through his black sunglasses. "Hey, relax," Sergei spoke softly. "You're with me."

Nexxa sighed. "I know, it's just hard."

"C'mon, let's take your picture."

Nexxa checked her photo on Sergei's phone. She approved, thinking her hair looked okay. Sergei insisted she looked gorgeous. The cold hit Nexxa, and she moved back into Sergei. He suggested they go for lunch.

Inside the shopping center, GUM, Nexxa took notice of the sparse patrons, the pink and white cherry blossom trees about the first floor, and an abundance of sunlight from the skylight ceiling. They were seated at the Abrau-Durso Champagne Bar. Sergei ordered, and Nexxa remained silent. When Sergei's phone buzzed, she was glad for the interruption. Only he chose not to answer the call. Nexxa drank her first glass, motioning for Sergei to pour her more.

"Nexxa," Sergei began as he reached for the bottle, "you seem like something is wrong." He refilled her glass.

"Oh." Nexxa took her glass from Sergei. "I'm happy."

Sergei took a sip of his champagne, placed his glass down, leaned back, and stretched his arm across the back of the sofa. "Are you having second thoughts?"

"No." Nexxa took a sip. "It's not like that." She touched her lips. Her mind went to the bag with Kilmer's urn which was resting beside her suitcase in their hotel suite.

"I've explained to you." Sergei sat up. "You're here with

me now," he said as he waved his hands around. In the same breath, he summoned the waitress over.

Nexxa observed how the waitress responded to Sergei. Overly eager.

Sergei ordered a Scotch and looked to Nexxa. "Another?" Nexxa nodded. The waitress brought a second bottle of champagne, Sergei's Scotch.

Nexxa realized that the first stage, initial taste, had passed. Of champagne—not Sergei, he still tasted great. Now it was the next stage: keep drinking to keep your buzz. Nexxa adjusted her hair behind her shoulder, massaging her neck. Sergei leaned in, and his lips took hold of her neck. Nexxa succumbed, her eyes closing, and she grasped Sergei's hand upon her thigh. The waitress approached their table. Nexxa opened her eyes. Seeing the waitress up close, she felt foolish. She was kind-looking, but there was no way Sergei had been flirting with her. Sergei lifted his empty glass, the waitress nodded, and he raised his phone, checking it.

Nexxa reached for Sergei's hand as he placed his phone down. She wanted to confess to him—the decadent champagne wished to speak. She wanted to tell him what had transpired in Rome. The man in the gray hooded cloak.

"So, in Rome." Nexxa began running a finger along his palm.

"Rome." Sergei reached for his second Scotch, taking a sip.

"Yeah." Nexxa looked to Sergei. "So…"

Sergei placed his drink down, moved his hand over his mouth and jaw, stretching his arm on the back of the sofa. He couldn't have been more confident.

"Thank you for taking care of everything. It meant a lot to

have my sister come with me."

"I'm happy that she went with you. You should bring her here for a visit."

Again with the waitress. Nexxa spotted her and another waitress by the hostess stand, giggling before looking at Sergei. Sergei poured Nexxa the last of the bottle, and he asked if she wanted more. Nexxa shook her head, indicating she didn't want more, as she took a final taste.

Sergei requested the check, and Nexxa stood and lifted her purse. Sergei cocked his head. "Bathroom," she told him. She hurried past the waitresses after they pointed in the direction of the ladies' room. Nexxa was quick. She smiled while walking back to Sergei; she liked the look he had had when she stood abruptly.

Sergei was standing, his back toward her. Blonde hair moved about in front of his body. A loud Russian voice enveloped them. Of course, why wouldn't it? Rochelle was there. Then a squeal defined the moment. A man approached Rochelle, and it was apparent she was introducing him to Sergei. Same coffin-shaped nails and tacky hair extensions. Sergei turned slightly; he grasped Nexxa's abdomen as if he had eyes on her as she approached him from behind. Rochelle was awkward, happy, and loud at the same time. She went in for a hug—Sergei, then Nexxa. Rochelle walked away practically attached like a Command Hanging Strip to her new beau, and Nexxa watched as Sergei grasped his forehead. Was the new boyfriend's name tattooed on her abdomen on the side opposite of Sergei's name?

Sergei pushed his phone into his pocket. He sighed, "Let's

get out of here."

Nexxa took a breath. "Yeah."

His pace was fast. "You want to shop?" he asked.

"No, no, I don't. Let's go back to the hotel."

"Yeah, I could take a nap."

"Yeah, I could go for a swim," Nexxa countered.

Sergei had been serious about the nap. He stripped down to his underwear, found a football game, and lowered the sound. Nexxa stripped too and he smirked, summoning her over to him. She stood before him holding her breasts, and he ran a finger across her abdomen. Next to the bag with Kilmer's ashes, she found her white Norma Kamali swimsuit inside her suitcase. She paired it with a white stretch skirt by Susana Monaco. Sergei was close to his nap but still suggested she wear a full robe to the pool. Nexxa obliged. It was January after all. He instructed her to take the elevator by their hotel suite door that was marked for staff only. Their room key would allow her access. This elevator would be more secure, taking her directly to the level the pool was on.

Nexxa took off her robe and skirt, laying them on one of the eggplant-colored pool loungers. She removed the clip holding her hair up, tossing it on top of her robe. Walking to the side of the illuminated pool, she sat on the edge before lowering herself in. She swam underwater, moving across the length of the pool. Nexxa emerged, resting her arms on the edge. She turned, pushing off the wall and swimming the length of the pool again. Reaching the shallow end, she stood and dabbed at her eyes. All this happened seamlessly.

"Is it cold?" The accent was ambiguous.

Nexxa turned; the voice came from behind her. She squinted in the dimly lit pool. The person wasn't very tall. "No, not really." She moved her head, hoping the evening sky would illuminate the figure. Nexxa advanced in the water, and the person was now to her left, by the loungers. Nexxa watched as her robe was lifted and tossed back down, her hair clip falling on the floor. The door opened from the other side of the pool, and a short, rather hefty, bald man in a robe and slippers made his way in. The rotund man eyed Nexxa as he disrobed and walked to the pool's edge. He looked like he probably ate a lot of stuffed sandwiches, and he made waves as he plopped into the pool. He grumbled something in Russian when his phone rang, yet swiftly he exited the pool and with heavy steps made his way to his phone, and with more heavy steps took his call to the men's lounge.

His scent gone, Nexxa inhaled something familiar.

Abruptly, Nexxa was dragged through the water by her hair. The scent—Crimson. Nexxa's eyes rolled, closing. Standing in the four-foot-deep water with only her bra and underwear on, Diane held Nexxa's unconscious body, caressing her forehead then her eyebrows. As she thought about her darling Uighur with fair skin and red hair that she desired, who was alive in another lifetime, Diane drew a finger with a coffin-shaped nail painted *Lavender Gliss* down Nexxa's décolletage. Next, she pulled Nexxa's bathing suit top, exposing her breasts. Diane circled a lavender nail around each of Nexxa's cold, erect nipples. She lowered her puckered mouth, and her tongue grazed her teeth as she licked Nexxa's nipple. Weaving a finger down between Nexxa's thighs she whispered, "One, two, three, four, five, and six." A sound came from the lounger where Nexxa's belongings were. Diane's eyes forced her head of dark hair to turn. Rosary prayer beads, which Nexxa had been given in Rome at the crematorium, had fallen from the pocket of Nexxa's robe. Nexxa's lavender pulsed—"Fuck!" Diane screamed, the force of her lavender caused her to release Nexxa's body. She realized that Nexxa wasn't just a pretty blonde with a lovely lavender glow, a glow Diane could see only because her malevolent soul made up for her lack of enlightenment.

Diane quelled her arousal—she hated something stronger than her.

Nexxa shivered. Water fell from the man's belly as he hovered over her, muttering to her in Russian. Nexxa managed to say, "*Khorosho.*" She didn't remember getting out of the pool. His fat hand moved toward her robe, Nexxa sat up. She reached for her robe faster than he could. She moved parts of the robe around, sniffing; the scent was the same. In Rome, she had detected a Crimson aroma using her wolfness, her special ability to track scents, while at the crematorium. Why was this scent here in Moscow? Nexxa pulled a long black hair from the robe.

Nexxa reached under the lounger, grabbing her hair clip. She thanked the man, patting him on the shoulder. He muttered again, handing her back her rosary. Nexxa left the pool carrying the robe. Back in the room with Sergei, she was glad he was asleep. She placed the robe on the floor by the bag with Kilmer's urn. She showered.

Staring at herself in the bathroom mirror, Nexxa noticed a scratch on her right breast. Touching the scratch, the scent pervaded the bathroom and Nexxa felt the events from the pool. Someone with the wolfness—like Nexxa—had been there. She wondered how she got to where she was. Not there in Moscow, but a place where scents, ashes, and a man who was most likely her soulmate were all converging.

SILVER | 2

MOSCOW

Nexxa observed his leather boots, his unshaven face, the way his jeans framed his thighs. His expressions during traffic. His hands on the steering wheel. Arriving, Sergei parked in his garage. There was another car, a paltry hatchback, dull blue in color. Sergei handed Nexxa her small bag, the one with the urn, and he pulled her suitcase in for her. Inside she saw boxes, some personal items she had mailed from New York. Sergei looked to the boxes. "Your stuff is upstairs." He left Nexxa's suitcase outside of his office and gave her a kiss on the cheek. Nexxa stood in the foyer, lowering the bag with the urn. She heard a woman's voice. Sergei was in his office, on a call already, so Nexxa walked to the kitchen.

"Hi, you're here!" Vlasta stood from her crouch behind the kitchen island.

Nexxa nodded, at least she thought she did. "Um, yeah."

Vlasta stood about the same height as Nexxa. Maybe—it was hard to tell because she was wide, wearing faded beige lounge pants, and had arms that hung heavily from her obnoxious sleeveless top. Her body pressed against Nexxa in a hug that felt like a light assault. Nexxa crinkled her nose. Vlasta leaned back, pulling her glasses down to her eyes. She smiled until Nexxa smiled as well.

"You're probably hungry."

"Oh, no, I'm sure Sergei—" Nexxa looked around for signs of Ankica.

"No, Sergei is busy." Vlasta frowned.

Nexxa scanned the kitchen again, and Vlasta pulled her glasses up, moving her head in sync with Nexxa. She couldn't help but notice. "So…" Nexxa said, looking down at Vlasta's shoes. Vlasta moved her head down. *How long is she going to keep this up?* Nexxa wondered. "Are you ready to eat?" Vlasta asked.

"Well," Nexxa sat on a barstool at the island. "Sure."

"How about some wine?" Vlasta poured two glasses of red wine. She maneuvered herself onto a barstool next to Nexxa. "Ugh, my feet hurt." She took off a shoe, pulling off something like an Ace bandage. Nexxa watched as she massaged her foot. "Oh shit!" Vlasta moved off of the barstool faster than Nexxa figured she could by her weight and war-torn appearance.

With the same hand that Nexxa witnessed her massage her foot with, Vlasta grabbed a large spoon and stirred in a stockpot. Sergei walked in the kitchen, past Nexxa. "Mmm, smells good." Nexxa looked to him. "Vlasta's here. I asked her to help—" Sergei looked in the stockpot, "help in the house now."

"Okay," Nexxa responded.

"She knew you were coming."

"Okay, okay." Nexxa lifted her wine, drinking the last of it.

"You want some more?" Vlasta eagerly offered, already on the move toward the wine bottle.

"Absolutely."

Vlasta filled Nexxa's glass. "And some for me." She continued smiling until Nexxa smiled. Vlasta took a gulp. The sound of baby Natina came across on the baby monitor. Vlasta started a heavy foot toward the monitor. Sergei held up his hand, and Vlasta's abrupt stop rattled the room. Nexxa's eyes moved from Vlasta to Sergei and back to Vlasta. She took a deep breath when she finally heard Ankica consoling Natina on the monitor. Vlasta moved about plating three plates and summoning Sergei back to retrieve them as he had just stepped over to Nexxa to give her a kiss. She insisted they all sit at the table. Nexxa thought, remembered, that Sergei liked to sit at the island, but she carried hers and Vlasta's wine glasses to the table anyway. Vlasta told Sergei that Ankica had already eaten, and that baby Natina only wanted baby cereal mixed with milk.

Sergei patted his abdomen, clearly expressing to Vlasta that he liked her dinner. Nexxa offered to clean up and Vlasta was thrilled. Nexxa hand washed the pots, loaded the dishwasher and wiped down the counters.

"You don't have to do all of that," Vlasta told her as Nexxa dried the last pot.

"No, it's okay." Nexxa pulled off kitchen gloves.

"You want some tea?"

"No," Nexxa said, yawning, "no, I'm just tired. Thank you so much for dinner."

"Sergei, you want some tea?"

Sergei indicated no. He stood from the table and took a sip from his glass, carrying it over to the kitchen sink. He hugged Nexxa from behind. Nexxa noticed how Vlasta purposely turned her head away from their direction as Sergei embraced her.

Upstairs, Nexxa saw her framed pictures on the dresser. Sergei was by his nightstand putting his phone and keys down. Nexxa lifted a frame, turning toward Sergei. "Thank you," she said as she looked at the photo. He nodded as he yawned. Nexxa went to the bathroom, and sitting on the toilet, she laughed. Delirium was setting in. The month had been long, and now she was finally back with the Russian but with a piece of her ex-husband.

Sergei hollered to Nexxa in the bathroom. He asked if she needed anything—did she need the smaller bag by her suitcase. Nexxa quickly finished on the toilet, barely rinsing her hands. She stepped out of the bathroom. Sergei was already lying down. Nexxa smiled. She removed her clothes, laying them atop of the small urn bag. She crawled in beside Sergei. Just her panties tonight. Sergei rolled over, grasping her breasts. Kissing the back of her neck, he told her he was too tired tonight. Nexxa was okay with that. She could feel his penis against her back. That was enough. Vlasta was nice; she wanted to get a good night's rest, unpack her suitcase, help her with breakfast. She anticipated learning baby Natina's routine.

Nexxa stood in Natina's bedroom doorway watching her stuff a doll into another toy. Baby Natina's hair was longer but looked dirty. She saw Nexxa and ran to her. Nexxa held her caressing the back of her head before Natina leaned into Nexxa, kissing her on her face. Nexxa told her she missed her, and she loved her. Ankica came down the hall using a cane. If she had grown to need it gradually, it would have seemed normal. Nexxa kept Natina on her hip while she gently embraced Ankica who felt like she had lost weight and smelled of stale clothing.

"Oh, it's nothing." Ankica wobbled the cane. "Nothing."

"Ankica, what happened?" Nexxa looked at her until Ankica looked past Nexxa shaking her head. Natina leaned toward Ankica, and Nexxa adjusted her grip, kissing her on the side of her baby face. Natina covered her eyes, mimicking playing peek-a-boo.

Sounds of exasperation and some moderate clanking came from downstairs. Nexxa remembered she had planned to wake early, be on hand in the kitchen. Ankica moved with her cane toward the stairs, and Nexxa followed. In the kitchen, Vlasta had quite a mess. Something was bubbling in the stockpot already. Nexxa noticed a teacup and a plate with a piece of bread on the table. In the daylight the kitchen cabinets, countertops, and island showed their despair—new but dirty. When Nexxa was first in Sergei's home, his kitchen, while Ankica had cooked up a mess, had still been orderly. Vlasta informed Ankica she had made her tea. Her bread was ready. *The bread is ready?* Nexxa thought. While there were many things going on in the kitchen, Nexxa couldn't smell anything. Natina fussed. Vlasta made a face.

"*Dobro utro.*" Nexxa wanted to smile first.

"*Dobro utro.*" Vlasta frowned.

Vlasta pulled the chair out for Ankica, patting her on her shoulders once she was tucked into the table. Nexxa watched as Ankica's shoulders slumped in as she took nibbles of the bread while looking toward the stockpot.

"And what about you, my baby?" Vlasta perked up and approached Nexxa and Natina.

"Oh," Nexxa moved her arm across Natina's body between her and Vlasta, "I can. I… planned to help, to feed her."

"No." Vlasta furrowed her brow, holding out her hands for baby Natina. "She loves to eat."

"Oh sure, but you know now that I am here, I can help out. I'm not working." Nexxa walked toward the fridge. There needed to be some space between her and Vlasta.

"I got you some more of that wine."

"Oh, okay." Nexxa saw that it was only eight-thirty a.m. "How—I mean, thank you."

"I've been up since four." Vlasta tapped the stainless-steel spoon loudly on the pot.

Nexxa twisted on the bottle nipple, handing it to Natina. "I can be up earlier tomorrow."

"Because you don't work?" Vlasta turned to Nexxa, looking down through her glasses.

Nexxa sighed. "Right, I don't work right now."

Ankica broke the tension, starting to cough. Vlasta dashed to her, pounding on her back. She spit out some bread. Vlasta frantically wiped Ankica's mouth, the front of her shirt. Vlasta sat with Ankica, tearing small pieces of bread and placing them on her plate. She lifted her teacup. "It's empty." She hopped up, poured a glass of water and swiftly brought the glass to Ankica.

"Ankica, are you okay?" Nexxa asked.

"She's good, she's fine," Vlasta barked before showing a delusional smile.

Fifteen more awkward minutes passed. "Okay, well then, I'm going to take Natina up for a bath since she finished her bottle," Nexxa explained, while keeping concerned eyes on Ankica.

Nexxa turned on the light, then the faucet. The water ran some, and she adjusted the temperature and closed the drain. Natina toddled out of the bathroom. Nexxa followed her. They returned and Nexxa undressed Natina. Nexxa lifted her to place her in the tub. "What?" Nexxa placed Natina down on the floor. Natina lifted her leg trying to get into the tub, but Nexxa held her back. Then, Nexxa reached her hand out before pulling it back, finally dipping her hand in the tub for what looked to be silverware holders that must have fallen from the ledge and would belong in a dishwasher. Natina made her way over the tub's edge, and Nexxa kept an arm on her while looking around the bathroom. She pulled the basket on the floor toward her which held Natina's toys. Natina stood and asked for a joobie. Nexxa held up several toys until Natina reached her hand out for one.

Nexxa stared at the silverware holders before lifting them and placing them on the bathroom vanity.

Natina was cooperative when Nexxa washed her hair. She knew to lean back as Nexxa rinsed the shampoo away.

Barely in her towel, Natina squirmed to get down running about her bedroom. Nexxa managed to get a diaper on but not any clothes. Once Natina finally had a baby shirt on and was occupied with her toys, she stepped back into the bathroom. The silverware holders were there; they were real. Nexxa lifted them, thinking they should just be brought back to the kitchen. She thought about how she would look carrying them downstairs.

It was evening again somehow. Nexxa had barely seen Sergei since he was occupied in his office—eating meals there, drinking a Scotch or two. Ankica didn't want dinner. Natina was already down for the evening. Vlasta found Nexxa and offered her some wine. With her feet up on a barstool, Vlasta began telling Nexxa about how she hated anything to do with social media. But that she liked to watch a Russian version of the American show *The Real Housewives.* She turned on the kitchen TV and insisted Nexxa "drink, drink," all that she wanted. When the show ended, she asked Nexxa if she liked travel shows, flipping around on the TV. When Sergei finally entered the kitchen asking if there was anything else to eat, she rolled her eyes laughing. Nexxa did the same before watching as Vlasta offered and plated him some cheese and crackers like a bossy older sister would. He seemed happy, giving Nexxa a kiss as he left the kitchen.

Nexxa watched three episodes of a travel show with Vlasta. Vlasta translated some for Nexxa. She understood most of the dialogue, but she let Vlasta translate anyway. Nexxa told Vlasta that she would clean up what was left in the kitchen.

Vlasta threw her arms around Nexxa, telling her good night, and Nexxa offered to carry up Vlasta's drink. Her room was the guest room Nexxa had stayed in, well, showered in, when she first came to Moscow with Sergei. Nexxa looked to the dresser where the seven flowers that became six had been placed. She hadn't thought about that in a few weeks. The longer she stood in the room the stronger the odor became. She turned to leave, but Vlasta was there. Another goodnight hug and a promise that tomorrow would be better before Nexxa was able to return to Sergei's bedroom.

Again Sergei was tired. Nexxa felt his penis against her back like the previous night. As she lay in the dark, she wondered when they finally did have sex, how she would feel with someone new in the house, someone like Vlasta just down the hall.

TEACHER MR. ALBERT | 3

UPSTATE NEW YORK

Iliada stepped up on the dais on the grounds of Mr. Albert's estate. She turned her head to the right where the sky was lending to lavender. She turned her head straight on seeing the woods were darkening. Iliada closed her eyes and blew out a long breath. She connected with Nexxa, and before her, she saw the evening during the Ice Queen party in December: the dragon eggs, Nexxa's suitors, and the white glow after the black cast. Iliada opened her eyes—Mr. Albert was standing with her.

"She is," he said, finessing the air with his hands, "with the one." Mr. Albert handled his Chinese accent. "The man with the white glow," he said.

Iliada stepped down from the dais. "How did you—" Walking toward the trees, she shifted her hands trying to mimic Mr. Albert.

"You want to know about the black?"

"Yeah. Like where did the white come from?"

Mr. Albert chuckled before saying, "The black is very powerful. Takes a long time to learn how to manifest it. To create the black cast, one must practice patience."

Can Nexxa do that? Did everyone see what we saw that night? Iliada lowered her face, pushing at her temples.

Mr. Albert heard Iliada's thoughts. Inquisitive, she reminded him of Nexxa.

He had first met Nexxa when she crossed the street from her apartment visiting his cigar lounge. He saw her glow, a smeared lavender against the night sky. He observed her from a spot behind the bar, watching her mind count the patrons and staff. Watching her mind determine if anyone could "smell her." Mr. Albert approached her table introducing himself. The months following, Nexxa continued to grace his establishment wherein he would continue to join her table, drink wine with her, and partake in her game of assessing the clientele.

Iliada knelt, running a hand across the winter ground. Mr. Albert knelt, and the grass before them began to turn black. Iliada jumped from her knees.

Mr. Albert grasped Iliada's hand. "Come inside." Iliada turned looking to the ground behind them as she walked inside. The grass had returned to its normal winter shade.

Inside, candelabras held flaming white pillar candles on the kitchen island. Mr. Albert neared the candelabra on the far end of the island. The candles slowly turned black. Iliada's eyes widened. "Wow!" An assistant entered the kitchen, removing one candelabra at a time. He set forth a few glass bottles filled with liquid and a variety of lip products. He presented Iliada with a black apron, and she gushed over how much she loved it.

"Knowing what exists, how it can work..." Mr. Albert separated the bottles on the massive kitchen island. "Then you will know how."

Iliada nodded. She tied her hair back and started to tighten her apron, so the attendant came around and assisted her. Flash, with his face of a snowy owl, no bill, used his petite wings, arms, and legs to hop upon the island. His voice rasped, "*Ad mundum pertinent.*" Mr. Albert held his palm out, and Flash rested upon it. "Between the manifested," Flash fluttered to the end of the counter and muttered, "unmanifested."

Iliada reached for one of the bottles and removed the stopper, sniffing and laughing as she pushed the bottle stopper back in. Mr. Albert pushed a tube of natural lip gloss across the island and Iliada grasped it with her always manicured hands. She smeared some gloss with the wand onto the rectangular piece of white marble in front of her, then poured some liquid from the bottle. As she mixed the substances, Flash fluttered over, lowering his head to the marble and inspecting. A powdery substance formed, and Iliada smiled with her shimmering cheeks. Flash folded in his wings rolling about the powder—he disappeared. Iliada held her face. "Whoa! Flash?" She felt around on the island. "Flash?" she called out again while bending looking down on the floor. She opened a few kitchen cabinets and drawers.

Iliada turned off the lamp on the nightstand and turned on

her side, and her eyelids closed. She heard breathing, raspy breathing. She sat up patting the covers. Flash winced. Iliada apologized. She asked him where he had been. He explained that once he rolled in the powder that it had a heightened effect on him. (Gargowls have the ability to make themselves invisible.) So therefore he was invisible until either the powder wore off or he purposely made himself visible, yet he wasn't able to see and had wandered off, getting lost in the massive house. Iliada pulled him into her. Flash wriggled, making his bed. "*Bonam noctem,*" whispered Flash. Iliada repeated the same as she pulled the covers over him.

Iliada popped in her Apple AirPods and spun herself around until she was dizzy. She began her fall, slowly—Mr. Albert raised the space between her and the cold ground. Flash hopped upon Mr. Albert's shoulder looking out of the massive kitchen window then asked Mr. Albert how long Iliada would need to be his student. Iliada returned upright, moving to the song "In Too Deep" by Eli & Fur. She knew she should have fallen to the ground. The song ended, Iliada took a step forward and did a front handspring. Now she was ready. Mr. Albert was waiting.

"We will train in the day and after, under the night sky."

Iliada nodded. She felt a tear and thought about Thomas, her first instructor of mystical things. She took a deep breath and quelled her fear. Nexxa was safe in Moscow and Iliada was with Teacher.

KOSHA (CAT) | 4

MOSCOW

Every morning Nexxa woke at seven a.m., Sergei was in his office, a stockpot boiled in the kitchen, Ankica hobbled down the hall, and a baby waited in her crib for Nexxa.

Nexxa dried her face, and she smelled Sergei's cologne on the towel. After she brushed her hair, pulling it up into a tighter ponytail, she used her finger to dab on some lip stain. Putting on her silk kimono, she tied the belt and twisted from side to side looking in the mirror. *No, no,* she told herself, pulling her hair down. It was easier for a man; he could shower, pull on tracksuit pants, spray on cologne, and look fuckable.

Natina looked taller than she did a week ago. Nexxa ran her fingers down Natina's spine as she dressed her in a clean yet stained white onesie she found in the laundry basket on the floor. Natina giggled, and Nexxa leaned into her, kissing her cheek just as Sergei appeared and said good morning.

Natina reached up for her, and Nexxa swooped her up on her hip moving over to Sergei. He kissed them both, and Nexxa started to ask Sergei something about Natina, but his phone buzzed, so he kissed Nexxa again and walked down the hall.

Nexxa decided to look through Natina's armoire. She had plenty of clothes, most of them looked unworn. She lifted one nice outfit at a time. In the back of the armoire, under some clothes, Nexxa found a framed photo of Demo, Natina's dad, with baby Natina. Nexxa pulled the picture out and placed it on top of Natina's dresser.

Ankica could be heard coming down the hall, and Nexxa chased after Natina, who ran from her room toward her great-grandmother. Ankica maneuvered her cane around going back toward her bedroom. Nexxa followed. "I want to show you," Ankica said. Nexxa noticed how Ankica's "want" sounded like she said "vant," as if it were becoming harder to speak in English.

Ankica had somehow managed to pull some clothes from her closet, and some jewelry was strewn across her dressing table. Nexxa encouraged Natina to stop rolling around on the bed. Ankica motioned with the opposite hand from the one holding her cane. Nexxa lifted a dress, and Ankica nodded. Nexxa removed her kimono, slipped on the dress and smoothed out the fabric with her hand. Ankica told her to keep it as she hobbled over to her dressing table. She shifted around some jewelry as if making it more detectable for Nexxa. Nexxa approached Ankica, placing a hand gently on her shoulder, before Natina pressed her way between them reaching up for a gold bracelet. "For you, baby," Ankica said, moving her head ever so slightly.

Natina held the bracelet tightly, and Nexxa helped her with the clasp and put it on her wrist as best she could for a baby. "For you." Ankica slid pieces of the jewelry closer to Nexxa. Nexxa only took notice of Ankica. How she looked gaunt. The cane.

The smell of soup preceded her and suddenly permeated the bedroom. "Oh, she's showing you that stuff. Her jewelry?" came the stern voice.

"Oh, hi." Nexxa looked to the doorway where Vlasta was watching them.

"Ankica!" Vlasta demanded.

Nexxa looked away before picking up Natina from the bed. Ankica pushed her jewelry toward the back of her dressing table. Vlasta scolded her in Russian, insisting that she come down for some bread. Nexxa heard Vlasta's tone—heard everything she barked in Russian.

The overcast sky lent to a calm afternoon, and a few hours later, Sergei found Nexxa rocking Natina to sleep. He stood in the doorway of Natina's room, looking at the framed photo of Demo and Natina. Demo was away again, another play in Europe, and he couldn't remember if that picture had always been there. Nexxa had fallen asleep with Natina on her chest. Sergei's phone buzzed and Nexxa woke, turning to see him. She placed Natina in her crib and stepped lightly toward Sergei, yawning before relaxing her head against his warm chest. Sergei turned, walking her to his bedroom. Nexxa sat on the edge of his bed. He spread her thighs, untied the belt to her kimono. His tongue was warm. Nexxa fell back onto the bed.

"Knock, knock."

Nexxa sat up. Sergei moaned. Nexxa pulled at his face.

"Can I come in?"

"I'm getting dressed," Nexxa hollered. "Going for a run."

"Oh, I don't mind." Vlasta's chuckle matched her boldness as she pushed open the bedroom door Sergei had forgotten to lock.

Nexxa sprinted to the closet and managed to pull on a padded bra top. Sergei was looking at his phone, as he walked past Vlasta and headed back to his office.

"I'm not dressed yet."

Vlasta was there, in the middle of the room. Nexxa peeked from the closet. The leggings she used for exercising were in the bedroom. She had no choice but to step out in her bra top and panties.

"I put all of your clothes away," Vlasta said.

"Huh?" Nexxa pulled on her leggings.

"I did it all by myself. I never thought about how you would need to bring panties and bras from New York."

"The clothes," Nexxa tilted her head, "I shipped here?"

"You need everything even when you move." Vlasta moved her head up and down.

"Uh-huh." Nexxa looked from Vlasta to the bedroom door that was closed. "Yeah."

"So you are going to get some exercise?"

"Yeah—"

Vlasta moved into Nexxa. She tugged at her top's strap. "It's loose. Take it off, I can tighten it for you."

Nexxa grasped the band of her bra top, slipping it over her head. She stood cupping her breasts, eyes looking up.

"Your breasts are symmetrical," Vlasta said with a smile.

Nexxa found another top, one that most likely fit better. "No hurry to mend my loose bra. I'm going for my run now."

"And I'll be here, Sergei will be here, and Ankica will be here," Vlasta informed Nexxa.

"Okay," Nexxa said. *Strange and strange. And you left out baby Natina.*

Nexxa found her running shoes, tied her laces super-fast, and tapped in the security code to exit through Sergei's bedroom door which led outside.

Her stride seemed to have a farther span, probably only because she wasn't running with Iliada. Nexxa reminisced on her first time in Sergei's home—seeing Sergei's trees, meeting Bogdan—his head of security in his izba, the Wi-Fi she remembered he called "Hi-Fi," the chic crypt. She decided she would only run to the cemetery where Sergei's parents were buried and back.

Nexxa slowed, catching her cold Moscow breath. *What?* Bogdan's house, his quaint green and white izba, was partially boarded up with a few weeds around the exterior. Nexxa took a few steps toward the door. She smelled something. Not just anything. *Vlasta.* Pulling on the door, it was for sure locked, Nexxa heard whispers. She turned, losing her balance. Then regaining her footing she turned again, listening for the whispers again.

Running at a steady pace, she balanced her breathing with her thoughts as a cloud moved away, and the sky was still gray. Reaching the cemetery gate she knelt and retied her right sneaker. Standing, she grasped the rods of the gate peering through at the tombstones. Sergei had handed her a Russian tea cake, noticed her eyeing the crypt; then they drank homemade wine from Bogdan, she wiped Sergei's pre-jack on her dry lips and Sergei's tongue warmed her between her thighs, all in the crypt.

Nexxa started back toward Sergei's home. The whispers began again. She stopped at Bogdan's izba, and this time she called out his name. "Bogdan, Bogdan." Nexxa walked through the weeds around to the back of the quaint home. She saw nothing but found a rusty wheelbarrow. Standing in the uneasy wheelbarrow, she peered through the window. *An animal. Is that a cat?* Nexxa questioned. The wheelbarrow cracked and Nexxa fell. "Shit!" she shouted. Blood ran down her leg and she looked around. Finding nothing obvious to wipe the blood, she removed her shoe and took off her sock. Stopping every few minutes to wipe the blood, she half-limped and half-jogged back home.

Nexxa saw Vlasta through the glass door. Removing her shoes first, Nexxa stepped cautiously into Sergei's bedroom while holding her sock to her wound. She had hoped to make it to the bathroom to find a bandage. "What happened? I thought you were only going for a run." Vlasta scowled.

"I…" Nexxa sighed. "I fell."

Vlasta lunged toward her shouting, "Sergei, Sergei!" as she grasped the sock Nexxa had pushed against her leg. Vlasta helped Nexxa over to one of the leather armchairs. Nexxa thanked her. She actually felt thankful, to her surprise. Vlasta retrieved her phone from the pocket of her cargo capris, pulled her glasses down from atop her head, and after what seemed like a long time, found Sergei's number and called him. Vlasta chuckled after she ended the call. Nexxa laughed too. She felt like it made sense. Something in common to laugh about.

"My love, my love." Sergei dashed to Nexxa.

"It's okay, I'm okay." Nexxa smiled at him.

"We have to take you to a doctor," Sergei asserted.

"What about your work?" Nexxa asked.

"It can wait. I'm sorry I've been so busy."

"You were only supposed to go for a run, nothing else." Vlasta scolded.

"Right, I just, I thought…"

Vlasta had an intense look, and she tilted her chin down. Lifting her chin, she seemed joyful again. "I'll run you a bath when you get back."

Sergei had Vlasta retrieve some gauze and bandage tape. He gently wrapped Nexxa's leg and helped her down the stairs. Vlasta shouted she would make *more* soup while they were gone.

The doctor's office turned out to be a home even bigger than Sergei's. Nexxa was in awe and now also in pain. A woman who looked more like a "sexy nurse" dressed for Halloween was waiting for them when they exited Sergei's Jaguar. She showed them to what looked like a home office and a tall slender man emerged from another entryway. He introduced himself to Nexxa. He stated his credentials. He asked her about her medical history. The sexy nurse handed Nexxa a pain pill and asked if she wanted white wine or sparkling wine. Nexxa thought for a moment, *This seems like what would happen before I'm coerced to make a porn.* "I'll…" Nexxa looked to Sergei. He smiled. "I will have white wine." The sexy nurse smiled and spoke in Russian to the doctor. They chuckled. "I like him too," Nexxa responded. She had understood that they had said "Sergei must like this girl." Sergei grasped Nexxa's hand. Then he asked the nurse for a glass of wine. Being there in the doctor's home, Sergei holding her hand, meant more to her than him going down on her. Even if she had to get hurt for some quality time.

On the ride back to Sergei's home Nexxa wondered, *Why that doctor? Why his home?*

"I know you are probably wondering," Sergei said.

"Yes, sure."

"I handle some investments for him." Sergei honked at another driver. "Sorry, some people can't drive." He turned to Nexxa looking at her leg. "It's better?"

"Yeah, yeah. I think the pain pill and wine helped," Nexxa laughed.

Vlasta had soup, more soup as promised, bubbling on the stove. Nexxa looked toward the kitchen. No Vlasta in sight.

Upstairs, Sergei helped Nexxa to his bedroom. "Knock, knock," said Vlasta as she pushed open Sergei's bedroom door. "Your bath is waiting," she continued in a sing-song tone.

Nexxa attempted to stand, and Sergei helped her up. "You're okay?" he asked.

"Yeah, just need my robe maybe." Nexxa pointed to the closet. Sergei started for his closet, but Vlasta beat him there.

"Okay, let's go now!" Vlasta ordered with Nexxa's robe slung over her shoulder. Sergei let them know he would be in his office. Vlasta insisted Nexxa lean on her shoulder on the walk to the bathroom down the hall.

The bathroom was steamy. Nexxa couldn't really see. She heard water running, she thought. Vlasta helped her over to the gray pouf and abruptly said she needed to check the soup. Nexxa felt grateful that Vlasta didn't insist on her undressing in front of her. Nexxa parted her way through the steam to the vanity. She turned off the sink, undressed and placed her clothes on top. Nexxa lowered herself to the edge of the tub, putting a hand in to feel the water. The tub wasn't full, and the water was hot. Nexxa felt for the faucet and turned it on before immersing herself into the tub.

She reached, feeling her bandage was still dry, and she heard meowing. She pushed up, bracing herself on the tiled wall. Meowing again. She leaned forward feeling for the faucet again and turned off the water. Parting the steam she saw, sitting on the inner ledge of the bathtub, two kittens. One was dangling, almost sliding into the tub, and the other sat curled up in the corner. Nexxa lifted the dangling kitten and placed it on the floor. She lifted the other kitten and placed it next to its brother or sister. Hobbling out of the bath, she took a towel and dried them off. "Now you're okay." She thought about the cat she saw in Bogdan's izba. "Where did you come from?"

she asked softly.

Nexxa sat on the edge of Sergei's bed. The two kittens were frolicking around his bedroom. She stood up. She sat back down. Standing again, she coaxed the kittens toward the towel on the floor. She scooped them up and headed to Sergei's office. Her leg hurt, but she thought about Ankica and how she used a cane now as she persevered down the stairs.

"Sergei." Nexxa tapped on his office door.

"Come in," he hollered. He stood from his desk and quickly made his way over to her. "What do you have?" His eyes were big.

"I found them in the bathroom." Nexxa accepted Sergei's help over to his leather couch. Seated with the kittens in her lap, she pulled back the towel and the kittens stepped out and meowed at Sergei.

Nexxa wanted to tell Sergei, ask Sergei about Bogdan's house, about how she saw a cat or some animal dash through it. But then she would have to explain how she *actually* hurt her leg and well, there was the scent of Vlasta and the whispers.

Sergei proudly carried the kittens into the kitchen. Vlasta banged a stirring spoon on the stockpot. "What do you have?" she asked as she pulled her glasses on.

"I found them—" Nexxa touched the nose of one of the kittens.

"No! No, Sergei is allergic." Vlasta stood with her hands on her hips.

"I'm not allergic," Sergei asserted. "They're actually cute!"

"No, Sergei can have a cat if he wants," Vlasta informed, shaking her head down and up, down and up.

Sergei placed the kittens down. He took some bread from the counter, tearing small pieces and gently, sweetly in "kitten speak," talking as he fed them. Nexxa stood watch over her Russian feeding the kittens that somehow were in the hot bath that Vlasta had insisted on running for her.

KNOW YOUR FEDERATION | 5

Sergei rolled out schematic designs on the table in his office. He moved a finger across the width of the plans and down to a place where his finger stopped and tapped. He never attributed it to luck, a lunar eclipse according to his babushka, when he came across Hoolihane in London a decade ago. Carlos Finch (Sergei) finally came to fruition because of Hoolihane, now so would Kozman Investments. Croatia's version of Moscow's Federation Tower, a smaller version of Tower West, was scheduled to break ground by the autumn. Sergei was privy to knowledge that the former USSR was going to face sanctions for their failure to implement their own KYC, Know Your Customer, regulations. (Hooli had accessed chatter between the CIA and the current administration in Washington.) Croatia was set to become part of the EU and foreign investment demonstrated that the young country was ready, which presented the Russian with a new playground, being that Beirut had been compromised.

With his muscular arms stretched out over his schematic designs, Sergei looked up and smiled at Nexxa as she stepped into his office. "My love, come here." Sergei motioned with his hand. Nexxa embraced him. He kissed her on the lips and then down her décolletage. Nexxa inhaled him. "Mmm, I want some Nexxa," Sergei breathed. Nexxa's leg brushed against the table and she winced. "Are you okay?" Sergei asked.

"Yeah, yeah." Nexxa reached down, feeling the part of her leg that was healing from her fall. It had only been about a week since she had injured her leg. "Can you sign me into your Bloomberg?" Nexxa wanted to peruse job listings, read the news, etc. Sergei had only just set Nexxa up on his computer, kissing her one more time, before Vlasta pushed open the door to his office with enough strength to send the door all the way to the wall—summoning him to the kitchen, huffing and huffing that she couldn't reach something in a top cabinet.

Nexxa typed in a colleague's name on Bloomberg. She backspaced. She sighed. Lifting her phone, she tapped on the app for her bank. Her balance was not impressive. She tapped on the app for her investment account. The numbers were in red. Philip had always helped her. She had not mentioned her investment account to Sergei. Telling a man everything would never be an option. Sergei was providing for her, paying for her travel and insisting on her using his credit card for anything she needed. Asking Sergei for money wasn't something she wanted to do. Yet the job listings available in Moscow to work in finance weren't that appealing. Sure she saw a listing with a British hedge fund, she could be a trading assistant again, and there was a listing for a Russian hedge fund where she could also be a trading assistant. Nexxa logged out of Sergei's Bloomberg account and turned off his monitors.

She looked over at his schematic drawings on the large wooden table. She stood and twisted her hair up, walking over to the table. Nexxa studied the drawing of what would be a mid-rise office building. She was familiar with some architectural industry terms from her time spent with Mr. Albert. Nexxa read the notes calling for bulletproof glass. Another note was for, she struggled with the translation, but it seemed something to do with a secret elevator or escape route from an office labeled with Sergei's name. Nexxa imagined Sergei being away in Croatia. She thought about being alone in the house with Vlasta. She thought about Ankica and Natina. Then she reminded herself that construction on the building hadn't even broken ground yet. Sergei's new venture was intriguing to Nexxa, something she would continue to be interested in.

I need a career change.

"What would you do, Nexxa?" she whispered to herself.

Even though her leg wasn't fully healed, the blood moon was almost visible, and she needed to run. Nexxa tucked her pendulum in one side of her bra top. She felt the scratch on her breast that she somehow incurred swimming at the Ararat Park Hotel when she had smelled the Crimson scent. It hadn't healed completely. She looked over at the bag that had

Kilmer's urn then over at her nightstand. She lifted the rosary she had received in Rome and tucked it in the other side of her top. She went down to the kitchen and grabbed a bottle of water from the refrigerator expecting to see Vlasta; to see soup bubbling over the large stockpot making a crusty mess on the vast range. However, the kitchen was bare, and no one was there. Nexxa exited through the back door. She took a sip of water then started along the back of the house. Looking up, she saw the light in Vlasta's room go off. She walked up the steps to the terrace connected to Sergei's bedroom. Taking another sip, she tightened her ponytail and massaged her injured leg.

She ran down the steps, leaping from the last one. She was off. Foot to the cold Moscow ground and breath to the chilly Moscow air, Nexxa persevered down the path toward Bogdan's house. Delicately the moon revealed its blood inspired crimson red.

She reached Bogdan's house faster than she anticipated with her injury. With her hands on her thighs, resting her lungs, she saw a scrap of metal from the broken wheelbarrow and after her pause, used it to pry open the window by the door. Window up, she hoisted herself through and into the izba. Nexxa covered her mouth and nose. The smell. It wasn't of a man nor a wood fire nor food. Nexxa pushed open the curtains on the side window, letting in the blood moon light. She pulled the bed sheet from the bed and formed a circle of white. She asked for a blessing, instructed her pendulum, circle for yes and back and forth for no, and began. "Has harm come to the home of Bogdan?" Her pendulum swung in a circle.

"Is Bogdan alive?" The pendulum idled. Nexxa reminisced about when Bogdan gave her the mezuzah with The Traveler's Prayer. "For keep you safe. Safe travel," he had told her.

Nexxa saw what looked like a person dash past the window. She jumped up, leaving her white circle, rosary, and pendulum, and looked through the window. The figure continued running, moving through the wooded area behind Bogdan's house. Nexxa swiftly stepped back into her white circle. "I call for protection around this property. Mirrored spheres, guards and angels!" Nexxa lifted her pendulum. It swung wildly. Her rosary slid across the white circle, stopping at her feet. Nexxa looked up when she heard a creaking sound on the roof followed by an animal screeching.

Diane perched on the roof of the izba. She had been so eager, but Jupiter was still in retrograde causing her to question her intentions, unwillingly causing her to reflect on her decision to take from Nexxa, take her soul. She was close to figuring out how to use the scientific aspect from her Wing Chun training to work around Nexxa's lavender glow. Maybe she should wait until then. She wanted to taste again, the lovely blonde. Sliding down the side of the house Diane pushed her tongue between her teeth. She stepped upon the steps of the izba and grasped the door handle.

Nearby, Vlasta dragged the Siberian musk deer with its white fangs and dripping blood shimmering in the light of the blood moon. "Now you'll be good. Now you'll be of purpose," Vlasta spoke to the dead animal. She stopped and adjusted her pants, and then burped. Laughing, she turned to the animal. "Did you hear that?" Vlasta dragged the animal to the edge of the front of the izba. She paused, hidden from the view of the front steps, to take a breath.

Diane leaned her head to the side, sniffed. She leaned her head to the other side, sniffed, smelling something sinister. She stepped down the steps of the izba moving over and seeing Vlasta. Their eyes met, and Diane detected Vlasta's nonsensical desire for Nexxa, *her* Nexxa.

"Well, look here. You're a China doll," Vlasta said. "Yeah, look at her," she spoke, looking down to the deer. When she looked back, Diane was close to her nearly sixty-year old worn Siberian body. Diane grazed her arm—Vlasta's eyes twinkled with lust.

Grabbing Vlasta by her sweaty hair, Vlasta still gripping the dead animal, Diane dragged them both around and around the izba. Vlasta used her hysterical strength, which heightened her pungent odor, to release herself from Diane's grip, and pulled the tusks from the animal, limping off toward Sergei's home. Diane gagged from Vlasta's odor. She looked to the stars. Was Jupiter weakening her? Diane had a new problem—a woman who had placed herself in the middle of her plan. She dashed off through the woods, taking a shortcut toward Moscow city centre. She needed a shower. She smelled of something she didn't like.

Nexxa lifted her rosary and her pendulum, which was swinging out of control, and flung open the door to the quaint izba. She detected Vlasta's scent. Faint, not as strong as before when she heard whispers and smelled Vlasta around Bogdan's house, this time with a hint of Crimson. She wrapped her rosary around her wrist like a bracelet, holding the cross in her hand, and tucked her pendulum back into her bra top. Off down the path, she persevered, inhaling the Moscow cold that carried a hint of Vlasta and Crimson.

Nexxa reached the back of Sergei's house. She stopped, holding her face in her hands. Vlasta's bedroom light went on. Nexxa looked to her window. She saw Vlasta, who peered down at her before closing the curtains. Nexxa entered the house through the kitchen door. It smelled of Vlasta with an undertone of Crimson in the kitchen, through the foyer and up the staircase. She held her breath the best she could considering how vast Sergei's home was. She knew Vlasta couldn't be Crimson. The scents were distinctly different and her intuition told her the Siberian housekeeper wasn't an international traveler.

   Upstairs, she found Sergei in the usual position. Lying on his bed, football game on, volume lowered. She tip-toed to the closet, undressed, and tip-toed to the bathroom. She showered. Drying off, she held the towel to her nose. She smelled Vlasta. Or she smelled soup. She dropped the towel and pulled out a clean one from the linen closet. It had an odor too. She pulled Sergei's towel from the hook and wrapped it around her. She wanted him now.

   Nexxa towel dried her blonde hair and dabbed on some red lip stain. With the Russian's towel around her, she made her way to his bed, stepping upon it. Sergei opened his eyes, and Nexxa let the towel fall. Sergei grinned, and Nexxa knelt. She ran her right hand along his leg up to his thigh, up to his groin, and positioned herself over him. Gripping his penis she moved her red lips over his erection. His hand on the back of her head, she went deep. Sergei moaned as he was close to climaxing.

Nexxa stopped. Sitting up, she held her chest laughing. Sergei panted. "Nexxa?" He looked at his erection. Nexxa glided a hand down between her fuckable breasts. Sergei panted more before reaching up to her. "My love," he spoke with a desperate face. Nexxa closed her eyes, hearing the sound of the animal screeching. She felt herself dragged by her hair, and she felt herself being scratched on her breast. Crazy, a little scary.

"Nexxa, finish me," Sergei pleaded. Nexxa lowered her body, lowered her head.

Nexxa watched as Vlasta limped, more like shuffled, around the kitchen. How she slumped against the kitchen counter as if one leg wasn't working. Usually Vlasta would make annoying eye contact in sync with her commands. This morning, though, Vlasta smelled of Crimson. Nexxa offered to help when she saw Vlasta struggling to lift eggs out of the pan. Nexxa plated everyone some eggs and cut the day-old bread. Vlasta burped and burped, barely touching her food, and instead announced that she felt a cold coming on, while shuffling over to the cabinet below the sink, withdrawing a bottle of Russian moonshine and downing two shots.

Nexxa cleaned up and helped Ankica back to her bedroom. After playing with Natina and straightening up her room, Nexxa asked Sergei to use his laptop since hers was sluggish.

Nexxa signed into her email. Then, she signed into her bank

account, which she could have accomplished from her phone. She perused Net-A-Porter for shoes, then Wildberries.ru for toddler clothes before shutting down Sergei's laptop. Nexxa assumed that Sergei was having Hooli monitor her online. She didn't believe there was a lack of trust, more that it was likely his protocol. Nexxa thought about how Vlasta was behaving, how something was different with her. But first, she needed to get away from the house so that baby Natina and Ankica would not be in danger. She needed to see if Crimson would follow her. Needed to see what it wanted from her.

While Sergei was nearing the end of his business for the day, Nexxa brought him a note and promptly left his office. Reading the note, he raised an eyebrow. Sergei leaned back in his chair, running a hand across his face, grasping his jaw. Nexxa kept her note flirtatious: firstly stating that he was "hella sexy," secondly, that he was her favorite Russian, and lastly, that she needed a few nights alone in a hotel in Moscow city centre. Sergei folded the note and carried it with him to his bedroom. He said nothing to Nexxa as she sat waiting for him on the end of his bed. He walked past her and retrieved a suitcase from his closet. He rolled the suitcase out and left it beside the bed. "Prove it," he said with *I want to fuck you* eyes.

Nexxa smirked. "You're my favorite Russian."

Sergei came intimately close. "You want a few days away?" Before Nexxa could answer he began kissing her, slipping his hand under her kimono robe between her thighs.

"Uh-huh," Nexxa breathed between kissing. Sergei began fingering her. She looked past him to the bag across the room that held Kilmer's ashes which had remained unmoved. She thought about the scent she had been detecting, Crimson. Sergei withdrew his hand from between her thighs, cupping her breast with the scratch. "What's this?" he asked.

Nexxa rubbed her lips together. "I... I think it happened when I fell running." The truth, the scratch was now more profound, was that Nexxa didn't know how she acquired it, but she was beginning to believe it had something to do with the Crimson scent.

GOOD GIRL+CRIMSON | 6

"You are good. They know you are taking care of them. You're a good girl." Vlasta stood before the mirror in her bedroom, staring at herself with an assuring face. Continuing with the look of a dark entity, she carried a communist era dark blue bag down the hall, down the main staircase, through the kitchen, down to the cellar, and through a rough looking wooden door that led to another room.

   Vlasta slung the bag down on a wooden tool bench. She withdrew the white fangs from the Siberian musk deer she had killed, placing them on the bench. She pulled out a pair of black lace panties, folding them in a tight, neat shape. She pulled out a tuft of animal hair then reached into her dirty faded beige cropped cargo pants, into her stretched-out and smelly underwear, and yanked out a pubic hair, placing it atop the lace thong. Vlasta told a joke. "That was funny," she said, leaning her head down looking at her specially curated items.

Vlasta had basically walked and hitched rides on trains from Siberia to Moscow, paying her way with manual labor and pleasuring not-so-feminine train attendants. Once she reached Moscow, she blackmailed a rather unattractive woman who worked at a temp agency after she had approached her with some chocolates and pleasured her in the bathroom of the office building where the agency was located. This tactic led to her name being placed at the top of the list for housekeepers in the Moscow area. Vlasta knew that the wealthy families, that the wives, would choose her in the selection process over the young or immigrant women. She was placed with Sergei because she had listed experience with elder care on her resumé. In truth, her "experience" was caring for her mother until she died. Her mother had succumbed to old age. No autopsy was performed, no poison was found under the sink in the apartment they had shared. Once her mother was gone, Vlasta felt the pull of city life. She felt the pull for a new victim of her human stain.

Vlasta heard sound coming from her CB radio. She shuffled over to the small makeshift table where it rested and adjusted the volume. A voice came on requesting EMTs to an address. Vlasta's eyes bulged, somebody was hurt or dying, and she smiled before she slumped down on the circular gray metal stool. When a second call requesting EMTs to another address followed, she managed to stand and nod her head with extra happy bulged eyes and withdrew a tattered looking notebook, making a few markings. She looked up and down and up and down her columns of markings. She counted, she recounted.

She forgot what the total was. Hearing Ankica on the baby monitor, she stuffed the notebook back in a box and plopped it down by the radio.

Back in reality, on the first floor of Sergei's home, Vlasta sloppily cut some vegetables while throwing back shots of vodka. She laughed, waving her butcher knife and making obscene comments at the show she had on TV, a Russian reality show about the struggles disabled persons go through to find love. She stirred the soup she was preparing in her stockpot. With the liquid coming to a boil, she lowered the heat and placed the lid on the pot before shuffling to the staircase.

"Ankica! Ankica!" she hollered as she slumped *up* the stairs. Natina came from her room, running toward Ankica as she hobbled out of her bedroom. "No, Natina!" Vlasta shouted, as she attempted to pick her up, but Natina clung to her great-grandmother's leg. Ankica spoke to Natina, calming her.

Vlasta gripped Ankica's forearm, talking about her crass thoughts on the reality show she had been watching while acting as if she was helping Ankica down the stairs. Ankica did her best to show she was listening, while trying to turn her head to watch for Natina coming closely, scooting down each step behind them. Vlasta stepped off the last step and Ankica struggled to place her cane on the tile floor at the bottom of the steps. "You can do it," Vlasta said. "No!" Not like that!" Natina started to cry and Ankica turned, reaching a slow arm out for her. Vlasta yanked Ankica off the stairs. "She'll follow." Vlasta leered back at Natina.

In the kitchen, Vlasta served Ankica some stale bread and soup. Natina shoved bits of dry cereal in her mouth. Ankica leaned toward Natina, attempting to give her some of her bread. "No! That's not for her." Vlasta lunged from her watchful perch and jerked the bread from Natina's reach. When Vlasta was preoccupied with her show, Ankica stretched her arm as best as her eighty-plus years of life could and handed Natina a piece of bread.

When her show ended, Vlasta announced dinner was over, and she ungracefully helped Ankica back up to her bedroom as Natina followed behind crawling up the stairs.

Sergei drove slower than he normally would into the city centre. "Just a couple of days?" he asked, looking over at Nexxa before reaching for her hand. His phone rang and he let the call go to voicemail, pointing out a few places along the way. He told her some history of Moscow, how it was named after the Moskva River. How it was the first and only capital of Russia.

They reached the city. "You should eat something," Sergei suggested as he pulled up to Vogue and illegally parked.

"I'm not hungry. I'll get a snack later," Nexxa said. And his Jaguar was so quiet she could almost hear Sergei's mind begging for answers.

"I'll need a few minutes," Sergei said before exiting the car. He met Hooli inside, at his table, where he was eating a bowl of mashed potatoes. "Track her phone." Sergei spoke with a flat tone.

"Okay, will do. You know, I never liked mashed potatoes until I had these. Moscow mashed potatoes," Hooli said without making eye contact.

"Okay." Sergei nodded his head, resisting the urge to pat his trusted advisor on the shoulder. Hooli had a proclivity for awkward moments.

Later, Sergei walked with Nexxa, pulling her suitcase to the elevator in the Ararat Park Hotel. He thought about when he had first kissed her in Beirut in her hotel and waiting as he watched her get onto the elevator. Thoughts of when he worried that he would never see her again and then of racing through Beirut to rescue her. When Nexxa kissed him and grasped her suitcase, moving onto the elevator, he realized she was really leaving. Sergei exited the hotel, then turned back, and the doorman asked if he could help. Sergei chuckled before withdrawing his phone and texting Nexxa—just to check the time he should be back to pick her up.

Nexxa wanted Crimson to show itself. She undressed and put on her black Wolford two piece, thinking of her last encounter in the pool. Was it an encounter with Crimson? Bathrobe and slippers on, she left her rosary, pendulum, and phone in her hotel room. In the pool area, she noticed that the loungers had been shifted around and that the lights had been changed to reflect a blue hue. Alone in the water, she floated on her back with her eyes closed. No one had entered the pool room, and not a soul had come or gone through to the women's or men's lounges. About three minutes later, Nexxa stood from floating and started to swim toward the other end of the pool. The water stung the scratch on her breast, so she abruptly stopped swimming and moved over to the pool steps.

Standing on a step she pulled her swim top down, feeling

her scratch. A man entered the pool area, slender with long dark wavy hair, noticing her partially exposed breast. Nexxa looked up and his smile told her he was excited to see his bonus. Nexxa pulled her top back up and walked to the lounger where her towel and robe were. The towel, her robe, the pool, nothing had a connotation of the Crimson scent. Mr. "I like your boob" motioned with his head for her to join him in the pool. *He's probably Italian—no, more like from Spain*, Nexxa thought as she dried off and tied the belt to her robe.

She returned to her room, sighing as she stood before the bed. She looked over to the nightstand and could see she had messages on her phone. After showering, she dressed in black leggings and a black fitted tank top. By the time she reached the lobby, she saw it had begun snowing, so she pulled on her hood. Looking around she saw a familiar porter, local expats in the hotel bar having drinks, and Mr. "I like your boob."

Fuck it, I'm going for a run anyway.

Nexxa put in her earbuds and started her playlist. She smiled at the doorman and ran down the block in the direction away from the Red Square. The sidewalk was filling quickly with snow. Nexxa reached the end of the second block and stopped. She reached down to where she had injured her leg. A woman approached her and asked her in Russian how to get to a restaurant. Nexxa explained to the woman in Russian that she wasn't from Moscow. The woman scoffed before huffing and walking away.

Nexxa ran back toward her hotel. The doorman made a remark that might have been a joke as she entered. Nexxa approached the hotel's front desk and asked the night manager for a map of Moscow. Back in her room, shivering, she undressed and stepped into the shower. She held her hand over her scar, shielding it from the water. The soap had irritated it. Sitting on the bed in her bathrobe, Nexxa unfolded the map. She withdrew her pendulum and asked for a prayer of protection. "Is Crimson in Moscow?"

Vlasta welcomed Sergei back from driving Nexxa into Moscow with a wide hug, telling him that she missed him and was afraid she had lost him. Sergei laughed. He had brought home some take-out and retreated to his office. After eating, he checked on Natina, she was asleep, and woke Ankica, who had fallen asleep in the rocking chair in Natina's room after she had gone in again to check on the baby. He helped her back to her room and with her clothes. She thanked him, her cracking voice exposing her weakness.

Sergei retired to his room and poured a Scotch. He checked his phone, seeing one reply from Nexxa. It lacked emotion. He scrolled through past messages between him and Nexxa going back to when she was in upstate New York.

Vlasta was good at one thing, and that was doing a whole lot of nothing at the same time. She decided to rearrange items in the pantry, feeling the need to label the shelves according to the color of the containers. Items were pulled out and left in total disarray on the floor. Next she decided to vacuum out the laundry room, but when she noticed a small bug scurry across the floor, she abandoned the vacuum in the middle of the room. Finally, she decided that a hot bath was what she needed, so she schlepped upstairs. She hunched over the tub sprinkling some powder cleanser before realizing she needed to take a shit.

Nexxa opted not to eat breakfast. She didn't shower or apply any makeup or beauty products. She kept on the panties she had slept in. With her hair pulled back in a loose ponytail, she wore her black uniform and left her suitcase with the front desk. Leaving the hotel, she turned off her phone. Outside, the sun was cast on the north side of Moscow. She headed in the direction of the gray. The snow from the night before was starting to melt. The first stop, where she would start her scent trail, was the Florarium.

Nexxa requested a private tour of the vibrant pink-hued greenhouse. As the guide showed her in the door, Nexxa slipped him the equivalent of one hundred U.S. dollars, telling him she would like to walk around alone. He looked to the money, smiled, and closed the glass door. Nexxa walked the path of the circular structure as it curved higher. She grazed the Hibiscus, ran the back of her hand along the soft Dragon's Breath.

Nexxa exited Partizanskaya Metro Station, which brought her to her second stop, Izmailovsky Market. The cold swirled around the mix of tourists and expats shopping for gifts to send home. Nexxa lifted a traditional Russian fox hat in white with some faint purple, placed it atop her head, handed the shopkeeper some cash and moved on. Nexxa moved along to the first café, where she ordered tea and a scone. She prepared her cup of tea, took a sip, and placed the glass down, before running her finger along the scone. Nexxa removed the hat she had bought and placed it on her chair before walking away.

Nexxa stood in front of Ivanovsky Convent with its white façade and soft glow. She took a mental picture then trailed a tourist group into the gift shop. There, she bought a black cross necklace and a purple egg pendant locket. She found her way to the museum bathroom and draped the cross over her neck, pulling on it so that the chain dug into her neck. She opened the window and removed the necklace, draping it with the purple egg pendant necklace upon the Orenburg lace curtains blowing in the wind. She pulled the hood to her jacket up, blessed herself, and dashed out past the last of the tourists. In the streets of Moscow she jogged, pushing herself, reminding herself of the perseverance she once spoke of in her past, in her life in Manhattan.

Nexxa retrieved her suitcase from the Ararat Park Hotel concierge and strolled with her bag to TSUM. Inside, she bought a bottle of Tom Ford Black Orchid *parfum* and a new black ensemble and lingerie. She undressed in the dressing room, doused her body with the Black Orchid, dressed and spritzed on more of the Black Orchid. She bought a new suitcase and a few more essentials. If her plan worked, Crimson would follow her trail and possibly be spotted wearing the black cross necklace, or the unique purple egg pendant locket with an enclosed small-winged cherub, and the fox hat with streaks of purple. She called Sergei. He answered on the first ring. "I'm changing hotels."

"Why?" he asked, standing from his desk taking the call off of speaker and lifting the phone to his ear.

"It's fine… I'll let you know where to pick me up," she

explained and ended the call. She knew he wouldn't be too worried; he had Hooli.

Diane sat straight from lying underwater in the tub. She removed her swim goggles and rubbed her eyes. She looked at the time on her lavender Apple Watch, she had ordered it specifically in a light shade of purple, before setting a timer and putting it back on her wrist. She had taken approximately fourteen baths since she dragged Vlasta and the Siberian deer around the small izba, but the smell—more like a stain—was still detectable.

 Diane threw a leg over the tub, and lying on the edge she rolled off onto the floor, yanking her towel down from the towel rack. She dried herself off while on the floor before scooting on her back out of the bathroom. When she reached the bedroom area, she rose to a backbend then stood upright. She maneuvered on her clothes before her timer went off. Diane's shoulders slumped and she rolled her neck before sniffing, moving, taking a step; then sniffing, moving, taking another step.

 A knock came on her hotel room door. She opened it, yanking the wheeled cart from the room service attendant, pulling it into her room. Boiled eggs sitting in their proper egg cups and British toast, she called it, were upon her room service tray. Diane wheeled the cart closer to the TV. The nightly news with a story featuring the Queen of England bestowing knighthood to some British bloke was soon to be on. She had watched a YouTube video of the proper etiquette for cracking and eating Dippy Eggs. Feeling prepared, Diane raised a butter knife to an egg, swung, and the egg flew from its perch, landing by the window. Diane rose from the end of the bed and crawled along the egg yolk stain. She grasped the broken egg. She heard the Queen's voice. Looking out at the dark Moscow sky, Diane flung her body against the floor-to-ceiling window, inhaling with her face pressed to the glass. She smelled *Smeared Lavender.*

Nexxa ordered the most expensive fish and an order of caviar. The waiter was insistent on explaining how the fish would be served, probably thinking he was going to sneak in a flirt with a pretty blonde "American" tourist. Nexxa thanked him and looked down at the map she held folded in her lap. She devoured the caviar before telling the waiter that she regretted she was too full to eat the amazing fish entrée. Alas, she needed a to-go box.

Nexxa carried her fish to the Matreshka Hotel. She was shown to her room. She had requested the room with the skylight, giving her access to the rooftop. Her room was meager with a slight hint of mildew. Perfect. She plopped the to-go container on the floor. Nexxa opened the skylight, and the frostbitten wind carried the scent of her Karelian pike perch around the room.

In one gulp, then another, Diane sucked down each of the boiled eggs. She licked her finger and drew a saliva heart on the picture of her love she had brought with her to Moscow which rested in a frame on the bed. Next, she decided on one of her new blonde wigs, which was parted in the middle and tied back in a low bun. This paired well with her belted winter green leather trench coat.

Diane trekked through the late-night crowd of tourists in her black, over-the-knee stiletto Christian Louboutin boots. She imagined Nexxa, imagined her covered in flowers. Effortlessly but forcefully, she moved the night guard and entered the Florarium where the sound of her stiletto boots climbing the circular structure competed with her pulsating heart. As Nexxa had done, Diane grazed the Hibiscus—running the back of her hand along the soft Dragon's Breath. Exiting the building, she tightened the belt to her trench coat and with care positioned the guard's head on the ground.

Diane stood at the entrance of Izmailovsky Market and inhaled. The market was mostly closed, with only a few shopkeepers still tending to their shops and stalls. She stepped into a shop, and behind the counter, a man shouted in Russian for her to "get out of here." She reached into his trash and removed a scone. Sniffed and licked it. The man made a face showing his disgust then motioned for her to take the food with her. Diane inhaled the scone, wiped the crumbs from her face, and squeezed the man's cheeks.

Diane stood all alone in front of Ivanovsky Convent with its white façade and soft glow. She knelt and pretended to bless herself. During her time living in the U.S., she had attended Roman Catholic masses as part of her undergrad work. She had convinced her economics professor that the Vatican was a racketeering business. So, she needed to "suss out" the extension to the source of her theory. Which in turn caused her to realize that Western religion and their relics were harmful to her powers. Her padded bra, with the insistence of Diane, pressed against the volunteer bishop as he was closing up the main entrance. He collapsed. Inside, the convent gift shop was locked. Diane tilted her head to her left side. Her stiletto boot, left foot, gently but forcefully opened the door. Looking down the length of the shop, she saw nothing she came for. She inhaled and darted out and down the corridor.

The Orenburg lace curtains fluttered in the intended Moscow air. Diane exhaled. She grasped the black cross necklace that Nexxa had bought and pulled so tight around her neck that it had left an almost bloody mark. The purple egg locket bounced along Diane's décolletage as she made her way outside. The night guard, the same volunteer bishop as before, rose, Diane's newly acquired necklace wrapped around his elongated beard—he gasped and went down. Diane leaned in, leaned down. Blowing along his beard, she spotted a piece of pork. Standing over his body, she held the speck of meat between her coffin-shaped lavender nails.

Nexxa stood on the nightstand and opened up the skylight. She used her core strength to pull herself through the opening. Her body, cold, faced the west. She missed Sergei. His strong embrace, the way he smelled in bed. The way his penis tasted in her mouth. His scent was still available to her, but she needed to suppress that. She needed this Crimson that was following her to present itself, preferably before the glow of the morning sun.

TEACHER MR. ALBERT | 7

Mr. Albert started life with his mother telling him, "All your experiences will be the result of your assumptions." He grew up poor financially but was never poor mentally. It was actually to his advantage that his parents could not send him off to school in China. Should he have been fortunate enough to attend Nanjing University, his mom worked as a cleaning lady in the southwest building on campus, he might have been recruited by the MSS. The Ministry of State Security is the principal civilian intelligence, security, and secret police agency of the People's Republic of China, responsible for counterintelligence.

When Mr. Albert was a young teenager, he came across a news article in the local university newspaper covering the first Buddhist temple to be built in upstate New York. If you were a monk you could apply for a six-month visa to the US.

So… Mr. Albert became a monk. At least on paper. He spent exactly six months at the newly built Mahayana Temple in the Catskills before making his way to New York City. Once in the city, he found work, not in Chinatown, and applied for permanent residency. He was able to get work as a janitor at NYU through his Chinese-American contact at the temple. He had learned some English by watching movies that were played on campus for "Western Night" in Nanjing. Sleeping in the janitorial closet and eating leftovers that were thrown out in the cafeteria enabled him to save enough to start college. His first year of school he sent a small portion of money back home to his parents and paid for his tuition. The rest he used to rent a cabin in upstate New York where he spent weekends studying the Buddha Fa.

With her finger, Iliada scanned the first chapter of *Opera Omnia Medico Chemico Chirurgica* by Paracelsus, a translated first edition. She looked back at the table of contents, then back to chapter one. She hadn't really been interested in reading, so when Mr. Albert gave her lessons which involved books, she was less than thrilled. Practicing alchemy was more fun, like when she applied lip glossimer to her finger and dipped it in her wine glass, transforming the wine to dust, and could feel her finger but couldn't see it moving.

She really just wanted to hang out with Flash, so she read, took notes, and read some more. When she left the library to make some herbal tea, she found Flash in the kitchen waiting for her with a pot already made. Flash spread out some note cards with Latin phrases, moving them in front of Iliada one at a time, testing her knowledge. When her mug only showed remnants of tea, Flash folded in his wings, and Iliada knew it was time to get back to studying.

Returning to Mr. Albert's library, she spotted a book in the grand bookcase. The cover was a vibrant fuchsia. *That's pretty. Has that been here all this time?* Iliada wondered as she let the sparkle in her eyes lead her to the book, taking it over to the leather sofa. She opened it, and the chapter that was revealed had a rendering of a swastika. Iliada's eyes widened. She read the passage beneath the depiction. It explained that this symbol was the Falun emblem, a miniature of the universe. The emblem has its own form of existence and way of evolution in all of the dimensions. She read further, realizing that Hitler took this emblem, turned it, changed it to black, and thus it became his symbol for the Aryan identity.

Iliada sat back and covered herself with one of the gray cashmere blankets. She yawned once, but the pages kept her interest, turning without the effort of her slender, manicured fingers.

"What you desire already exists," Mr. Albert said, as he and Iliada walked along the perimeter of his estate. Iliada thought about the life she had had in New York City with her sister. Their past together in Canada. She had never really thought about what she wanted. She had spent more of her life following her sister than making her own decisions. Now she was here learning from Nexxa's confidant, but she was okay with that. It had more of an impact now, the thing Nexxa would say: "Someone always has less than you have, and somebody will always have more." She could now apply this concept even more seeing how something so profound as the symbol for the universe was taken, stolen more like, and used by the nefarious Hitler.

Iliada watched as Mr. Albert pulled some leaves out of a potted topiary and crumpled them, letting the bits fall to the ground, where they vanished. Mr. Albert offered no explanation as they continued walking down a set of steps to the lower area of the grounds to stand where they both looked over the steep slope to the horizon. "Your assumption places you psychologically where you are not physically," Mr. Albert spoke as he stood in his all-gray ensemble, pants and a long-sleeve t-shirt, which gradually turned to black. "Then your senses pull you back from where you were psychologically to where you are physically," he continued, turning with a barely detectable smile, while his clothes returned to their original color, shadow gray.

Iliada had seen "black cast white glow" and shook her head wondering how this all made sense. Her mind brought forth her first days in New York City. How Nexxa took her shopping for her "black uniform." The right shades of city wear. *Does Mr. Albert simply wish to be in the men's department in Saks perusing the black cashmere sweaters from this season's Zegna?* Iliada couldn't help but laugh to herself.

Now her time with Mr. Albert in upstate New York was giving her the confidence to accept that her innate gifts were becoming more powerful. She wanted to go back to the night she had whacked Kilmer on the head in Rome. Connecting with Nexxa telepathically that night had been off the charts.

She knew something was different at the time, at the moment she stood from the table abruptly leaving her new friends in Rome to return to the villa she and Nexxa were staying in.

"You can go to Rome," Mr. Albert said.

Iliada's eyes widened.

"You can whack him." Mr. Albert touched the back of his head. "Again," he continued, laughing.

"How? I mean, I can telepathically. I mean, with Nexxa." Iliada stood with a leg out, hands on her hips looking to the sky.

"In Norse mythology, it is said that in the beginning there was only a deep, deep sea," he said.

Iliada's eyes closed. Mr. Albert broke her fall.

She saw Nexxa. She saw Nexxa running for her life in Moscow.

LAVENDER | 8

Nexxa maneuvered onto the ledge of the Matreshka Hotel's rooftop deck. She walked to the northwestern corner of the building. Facing the direction of the Ararat Park Hotel, she stood breathless watching the people around Moscow's city streets. Was she looking for someone who was Russian? Whoever it was, it was attracted to her. Nexxa realized that something about her held the attraction, and at the same time repelled this person enough to have kept her safe so far. She tilted her head to the side. She saw a woman prancing along the street. This woman seemed out of character for a native Muscovite. Nexxa walked along the ledge going south, attempting to follow the woman before she turned the corner and was out of sight. No detectable Crimson. Perhaps the woman was only prancing because of the shopping bag she carried along with her. This section of Moscow was littered with high-end ateliers and luxury department stores.

Nexxa jumped down from the ledge. She walked over to the skylight and placed her right leg in and began to swing in her left leg. Then—Crimson. She smelled Crimson.

Dashing to the southwest corner again, she felt her lungs moving. She stood suppressing her breath and looked down below to the passersby. A woman with blonde hair and a winter green leather trench coat walked with her back to Nexxa. Another woman with blonde hair walked in the same direction wearing a royal blue wool wrap coat trimmed with fox fur. Both women stopped when a man walking a Siberian Husky passed by. The woman in the winter green coat slightly turned toward the man bending to pet his dog. The woman in the blue coat also put a hand out to the dog. The animal sat, then laid down on the sidewalk. The owner spoke to the animal, commanding him. Nexxa looked from the woman in the winter green to the woman in the royal blue and to the man who was attempting to entice his dog from its lying position. The blonde woman in the royal blue wool coat moved along before embracing a man on the street. The woman in the winter green leather coat stood, and as she turned to walk away, Nexxa noticed her necklace swing in the air. Could it be a black cross? Was it the purple egg locket? And then she was out of sight.

Nexxa stared at the fish in the takeaway box on the floor in her small dowdy hotel room. It was all she could smell now. No Crimson. No decadent perfume. No Sergei. She knew she would need to go back to Sergei by the morning.

Nexxa unzipped her suitcase and pulled out her pendulum.

She heard Iliada call her name. Moving over to the skylight, letting the pendulum swing, Nexxa asked if Crimson was human.

Diane told her she could come into the bathroom while she showered. She had noticed Karyna sitting alone at the hotel bar, so with an awkward gulp of excitement, she entered the bar of her hotel and approached the young woman. She was wearing a tacky, sparkly, low-slung dress in a horrible shade of turquoise and was sipping a libation that looked more for show than for enjoyment. Sure, she had a snaggletooth or two, but her breasts were perky. Diane detected a spot of ginger in her. More like auburn hair that she had tried to dye sultry dark, but pieces of the naturally blended red begged to shine through.

Diane removed her blonde wig but kept on her thong as she entered the shower. The brownish Moscow water fell onto her petite Asian frame. She looked over her shoulder as the steam started to fill the room. She called out to Karyna. No answer. Diane pulled at her thong so that it glided along her clitoris. She mouthed *Reyhan*, her love's name. Careful not to climax, she turned off the water, removed her thong and patted her vagina with a powder puff. She used a hand towel to wipe the mirror and then adjusted her hair. She pushed her tongue along the bottom of her top front teeth. She was ready for Karyna.

Karyna was perched on the end of the bed. She held the framed photo of Diane's love. She laughed looking at the picture, and in broken English she asked who the Asian woman with red hair was in the photo. Diane stepped closer, smiled, and snapped her neck. She was careful to remove the photo from her hands before she tossed her body into the bathroom. Diane dressed in the clothes she had had on that night, and then standing over Karyna's body, she used the bathroom mirror to put on her blonde wig. Kneeling, she pulled down the top of Karyna's dress. *Hmm, she has nice breasts.* She tilted her head. *Not as nice as Nexxa's though.* With her winter green leather coat on and her black, over-the-knee stiletto Christian Louboutin boots, she left her room wheeling her suitcase with the picture of her love inside. Jupiter was still in retrograde, but she could pass the time by executing a transaction for her father. Something she needed to do in the land of the leprechauns.

Nexxa sat on one of the pitifully dressed twin beds that flanked the skylight in her hotel room. She exhaled. She looked through the still open skylight. The daylight would be there soon.

In upstate New York, Iliada walked in a pair of black stilettos in Mr. Albert's grand foyer. She stopped at a mirror, applying some lip glossimer.

Nexxa stood. Their minds connected.

This time Iliada directed Nexxa. She walked them through her thoughts whilst wearing her new Balmain black leather heels, courtesy of Mr. Albert. Iliada showed Nexxa running, running around Moscow. Her determination was racing against the cold. Then—Mr. Albert crumpling leaves and a swastika.

Nexxa closed her eyes and let herself fall back on the bed. The break of Moscow's dawn was coming.

Nexxa examined the bathroom which looked more like a latrine. She reluctantly peed, lining the seat first with toilet paper. She regrettably brushed her teeth with a disposable toothbrush, careful to place it back in the plastic wrapper. She stripped the bed and, on her way out, tossed the linens and the wrapped toothbrush in an open room that was being cleaned. Staring at her reflection in the elevator going down, Nexxa noticed the mark on the back of her neck from the black cross rosary. Licking two fingers, she rubbed along the spot.

Sergei stopped in front of the hotel and stepped out of the car. He smiled at Nexxa. He looked to the hotel then back to Nexxa with a scrunched forehead. Nexxa let her head fall to the side and smiled, saying, "Hi." Sergei embraced her, and Nexxa flinched. Sergei took a step back. "I'm sorry. I'm tired and I smell. Need a shower," she explained. Sergei took her bag, he had already retrieved her other suitcase from the Ararat and placed it in the back. He put the car in drive, took hold of her hand, and sped off way faster than Nexxa was prepared for.

The streets leading out of the city were a blur. Nexxa moved her hand up to her chest almost to her neck. Sergei looked over at her, so Nexxa pulled her hand back down. Sergei maneuvered through traffic in and out, in and out of lanes. "How are—" Nexxa asked with guilt in her heart.

Sergei shouted at another driver, "Fucking move!" Looking out of the passenger window, she decided she would let him be angry, just a little bit.

Nexxa knew Sergei was the one, the man that emitted the white glow, but she needed to be reminded of that. Reminded of when Mr. Albert had cast the black to reveal the man with the white glow. Sergei presented himself as a self-made man, with a formal higher education, and as someone who could respect the fact that Nexxa had made a career from nothing with no formal instruction. Yet, he hadn't inquired as to why she had a lavender glow, or as he put it, "There's purple around you." She felt uneasy bringing it up. Was now even a good time?

Nexxa looked down the hall toward the sounds of Natina whining in her room and Ankica attempting to calm her. Nexxa turned to thank Sergei for carrying up her suitcase, and their eyes met briefly, before he trotted back down the stairs off to his office saying, "Sorry, my love, gotta make a call." Nexxa pulled her suitcase across his bedroom. She properly brushed her teeth with her electric toothbrush and stripped from her clothes, folding them and placing them in the corner of the bathroom. She lifted Sergei's bath towel to her nose. In the shower she thought about when he had said "I ya tebya lyublyu" as he kissed each of her hands then each foot. Nexxa lathered her hair. She leaned back, and the warm, slightly dirty Moscow water pulsated from her head down her back.

  Sergei stepped into the shower and Nexxa smelled her Russian just as she felt his hands grasping her abdomen. She turned; he began kissing her. Sergei pushed Nexxa against the tile. He continued kissing her down her neck with one hand between her thighs. Nexxa lifted his head. She breathed his name. Sergei spun her around and bent her over.

  The ensuite door opened. Nexxa heard, "Mommy." She

jumped from Sergei's grasp. "Did you hear that?" Nexxa asked.

"Hear what?" Sergei looked toward the door. Nexxa turned off the water and stepped out of the shower. She saw one of the kittens she had found in the tub a few weeks prior. The kitten was rubbing against the bottom of the bathroom vanity… only the kitten was much bigger, more like a full-grown cat. Sergei stood with his erection. Nexxa grabbed a towel and wrapped it around herself. She bent, petting the cat. Looking back to Sergei, she smiled. He stepped out of the shower and dried off.

"Nothing like a pussy to ruin me getting pussy." Nexxa looked down, shaking her head. "I'm getting a Scotch." Sergei pulled on his underwear and pants.

Nexxa sat beside the cat asking it gently, "Did you say mommy?" The cat looked Nexxa in the face and meowed before darting out of the bathroom, through Sergei's room, and out of the bedroom door.

Sergei stood next to his leather armchairs as he sipped his Scotch eyeing the door. He knew he had locked his bedroom door.

Nexxa towel dried her hair, examined her neck as best she could in the fogged-up mirror, and applied some lip stain. She lifted her forearm, sniffing it. She pulled a section of her hair up to her nose. She grabbed her Moroccanoil dry shampoo spray, spritzing her whole body with it. It was undeniably decadent.

Sergei stood with a bulge in his tracksuit pants. He poured more Scotch, took a taste, set his glass down, and started toward his bathroom. Nexxa adjusted the towel around her and stepped out. Sergei smiled. Nexxa removed her towel, and Sergei put a hand to her breast. "Wait," he said as he dashed over to his bedroom door. He locked the door and turned, seeing Nexxa sitting in an armchair. She had her legs gracefully draped over the arm. He watched as she lifted his glass of Scotch, taking a sip. With vampire*ish* speed, he was upon her.

Sergei grasped Nexxa by her ankles, pulling her legs around to the front of the chair. His eyes narrowed as he pushed her thighs apart, knelt, and pulled her to the end of the chair and onto his face. Nexxa braced herself, letting her head fall back. She grasped the back of Sergei's head, and he pulled on her hips, pushing his face deeper. Nexxa heard the door creak; she opened her eyes, but feeling Sergei's stubble against her thighs, she closed them. Sergei groped her left breast and used his right hand to maneuver Nexxa onto the floor, and she moved her legs apart, allowing his well-endowed erection to thrust.

When the sun shone the next morning, Nexxa could see dust accumulating on the bag with the urn. She had *almost* forgotten about his ashes. Sergei's bed was massive, his master bedroom was spacious, and yet she could still see the bag that held Kilmer's urn from any angle in the room.

Nexxa was making her way to the bathroom while Sergei was already up getting dressed. He leaned out of his closet, grabbing at her for a kiss. Nexxa lowered her head into his chest before squirming. "I need to brush my teeth."

Sergei chuckled, "I'll *lick* your toothbrush." Nexxa smiled before glancing over at the urn. Peeing, Nexxa counted. There were two seasons she had known Sergei in, autumn and winter. Two smells, Crimson and Vlasta's. Five countries they had been together in: Lebanon, Turkey, Russia, Italy, and the U.S. One death.

In his bedroom, Nexxa stood looking through the glass doors. She saw birds flying in a pattern an equal distance from one another. Eight in total. Nexxa counted how many times she and Sergei had had sex. How many times he had gone down on her. How many days it had been since she worked for Kuretz Investments. How long she was married to Kilmer. She reached into her bra, touching the scar on her breast. She reached to touch her neck, running her finger along the part where she had pulled so hard on the necklace with the black cross. This time in Moscow she had acquired two scars which had manifested in a span of two months. Nexxa crossed the bedroom and picked up the urn with Kilmer's ashes. Standing in the sunlight by the glass doors, she held the urn next to her chest. Her lavender pulsed.

PETIT OLIGARQUE | 9

Sergei scrolled through a list of names on his computer. Some you could call "little known oligarchs." Some you could call "semipermeable rich," meaning they were vulnerable to the effects of war, global pandemics, or just ignorance. Some you could classify simply by their generation, Gen Y.1, making money being twats on social media.

Sergei was one to gamble and Croatia's football team always lent to a favorable profit hedging against a long shot. So when Hooli approached him about the potential of sanctions against Russia for their lack of domestic policy on investing, he knew instantly where he would continue to play the game. Working with Hooli, Sergei now had a new shell company which enabled him to establish a presence in Croatia.

Rising from his desk, he walked across his office and poured himself a Scotch. Sergei stood intimately close to the painting he had of former President Mikhail Gorbachev. He raised his glass to the former president: the person who was *numero uno* in a series of events that changed the political trajectory of Europe marking the demise of the "Coldest War" ever. Sergei had been a teenager when he and his father watched Gorbachev accept the Nobel Peace Prize on TV. Oh, and Gorbachev made it into Louis Vuitton's 1999 Fall campaign; so Sergei owned an LV suitcase, briefly. But now, with Putin in power again, the only business Sergei wanted to keep in his homeland was his restaurant Vogue.

Sergei ran his hand along the bottom of the painting which years ago he had commissioned from a local artist, a portrait of his favorite president. When he received the final work of art, it included not only the artist's signature but the words *glasnost*, open voice, and *perestroika*, rebuilding, on the bottom.

Nexxa stood on the staircase with Natina as she giggled scooting down the steps. As she ran into Sergei's office, Nexxa retrieved her so Sergei would not be disturbed. Looking at the Bloomberg terminal, she saw a career in the past. Lifting Natina, who threw her arms around her, Nexxa felt her baby fingers run along the red mark on her neck; a reminder of an unaccomplished mission seeking out the source of the Crimson scent. And, as Natina dashed into the kitchen getting a verbal reprimand from the woman making soup, Nexxa was reminded of the unconventional housekeeper lurking about the house.

Natina whined, struggling from Nexxa's grasp and running

out of the kitchen and back into Sergei's office. In a successful swoop, Nexxa lifted Natina, carrying her all the way upstairs wherein Natina tugged at Nexxa's shirt, revealing her bra. Sighing, Nexxa examined a tattered piece of lace on her bra. With Natina sitting on the bed watching a cartoon, Nexxa undressed and stared at her clothes in the walk-in closet, about thirty pieces in total. Most of what she had was what she used to wear to work. Nexxa pulled out the Hervé Léger dress Sergei had bought her when they first visited Moscow.

"Isn't this pretty, baby?" Nexxa asked while stepping out of the closet and holding the dress against her body. Natina giggled, pointing her tiny finger at Nexxa.

When making his proposal to potential investors, Sergei had insisted that having retail space on the first floor, the only floor accessible to the public, would be necessary. Implementing this into the design of the building would encourage any sovereign state's local government to issue permits. A steady revenue of VAT, value added tax, also known as sales tax, would make the project more desirable. It was a delicate balancing act whenever working with state officials whether from a former communist country or from the modern democratic West. Sergei had learned that no business venture was as simple as filing the correct paperwork: applications, work permits, building permits, visas, etc. For Kozman Investments to operate, he needed help from Hooli and for Croatia's version of Moscow's Federation Tower, on a smaller scale, he needed to foster friendships with the elite and within the government in Croatia.

The most important relationship he had to caress was with the Minister of Physical Planning, Construction and State Assets. Fortunately, Ivan Jubić, the newly appointed minister, was the cousin of Sergei's friend Srđan. Srđan and Sergei had met when they were both in their early twenties in Canada at Skip Barberton Racing School, where a Russian and a Croat formed a bond over fast cars and their love of Western blondes, Christina Applegate and the fuckable Sharon Stone. Croatia's various department ministers seemed to be in competition with one another to prove to the EU that they were like the rest of Europe. Sergei was armed with his initial boost, Hooli's intercepted CIA chatter about potential sanctions against Mother Russia, his entrepreneurial spirit, and last but not the least, his babushka's visions.

Sergei looked at the calendar on his phone. A meeting with a Croatian state official. A meeting with one of the project investors. A meeting with the contractor. He sighed heavily, partly growling, and put down his phone. *I will need a lot of Scotch and a good fuck after all this.*

Sergei made his way up the stairs, and in his bedroom, he found Natina on his bed. Smiling, he sat beside her. She leaned into him, and he stroked her head before she leapt up quickly and started jumping on the bed. Sergei laughed. Nexxa stepped out of the closet, she was in a bra with tattered lace, and Sergei grinned. Nexxa turned around and slipped on the silk kimono over her bra and leggings. Somewhat dressed, she moved from one side of the bed to the other trying to grasp Natina. Sergei put his arms wide blocking the baby, catching her. Natina squirmed, laughed, and fussed. Nexxa held her arms out to her, and Natina fell into her. Down the hall, Sergei watched in the doorway as Nexxa rocked Natina to sleep.

Later in his ensuite, Sergei kissed Nexxa on the forehead. "I'm heading out. Here, take this." He handed her his credit card. Nexxa slipped it into her bra. Sergei pushed open her kimono, revealing her brassiere. "You need a new one," he said, looking down at her.

Perched on the pouf, Nexxa crossed her legs and leaned back with a tempting look. "Okay, so when can you take me?" Nexxa knew he was going to a meeting.

"I'll have a driver bring you later." Sergei faced the mirror, adjusting his tie.

Nexxa nodded, forcing a smile.

"You alright?" Sergei asked.

"Yeah, yeah." But in truth Nexxa really had no desire to go back into the city centre. Sure, she couldn't have been happier upon her return to Moscow. The anticipation on the ride from the airport to the Ararat Park Hotel. The surprising and humorous Rochelle sighting. But then, her incident in the pool resulting in scar number one. And... running herself around leaving her scent for Crimson to follow, which she hid from Sergei.

Sergei bent over again, kissing Nexxa on the lips this time. Nexxa grasped his arms, pulling herself up and into him. She ran her hand along his navy-blue Canali silk tie. Sergei looked her in the eyes. Nexxa moved her hand down his abdomen, stopping at his endowments.

"Later," Sergei whispered into her ear. "Definitely," he

breathed heavily.

Sergei pulled his Jaguar into the alley and exited the vehicle, handing the key fob to the young valet, and stood looking to the sky. It was unusually warm for late February in Russia. He thought about Beirut. How calmly warm it had been when he was there last October. He lingered outside the back entrance for a few minutes inhaling the secondhand smoke from a few local homeless men. After laughing at a few of their lewd jokes he handed them each some pocket money, money for booze, then tucked his leather case that held his tablet and some documents under his arm and headed inside the door that led to the kitchen of Vogue.

Sergei greeted each staff member as he moved swiftly, grabbing a raw potato and taking a bite before tossing it into the large trash bin as he exited the kitchen into the dining room. He had instructed the staff to set up a table near the back corner for him. He chuckled as he approached the table. A stack of Bloomberg magazines had been placed on it. Sergei lifted the magazines and carried them to the kitchen. He plopped them on the floor.

"Minister." Sergei stood and shook Ivan's hand.

"Sergei," Ivan said.

Sergei waved over a waiter. He approached, holding his head down. The minister, Ivan, began rattling off his order. The waiter tapped and tapped on his tablet, losing his grip. Sergei stood, and the waiter clenched his shoulders. Sergei reached for the tablet. "Technology," he chuckled, as he placed the tablet on the table next to them. He repeated Ivan's order and walked with the dark-haired, clean shaven, lanky waiter to the kitchen. The waiter apologized. Sergei asked a kitchen staff member for a bottle and two glasses. A man swiftly complied. Sergei poured them each some vodka. The waiter threw back the shot. Sergei patted him on the back and returned to his Croatian minister.

The Minister of Physical Planning, Construction and State Assets, Ivan Jubić, had taken his first trip on a private aircraft. His destination: to see his cousin's friend, Sergei Kozlov, in Moscow, Russia. He had hoped, in his wet dreams, that it would have been to see the man who had served as U.S. President Barack Obama's Chief of Staff, Rahm Emanuel. While he could easily fancy Sergei, it wasn't his style to be interested in straight men.

Sergei led the conversation into business, stating figures from the projected revenue the preemptively approved project would bring into the city of Zagreb. He mentioned notable buildings the architect had worked on in Eastern Europe. When he saw Ivan nod with an unenthusiastic face he mentioned Srđan, Ivan's cousin. Sergei mentioned how his fondness for Croatia, at the time Yugoslavia, came about because of his friendship with Srđan. Ivan gave a nod. Then, Mikhail Sergei's partner in his restaurant, approached the table introducing himself. Sergei noticed how a glimmer of delight appeared in Ivan's eyes as he spoke to Mikhail. Sergei took a sip of his vodka, wiped his mouth, then placed his napkin next to his plate and suggested they take their meeting elsewhere.

Having done his research via Hoolihane on the minister, Sergei had asked Mikhail to approach their table approximately thirty minutes into his meeting. Mikhail had that pretty boy look that matched the porn Ivan watched. Sergei invited Mikhail to go with him and Ivan to a dancer's lounge. Mikhail clapped his hands together saying, "Yeah, yeah."

Sergei wasn't a regular at the dancer's lounge, but he had brought clients there in the past for some "encouragement." He watched as Ivan leaned intimately close, saying, "It's so loud in here," speaking incessantly to Mikhail. And how Mikhail drank incessantly on Sergei's tab giving a cheer, clapping his hands here and there for each dancer. Mikhail wasn't the brightest... He would talk to a Siberian snowwoman.

Sergei looked at the calendar on his phone. His next appointment was going to be with his Russian investor. Then he checked his text messages. The investor's personal secretary had sent a message with a link to coordinates for the meeting for the next day. Sergei messaged Hoolihane that he should look at the text that he had been sent. (Hooli had access to Sergei's phone.)

When Mikhail excused himself, sloppily with the imminent smell of pussy on him, to go to a private room, Sergei used the opportunity to escort Ivan out of the club. Sergei stood and waved over one of the security men that worked there. With the brute's assistance, he helped Ivan out of the club and into a cab. Sergei handed the security from the club a tip and walked down the street.

Reaching the corner, Sergei stopped, only a few minutes to five p.m., dark already. He breathed out and his breath billowed through the evening lights of Moscow. Sergei spotted another homeless man he knew, the light changed, and he stepped into the street. A black Mercedes S-Class started down the street. Sergei stopped and turned; he looked the driver straight on. The car accelerated, and Sergei cocked his head. The thought of Nexxa flashed in his mind, so he picked up his pace, and the sedan narrowly missed him, driving away. Sergei cuffed his mouth and exhaled.

Sergei removed his phone, giving it the command to call Hooli. He walked briskly telling himself he was just *cold*. Hooli's phone went to voicemail. "Fuck!" Sergei shouted.

Sergei made his way toward the Ararat Park Hotel. He was under the impression he would meet his investor in an office building nearby the next day. Sergei's phone vibrated and he answered.

"The coordinates *were* for the Barvikha Hotel and Spa," Hooli said.

"Were?" asked Sergei.

"Yeah, so, they keep changing every fifteen minutes," answered Hooli.

"Changing?" Sergei asked. "Fifteen minutes?" Sergei looked at his watch.

"This is typical," explained Hooli.

"Typical? Fuck!" Sergei responded, thinking about Nexxa. His driver would have already left to retrieve her. "I have to call Nexxa."

"Yeah, man. I'll, wait a sec, man."

Sergei could hear Hooli typing and typing. The silence was annoying, the typing even more so. Sergei lowered the phone until he heard Hooli again.

"So... so we've got, okay. Yeah, got 'em."

"Got 'em? Got who?"

"Dude, hold on!" Hooli spoke in a trying-to-be-commanding voice before apologizing. "S—sorry. I reversed the coordinates and plunked them into a fresher no dot com file."

"Uh-huh." Sergei scrunched his forehead.

"So yeah, you'll be meeting basically by your house. Is there a Starbucks there now?"

"No. I know the location. This is about my land. I'll get back to you." Sergei ended the call.

Sergei knew that the location was the empty lot past the forest behind his home. The plot of land his home was built on and the lot behind it were land that he inherited from his parents. Land that he had to almost buy out of probate. While his father had had a will, there were complications. Basically, his father acquired the land because he had produced documents showing the land was his great-grandfather's property. Property records from WWI had been difficult to acquire, and when Sergei's father presented birth certificates and requisitioned land documents, he was able to prove ownership through his lineage. Then, when it came time for Sergei to build, he needed permits and to prove again that he owned the land, and that's where the problem incurred. Rather than produce what he wasn't sure he had in his possession, pre Hooli, he took everything he had in the bank plus a loan from a family friend—a short, fat, and old Russian bear, his now-investor for his project in Croatia, and bought the land that he legally should have inherited.

Sergei called his driver, but he had already retrieved Nexxa to bring her into Moscow. He turned around. Walking back to his car, Sergei spotted Mikhail trying to make his way into the front entrance of Vogue. Sergei quickened his pace and reached Mikhail just as he approached the door. He walked him around to the back entrance, and with Mikhail's arm slumped over Sergei's neck, Sergei helped him into the restaurant. A kitchen prep ran over to assist Sergei with Mikhail. Together, they got him up to the office. Sergei's phone rang. It was Nexxa, and another call was waiting—it was Hooli. In one breath, Sergei explained, "I have something I need to take care of with Hooli. I can't take you out tonight. I'll be home as soon as I can."

Nexxa said nothing, hushing her mind of thoughts of him out with the women from his restaurant that eyed him like a Spartan sport.

"Nexxa? Nexxa?"

"Yeah... yeah, I'm here," she finally spoke but was glad he couldn't see her grasping her chest willing herself not to throw up.

"Stay in the house when you get back. I'll see you when I get home."

He switched over to Hooli. Hooli said he was monitoring the area for cell phone pings and that he had activated the drone that Sergei kept on standby outside of his home, sending it over to the area of the coordinates they were given.

Not wanting Nexxa to see where he was going, Sergei drove past the exit for his home and took the next one. This exit led him to the same road his home was on, but much further down. Sergei parked in a lot meant for people accessing a hiking trail. He began down the path. In the distance he could see the drone Hooli had activated. Sergei called Hoolihane.

"You right, man?" asked Hooli.

"Yeah." Sergei cleared his throat. "I just started down the path."

"So, man, they've got, I'm detecting two individuals."

"Okay, so what else?"

"Well, one individual is definitely short and round. The other is really taller, yeah taller than the short one."

Sergei chuckled, "That's how taller would work."

"Dude. Bogdan?"

Sighing, Sergei said, "He's still gone." Sergei thought back to the day he had gone out to Bogdan's izba on his land. Bogdan was simply not there. No more "Hi-Fi." No more Russian tea cakes. It all happened like a bad breakup when one party sends the other a "breakup" text. Only Bogdan, his head of security, just simply wasn't there anymore. He didn't answer his phone, and he hadn't withdrawn any money from his account. (Sergei paid him well.) When Bogdan vanished, Sergei had Hooli search for him. The trail went cold. Sergei went through two different security firms, not liking either of them. Without Bogdan, the few other freelance security personnel that were on his payroll just seemed worthless. He found Vlasta, hired her, moved her in, and after upgrading his security surveillance—hence the drone and investing more into Hooli—he decided with the insistence of Vlasta that he didn't need security anymore.

Sergei had his gun, he had his bravery, and he had a drone overhead with Hooli looking down on him. The path ended.

Sergei blew into his hands and rubbed them together. He withdrew his gun, slid the hammer back, and walked into the view of the moonlight.

DR. DIANE MARTENS | 10

Diane boarded the train, took her seat, and popped in her earbuds. She bobbed her head to her playlist, singing out loud. When an older man lowered his newspaper and gave her his "you youth" look, she began to exaggeratedly mouth the words. She only knew a word here or there, so she began ad-libbing. She took out her snack, Peanut Flips, *Erdnussflips* in German, and ate it while mouthing, letting crumbs fall into her lap and brushing them off onto the floor beneath her feet. The old man scowled before raising his newspaper.

The toilet in the passenger cabin was itsy bitsy. When the train rounded a curve right as Diane withdrew her tampon, it wiggled loose from her grip and dropped on the floor next to her shoe. Huffing, she lifted the tampon, read the sign on the mirror, in Deutsche, to not flush feminine care products, and plopped the tampon in the toilet, flushing it down the drain, and down went the *damen hygiene produkte*. Diane licked her hand and rubbed the spot of blood on her shoe.

The Draco constellation, dragon in Latin, was Diane's preferred constellation. So… she chose an itinerary that was as close to the shape as possible for her trip around Europe. Berlin, Prague, Munich, Luxembourg, Paris, London, Birmingham, and Dublin, five stops less than the exact number of stars in the constellation.

Sitting in the restaurant railcar, Diane let a genuine smile occupy her face as she thanked the server for her breakfast. Two boiled eggs and some toast. She let her genuine smile transform into the smile of an innocent teen girl as she listened and smelled. She could smell the passengers' fluid within their Cowper's gland, the little bit of fluid that leaked out as they each became aroused, as they spoke about their destination. Borovets. *Borovets, Borovets, Borovets!* Five lads on their way to a stag party in Borovets, Bulgaria.

Diane tucked away her photo of Reyhan in her suitcase and closed the door to her private cabin as the train was pulling into Prague. She decided she would take a detour to Borovets as well. Seven strip clubs, five stags and one with the wolfness.

Once in the Sofia train station Diane wheeled her suitcase like she had a destination. She noticed the group of five men negotiating for a taxi to the town of Borovets. Diane maneuvered into the women's bathroom and exited as KitchenGod. Approaching the lads, she explained in the persona of a horny Asian man that "he" needed a ride. That he could pay taxi fare. They all chuckled. Then, they obliged.

Later, "They can't break my heart. They can't break my heart," Diane whispered, standing on the dark, snow-covered ground wearing a new pair of ski boots outside of an exotic dancers club. Inside the door, she whispered something else. "Please break my heart."

Sitting with her back against the wooden wall in the quaint club, wearing Bulgaria's finest ski gear, she watched, sipping her vodka, as a dancer spread her legs. As she spun around the pole. As she, the one with lovely auburn hair, licked a blow-up penis.

The next morning, Diane awoke next to the only lady lover with auburn hair in Borovets. Out of the twin bed, Diane placed her ski gear, pants, top, and boots on the floor. She wrote a note, in Mandarin, that said she had a good time. She looked to the woman she had spent the night with. She looked to her tousled auburn hair, then to her panties on the floor. Diane lifted the panties and placed them atop the ski pants. She then leaned over the lady in the bed as she slept and using a pair of tweezers pried one of her fingernails off. The nail was painted lavender. A fake press on.

Someone with the wolfness was waiting on the platform. Diane conspicuously whiffed each person as she rolled her suitcase through the passengers. *Right here.* Diane stopped. Boarding began and Diane followed a short and round older woman onto the train. The woman approached her seat and attempted to lift her worn luggage. Diane's hand grazed the woman's as she lifted the suitcase for her. Sitting together,

Diane saw the old lady's ticket was for Serbia. Three hours.

Diane circled her lavender coffin-shaped nail around the older woman's wrist. The woman woke and began muttering in Serbian. Diane smiled, tilting her head. The woman smiled, tilting her own head toward the window. Diane pressed her fingernail harder into the woman's wrist. The woman said, "I know what you are," and Diane withdrew her hand before the woman closed her eyes again and returned to snoring.

Exiting the train in Paris, Diane followed a scent. The scent led her to a bakery in the second arrondissement which sold *American* cookies. The woman who owned the shop happened to have lived in the U.S., so Diane chatted with her in American English as she chose seven delectable cookies. Wheeling her bag with one hand, carrying a mojito cookie in the other, and with her mouth holding onto a vanilla cookie, Diane made her way north on Rue d'Aboukir.

The entrance was narrow. The hallway leading to the elevator was narrow. The elevator was ever so cozy. Diane looked around the apartment she had arranged for her stay in Paris. Modern, small bedroom with direct access to the elevator, and the best was the view. Diane opened a window shutter in the living room, exposing her to the nightlife below. She reveled at the colorful women below. One was transgender. *Not that one, but the rest*, she thought. She held up two hundred euros; one woman began walking toward Diane's building. Diane shook her head no; the woman was too big. *Won't fit, narrow accommodations.* Diane extended her arm, pointing with a lavender coffin-shaped nail. The woman, a blonde, smiled.

Diane removed her top, sitting in only her thong with a leg propped up on the sofa. She had left the door open for the French hooker. She moaned as the lips of a blonde French woman licked her clitoris. Pushing her head in further she saw the blonde was actually a redhead. Diane pushed the woman from her body and pranced around the apartment. "*Ma cherie, ma cherie, ma cherie* redhead in Paris."

Paris had been busy. Cookies, someone eating Diane's pussy. Now it was off to the Queen! Had she only been into ginger men, namely the party boy of the royal family, Harry, this would have been an ever-anticipated stop along her way through Europe. For surely Diane could be very persuasive. She could flash her Hong Kong Convention Ambassador credentials working herself all the way to a meeting with Prince Harry. But no, nope, she didn't like the feel of ginger stubble between her thighs.

A Harry Potter Black Cab Tour, a photograph in front of a red telephone box, a bad meal or two and Diane was done. Oh, she did watch the guards at Buckingham Palace. Rather boring. She stood looking one in the face wishing she were an actual vampire and could suck his boring bland English blood. But no, no, she could only suck his breath if he had the wolfness. None of that sordid stuff probably ever happened in London. Of course, sordid stuff did happen in London. "For fuck's sake!" Diane shouted. "Jack the Ripper?" Diane questioned, leaning into a man who walked past her. He scoffed. "Jack the Ripper?" Diane asked, leaning into another passerby.

Finally a man selling souvenirs hollered to her, "Take the

tube to the Tower Hill tube station. That's right. You'll see the Jack the Ripper Museum."

"Killed five prostitutes, sadistic butchery, grandson of Queen Victoria," Diane read aloud from a plaque on the wall of the museum. A tear, then more, came to her dark eyes. She walked backward bumping into the front entrance. Outside, pubs, shops; Diane didn't look right, look left. That was for tourists. She threw herself against the air in the street. She did several cartwheels, round-offs, and a back handspring. Landing, she knelt and screamed holding her chest. A shop owner came out and approached her. A young teen boy laughed, taking out his phone to video her. A car came to a screeching halt. Diane stood. She looked directly into the dark-haired, middle-aged British woman's eyes. She thanked her.

In her private cabin on the last leg of her trip to her destination, Dublin, Diane cozied up in her lavender pajamas holding the framed picture of her love, Reyhan. She told Reyhan about Jack the Ripper. She told her she would have protected her from a man like that. Diane flipped over on her stomach on her bed and leaned into the picture of her love, lying on the pillow. She whispered her plans. Her plans were to procure a private jet. And possibly to try mutton.

The cabbie talked non-stop, pointing at landmarks and laughing at his own jokes. Ick, he smelled repugnant. Like the dirty, dirty smell of piss and beer on the floor of the loo in a pub. Diane smiled at him in the rearview mirror. He swerved the taxi. The ad nauseam continued, endless ramblings about

Dublin and its remarkable history. Diane spread her legs, leaned closer, and when the bloke caught view of her, Diane circled her lavender coffin-shaped nail around the back of his neck. The talking stopped.

The porter for the Dylan Hotel was sweet. Yeah, Diane really felt like this Irish bloke was nice. She tipped him. She thanked him. She had been thanking a lot of strangers lately. Maybe she wasn't so upset anymore that she hadn't been effective at taking what she required from Nexxa, yet. Or… maybe it was having a blonde woman go down on her. She had always liked redheads. Auburns. But who could resist a pretty blonde.

Diane had reserved a suite with baroque furnishings. She adjusted the Irish-designed bed cover in a gorgeous hue of dragon's blood and wallowed in it.

Diane tapped on the app for her notes and scrolled with a lavender coffin-shaped nail. "In a western town with dead end walls," Diane sang as she stood looking in the mirror by the bedside, brushing her black hair. *Where do I find a Pet Shop Boy?* She looked to the empty bag of chips on the dresser. Now it was time to find that mutton.

Diane walked with the lyrics of Pet Shop Boys in her head: *For everything I long to do, no matter when or where or who, has one thing in common too, it's a sin.* Diane moved along St. Mary's Road. *Tis gray here. I kind of like it*, she thought. The sky kept its true color which was different than the smog gray cover Diane was used to in China. This gray was calm, familiar. Maybe addictive. Round the bend she went. Diane walked into Sutherland Interiors and properly lay on a gorgeous gray begging-to-be-touched modular sectional sofa.

Her Balmain high-top sneakers had a bit of Dublin dirt on them. His face cringed, the sad Mr. Bean looking salesman, as he approached her. He looked to her feet, and Diane lifted her head. She imagined him decapitated. No, she imagined the other salesman, a gorgeous redhead, the one with the red Irish pussy sitting with her skirt around her ankles.

Diane showed off her dance body. Petite, but it moved well to the '80s tunes bouncing around the Dr. Martens shop. The redheaded salesman from the furniture store put her hand on Diane's lower back as she pointed with her right hand to a pair of black leather platform boots. Diane left the store wearing her new Dr. Martens. The redhead suggested Diane come to her flat for dinner. She wanted to thank her for buying the gray sectional, as it gave her enough commission to pay her rent for the month.

   Diane thought the flat would be filled with old lady stuff. Like crocheted doilies and a few crosses. The flat turned out to be in a modern building. As the microwave worked on "dinner" Diane sipped a glass of stale chardonnay on the terrace. The microwave dinged. A guy emerged from the bathroom. He opened the microwave, removed the food and plopped down with a plateful, turning on the telly. The redhead shouted from the bedroom that she would only be a minute and not to mind her roommate.

   Diane squinted her eyes. She stepped in from the terrace, and the dude said, "Oh hey." Diane hovered over him as he took a bite. He chuckled. Diane circled her nail around his thigh, then he moaned. She dragged him to the terrace and flopped him over.

Diane pushed open the bedroom door. The redhead was smoking a cigarette out of the bedroom window. Diane took the cigarette from her hand; the redhead blew smoke out, and Diane tossed the cigarette butt. It landed on the duvet. She bent her over, and down came the redhead's skirt. Tongue in and out of her vagina. The redhead orgasmed. Flames erupted from the bed. The redhead screamed.

On her way out, Diane stopped and thought about how the roommate dude had blonde hair. Like the blonde-haired male she had found in Rome and spork fed soup. She lifted her bag with her Balmain sneakers and jumped from the terrace, landing next to the blonde dude's body in the landscaping. Diane stood for a moment admiring the solar lights that were weak but emitting a subtle lavender glow. Screaming could be heard from the apartment building. Sirens were coming. Diane moved her tongue across her teeth. *Now, where can one find mutton?*

Diane stepped into Spar. She walked down the first aisle. Back up the second aisle. No mutton. The gangly teen behind the counter asked her something in his thick brogue. Diane stopped. She pushed her head forward. She sniffed. The teen asked her the same question, changing his tone to sarcastic. Diane held her arm out, pointing to him with a lavender coffin-shaped nail. The embarrassed bloke lowered his head.

Down the block and around the corner, that's where Diane followed the scent to. The bouncer told Diane, "Proper attire is required." Diane jumped in front of a woman trotting in black heels. The woman remained stoic as Diane whispered in her ear. Diane's Balmain sneakers were pulled out of her bag, and the woman eagerly took them. Then, Diane stood before the doorman in her recently acquired black heels. She pulled out a mauve lipstick she had swiped from her lovely redhead and applied it, making a pucker sound for the brute.

A few steps inside, Diane stood before an impenetrable black gothic door. The desirable Irish doorman opened the door. "Down the corridor and to the right." Illuminated modern gray planters with floating purple orchids lined the walls which guided her along the dimly lit corridor.

The creatures were gorgeous. The gents. The ones with the sights of heaven between their legs. The *vampire* model-esque wait staff. Diane touched her lips, *I wish I drank blood.*

Diane skimmed the menu twirling the options with her fingernail. *Something about this room. The scent, mmm, I smell something I like.* "I will…" Diane spoke, and as the breath exited her lips where her desire rested, she spotted something. He was there: a striking, better-than-she-could-have-described living being with dark salt and pepper hair. He appeared with a cigar and was speaking to the maître d´. The striking man looked in Diane's direction—took a draw from his cigar—and disappeared, probably following the path along the orchids. Stroking her hair with a huff, Diane responded to the waiter, "Take the mutton." He looked to the maître d´, then tapped on his tablet.

Later, Diane sat with crisscrossed legs on her hotel room bed reading an article about the latest model put out by

Rolls-Royce. She imagined spending the money her dad had allocated to buy his new private jet on this car instead. She imagined herself driving the Rolls all the way back to China despite the fact that she had never really driven anywhere other than in a car park. She thought it could be like that dude who played Forrest Gump. "I just started running." *If I could make it through the tunnel from England to France, yeah, I could just keep going.*

Diane opted for her blonde ponytail wig for her meeting the next day. She wore her black iridescent Versace blazer. She had on a lavender panty and bra set from some French brand. Black riding pants with stirrups that fit nicely with her newly acquired heels. The pumps she brokered from the lady on the street turned out to be not so cheap. Some guy named Stuart Weitzman. They must sell those at Marks & Spencer, Diane figured.

Sitting tapping her lavender nails on the table, Diane took a sip of her PG Tips tea. "Ick." Diane plopped the teacup down. The waiter came around, suggested a more refreshing caffeinated beverage, which she declined.

"You're late, *Karen*," Diane said as she eyed the man who was sent to drive her.

"I'm not late, ma'am. You're early."

"Hmm, well let's get on," Diane huffed in a pompous accent.

"This way," Kieran said as he motioned toward the front entrance. Diane stood and followed him. Sitting in the back of the car, Diane smoothed her long blonde ponytail. Closing her eyes, she saw herself snapping Kieran's neck and taking over the wheel of the black Range Rover. You know, for practice in case she did buy that Rolls-Royce.

"You right, ma'am?" Kieran inquired.

Diane threw her head back, opening her eyes. She looked out of the car to the right. A car sped past them. She looked straight ahead. *The other side of the road. Maybe I shouldn't do him in. I can't drive on the other side.* "Yeah. I'm okay."

"There are cold drinks if you need one."

Diane smiled. Insincerely.

"When I travel, me stomach bothers me. Thought maybe you might—"

"Yes." Diane struggled with the opening in between the seats. After the last curve she did feel like, instead of snapping his neck, she might actually throw up on her Versace jacket. No worries about the Weitzman shoes.

Kieran walked Diane into a hangar at the FBO, Fixed-Base Operator. Two jets, one in the front and one in the back, and a spot straight on complete with ambiguous furniture imported from Italy. The rug strewn beneath looked like a Persian rug from a distance, but up close, if one were to stare at it, had a modern geometric element. She spotted the person she was to meet with, Tolya. A tall broad woman with gray hair that was braided with perfectly placed purple strands. Diane had been corresponding with her via email for a few months. Very welcoming, borderline theatrical in a subdued German accent as she greeted Diane. The woman offered Diane a cocktail. It was all of ten a.m., but Diane obliged. Her emperor would approve. Her dad would not.

Her drink was carried for her while Diane followed the

theatrical German woman up the stairs of a Lear Jet 2000. The jet looked just as it did in the photos. Diane asked to see the loo. In the loo, she sat on the closed toilet. She spread her legs, then kicked off her heels and propped up her right leg on the vanity. *Okay, this could work.* Diane emerged from the bathroom. She adjusted the lapel of her jacket, exposing her lavender brassiere. The broad German woman stood and asked her how she liked the toilet. Diane took a seat in the front row which faced the back of the plane. "This will meet our needs." Diane pulled out the lavender fingernail she had graciously transported with care from Borovets and held it out for the woman. "This shade." The woman asked her what she needed that shade for. "For whatever else do you think? The plane, of course," Diane responded effortlessly in a British accent as she tossed the fingernail.

Diane could feel her lavender thong with each step she took down the jet's stairs. He stood there waiting for her. This time sans cigar. Diane slipped from the last step enamored by the striking Irishman, and he caught her.

The owner of the company introduced himself then said, "My apologies, I've been tending to an issue with the redesign of the client accommodations. You're in great hands with my assistant Tolya."

"Lavender. Uh, I like it, for the seats," Diane responded, touching her face, avoiding eye contact.

"Come, come, I'll make you some tea," he offered, escorting Diane to his private office. She sipped her tea, and as the owner of the private jet company stepped away to speak with his assistant, Diane noticed an old issue of Forbes Middle

East. She flipped through to the article about her. Her thong tingled in the front. She walked around the office with her teacup in hand. There he was on the wall. The same striking, better-than-she-could-have-described Irishman from the night before. Dublin's Businessman of the Year, Quinn Osian Kane.

BEAR'S MOONLIGHT

Nexxa was dressed for the *Sin of Lust*. Really, she dressed for Sergei. When Sergei's driver turned around and headed back to Sergei's house away from Moscow, Nexxa saw three faces in her mind. The woman didn't have a good complexion yet was still attractive. The man had the face of a fat older man. And the third face—was her own.

On the floor in Sergei's bedroom, she made a circle with some white towels she had retrieved from the laundry room. She said a prayer for protection, placed a map of Moscow in the center, and lifted her pendulum. The pendulum swung in a circle indicating yes when Nexxa asked whether Sergei was coming home. She knew he wasn't coming *home*. Nexxa dressed for a run. Really, she dressed for a mission.

Nexxa stepped outside onto the terrace attached to Sergei's master bedroom. She placed two fingers on her wrist taking her pulse—it was heightened. The moon was casting an amber glow, and the air was changing. Nexxa cut through the wooded area behind Sergei's house, opting not to take the cleared path that led to Bogdan's house or the cemetery. Each tree led her to the next like the messy strung power lines of the Haret Hreik in Lebanon.

Images flashed again of the faces of the unknown man and woman. Nexxa sprung into a sprint when a clearing allowed and latched onto branches, climbing over them when needed, aligning her movements with Mother Earth.

Flurries began falling, reflecting the light that the Russian bear was so kindly letting into the thick part of his forest. Nexxa pulled on her hood and turned off her flashlight. She returned to a slow-paced jog, continuing to follow Sergei's scent. Nexxa thought about their drive from Beirut to Tripoli. How it was impromptu, fast and necessary. Now her enemy was the Russian cold that penetrated her skin through her black leggings and jacket. Without a proper invitation, Nexxa tripped over the remnants of a campfire accompanied by some beer bottles, sliding down a small decline. As she stood at the edge of a trail, she smelled something that was out of place—an irritating perfume.

Nexxa wiped the debris from her hands and pulled up her legging, touching her scar. She tightened her ponytail. Looking up she saw a drone moving around. Running this time on a trail that went both north and south, Nexxa chose south. Forced to slow her pace to a jog by the irritating smell, Nexxa continued toward the drone. And then she was upon the intended scene. A black Range Rover sped south through a cleared lot before coming to a stop. A tall woman with a bad complexion and a short older man emerged from the vehicle. The third person from Nexxa's vision was herself.

Where is Sergei?

The cold was becoming frigid and carried the sound of a phone vibrating, the scent of a recently waxed vagina and the feeling of old Moscow money. Sergei stepped into Nexxa's view; he couldn't see her from the other side of the clearing walking toward the older man and taller woman.

The drone circled the open area. Snowflakes stopped falling. Sergei shouted in Russian. Nexxa understood he was speaking to the older man. The woman withdrew the rifle she had slung over her shoulder, aiming as a sniper would. The older man withdrew a cigar and lit it himself. The Range Rover huffed exhaust. Sergei raised his gun.

Nexxa withdrew the flashlight she had and tossed it toward the woman and man. Landing, it emitted a pulsating light. The lady fired in Nexxa's direction. Sergei fired at the woman.

The tall woman with the bad skin was hit by a bullet. Of course Sergei was a good shot. The old man's daughter turned, aiming at her father. Sergei shouted, "Lower your gun!" She limped to the Range Rover. It sped down the hiking trail, taking her stench with her.

Nexxa ran.

Sergei ran looking up at the drone. Nexxa blew a long breath as she reached the older man. He took a draw from his cigar and raised his pistol aiming at her. Sergei reached them, his eyes shocked and worried, as he reached for the woman he loved. The old man barked, "Stand back now and put down your gun!" Sergei adjusted his stance, lowering his gun halfway. Then all the way.

"This has already happened. It ended well for all of us but one," Nexxa said, standing with her body grounded to the earth and her brown eyes going straight through the old man's tough but worn eyeballs. He chuckled, his hand with the gun going low, and took a draw from his cigar. Nexxa knew the older man wasn't going to shoot her. His ride home was gone, and he was short, old, and bore a Russian bear belly. The man lowered his gun, compensating his ego with a confident laugh. Nexxa envisioned her abduction by Medan. She remembered how it felt when Klarin hit her face with a glass. She felt the force of Nahil's pocketknife striking Klarin. The older man's laugh over, the moment was ready to change.

He lifted his gun. Nexxa whispered in the air, "I call for protection, lavender."

Her lavender pulsed, and he fell to his knees then slumped down. Nexxa knelt. She lifted his arm feeling for a pulse, catching her reflection in his oversized Cartier watch.

The ride was a little rocky at first then smoothed out on the main road leading to Sergei's house. Nexxa looked to Sergei. He kept his eyes on the road and on the old man in the back. Nexxa shivered from the cold and from the exhilaration leaving her veins. Sergei reached for her hand, gripping it tightly. He finally looked at her when they pulled into his driveway. His expression was that of a parent that was happy their child was alive but irritated at the same time that they had put themself in danger. Sergei summoned Vlasta, who helped him carry the old man in. He called the doctor who made house calls for sensitive situations, the same doctor and nurse that he had taken Nexxa to when she hurt her leg.

The next morning, the old man woke and with a defeated voice said, "Scotch, cigar."

"You're up," Sergei spoke, sounding ready to go, and helped the man into the wheelchair that the doctor had brought and wheeled the old man over to his desk. Sergei knew that this old Russian bear of a man would never give up requesting the land back from Sergei that he loaned him the funds to buy. He had been persistent with his requests for the land so that his daughter could build a house and possibly some apartments. The loan had been paid back in full.

"It has come to this," Sergei sighed, handing him a pen. Sergei preemptively had a one-hundred-year lease drawn up wherein the old man, his investor for his project in Croatia, could lease his land. For a price, of course. Business in Mother Russia was never kosher. More like the Wild Wild West. Sergei knew this, lived this. He knew, he had no choice but to continue their partnership, contracts had been signed in Croatia. "Manushka can build her house on the land," Sergei offered as the old man lifted the document.

"No! No deal. Give me my phone," the old man growled, waving his hand around. He made a call. His daughter was shot dead. He signed the lease. He decided to build apartments.

PURPLE FLOWERS | 12

Sergei laughed while watching the TV in the kitchen. A game show was on, the one where contestants put a card on their forehead with a word written on it. Then the other contestants give clues so the one wearing the card can guess what it says. One contestant used a color to describe the word. "Lavender—I mean, purple!" shouted the contestant, giving a clue. Jeers erupted from the game show host and the audience since the card had the word *lavender* written on it. The host went on to explain that the contestant could have said "An aromatic plant native to the Mediterranean with light purple flowers."

Sergei turned to Nexxa as she was preparing a cup of tea and they made eye contact.

"Interesting show, huh?" Sergei remarked.

"Yeah, I guess so," Nexxa said, looking down at her tea.

"I like purple. The color," Sergei said. Nexxa looked up, and their eyes met again. Sergei motioned with his head and Nexxa followed him out of the kitchen. Upstairs, Sergei closed and locked the bedroom door behind them. Nexxa sat in one of the leather armchairs. She took a sip of her tea and placed the mug down, watching as Sergei crossed the room and back and then again.

"So you have a… You have a vivid aura? Is that what it is?"

Nexxa bit her bottom lip. She heard, "I mean purple!" She stood saying, "Should I start with when I was younger?"

"Sure." Sergei nodded.

"Well, my mom has gifts. She can see things that will happen."

"And you?"

"Well, I can't always see things. It's more like I can smell some things. And I can connect with my sister."

"Smell?" Sergei asked with a confused look. Nexxa sat down again and took a sip of her tea. "Do you want to sit?" she asked Sergei, motioning with her hand to the other chair. Sergei sat slightly hunched over with his hands between his legs. "I, well you know that I grew up in Canada and was raised by a Native American, Thomas." Sergei gave one nod. "He taught me about the spirit world. He helped me harness some of what I would say are my natural gifts."

Sergei stood. He poured himself a Scotch and rubbed his hand over his head, then walked across the bedroom to the glass doors that led to the terrace. After taking another drink, he unlocked the door and stepped outside. Sergei ran his hand along the ledge, before wiping his hands together, feeling some snow. The wind blew, shimmying some snowflakes from the limbs of the trees. He could see in the distance his nearest neighbor had installed some new outdoor lights. Lavender, the lights emitted a lavender hue.

Nexxa felt the cold since Sergei had left the door open, so she retrieved a wrap sweater from the closet. Sergei's phone buzzed, and she figured he would step back in and answer it. After a few moments when he didn't and his phone buzzed again, she decided to go out to him. The cold on her bare feet was her courage. Sure, a glass or two or three of wine would help. Nexxa wasn't afraid to tell him about herself—she was afraid that Mr. Albert could have been wrong. That she and he didn't actually see the white glow around Sergei during the game of Winter Tag. He had been distinctly away from Quinn when the white glow emitted.

Or had he?

They had all been running around looking for dragon eggs and Nexxa's mind had been pulled in different directions. First with seeing Kilmer's apparition in New York City. Then being awkwardly pursued by Mr. Ball Snow. And the shock of seeing Quinn during the Ice Queen party with his energy competing for her. She and Mr. Albert never actually had a conversation about what they saw. She only had his subtle encouragement to believe.

Sergei turned as Nexxa approached him. His face was genuine. The same as when Nexxa had first seen him at the Beirut Horse Track. "My lavender glow protects me from spiritual attacks," Nexxa blurted out.

Sergei pulled her into him. "You're barefoot. You're going to catch a cold." Nexxa kept her breathing still in his embrace.

"Unless your gifts keep you warm too," Sergei said with a smile. Lifting his Scotch, he said, "Let's go inside." Nexxa exhaled seeing him smile, and took a step, slipping as it seemed the temperature must have instantaneously dropped ten degrees, the terrace beneath her bare feet icy. Sergei swooped her up and carried her into his bedroom. His gift of strength.

Inside, the Russian placed Nexxa down in one of the leather armchairs. He went to his dresser, opened a drawer, and returned to Nexxa. He insisted she put on a pair of his wool socks, so Nexxa pulled on the socks. Sergei sat beside her in the other armchair. "Do you want me to get Vlasta to make you another cup of tea?" Nexxa shook her head indicating no and leaned forward, lifting Sergei's Scotch. A sip. A rough swallow. Nexxa thought for a moment about how she had trained with Thomas, learning to use her heightened sense of smell in the Canadian woods. How she had recently traversed the woods behind Sergei's house following his scent. How she had literally run around Moscow city centre looking for Crimson. And now, she had just stepped out into the cold with bare feet onto the accumulating snow in Moscow just as the guests had in December at her Ice Queen party playing a game. All events were connected purposefully.

"I wondered when you might ask me. You said when we were in New York that there was purple around me."

"Yeah. I saw it," Sergei replied in a tone of agreement.

Nexxa smiled in her mind hearing his acknowledgment. "You said something about a smell." Sergei's eyes asked the question. "I didn't want to say anything. Last night. I had things to take care of. My investor." Sergei lifted his hand from his thigh, motioning. "How did you know where I was last night?" Sergei's tone now turned interrogative.

The thought crossed Nexxa's mind that she could joke about checking his phone, knowing his whereabouts like a jealous girlfriend. She knew that he knew she didn't have access to his phone. But it would be an easier explanation. "I... I can smell—you."

Sergei abruptly stood. "What?" he asked as he rubbed a hand over his face. When Nexxa remained seated, stoic face, Sergei sat back down.

Nexxa looked to him. "Yes, I can smell people. I can smell them from afar. I can smell what others can't."

"So what does that mean? For you. For me."

"It means..." Nexxa smoothed her hand along her ponytail. "I have a heightened sense of smell." Sergei was looking up like he was trying to process what she was saying. "Not like I can sense when people smell bad." Nexxa laughed with her tempting eyes. "It's more that I can track them. Find them," Nexxa said quickly. She didn't mention that at times something—what that something was, she didn't know yet—prevented her from smelling.

Sergei grasped his jaw. Nexxa knelt before him saying, "It's okay," as she grasped his hands. Sergei chuckled. "No, really. It's a good thing. I found you last—" Nexxa stopped herself. She didn't want to emasculate him. Sergei released her grasp and leaned back in the chair. Nexxa kept her hands on his thighs, feeling his warmth. "I was going for a run. I just headed through the woods. I knew it was stupid, but my intuition told me to run, and that's the way I went." Nexxa knew there was more she needed to explain, like the new scar on her breast and the mark that was going away on her neck.

Moreover, she had questions about the mysterious kittens that manifested themselves a new home in Sergei's house and the silverware baskets that must have hopped and skipped to the bathtub. The new housekeeper. But she also wanted to feel closer, intimately closer to Sergei. She had dressed for him the night before, dashed through woods for him, and now was exposing her coveted self.

Nexxa pulled her breasts from her bra. Sergei let out a breath as he moved his hand along his neck. She moved her hand along his thigh up to his groin. He shifted himself in the chair to spread his legs apart. Nexxa leaned forward with her breasts pressing against him. She started pulling the waistband of his tracksuit pants. Sergei helped her. Nexxa wet her hand with some saliva and stroked his penis gently. Sergei let his head fall backward.

Nexxa remembered that she chose to end the night by pleasing her Russian. She wished she had taken notes, had things in writing—what she had explained to him—an old habit from working in finance. He was snoring unusually loud this morning. Was that a good sign? Or a sign of louder snoring to come? Nexxa counted his deep inhalations—she counted how many guns she had seen the night before last.

Nexxa craved a good cup of tea. One worthy of calling it a "cuppa." Tea was good in Russia, but still not the same as good ole Irish or British tea. Downstairs in the kitchen Nexxa prepared herself a cup of tea and some toast. When looking for more paper towels in the pantry she noticed that Vlasta had restocked the red wine. Usually Nexxa would have Sergei pick her up a bottle or he would just bring some from his restaurant. Vlasta entered the kitchen, and before Nexxa could say good morning, she turned on the TV. She was always in the kitchen, or at least there were always obvious signs of her presence: soup boiling, grunting coming to and fro the pantry, some meat defrosting in the sink.

"I love this show," Vlasta said. She hunched over the sink running water over some meat, thawing it.

"Yeah, this was on yesterday," Nexxa commented, wishing the show hadn't been on. The whole, "Lavender—I mean, purple!" dumb contestant giving a clue which in turn spurred Sergei and Nexxa to have a much needed yet uncomfortable discussion. Nexxa had wanted or hoped to sort out the source of the Crimson before she and Sergei discussed things like her lavender glow.

"The show is good. They're good," Vlasta asserted. In her slouchy stance, she continued picking at whatever she had in the sink.

"Thank you for the wine," Nexxa said as she approached the sink with her mug and plate.

"You had a busy night," Vlasta said as she looked up, still hunched over the meat.

Nexxa looked in the sink. She had intentions of rinsing her mug and plate before putting them in the dishwasher. "Uh, yeah." Nexxa's shocked eyes reflected back at her from the large stainless-steel sink.

"You can put that in," Vlasta told her as she motioned with her half closed, twisted and blood covered hand.

"I'll just put it in the dishwasher." Nexxa opened it. She put her mug and plate in, her eyes shifting to the silverware baskets.

"So do you ever deep clean the dishwasher?" Nexxa asked. "I mean, like take parts out to scrub." Nexxa searched her mind for a way to rationalize why the silverware baskets could have made their way up the stairs. It seemed like something she should address now, being that she and Sergei were finally discussing other matters.

"I have a brush under the sink you can use. But the proper way is to take the baskets up to the bathtub," Vlasta said as she tossed an eyeball from whatever animal head she had in the sink into the trash can she had pulled over by her.

Nexxa held a hand over her chest. "Okay, okay."

"I'm making soup," Vlasta hollered over her shoulder.

"Okay, sure." Nexxa looked to the TV again, thinking that if something else normal was happening then she could reconcile that with whatever the fuck Vlasta was picking and cutting on in the sink. But nope, all she could hear was Vlasta pulling on the animal carcass and the annoying jeers from the reality show. Ankica entered the kitchen and Nexxa offered to help her with her morning routine. The past few weeks Nexxa had told herself to let Vlasta do her job until she had settled her business with Crimson, then she could fully integrate herself into the lives of Ankica and baby Natina. She also had Sergei to concentrate on.

Nexxa helped Ankica with a cup of tea, and Vlasta didn't

object. Natina was still up in her room. She was finally sleeping until about eight in the morning. Ankica asked what was going to be for dinner. Vlasta replied, "Soup!" Nexxa never ate the soup, but Sergei did most of the time, usually only a few spoonfuls. Ankica always had the soup. Meat and a vegetable were always on the menu too, and bread, naturally.

A commercial advertising vitamins came on and Vlasta chuckled loudly. "My soup is better nutrition!"

Nexxa thought about her own health. Her own immunity. Her lavender glow that kept her safe, healthy. "The red wine is good too," Nexxa added while she cut Ankica some bread. Vlasta looked to Nexxa with a grin. "Thank you, again," Nexxa said louder and clearer than she thought she did the first time she thanked her for buying more red wine. Vlasta looked back down to the carcass in the sink.

Soup. Soup's for dinner, Nexxa thought as she watched Vlasta continue to chuck pieces of an animal's head into the kitchen trash. *At least there is always some bread and wine*, she thought further through the sound of the now-louder reality show. "In Arabic *qirmizī*. Deep purplish reds," spoke the game show host to the contestants.

"Crimson!" answered the contestant.

"You're correct!" the show's host said jubilantly.

Later that night, dinner was served. Soup to start, which Nexxa declined, and an unknown meat source which turned out to be not so bad. Potatoes that Nexxa had expected to be mashed because that's what Natina liked and really all that Ankica could eat along with tiny cut up pieces of meat. When Ankica asked what was wrong with the mashed potatoes, because they were under cooked and had pieces of tough skin, Vlasta announced, "They are smashed potatoes." Natina didn't eat her potatoes either. Nexxa looked around in the pantry, finding some cereal. Ankica asked Nexxa if she would fry her an egg. Vlasta protested both the cereal and the egg. Nexxa fried an egg for Ankica and prepared a bowl of cereal with some milk for Natina. When they were finished eating, Nexxa insisted she would help Ankica back upstairs and also get Natina down for the night.

Upstairs in Natina's room Nexxa watched as Ankica held onto the dresser with one hand and using her cane in the other lowered herself onto the beige pouf. She muttered, "No, baby, babushka can't," when Natina held her arms out for someone to pick her up. Ankica motioned for Nexxa to hand her the clean clothes that were piled on top of the dresser. Nexxa handed her a few items and Ankica straightened her fingers as best as they allowed to fold and smooth out the baby clothes. Nexxa looked around Natina's nursery. She imagined how it would change. A toddler bed was needed. Eventually, a rocking chair would not be needed. Nexxa lifted Natina, telling her that it was time to put on her night-night clothes. Natina fussed, but Nexxa managed, with the encouragement from Ankica, to get her changed and change her diaper too.

Nexxa turned on the light that emitted stars around the room and carried Natina while helping a slow-moving babushka to her bedroom. Nexxa placed Natina down and she played a bit with a shawl that had been strewn across the foot of the bed. Ankica managed to take off her top and Nexxa helped her maneuver on her pajama top and pants. Nexxa asked if she needed to go to the bathroom and Ankica informed her that she now wore diapers that were for women of her age. Natina rested her head on Nexxa's shoulder as she carried her to her bedroom. She placed her in her crib which, while the mattress had been lowered for a more mature baby, she had already outgrown.

Nexxa remembered how her mother would tell her that she "could feel the weight of the world." Nexxa felt it now. For real this time in her new normal in Moscow. She felt the weight when dressing Ankica—she felt the weight seeing how Natina had grown—yet, they were a weight she wanted to bear.

Nexxa walked down the hallway and sat in the sitting area between the hallway and Sergei's bedroom. She took notice of the lace runner on the coffee table. The decorative items on the table with the lamp. The lamp looked like home. Its light was soft. Nexxa sat on the loveseat and pulled her legs up. She pulled the blanket onto herself, remembering when she and Sergei spent their first night together on the ferry from Lebanon to Turkey. Nexxa leaned her head back; she needed to rest her heart.

WOLFY | 13

"Who's afraid of a bad wolfy. Baby, baby are you drunky. The bad wolfy will come and nip you in the bum. Who's afraid of the bad wolfy. Baby, baby are you drunky," Vlasta sang.

Nexxa sat upright on the sofa. She touched her forehead, her eyes adjusting to the lack of light. She heard Natina cry out. With precision, as if she had done this before, she made her way down the hallway in the dark, as it seemed all the perfectly placed lights had been turned off. As she took her first step into Natina's room, she heard, "Who's afraid of the bad wolfy?"

A sliver of moonlight brightened through the drapes, providing Nexxa with enough light to see the sadness in the room. "Vlasta!" Nexxa called out as she felt on the wall for the light switch. Natina was standing in her crib with one leg swung over on the lift gate. Nexxa leapt to the baby and swooped her into her arms. Vlasta gave no resistance, continuing in her sing-song voice. Nexxa stalled for a moment watching Vlasta still singing into the empty crib, before she carried Natina to Sergei's bedroom. She placed Natina on his bed cradling her, soothing her to sleep, and each time Nexxa's eyes threatened to close she scooted herself up against her pillow.

Quietly, with little movement, she finally leaned to see the time on the tablet on Sergei's nightstand. He wasn't in bed yet and it was almost one a.m. Nexxa heard the toilet flush in the bathroom, and then she felt Sergei get into bed. Natina turned and pushed closer to Nexxa. "What? Oh, there's a baby in the bed," Sergei said, feeling for Nexxa.

"Yeah," Nexxa spoke softly.

"What happened?" Sergei asked louder than before.

"Shh." Nexxa placed her hand on Natina, stroking her head. "Why is she in here?"

"Don't you love her? I love her." Nexxa huffed. "She was crying."

"Of course. Of course. My babushka. She—"

"No!" Nexxa said sternly before calming her tone. "Sergei, come." Nexxa pulled on his arm. Natina remained asleep.

Nexxa yawned as they stood in his closet. A hanger was protruding. Nexxa couldn't help but reposition it. "Natina was crying. I had fallen asleep. Then I heard—"

"Why are we in the closet?" Sergei wore a baffled expression.

Nexxa's eye widened. "So we don't wake her up."

"Oh right." Sergei nodded, looking up.

Sergei's phone buzzed. Nexxa looked toward the sound. She knew it would wake Natina if it persisted. The thought about who would text Sergei in the middle of the night wasn't even a worry. It was only a text from a sports betting club.

Nexxa leaned out of the closet looking toward the bed. "Vlasta was singing some… some fucked-up song. A song about wolves or something."

"What?" Sergei asked as he yawned.

"Never mind. But she has to sleep with us."

Nexxa recited the Hail Mary in her head until she fell asleep. Sergei was already snoring.

Two things that Nexxa had not experienced on another continent: Daylight Savings Time and Easter. Another month had passed and Nexxa had managed to convince Sergei to let Natina sleep in their room, in a cute toddler bed Nexxa had ordered online. Though Natina was sleeping well, Nexxa had been setting her alarm to wake herself every night a few minutes before three a.m. She would touch Natina on her forehead: first one done. She would then make her way down the hall to Ankica's room; by the light of a dimly lit lamp, she could see Ankica asleep: second check done. Once she heard snoring from Vlasta's room, she would go back to bed.

Nexxa had suggested to Sergei that he give Vlasta a few weeks off. Perhaps she had family she should visit. The grunting and confusion of her packing, the sound of Vlasta's car starting up, the tension that she gave off driving out of his driveway, was all worth it.

Sergei stood lost in his own kitchen. The stove was dirty. The floor was gross. Nexxa directed him to entertain Natina with an Easter basket of new trinkets she had ordered for her online while she began cleaning the kitchen. She managed to get the floor clean and the kitchen table cleared. The stove was going to take more time, so she sprayed a cleaner in the sink to help dissolve the muck. Taking a break, Nexxa retrieved the eggs she had asked Vlasta to boil for Easter egg dying. She helped Natina hold an egg and dip it into a bowl with pink dye. Natina giggled. It was the best sound Nexxa had heard in months.

Nexxa sat with Ankica as she watched Easter Mass on TV. "What should we do for food?" Sergei asked, looking at the time on his phone.

"I took care of that," Nexxa responded, and not long after Lavka.Yandex delivered their Easter meal. Nexxa plated each of them. Ankica said a prayer in Russian. The house was allowed true love.

Outside Nexxa hid the eggs for Natina's first egg hunt. The eggs had dried, changing to a lovely shade of lavender. Sergei carried her outside. Demo was supposed to have made it home for Easter, but he had fallen ill while on set in L.A. It was such a big opportunity for him, landing a spot in a new comedy for Showtime after the play ended in Europe. He couldn't risk travelling and chose to stay and recover so he could keep filming. Natina ran around. Sergei followed her, pointing to the colored eggs hidden just inconspicuously enough for a toddler. His face was grand as Natina smiled up at him, holding up an egg each time she found one. Nexxa took a few pictures and a video to send to Demo before standing beside Ankica, who sat in a chair watching. Ankica pointed to Sergei. "Is that man with the baby Demo?" she asked Nexxa in English.

Nexxa laughed, "No, that's Sergei." When she saw Ankica's reaction, the hurt that shaped her face, Nexxa knelt grasping her hand. Ankica turned to Nexxa. She asked in a low voice, "Has the bad wolfy gone?"

Later that evening Natina played with the dyed Easter eggs. An egg cracked on the couch. Some had never been boiled. Nexxa worked to clean the mess while trying to sooth Natina all the while trying to assist Ankica, who had made her way downstairs looking for a digestive concoction that Vlasta had made for her. Nexxa found a jar in the fridge. She removed the rubber band, the foil and finally the plastic wrap that was covering it. The liquid had sediment and an unhealthy odor. Nexxa requested another Lavka delivery, for the Russian version of Mira Lax for Ankica.

Vlasta had sat in her car for two days in the parking lot of the Petrovna Spa eating take-out and listening to the only radio station she could tune in to, Siberian Top Hits. On the third day she called Sergei asking to come back. He re-informed her that he had prepaid for her to spend two weeks at the renowned spa retreat. Vlasta huffed. Sergei started to tell her that he needed to take another call when Vlasta spotted a curvaceous white-haired woman walking into the spa and hung up on him.

Seven days had passed with Vlasta gone. Nexxa continued to burn scented candles and open a few windows around the house, which Sergei made sure were closed and locked before bed. Nexxa divided her energy between babushka and baby. Ankica showed improvement. She was no longer constipated and seemed to walk much better, even unassisted by her cane at times. Nexxa wondered if it was from not eating Vlasta's cooking, the stale bread and half cooked potatoes. Standing in the midst of Natina's room, Nexxa looked to the tent with play toys which still worked, but something seemed missing. Nexxa presented her case to Sergei. She stood before him with a teething toy saying, "She's got a full mouth of teeth."

   Nexxa was successful and had managed to get Sergei to take a day off from business and take her to shop for a toddler table and chair set for Natina's room along with some age-appropriate educational toys and books. Nexxa also hung some framed photos that she found in the bottom of her dresser and worked with Natina, getting her back to being comfortable sleeping in her room in her new toddler bed. Demo would call often when he could take a break on set, but Natina was too shy to talk, so Nexxa decided she would email Demo weekly with updates and photos. She had come across articles regarding toddler milestones when searching for children's toys and books and wanted his approval in taking Natina to her annual pediatrician appointment, being that Sergei was really busy and Ankica was no longer able to keep up with Natina's changing needs.

   One night after she got Natina down for bed, Nexxa sifted through the pile of books and pads for scribbling in Natina's room. She lifted one that had a pattern of flowers with sparkles on the cover. Sitting in bed in Sergei's room, Nexxa began to journal anything and everything she could about beautiful growing Natina. When she was done with that, she scanned her LinkedIn account. A few job listings in finance that she would be qualified for. After looking on LinkedIn, she searched online for signs of dementia in the elderly. Back to searching for jobs, but really she looked up former colleagues, Philip and Dan.

Tired of looking at her phone, Nexxa quietly made her way down the hall, first checking on Natina then Ankica, both asleep, so she made her way downstairs for a night cap. She saw Sergei's office door was closed with light emitting from under it, and she entered the kitchen, which smelled of vanilla. Standing in the walk-in pantry she found a red blend and looked over her shoulder when she heard footsteps. Nexxa pulled open a drawer and found a corkscrew. Looking out of the kitchen window, she took a sip of her wine before she reached to close the window when she felt someone against her backside.

Sergei whispered in her ear, "I've never fucked you in my office."

Nexxa laughed, turning around. "What makes you think you ever will?"

"I want you. So I will. Fuck you. In my office."

Nexxa placed her wine glass down and walked to his office.

"What do you want?" Nexxa asked as she removed her chemise.

"What do *you* want?" Sergei asked.

Nexxa replied, "Some more wine. That bottle is really good!" They laughed.

Sergei had begun hard in his pursuit but was tender with his touch. He stepped toward her and bent, picking up her chemise. He placed it on his desk. "Do you want to give me your thong?"

Nexxa blushed, turning her head to the side. "Okay." She removed her thong and handed it to him. Sergei tucked it into his back jeans' pocket as he had done on their ferry ride from Lebanon to Turkey. Nexxa quivered as Sergei ran his hand down between her breasts. He pulled her into him, kissing her. She liked the feeling of her naked body against him in his clothes; it felt naughty, like she was having sex somewhere she shouldn't. Sergei walked Nexxa over to the leather sofa. He began to remove his jeans. Nexxa pushed him onto the sofa and straddled him, feeling warm denim against her skin. She slid her hand between her thighs as she leaned over kissing him. Sergei breathed heavily, and in one swoop lifted her off and removed his jeans. He told her to stand and bend over.

Sergei climaxed. A short minute later, his stomach rumbled. Sergei looked around his office and said, "I need something to drink. I need a snack too."

"Really? You're hungry *now*?"

"Yeah." Sergei confirmed.

Nexxa burst out with a laugh. "Oh." She grasped her stomach and said, "I think I am too."

Sergei started walking toward the kitchen. "Come, let's eat."

Nexxa felt around on the floor for her panties. "Sergei, where are my panties?"

"You don't need them," he hollered from the kitchen.

Nexxa looked to her chemise on his desk and picked it up. She peeked out of his office and into the kitchen. She saw him standing there peering in the fridge. She thought about babushka and baby, knowing they were asleep. She plopped her chemise down and followed the sound of Sergei humming in the kitchen. Sergei turned on the pocket lights. Nexxa quickly dimmed them. Sergei chuckled but kept his rhythm rummaging through the pantry.

"This and little of this," Sergei said, placing some salami, cheese and olives on the counter.

"Where is the bread?" Nexxa pointed to the pantry.

"Ah, how did I miss that?"

Yeah, how did he? Nexxa wondered. She had managed to straighten up the mess that Vlasta had made of the pantry. The bread was fresh and on a shelf at eye level.

Sergei made some sandwiches and placed the plates in front of the barstools. Nexxa watched as he sat and took a bite. "Sit, eat," Sergei said with food in his mouth. Nexxa approached the barstool and pulled it out. Sergei dropped an olive, and it landed in his crotch and they laughed as he stood, wiping his mouth. "I think I'll just put on my pants." They laughed some more.

Nexxa trotted to his office and slipped on her chemise with Sergei following her and picking up his jeans from the floor. He walked over to her by his desk and held out her panties. "Thank you," Nexxa said as she looked down then shimmied them on.

Sergei took ahold of her hand. "Let's try it again." Nexxa leaned her head on his shoulder as they returned to the kitchen. Nexxa grasped her abdomen, not because she was hungry, but because she felt the same white butterflies as she had on their first date in Beirut.

Vlasta sat perfectly plopped in a leather armchair in the golf course clubhouse with her martini. She took a drag from her cigarillo. She liked vodka, not necessarily martinis, and she didn't even smoke. She made a jarring motion with her arm, summoning over the waiter. "Shouldn't the service be faster since I paid more?" she asked when he approached.

The waiter looked at her then looked back to the bar manager, who shook his head. The manager tugged at his jacket before making his way over to her table sending the waiter off. "No ma'am, you actually did not pay more." He had heard her scolding complaint from across the room.

Vlasta shifted her extra pounds, grunting in the chair. "I—"

The manager held up a hand. "Actually, *you* didn't pay more. Your employer booked your stay and we've done everything to accommodate your erratic behavior."

"My—" Vlasta began as she started to push herself up in the chair.

"Yes, we've had complaints about you from other guests. Namely female guests."

"I've made some friends here. Everyone needs friends and that's how you do it. You make friends. And people want to talk and socialize and social. The social is important. I need to be with other people. We are all humans and the Earth is important."

The manager rolled his eyes. A couple walked in from the golf course. He turned toward them and smiled. Vlasta had pushed herself all the way up. She stumbled when she bent for her drink. "We'll have your drink brought to your room."

Vlasta burped. "Yes, you should. I think a new drink with

some olives on the side."

The manager took a deep breath. He glanced over at the waiter. The waiter shook his head in disgust. "I need an escort for a guest," the manager spoke into his two-way radio.

"Oh, you have escorts?" Vlasta asked with surprised googly eyes through another belch. The manager squinted his eyes, thinking.

They managed to get her off to her room. Vlasta sprawled out on her bed and turned on the TV. She found the Russki porn channel. She watched while sucking down her fresh martini and licking the olives imagining they were breasts. She licked her fingers and pleasured herself.

"Well, I need a real escort," she said, hobbling over to the bathroom. After she had a blowout on the toilet she wiped her butt with a hand towel and plopped down on the bed in only her sharted underwear. She started to sing: "Who's afraid of a bad wolfy. Baby, baby are you drunky. The bad wolfy will come and nip you in the bum. Who's afraid of the bad wolfy. Baby, baby are you drunky." Too drunk to find that "escort," Vlasta passed out and slept from that afternoon to the next afternoon. The staff were happy.

The next day, Vlasta continued to look for victims to socialize with. When she wasn't successful following women around the dressing room in the spa she wandered down to the cellar level, finding the chambermaids. She coaxed a younger woman into an area that had supplies, asking for help finding some towels. The maid was more than helpful. Vlasta offered her some rubles and the used hand lotion she had in her bag. The woman thought for a bit then grasped the money. Vlasta told her that she would need to take off her underwear. The woman told her she thought she just wanted to massage her. Vlasta pulled another US hundred worth from her bag and locked the door. The woman took off her underwear.

Nexxa continued her nightly check a few minutes before three a.m. for the baby and babushka. Natina was asleep, so Nexxa adjusted her blanket and stood for a moment as she pulled the door almost closed. She heard Ankica muttering in her room. "Is, is Nexxa?"

Nexxa gently approached Ankica's ajar door and pushed it open. "Ankica?" She saw she was trying to push herself upright. Nexxa came to her side. "Ankica, are you okay?"

Ankica pointed toward the door and asked, "What will you do when the bad wolfy comes back?"

NURSEY+WOLFY | 14

The sexy nurse arrived, pulling into Sergei's driveway in a Mercedes G-Class SUV. Nexxa watched from Natina's bedroom window as she exited the car and Sergei greeted her. She observed how he was professional when he welcomed her. *No flirting*, Nexxa thought. She brought Natina and her diaper bag downstairs. The sexy nurse warmly acknowledged Nexxa and escorted them to her Mercedes. Sergei had arranged for the nurse who worked with the private doctor to assist Nexxa in taking Natina to a pediatrician. The next day she came back and did the same for Nexxa so she could have Ankica seen by a specialist.

The last few weeks had been busy, in a good way, but Nexxa was exhausted. She stood in Natina's room watching her sitting at her toddler table scribbling. She heard Ankica, who had started sitting in her chair in the upstairs sitting area again, muttering an Orthodox prayer. Nexxa came to her and asked if she wanted something to drink. Ankica pointed toward the window that overlooked the front garden. Nexxa walked over to the window. She pushed the curtain aside and could see a car pulling into the driveway. It looked like Vlasta's car. Nexxa looked down and held her stomach. With dread, she looked again. The car was only a courier. She saw Sergei take an envelope from the young man, who barely stopped his car before hopping out.

Nexxa turned over her shoulder and, looking at Ankica, shook her head, saying, "No bad wolfy." Nexxa stayed by Ankica's side for a while before checking on Natina. She peeked into the room that Vlasta slept in—the room smelled of stale awfulness—and promptly closed the bedroom door. She informed Ankica that she was going downstairs to start something for dinner. Thankfully, getting provisions delivered hadn't been a problem in Moscow.

Nexxa served everyone dinner and cleaned up the kitchen. She got Natina into bed and read her a bedtime story. Next she poured Ankica her nightly tonic, cherry brandy, and sat with her in the sitting room upstairs. Ankica sipped her brandy. Nexxa drank her red wine. Ankica moved her hand along the cloth on her side table. She closed her eyes. "*Krasnyy*," Ankica said in a cracked voice. Nexxa leaned closer to her. "A *Krasnyy*," Ankica repeated and jerked her hand away from the lace cloth.

"What is *Krasnyy*?" Nexxa asked. She knew it meant red, but red... *Crimson? Did Ankica smell the Crimson scent too?*

Nexxa's phone vibrated. Then again. She lifted her phone

and saw that Vlasta had sent her a string of texts, each full of jargon with flower and heart emojis. "What?" Nexxa said as she read some of the messages.

"Bad wolfy," Ankica whispered as she took a sip of her brandy.

Nexxa nodded. "Yeah. Yes, it's her."

The next day was exactly three weeks since Vlasta had been sent on her trip. Nexxa had convinced Sergei to extend her stay at the spa resort by one week. Nexxa reached the top of the staircase and it began there, the scents: broken spices, decayed herbs, lifeless florals. Baked foods and scorched cuisine. Only together it was like a pungent kill. Nexxa made her way to the kitchen. A floral arrangement in a vase was on the kitchen island. Vlasta popped up from her crouch. "I'm here!" Vlasta sang. "I'm here! I got you flowers," Vlasta motioned with her head to the arrangement before saying, "since I was gone for Easter."

"Hi." Nexxa looked to the stove. Soup was already boiling, making itself home again. Nexxa looked back to Vlasta. She had a postcoital look in her eyes and was making *herself* home again.

Later that day, Vlasta insisted on playing music at dinner, asking Nexxa to help her play ABBA on her "speaker boombox." She had made fresh bread, making a point to tell Nexxa that she remembered sourdough was her favorite. She gave Natina a toy at dinner. Vlasta presented Ankica with a box of chocolates. Lastly, she abruptly stood from the table and schlepped over to the back door in the kitchen where her suitcase was on the floor. She rummaged through, grumbling. Nexxa wondered if she was going to pull out her dirty panties. Instead, Vlasta pulled out a bottle that was shrink wrapped, looking like she had gotten it in a Duty-Free shop. Sergei took the bottle from her and thanked her before placing it down. Vlasta hovered over him insisting that she open it for him. The gift giving over, Nexxa suggested it was time for Natina to go to bed, while Ankica said she was tired and wanted to go upstairs with them.

Nexxa turned on Natina's starry light and cracked her door. She tiptoed to the sitting area and poured Ankica her drink. Then she sent Vlasta a text, she was still in the kitchen, inviting her to join them tonight. Nexxa retrieved her stones from the bedroom and placed them on the coffee table, visibly. She put on her crystal necklace, one that she used at times as a backup pendulum, and turned it so that the crystal hung in the back. Time away from Vlasta had given her the space to think. And time to recall an outing with Thomas in the forest. He had described a nonsensical human with a distinct pungent odor—a sociopathic creature with hysterical strength. But, Nexxa felt like she could handle Vlasta, so with Natina in bed and Sergei occupied watching a football game, it was time for Operation Bad Wolfy.

"Ugh. I forgot how hard these stairs are," Vlasta growled as she reached the top of the staircase. Nexxa calmed her breathing. Vlasta rounded the corner to the sitting room. Ankica took a sip of her brandy and reached out to her cloth, which rested on the table. Nexxa held a hand behind her back, feeling her crystal. Vlasta huffed and plopped down her communist era dark blue bag, bottles inside clanking, and then plopped herself down on the sofa opposite them. Nexxa smiled; it was difficult to and surely looked unnatural. She thought about the carcass Vlasta had in the sink weeks before. Turning her head to Ankica, she thought about *"Krasnyy,"* and what she had meant by red. Vlasta unzipped her bag and pulled out a bottle. "This is good stuff," she said with encouraging eyes.

Nexxa took a sip of her wine and said, "I'm okay." Vlasta drastically moved her head from right to left to dead center. "I need a glass." Nexxa pointed to the sideboard that held glasses, Ankica's tonic, and accessories.

Vlasta nodded. "Yeah, uh-huh. Yeah, uh-huh, I see now."

Nexxa liked triangles. She liked the triangle of coveted spots she left on the continent that housed New York City. Her apartment, *le office*, and the spa at The Peninsula Hotel. But here in the upstairs sitting room was a new triangle: The Housekeeper, The Babushka, and The Nexxa Davoren. Nexxa wished she could close her nose to the heinous unsolved crime that wafted directly from Vlasta's area, from her communist era bag.

Vlasta stood at the sideboard and poured her drink into a glass. Pouring, pouring; it sounded like water running. Ankica looked to Nexxa with a perplexed face. Nexxa leaned, trying for a look at Vlasta's glass. "There, my drink is done!" Vlasta announced turning to her new comrades. Nexxa struggled to smile. "Oh no!" Vlasta dashed to Nexxa. "Your necklace is backwards." Nexxa's head fell back and Ankica grasped her cloth. Vlasta turned Nexxa's necklace. The crystal lightly swayed, landing in-between Nexxa's breasts. Vlasta jumped, narrowly catching herself on the coffee table. Nexxa moved her head upright just as Vlasta laughed a hearty laugh, letting out a "toot" as she called it.

Nexxa watched every part of Vlasta. How she had poured her drink. How she dashed to Nexxa. How she managed to catch herself. This was contrary to the Vlasta that schlepped around the house. The housekeeper that huffed and moaned with heavy arms. Vlasta popped her neck, took a gulp of her drink, and said, "Mmm, this is good." Nexxa didn't believe, as Vlasta eyed her, that she was referring to her drink.

Nexxa looked to her stones on the table. Vlasta followed Nexxa's move. She hunched over and lifted Nexxa's black opal stone. "If you warm the stone in your hand and then move toward light, you should see something," Nexxa explained to Vlasta. Vlasta vigorously rubbed the stone in her palms, the stone practically leaping from her hands. She darted after it as it rolled around the corner to the stair landing.

"Ah! Oh! Ugh!" Nexxa and Ankica heard her grunts and a thumping sound. Nexxa stood. Vlasta lay sprawled with half of her body on the landing and the other half on the top step. Nexxa stepped over her. She calmly made her way, through Vlasta's groans of pain, to Sergei's office. She tapped on his office door. He hadn't heard a thing as football was still on. She told him that Vlasta would need a doctor.

Thirty minutes later, the sexy nurse arrived with the physician. Vlasta was loaded into a new Mercedes G-Class SUV, this one dark green.

PUNKY SHAMPANSKOYE | 15

Nexxa ran a finger along Sergei's palm. She knew it probably tickled. She drew her finger up each of his and back in a circle around his hand. Sergei grasped her hand—their fingers interlocking. Nexxa caressed Sergei's face, moving her hand along his jawline before resting her hand on his manly thigh. Sergei grasped her hair, pulling her, and Nexxa allowed her head to fall back—not so much that her heart could break, his love felt so intense it almost hurt, but just enough to allow Sergei to move his mouth along her neck.

"What is today? It's Thursday, right?" Sergei asked as he lifted his phone from the side table. Nexxa nodded, as she knew exactly what day it was. It was four days since Vlasta had returned and left again for rehab for her broken leg. "I need to take you out."

"But what about babushka and baby?" Nexxa asked.

"They're okay." Sergei stood, and before walking to his ensuite he turned and leaned to kiss her on the forehead.

Nexxa thought for a moment, *How will Ankica and Natina manage with Vlasta gone again if I go out for the night?*

"There's leftovers!" Sergei shouted from the bathroom.

Nexxa tilted her head thinking, *Okay sure, leftovers, but can Ankica get her down for bed?* Nexxa sighed. Sergei popped his head out from the bathroom doorway and said, "I'm already naked. Taking a shower."

Nexxa walked to the closet. She pulled out a dress she had brought with her from New York. The tag was still on. She had got it on sale, cheap almost, but it looked more than it cost. Nexxa slipped it on and stood in front of the mirror. She heard Natina cry, so she dashed out of the bedroom and down the hall. She was fine. Playing in her room with some kitchen playset toys and had managed to soothe herself.

Nexxa trotted back down the hall and into the bedroom. Sergei emerged from the bathroom with a towel around his waist. "You look great!"

"Oh, no, I only tried this on," Nexxa explained, pointing toward the door. "I heard Natina, so I went to check on her."

"Come here." Sergei walked over to her and pulled her into him.

"You're wet," Nexxa laughed.

"Are you?" Sergei moved his hand through the slit of her long black dress with its nude lace accent.

Nexxa smirked. "Maybe."

"Maybe we should just stay in," Sergei whispered before he licked his fingers and moved his hand back under her dress.

"No. You're right. Let's go out." Nexxa moved Sergei's hand from under her dress. "Besides," Nexxa licked the tips of his fingers, saying, "I'm hungry."

Sergei chuckled. He smacked her on the butt. "Get dressed."

Nexxa found Ankica and told her that she would feed Natina and warm up leftovers for her. Ankica waved her off telling her to "go, go." Nexxa kissed her on each cheek. As she walked away she thought about how babushka's hair looked more vibrant and the color in her face had come back as well.

Sergei parked behind Vogue and hopped out to open Nexxa's door. Nexxa stood by his Jaguar looking down, fidgeting with the slit in her dress. She wanted to hide the face that didn't want to see the patrons inside, Sergei's admirers. "Okay, let's go," Sergei said, taking hold of her hand. Nexxa watched as a Mercedes S-Class pulled up to them. The driver took them to the other side of Moscow, maneuvering with grace around the traffic.

Their destination had a falafel style restaurant on one side and a *pharmacie* on the other. There wasn't any signage above the door that Sergei held open for Nexxa. Inside was a brute, and Sergei gave him a nod. They made their way down the hall and through what looked to be an older woman's apartment. Three rooms in and Sergei pulled out a chair at a table by a quaint looking antique dresser decorated with Russian heirlooms. Sergei walked to the opening for the kitchen and shouted in Russian, "Champagne and two Hibiscus flavored vodkas!" Nexxa leaned in her chair as much as possible without falling out and saw a rotund woman, two of them, in the kitchen.

Nexxa repositioned, her red lips smiling, waiting for Sergei to turn and step back to their table.

Sergei seated himself and reached across the table for Nexxa's hand. "Don't look now, but that table in the corner is Putin's brother that he doesn't acknowledge."

Nexxa leaned down to adjust the slit that she wore so well with her creamy toned legs and used her fuckable almond-shaped eyes to catch a glimpse of the Russian misbegotten. "Hmm… he looks like him. Different mother, right?" Nexxa remarked in a tone that sounded like she had it all figured out.

"No, actually, he's adopted," Sergei said with his undeniable sexy smirk.

Nexxa used her left foot to take off her right Prada heel and positioned her foot against his crotch. "Adopted?" she asked. The shots were served. Sergei lifted his. Nexxa lifted hers and swallowed. "Now," Nexxa asserted as she pressed her foot into his penis, "I know he's not adopted."

Sergei reached into his lap. He caressed Nexxa's foot, and she relaxed. He could lie to her all he wanted. "He's actually nobody. Just a second or third cousin." Sergei leaned in closer. "The story is he has something on him, Putin," he whispered.

"I'll think of what the secret is, while you check on our champagne," Nexxa instructed Sergei while moving her eyes toward the kitchen. She had already determined that Sergei was a regular and that he personally knew the owners. It was easy for Nexxa to count the patrons and staff. The bastard Putin brother-cousin with his unfortunate looking whore. An older man with white coiffed hair who was in a military uniform dining alone. The brute at the door. Two seemingly sisters in the kitchen donning the same wide rolled dishwater blonde hair, waist aprons, and Crocs-looking clogs.

"I hope this will do for my love," Sergei said as he poured a champagne that they each had never tried, which flaunted a Russian label. After they clanked flutes Sergei explained, "There's talk that the president doesn't want any imports to bear the name *Shampanskoye.* The labels will have to say sparkling wine unless it's made in Russia."

"Hmm." Nexxa shrugged a shoulder then took a large swallow.

After they ate homemade lobster pierogi, Nexxa asked how to get to the ladies' room. Sergei walked her through the kitchen. He tapped on the door of the single room toilet, and once she was in, he asked if she was okay if he went back to the table; he wanted to catch General Raznikov before he left. The general had been friends with his grandmother. Although retired—long retired—he still dressed in his uniform and ate at the same restaurant, owned by his younger twin sisters, who had transformed the home they all had grown up in into a restaurant. Sergei asked the general about his meal. He said it had been fine but a bit too salty. Sergei laughed.

The general asked about Ankica. "Ankica, the one with—"

Sergei finished his sentence: "The one with lovely brown eyes that got away." Sergei patted the general on the shoulder and said, "She's good. She's good." Sergei looked to the Putin reject and his girlfriend. He noticed her snaggleteeth when she flashed Sergei a smile. The general coughed. Sergei patted him on the back and handed him an extra cloth napkin from the table. He looked at the time on his watch. It was ten past nine. He thought about brown eyes.

Back in the kitchen, Sergei knocked on the bathroom door. One of the sisters, Slava, shook her head no. Sergei twisted, looking back out of the kitchen toward the dining area then back to her. She pointed toward the back door that led to the alleyway. "This way?" he asked her. She nodded, this time with big eyes indicating *yes, yes, you idiot*. Sergei pushed open the heavy metal door.

Nexxa paused her chatter. "Oh hi!" She gleamed at Sergei and pulled him toward her. She took a drag from the cigarette in her hand and handed it back to the young man standing across from her.

Sergei gave the young man wearing street clothes a scowl. Then, "Pushkin baby!" as he grabbed him in a mock choke hold and rubbed his closely shaved head.

The kid wrestled out of Sergei's grasp saying, "I'm twenty-five years now. Am not a baby." Sergei pulled out some money and handed it to him, the grandson of Petra, Slava's sister. The kid offered Sergei a smoke. Sergei declined, then changed his mind.

"So how did you meet?" Sergei asked as he blew from his first puff.

"Oh, him?" Nexxa looked with serious eyes toward Pushkin baby. "He helped me. I needed more toilet paper." The twenty-five-year-old baby looked down.

"What? Toilet paper?" Sergei responded with what looked like angry eyes.

"Well, it's not like I asked him to help me wipe," Nexxa answered, laughing. Sergei stood stoically for a moment then chuckled as he moved over to Nexxa, putting his arm around her and kissing her on the cheek.

Punky, "Pushkin baby," whose mom had named him after the popular American TV show Punky Brewster, said, "I, I didn't!" Sergei took a drag and held up a hand as if to say, *It's okay. I believe you.*

Leaving the restaurant was just as interesting as arriving. Sergei told Nexxa to follow closely. They walked to the back of the adjacent building, and Mr. Brute was waiting to let them in the back door. Sergei told Nexxa to remove her heels. He grasped her hand and they trotted up three flights. "You ready?" Sergei asked with ease of breath. "Yes," Nexxa replied. He pulled out a key and unlocked a door. The inside was dark and cold. Nexxa started to make an assessment. She only saw that there weren't any curtains in the window in front of them and that the doorway to the kitchen was to the left. A small loveseat that was low to the ground and opposite a blank wall was flanked with only a slim table. Sergei led her to the bedroom. Nexxa paused her breathing.

Sergei pulled on the bookcase, and when it opened before them was a room with a spiral staircase. Gripping her hand tighter, Sergei led Nexxa up. He slid a lock open and pushed open a hatch. The swirling Moscow sky was there, and the air was sultry. They emerged, and before Nexxa could ask her Russian what they were doing a helicopter hovered over. Nexxa buried her head into Sergei and the helicopter landed. She barely felt her feet as she was running again with Sergei. They buckled in and put on the headsets. Nexxa held her stomach. She wasn't sick—she was feeling the white butterflies, from the man that emitted the white glow.

Sergei huddled with Nexxa and pointed out a few sights. She knew, but she let him tell her they were flying over the Red Square. They went over the river and then back toward where they began when Nexxa had a heart stopping view, a view of an illuminated billboard for De Beers. She smiled, thinking *who wouldn't* while looking at the brilliant cut diamond engagement ring that flanked the woman from the advertisement. The time spent as a family the last few weeks without the strange housekeeper felt right.

Nexxa gripped Sergei's thigh, and Sergei placed his hand atop of hers. He thought about the general, how he had talked about the woman with brown eyes that got away. *That will never be me*, he scoffed in his mind.

"Are you sure?" Sergei asked, looking over at Nexxa before he started his Jaguar.

"Yeah. I couldn't." Nexxa shook her head. "I would be worried if we stayed in a hotel."

"Okay." Sergei touched her dress, feeling for the slit. He found it. "You're mine when we get home, right?" Nexxa pushed his hand further and looked out of the passenger window with a naughty thought.

After a quiet drive home, Sergei pulled into the garage. Nexxa looked over and saw Vlasta's car was still there.

Upstairs she checked on the baby and babushka and they were both asleep. She smiled as she passed the sitting room between the bedrooms thinking about her conversations with

Ankica.

Sergei was waiting for her. She had expected to see him with his clothes off. He motioned for her to come toward the bed. Nexxa slipped on her heels and walked toward him. Sergei pushed her on the bed and removed her heels. One side at a time, Sergei pulled her dress from her shoulders; Nexxa stood and he pulled her dress down to where she could step out of it. Sergei went to his closet and came back with one of her chemises and one of his oversized sweaters. He said nothing, so Nexxa dressed. Sergei grabbed the cashmere blankets he kept on his leather armchairs and said, "Great, let's go." Nexxa looked from one side of the room to the other. Sergei motioned with his head to the glass doors. Outside on the terrace he had a fire going in a gas fire pit. Chairs were positioned and a bottle of red wine was waiting. They sat and covered themselves with the blankets. "I got chips too!" Sergei lifted a bag and handed it to Nexxa. They laughed. Nexxa "mmm'ed" as she drank the first sip of the cherry-tasting red blend Sergei had found just for her. The fire wasn't that warm, but the air was still humid and the alcohol helped. Sergei tapped his phone and a song that Nexxa recognized from the Hôtel Costes playlists started playing.

Nexxa shivered. "Come sit in my lap," Sergei told her as he reached his hand out. Nexxa handed her wine glass to him, which he placed on the terrace by his chair, and she sat in his lap leaning her head on his shoulder. "See, I told you, you would be mine tonight," he said before kissing her.

The next day Nexxa went for a run after she handled the

morning routine. A little hungover, but she pushed herself because that's what she would have done if she was still in New York working for Kuretz Investments. When she returned, she entered through the kitchen door and grabbed a water bottle from the fridge. A beeping sound started to emit, so Nexxa went to the fridge, checking the door. It was closed. The beep changed to a high-pitched sound. Nexxa looked around for the sound, maybe from the dishwasher or the house alarm. She heard static and voices, so she crossed the kitchen to the butler's pantry where she found the baby monitor. Lifting the monitor, she adjusted the volume, but nothing there.

The sound came again, and Nexxa turned following the sound to the cellar door. She opened the door and said, "Hello." She looked over her shoulder. Hearing Sergei on the phone in his office, she felt comfortable knowing he was close by, remembering Sergei had mentioned never finishing his cellar. She took a deep breath and started down the steps.

The sound of static, sirens perhaps, and voices.

Nexxa stepped off of the staircase and turned in a circle. She saw some dusty bottles, some old boxes, and a door. She moved a box off of another and dragged the heavy box away from the door. Nexxa pulled on the handle; the door didn't budge, but there wasn't a lock that needed undoing. She felt along the door frame then pulled the door handle down and toward her. The door bounced back on her and she felt dust in her mouth. The first thing she saw was a round metal stool positioned before a wooden bench style worktable surrounded by cinder block walls which gave the feeling of an unlucky hostage. There on the worktable was a CB radio.

"Well okay, this is fucking weird, but whatever," Nexxa said as she took a few steps forward and adjusted a knob. Crackling, the voices started again. Looking around, she saw a tattered box. Inside she found a notepad. "Like, what?" she questioned, shaking her head looking at the mostly illegible handwriting. Some markings read "NEXXA" by days of the week, with either *like* or *don't like* beside it. She plopped it down, and a short black hair clung to the spiral edge of the notepad.

One more look around, then Nexxa lifted the notepad with just her finger and thumb, placing it back in the box where she had found it. *This isn't a cellar. This is a room fit for a victim. Or a victim of a victim*, she thought and hated her assessment as she left climbing the stairs to the kitchen. She pulled the door shut and before she let go of her grasp, she felt the lever jiggle.

Out in the garage, Nexxa rummaged through a toolbox on the perfectly organized garage shelves for the very specific tool to tighten the door handle. (She knew what to look for because of a man she had dated in New York. Brief, but after a night together he let her stay the next day while he did some house projects.) Tool in hand, Nexxa bent to tie her sneaker and it slipped from her grasp, landing under Vlasta's car. *Ugh,* Nexxa crawled on her knees and reached under the car. Standing, she looked around for a broom or anything to retrieve the tool but the urge to look into Vlasta's car took over. Cupping her face with her hands looking through the passenger window, she saw the front seat had some takeaway boxes, crumpled napkins and a mangled spork with a piece of meat poked through the handle's end. And, on the floorboard was an urn from Rome.

"What?" Nexxa screamed as she yanked on the door handle of Vlasta's car. She grabbed Kilmer's urn, holding it securely as she ran through the house. Upstairs she sat on the edge of the bed. She stood again and put the urn down, then picked up the urn and moved it back to the corner of the room where it had rested for months. *How did I not notice it was gone?*

Later, when Sergei came up to his room, he found Nexxa sitting in one of the armchairs. She was staring at the urn on the floor. "What are you—" Sergei began to ask when he noticed the urn in his room.

"Why was it in Vlasta's car? I mean, I get it was morbid having it in here, but why?" Nexxa asked without looking up to him.

"Nexxa, the urn was in here way too long. Why was it ever here?"

Nexxa looked up. "Why? Because I brought it here. You knew what I was doing in Rome. You knew I had no choice but to bring it with me."

"It's your dead ex-husband's remains, ashes or whatever!" Sergei responded with haste.

Nexxa began nodding her head. "Yeah, yeah that's what it—"

"This is my room. MY house!" Sergei yelled. "What the fuck were you thinking?!"

"Thinking? I moved here for you. I left my sister, my j—"

"Fuck me!" Sergei shouted over her.

"My job," Nexxa said under her breath.

"I work! I provide, a housekeeper, money. Everything you need!" Sergei scoffed raising his hands.

"A housekeeper? She's crazy! She fucking put kittens in a steamy bath and then, then fucking said you couldn't have a cat or kittens. Then put silverware baskets in the fucking tub! She's rude. Your grandmother—"

"This has nothing to do with my babushka. Why are your bringing her into this?" Sergei questioned with continuing hostility.

"Vlasta is not normal! She's not good for this family. She doesn't fucking treat baby Natina right. With love. I've wanted to talk to Demo. Tell him—"

"What the fuck? I take care of this family! Me. Me! I take care of this family!"

"Really? Have you seen how much better babushka is with Vlasta gone? And think, did you really want me to spread his fucking ashes here? In Moscow? On your land?" Nexxa didn't have a plan for how to dispose of the ashes. The shock had not fully subsided since she first collected them in Rome. She was honestly waiting for a sign as to what to do with them.

"He fucking tried to rape you! Tried to kill you!" Sergei shouted.

Nexxa's eyes glassed over and she stood, taking a step away from the leather armchair toward the urn in the corner. Sergei reached for her, barely grasping her arm. He thought she had gotten up to embrace him; but when she walked past him, he wore an expression of betrayal.

"I should take this and my clothes and..." Nexxa closed her

eyes, holding back a feeling she had never had with Sergei. "And go." She bent down and lifted the urn then started toward the closet.

"So you're going to leave now! Leave me? Fucking go!" Sergei's chest expanded up and down as he paced, before kicking the table that housed his Scotch. Nexxa heard only his anger and the table falling over, glasses breaking. What she didn't hear was the underlying tone of: *I'm worried I will lose you, lose you like the general lost his brown-eyed girl.*

Nexxa placed the urn on a chair by the fallen table. From the closet, she pulled out her suitcase.

IRELAND

Nexxa looked over her shoulder at the carry-on bag that once again contained Irish human remains. She had told the man pushing her luggage to keep pace with her, for she didn't want to lose sight of the ashes that had slithered their way around her lavender.

The driver pulled up to the entrance of The Westbury. Nexxa exited the car, looking at the façade, and thought, *This gives me a familiar feeling.* A porter unloaded her luggage, and the doorman directed her inside. Nexxa approached the front desk and gave her name. The woman informed her she had been upgraded to a junior suite courtesy of management and handed her a room key. Nexxa didn't question since she knew Sergei had used his concierge service to book her travel. With her room key in hand, Nexxa dashed to join the porter on the elevator. "I have expensive shoes in my luggage," she said, unsettled. The porter nodded.

Nexxa ordered a bottle of wine from room service and undressed to shower. The water smelled of fresh green grass but in a good way—that didn't stop her from collapsing to her knees and crying. Dressed in the hotel robe, which smelled of the hotel's signature scent, Nexxa quickly twisted her blonde hair up and answered the door. The wine was delivered with chocolate. Nexxa asked the server if he had any bread. Her eyes held more tears waiting to be unleashed. He noticed.

The server unwrapped a napkin-covered basket and said, "I always have a mind to bring bread with the wine, ma'am." Nexxa braced herself on the room service cart and grasped her abdomen. The kind young man patted her arm. "You right, ma'am?" Nexxa held back her tears and nodded. "I'll open the wine." The server twisted the corkscrew, twisted quickly and the cork was out. He looked to her for direction of where to place the bottle. Nexxa pointed to the nightstand. He moved across the room, then back again to retrieve a wine glass. He placed the glass down; it wobbled. "Oh no," his voice shook as he balanced the wine glass. Again across the room to the room service cart, he lifted the bread basket and handed it to her. Nexxa laughed. Cried. Tipped him. She drank a glass of wine. She thought about drunk texting Sergei: *Sergei, you are... I mean. I love...*

Instead—she drank the entire bottle and then texted Iliada that she was feeling like a failure.

The next morning, Nexxa sprayed herself with the new *parfum* by Sisley that Sergei had gifted her the day before

Mother's Day. He had told her that she looked even sexier when taking care of his niece, and she wanted to be reminded of the feeling she had had before the argument that caused her to leave Moscow.

Dressing, she realized she had only packed her Vampy black Prada heels. Not exactly the shoes she felt like wearing for her trip's intended purpose. Nexxa stepped out onto the suite's quaint terrace and smelled part of her past, inhaling and exhaling. Back inside, she changed into a pair of her black Splendid leggings and sneakers, then called the front desk and requested a driver to take her around.

"They look gorgeous, love. Quite a good look for you." The sales attendant in all of his twenty-two years tried hard with the flattery, flirting. Nexxa smiled. *Stop imagining fucking me and just ring up the shoes.* She did like the look. An open toe sling back with a block heel. Black.

Nexxa rode the escalator up, seeing a mannequin donning the loveliest red lace ever. A sales lady promptly approached informing her, "It's just arrived. A new designer. Shall I arrange a room for you?" In the dressing room, Nexxa looked at herself in the red brassiere and panties. She thought about Sergei telling her she needed something new. *How did I get here? Standing in a dressing room, alone. It's like I'm back in New York, still single.* So, she bought the expensive Kiki de Montparnasse matching set in a color called *Blushing Cherry*.

Mr. Kane, perfectly positioned with his dark salt and pepper hair in the lounge of The Westbury, stood when Nexxa made her way through the lobby. He watched her as she thanked the porter for carrying her bag to the elevator. He chuckled at how smitten the poor lad was. Then when an attractive man attempted to strike up a conversation with Nexxa, positioning himself to block his view, Quinn realized he was the poor lad now. Quinn moved quickly in his blue check print Tom Ford shirt, jeans, and black suede loafers toward the entrance to the lobby. She was gone, going up to her suite in the lift with that douche.

Mr. Kane cleared his throat and looked around at the guests and staff. He laughed at himself realizing that no one but he knew his newly divorced heart was pining over a gorgeous woman he had thought about for over a decade. Outside, he bummed a fag from a guest. On the phone with Kieran: "I saw her."

"What now?" Kieran asked without emotion.

"Me fuckin' bollocks. I don't know." Quinn rubbed his hand over his head.

"Ya do."

"It's not how I expected." Quinn took a drag and continued. "I mean if she had fuckin' told me. Told me that she was coming to Dublin."

"She's here now. Nexxa's here." Kieran sounded empathic.

Quinn handed his cigarette butt to a porter and pulled fifty quid from his pocket, giving it to the young lad.

On the fifth floor in her junior suite Nexxa stood in her new shoes and looked at herself in the mirror. She moved the urn and lifted her phone, opening her music app and downloading the Pet Shop Boys while pulling off her leggings and top. In her bra and panties Nexxa danced to "It's A Sin." As the song was ending, Nexxa fell to her knees before the mirror, she could see the urn behind her, and cried. Standing, she screamed, "Fuck, fuck, fuckity fuck you!" A song that had lyrics about never being alone in the afterglow played. Nexxa went to the bathroom and came back with her manicure bag. She removed her cuticle trimmer and drew it along her lifeline on her right palm. Blood dripped from her hand, which she caught in a cotton round. Nexxa looked to the urn. Stepping slowly to it, she lifted the lid and reached her fingers in. She sprinkled her cut—her blood—with Kilmer's ashes; a spot of blood pooled and turned lavender.

Nexxa gasped. She ran a finger along her cut, smearing the lavender spot of blood. Without thinking, she sprinkled more ashes, on the gash, and more lavender blood appeared. Standing over the bedside lamp, she moved a hand over the light bulb. Lavender. Her blood vessels were reflecting back a lavender tone.

QUINN OSIAN KANE | 17

"Take a deep breath."

Quinn's chest rose.

"Good, and again," instructed Dr. Murphy, Quinn's primary care physician.

Quinn took another deep breath.

"You're good, Quinn." The doctor pulled the stethoscope out of his ears. "I could run tests," Dr. Murphy continued, "but," he shook his head, "you want to tell me what happened."

Quinn buttoned up his shirt. He lifted his phone from the side medical counter and said, "Nexxa."

"Who?" the doctor asked with a lost face. He had known Quinn since he was in his twenties and even knew Quinn's wife. While he was aware of Quinn's divorce, he hadn't any idea of anyone new in Quinn's life or heart.

Kieran was waiting for Quinn, leaning against his Range

Rover with folded arms. "Was it a heart attack?" he questioned with a smirk.

"Fuck off!" Quinn spat at him.

Kieran handed Quinn a bottle of water as he pulled into traffic. "Where am I takin' ya?"

"He said it was most likely a panic attack," Quinn offered.

"Really now. Are you jokin'?"

"The hotel," Quinn said after a sip of water.

Kieran started to say something when he looked over at Quinn and saw him gazing out of the window. He wanted to ask what his obsession was with this woman. He knew Nexxa was irresistible, but Quinn hardly knew her.

Kieran drove Quinn to his home in Dublin. While it was meager, he could afford better from what Quinn paid him, he refused to move. His home was old but actually worth about a million quid. "Is your navigation broke?" Quinn asked as he lowered his window, peering out at the old row house.

Inside Kieran warmed up some soup he had made. Sliced some day-old bread and poured some Scotch. He ushered Quinn outside. They sat at a small round table, plastic white chairs. Quinn took the Scotch before he ate. Kieran pushed a bowl of soup toward Quinn. Kieran tore a piece of bread and dipped it in the soup. "Tomorrow," he said with caring eyes.

Quinn nodded as he sipped and leaned back in his chair.

Mr. Kane, I would love the opportunity to—

That's all Quinn could entertain while reading an email from a reporter. So he forwarded the email to his new assistant. Quinn pushed on Kieran's back. "Get up." Kieran rolled over on his couch and opened one eye. Quinn stood over him. "Your hot water sucks and your coffee doesn't work."

"Me coffee doesn't work?" Kieran sat up and pulled on his tracksuit pants and sneakers.

"Let's go." Quinn was eager.

Kieran smoked in the car on the way; Quinn had insisted on driving since he was the one with the "lesser" hangover. When Quinn exited the SUV and Kieran stepped over to the driver's side, Kieran said, "You know she never actually broke your heart." Right there in that moment hearing Kieran's words, Quinn realized something he hadn't in a long time. That he had never had his heart broken because he had given it to the UVF and to proving that he was worth something in business. His ex-wife never really had his heart because she had never really given hers, except to renovations on his home and herself. So as he stepped into The Westbury, the hotel that he had bought with two other investors five years ago and renovated, he wanted something more than a false alarm heart attack, but not quite a broken heart either.

Quinn made his way into the hotel doing his best to smile at the staff that greeted him warmly. All the women working there had a crush on him and a few of the lads too. A night spent drinking Scotch with Kieran hadn't given him any ideas of how to approach Nexxa. His phone pinged and pinged, and for the first time he felt like dropping it in one of the vast flower arrangements in the hotel. The Westbury was one of his three ventures. It felt like having three children at times. When he would be done for the day with one business it never failed that one of the others would need attention.

Sitting in the lounge with a bottle of sparkling water, Quinn waited, using a copy of the Irish Times to hide himself and hopefully his conspicuous feelings. A song from a Hôtel Costes album played. Quinn noticed and tried to focus on the article he was reading about a Croatian version of Moscow's Federation Tower to be built in Zagreb. Next, a song about Paris colliding with love across the horizon and more about forming circles in your mind came on. Quinn exhaled and folded the newspaper. He leaned on the table and moved his hand along his jawline.

The day in Paris that Quinn and Nexxa parted ways had always haunted him. Once he recognized Kilmer he had felt disbelief in who Nexxa really was. Being honest at the time, he told himself he was too old for her. Really, she was just beginning her life. If they had started up a relationship then, they most likely would not have stayed together. Still, he had regretted not letting Kieran handle the situation with Kilmer at the time, removing Nexxa from his control. His first impression was right though. That Nexxa was remarkable: she had had the bravery to train with the IRA, she had been able to infiltrate his inner circle, she had made her way from Canada to the U.S. and established herself with a career in finance later. All this while looking fuckable.

After Paris, Quinn had hired a design team to refurbish his wine cellar, swimming pool, and guest house. Through this, he met a lovely Irish woman with shiny brown hair and fair skin. He asked her to marry him a month later and she moved in, working full-time on his mini chateau. In fact she never stopped renovating his home right up until he served her with divorce papers. Their split was mostly amicable as they had formed more of a friendship over the years. She had been well educated and had an affluent group of friends she spent plenty of time with between Dublin and London. And when they couldn't conceive and neither of them persisted with the usual route of IVF, surrogacy, or adoption, they settled into their own routines. Quinn with his businesses and her with her design agency, which Quinn graciously funded.

"Mr. Kane, is there anything I can get you? You haven't eaten anything, and you've been here all day?" asked the hostess. Quinn looked down at his watch—he had been there for five hours—then shook his head. "Anything you want, I'm only over there," the hostess said, smiling as she motioned with her head toward the restaurant.

He felt like a fool. Now the staff were noticing him sitting around doing nothing. He took one more sip of his sparkling water and headed out to the valet. Standing outside waiting for his Obsidian Black Mercedes S-Class Sedan to be brought around, he spotted Nexxa emerging from the hotel. Quinn's heart quavered. He watched intently, wondering what she was asking the doorman as he pointed and shook his head. Quinn's car was brought around, and the valet handed him his key fob. He took no step toward his car, not wanting to miss her next action, and the valet politely asked him if everything was alright. When the doorman hailed a taxi and helped Nexxa in with her shopping bag, Quinn sprinted around to the driver's side and sped off following the taxi.

HOWTH | 18

Nexxa had planned to go to an area known as Howth to release Kilmer's ashes. She hated him. She also didn't hate him. She was smart enough to realize that without meeting him she wouldn't be who she was now. Something about pain teaches you, and she knew this. It wasn't in her to use her energy on hating someone—she was more of the personality to spend her energy ending someone if needed.

Quinn pulled into the parking area by the seaside park waiting and watching as Nexxa exited the taxi. When a car honked behind him, he was forced to find a spot and park.

Nexxa looked around, catching her hair in the wind, as it felt colder than she had expected. The area was crowded with tourists, mostly families it seemed. She had imagined having more privacy when she was to spread Kilmer's ashes. She walked toward the access down to the seashore, and just as she took her first step down, Quinn exited his car and had eyes on her. He wondered what she could be doing, especially since she had on heels and a black dress and no jacket or sweater. Another step down and she was quickly out of his sight. He dashed in front of a car, another honk, but he reached the top of the stairs, quickly on her heels.

Nexxa took a few more steps and lost her balance on a slippery step. Quinn caught her. She practically fell into him. Nexxa felt strong arms, smelled a familiar cologne. He helped her stand, and she turned, grabbing ahold of him to maintain her balance in the strong seaside wind. "Quinn?" Nexxa gasped.

"I won't let you fall," Quinn said, hoping his own emotions wouldn't break him.

Her eyes swelled with tears. Quinn pushed her hair from her face. "Will you come with me?" Quinn asked with longing eyes. Nexxa looked over her shoulder to the water then back to him nodding yes. She had felt so alone and now was cold; he was warm and his hand felt strong holding hers as he guided her up the stairs.

Quinn opened the passenger door for Nexxa. Getting in the car, she then placed the bag she held with Kilmer's ashes by her feet. Quinn exited the car park and knew he didn't want to drive her back to The Westbury. "You're cold," Quinn said and rubbed her right arm. He wished he had worn a jacket, but a long sleeve shirt was enough during the day for him to stay warm. Nexxa looked down at her feet, seeing her new block heel, open toe shoes weren't scuffed during her slip, but her toes were slightly red and cold. "You have nice shoes."

Quinn glanced at her, then immediately felt stupid. *Get a grip, man*, he thought. Nexxa shivered and tugged at the hem of her dress. Quinn turned on the heat. He was warm, his blood was excited from touching her, but he didn't care; she was cold, and he had her in his car.

Arriving at her hotel, Quinn's hotel, Nexxa wondered how he knew where she was staying. Quinn raised a hand as if to say, *not now*, when the valet came to his door. "Is this your hotel?" Nexxa asked stoically, looking straight ahead through the windshield.

Quinn lightly nodded. "Yes." Nexxa felt nauseous, lowering her head. She managed to pull herself together, and just as Quinn began to speak, she opened the door and was gone with her ex-husband's ashes. Quinn closed his eyes and slammed his fist against the steering wheel. "Bloody fucking hell!"

Quinn practically opened his door into the valet as he exited the car running after Nexxa. He barely saw her, their eyes meeting as the lift doors closed. Quinn screamed, "Fuuuck!" Staff paused and one or two guests were in earshot. He smiled, laughed, and nodded. His car was still waiting for him when he made his way through the lobby and outside. He sped off, narrowly missing a lorry.

Quinn drove straight to Kieran's. He didn't want to stop for petrol in order to get outside of the city to his home: that was a lie he told himself. He banged on the door. It was Kieran's day off. Kieran had told Quinn a decade ago that he should get one day off a week, which really meant that he would just be on call unless it had to do with real business, UVF business. Not being Quinn's personal bodyguard, or therapist as it had been recently.

Nexxa closed the door to her room. She looked around her suite realizing that Quinn was probably the reason why she had been upgraded. Or maybe it was Sergei's concierge service or his points or just his money that put her in this room. Her mind felt heavy like she had been drugged. She plopped Kilmer down and steadied herself with a hand on the wall to remove her new shoes. The wine she had ordered her first night there and crying to the room service waiter, did Quinn know about that? Did he follow her when she went to Marks & Spencer shopping? Nexxa took her phone from her purse and looked at her recent calls. She saw Sergei's name. She screamed a little and sat on the bed.

Nexxa undressed, pulling on the hotel robe. It was soft, the feeling of a luxurious item designed for a hotel brand. She stood before the mirror in the bathroom and took off her makeup. She glanced down at her phone. Sergei was calling. She knew she couldn't lie to him about Kilmer's ashes. She imagined the conversation: *I couldn't let his ashes go because it was windy, and I slipped. Then Quinn, the man you met in New York at Mr. Albert's house, appeared and practically caught me. And guess what? I'm staying in his hotel. The hotel you booked for me. Then he drove me back here and chased after me when I got mad at him and got out of his car. His lovely Mercedes.* Yeah sure, how was she going to tell him that?

And she was still hurt.

DUBLIN'S TURN

A knock came on her suite door. Nexxa pulled on her robe. Outside was a long rectangular box, no bow. Nexxa placed it on the desk and opened it, pushing back tissue paper to reveal a pair of navy-blue Hunter wellies and a pair of blue Sweaty Betty cashmere lounge socks. Nexxa stood back from the box. She held her chest and closed her eyes thinking about when Quinn had *parfum* and a white dress and more delivered to her room in Paris.

The room phone rang. "Hello," Nexxa answered, barely holding the receiver to her ear.

"Can I take you back to Howth?" Quinn asked in a calm, hopeful tone.

Nexxa could feel Kilmer's urn slumped in the corner rotting away. The new boots smelled of fresh rubber. Outside would be better with the aroma of Dublin. "Okay," she answered, waiting for what he would say next.

"I'll have Kieran come to your room. If. If that's okay?" Quinn sounded like he was waiting for more from her.

"That's fine."

"Okay, good." Quinn remained composed.

"Oh, what time?" Nexxa sounded panicked, looking over at the boots. It was nine a.m. and she hadn't showered yet.

"One hour?" Quinn grimaced as he spoke. Was he being too pushy? He fucking wanted to see her and it was so hard to think about waiting any longer. Last night had been hard. He had stayed at Kieran's again subjecting him to his what-ifs reminiscing on their brief time in Paris together. He hated that he had been so stupid. Being more of a show-off flying her there, giving her money to shop with Klarin. Had he known that she was working with Kilmer, under his control, he would have handled Nexxa differently. He would have let go of his ego and stepped up.

"I can see your toes. Where are the boots?" Kieran asked, sounding playfully irritated.

"Kieran." Nexxa acknowledged him standing at her suite door. "You're the same. I mean you are mean and nice at the same time," Nexxa said laughing, and it felt good.

Kieran moved in for a hug. Nexxa let him. She wondered if Quinn was close by, in his car downstairs perhaps. She figured he might not want to be seen with her since it was his hotel. She assumed he was still married*ish*. Nexxa moved her neck around and blew out a breath. Kieran pulled the door shut behind her, and just as they had a decade ago, he escorted her to Quinn.

Kieran opened the passenger door, and Nexxa slid in. Kieran moved over to Quinn's door. They spoke in Gaelic. (Kieran told Quinn that he would follow them.) Quinn pulled off and Kieran hopped in the Range Rover that had been waiting behind with the engine running.

Nexxa adjusted her hair after she buckled her seat belt. "Thank you for the boots. I didn't wear them."

"It's ok," Quinn said as he cleared his throat. "Did you get the socks?" Quinn quipped with a nervous thought in his head.

Nexxa laughed. Quinn looked over at her. "I, I don't want to go back to Howth."

Quinn nodded. "Sure, okay." He signaled and switched lanes. Kieran did the same. "Where would you like to go?" Quinn asked, sounding more relaxed.

"How about a pub?" Nexxa said spontaneously.

"Okay," Quinn chuckled. He looked over at her. Nexxa kept her gaze on the scenery out of the side window.

Quinn drove and Nexxa leaned her head back, closing her eyes. This was the first time in six months that she had felt peacefully out of place. She hadn't even noticed how much time had passed. The roads felt so smooth, and Quinn hadn't spoken. He had looked over at her a few times as she sat with her eyes closed and her blonde locks flanking her shoulder. He struggled to stop himself from looking at her legs even though she wore skintight black pants with her black open toe shoes. Her top exposed her breasts just the right amount. Quinn adjusted his arms, switching to steering so he was faced more toward his window. Looking at her made him feel as if his muscles were broken.

Forty-five minutes later Quinn pulled into a gravel-paved car park. He parked and turned off the car. Nexxa sat straight and finally had the courage to turn to face him. "So, we're here for a beer?" she asked, smiling.

Quinn reached, touching her cheek with his key fob in hand. "Yes, yes we are," he said with his own smile.

Quinn held the door open for her. The establishment was an old one-level stone building with a thatched roof. The hanging planters were filled with fresh spring flowers in fuchsia and white. They were seated at a booth in the corner by the fireplace. Quinn ordered a Guinness for each of them. "So how did you know where I was?" Nexxa started with an assertive tone.

"I had my hotel, The Westbury, tell me that you had booked a room," Quinn offered right away.

"No." Nexxa shook her head. "The seaside area, Howth. How did you know?"

"Yeah." Quinn started as he spun his glass of beer around. "So, I actually waited for you in the lounge." Quinn rubbed his hand along his chin. "True story." He added, laughing.

"Okay," she responded, not knowing if her mind wanted her to laugh or if her heart wanted her to be sad.

"You're worried about something." Quinn was sincere as he looked into her perfectly accentuated brown eyes.

Nexxa took a sip of her beer. "Oh," she said, grasping her chest.

Quinn lifted up from his seat. "Are you okay?"

"Yeah, can I just have a glass of wine?" Nexxa continued

holding her chest, eventually letting her hand slide along between her breasts. Quinn turned motioning for the waitress, and Nexxa slumped over in the booth.

Nexxa opened her eyes and saw flames crackling before her. She could smell the burning wood and lifted her hands, looking at her right palm which she had cut and added Kilmer's ashes. Quinn stood up and hovered over her in the armchair he had moved her to. Nexxa looked at him and he grasped her hands.

"What happened?" Nexxa spoke lightly.

"You fainted," Quinn told her in a comforting voice. "I've called a doctor."

"Kilmer's ashes," Nexxa said as she pulled her hands down from his grasp, resting them on her thighs.

"Kilmer. You have his, his ashes?" Quinn questioned, furrowing his brow.

Nexxa grasped the back of her head; it felt heavy. She thought about cutting her hand, looking at Kilmer's urn in her room and screaming, Fuck, fuck, fuckity fuck you! "No, no. I don't need… a doctor."

Quinn leaned down to her, stroking her face. Nexxa reached for his hand. She slumped again into his grasp. Quinn motioned with his head for Kieran to come over.

RUSSIAN'S ROME | 20

ROME — OCTOBER 2013

Sergei stood outside of the large windows that gave a view into the living room of the Italian villa in Rome. He watched as an Asian man wearing a ball cap left with a crumpled brown paper bag, presumably takeaway.

Sergei let himself in through the unlocked door. The villa smelled of Chinese soup and something else. Something that smelled like a color, reddish if he had to describe it. He dismissed the odd odor and made his way over to stand before the man slouched in a chair, seemingly asleep in skinny red jeans, a black V-neck t-shirt, and—a blonde wig.

Crouching before the man, Sergei assessed his height and weight before he removed the tie that bound him. Sergei knew this was Nexxa's ex-husband, who had ties to the IRA and a connection to a man in Beirut named Sal, SalKiss4U. "What the fuck are you doing here?" Sergei spoke to himself as he thought back through events he had been told by Demo.

Sergei had narrowly facilitated Nexxa's release in Beirut, but he enjoyed every bit of it. The possibility that he wouldn't have been successful was always there in the universe but wasn't meant to be part of his journey. He knew that he relied on fundamental help, but the real truth was that he had always suppressed the supernatural that he possessed like his babushka.

Kilmer opened an eye. He asked, "Who are you?"

Sergei stood from his crouch and slowly rubbed his hands together saying, "I'm Sergei. I came from Moscow."

Kilmer touched his head and winced. "Russia. Did you bring me a Russian hooker?" Kilmer spoke through a struggled cackle. "How about that baby from Babies "R" Us. Where is it? I liked it."

Sergei slowly lowered his arms. He recognized that his amygdala, the part of the brain that attaches emotions to memories, was being assaulted. Kilmer shifted slightly in the chair touching his chin, wiping soup drippings. He remembered KitchenGod now and the spork of soup. His facial muscles slumped, but he moved his eyes toward the hallway where the bedrooms were. "Where's Nexxa?" He half-lifted an arm, pointing, "I need her."

Sergei briefly looked behind him toward the bedrooms, and when he looked back, Kilmer was standing eye to eye with him. Kilmer drew in a breath with his neck sinking in and his eyes bulging. He grasped Sergei, speaking in a hoarse *daemonicus* voice, "I want Nexxa." Sergei grabbed hold of Kilmer's neck with one arm, the other on his head, and just before he broke his neck, Kilmer said, "Tell her I love her. Crimson is coming for her soul."

Quinn lifted Nexxa and carried her over to the emerald green velvet couch. Holding her in his lap, he stared into the fireplace. He told Kieran to have them add a log to the fire. An older man carried in some wood and Kieran assisted. Quinn had Nexxa lying against his chest, and feeling her heart beat, his confidence competed with the fire. Kieran crouched by the fireplace poking at the burning wood, and as Nexxa came to and opened her eyes, she saw sparks of lavender in the flames.

Quinn ran his hands along Nexxa's bare arms. "You're cold." He assessed, worried.

"Yeah, I feel cold even though it's supposed to be spring." Nexxa's voice was tired, and she took a minute to realize she was in a lap that wasn't Sergei's.

"Love, it's spring in Ireland!" Quinn let his happiness come out.

"I like this place, it's old. I like old," Nexxa spoke as she adjusted her hair, determined to reposition herself *next* to Quinn on the Louis the Fifteenth era sofa. She ran her hand along the velvet and then her mind flashed back to being in the crypt with Sergei on his Louis the Fifteenth furniture that he had styled after Hôtel Costes, where she had spent time with Quinn. Nexxa turned and asked, "Can I have a glass of wine?"

Nexxa drank a red wine she described as gorgeous and her embarrassment faded, giving room in her mind to admire how strong Quinn looked. The restaurant had only a few patrons in neighboring booths, just enough background noise to allow her and Quinn to sit in each other's company on the velvet sofa flanked with tartan upholstered pillows by the welcoming Irish fire.

"Why did you come to Dublin?" Quinn had switched to Scotch and couldn't wait any longer.

Nexxa looked away, then back to Quinn. "I, I have Kilmer's ashes." The waitress approached, and Quinn ordered her another glass. Nexxa smiled. "Thank you, thank you for everything, Quinn."

"I would do anything—" Quinn stopped himself as he reached for his Scotch. He threw back the last sip and placed his glass down on the coffee table.

"Seeing you in New York, I, I didn't think I would... I don't know," Nexxa said.

"Are you with him? The Russian," Quinn asked.

Nexxa nodded. "I'm with him in Moscow."

Quinn reached for his glass of Scotch before the waitress could place it down. He took a sip. "One question." He took another sip, asking, "is that what you want?"

Nexxa rubbed her lips together. She thought about Sergei. His voice, the first time she had heard it. Him driving her to safety out of Beirut in a Jaguar. Their first night together in the Ararat Park Hotel in Mother Russia. Seeing him shoot a gun. All that was sexy as fuck. But then again, Kilmer had taught her many things, exposed her to a different lifestyle, and she knew that Quinn was powerful—intriguing. Nexxa heard a baby cry, and she turned her head and thought about Natina. She did want to be with Sergei, and yet she was sitting across from Quinn. Quinn didn't have a creepy housekeeper and hadn't been angry with her over Kilmer—ever.

He seemed uncomplicated and safe.

Nexxa looked at Quinn's hand as he pushed the button for her floor in the lift. "The ring left a mark." Quinn knew what she meant.

He turned, moving closer to her, and said, "My divorce is final." He wanted to say, *You left a bigger mark on me.*

Nexxa stood on her balcony alone. She was wearing the cozy hotel robe and the socks Quinn had given her. She held out her hands. She didn't have a line from wearing her old wedding ring and she wasn't wearing the ruby ring that Sergei had given her. In her mind, wearing a ring didn't symbolize one's love. *Or did it?* she wondered after seeing the mark on Quinn's finger. Your character was supposed to be the symbol of your love unless, she laughed to herself, you had the large diamond ring the woman from the billboard did in Moscow.

Iliada answered Nexxa's Skype call. She was sitting with Flash, and they were eating strawberries and listening to Britney Spears. "Hi." Nexxa smiled at them.

"Hi, how is Ireland?" Iliada asked enthusiastically. Flash fluttered around.

"Hi Flash," Nexxa laughed. "Um, well, it's good."

"Yeah, like, you were so sad the other night," Iliada recounted, adjusting her laptop.

Nexxa held her forehead. "Well, okay. So Quinn is here. I mean, of course he's here. He fucking lives here!" Nexxa huffed, letting her head fall back.

"Uh-huh." Iliada grinned and lifted a strawberry, took a bite of it and handed it to Flash.

"No, it's not like that," Nexxa insisted, shaking her head. "Oh hold on, let me show you the new shoes I got here." Nexxa walked away from her laptop. In her bedroom she heard her mobile ringing. She almost didn't look, assuming it would be Sergei calling to tell her something she didn't want to hear. As she picked up her new black block heels, she glanced at her phone; it read *Private*, and only a few people had Nexxa's mobile number. She stepped back out onto the terrace. "So I got these the other day to wear when I disperse Kilmer's ashes," Nexxa said, holding up a shoe.

"Ooooh, I like those!" Iliada beamed before turning and looking at Flash. He told her he wanted more of the berry.

Nexxa heard her phone again and looked away from the video call. "Let me call you back. My phone is ringing."

"Wait, wait!" Iliada called out. "Tell me about what happened with Quinn."

"I have to go. I love you. You too, Flash." Nexxa closed her laptop and walked back into her suite. She lifted her phone. She saw that Sergei had not called her since earlier that afternoon. "Private" had called again.

Nexxa tapped on the call she missed and it rang. Quinn answered, saying, "I have an idea, Nexxa."

Nexxa heard his voice, his Irish accent, realizing that Quinn was *Private*. "Okay."

"The Rosleague Manor in Connemara. Galway. It's by the sea," Quinn continued. Nexxa remembered going on a day trip to Galway with Kilmer. "I'll take you. You can take his ashes there." Quinn's voice sounded sincere but direct.

Nexxa looked at herself in the mirror. She started to let the feeling of guilt slip in, but she really needed to get rid of the ashes. She wanted to accomplish what she came to Ireland for even if it meant staying mad at Sergei and allowing Quinn to help her.

Hours later, after they arrived and checked in at the Rosleague Manor, Nexxa changed into her Wellies and carried Kilmer's urn in her arms for the last time. She made her way across the landscaped green space adjacent to the manor and continued toward the sea which held a view of the mountains, and with the luck of the Irish, found herself in a quaint forest most likely put in her path by fairies. "This seems fitting. Not the sea," she said to herself. Kneeling among the elegant greens that competed with and complemented each other, Nexxa opened the urn. She reached in and pulled out some ashes, sprinkling them along the base of a tree. Standing, she spun with the urn and let the remaining ashes flow out as it began to mist, and a ribbon of fairies swirled around her. Kilmer was in the Celtic air—and always in her.

Quinn was waiting at a table outside when Nexxa returned from her walk. He stood when she approached him. Her face told him it was done as she said, "I'm going to go to rest."

"Will you have dinner with me?" Quinn asked, so badly wanting to reach for her hand.

"I'm not really hungry." Nexxa turned, watching an older couple emerge from the manor.

"I can have it delivered to your room," Quinn came back with quickly.

Nexxa thought, looking around and seeing the older couple gliding along the green space. They looked so easy. She sighed internally. "Okay, sure."

"I'll have them ring you later for a time to bring it up." Quinn covered his disappointment well.

"Oh," Nexxa held a hand to her chest, explaining, "no, I meant I'll have dinner with you."

"Come on, I'll walk you up." Quinn motioned with his head while he told his heart to be still.

Nexxa thanked Quinn when they reached her room. She pushed on the door to close it and then pulled it to a crack watching Quinn walk down the hall. When he stopped at his door, she quickly shut hers with a piece of her hair stuck in the door jamb. *Fuck*, she waited a few seconds then re-opened her door and let her hair loose. She then slipped on a chemise, pulled back the duvet and allowed herself to sleep.

When Quinn had knocked on her door, Nexxa's stomach flipped. *It's not a date; I have to eat dinner*, she reminded herself. Quinn pulled out the chair for her, and after he sat down, promptly ordered a bottle of wine. This was something that they never had the chance to do a decade ago. But it wasn't a date.

After they finished the first bottle of wine Nexxa excused herself for the ladies' room and Quinn called the waiter over for a second bottle. Nexxa caught a glimpse of the shimmer she had applied to her cheeks in the bathroom mirror. She wondered why she had done that. Was she trying to look pretty for Quinn? No, she shook her head as she washed her hands. The hand soap was a specifically curated scent for the hotel. The label on the pump read: Lavender & Irish Souls. Nexxa laughed before reapplying her lip stain.

When they finished dinner Quinn escorted Nexxa to her room. He stalled by asking, "Does your telly, TV, have cable?"

"Well, I don't know yet." Nexxa looked toward her door that was still closed. She thought about a question to ask him. "Where is Kieran?" she questioned, looking past Quinn.

"He's not here," Quinn replied calmly. Nexxa laughed, shaking her head in acknowledgment. Quinn moved in and gave her a kiss on each cheek. Nexxa felt her shoulders tense up. "Good night," he said, looking into her lovely brown eyes. Nexxa turned to let herself into her room as he walked down the hallway. "There's this place..." Quinn sounded boyish as he turned, walking a few steps back toward her.

"Yeah." Nexxa held her door ajar.

"Tomorrow, I want to show you," Quinn said, smiling big.

"Okay," Nexxa smiled back.

In her room Nexxa mentally chastised herself for agreeing. She knew that she needed to sort things out with Sergei. That's where she belonged. She had accomplished getting closure on a tough time in her life and Sergei had told her to take the time she needed to do what she came to Ireland for even though it pained, angered him. Nexxa changed and got under the duvet. She lifted the remote and turned on the telly. She thought about Quinn. Settling on a British sitcom, she was content. Her eyes barely open, she turned the volume down and turned on her side.

THE FARMERS | 23

The first thing that greeted Nexxa was a donkey that waited for her behind a three-foot-tall century-old stone wall. Quinn spoke to the donkey. Nexxa tilted her head, asking, "Did you just call the donkey Pearl?"

"Yeah, she's a jenny." Quinn smiled as he petted her. "C'mon." Quinn motioned with his head, leading Nexxa down a gravel driveway toward a modest farm. Two men stood at the entrance. One was older than Quinn; he had white hair and reminded Nexxa of Kilmer. The other looked to be his grown son. Quinn wasted no time introducing Nexxa and they each shook her hand. Their hands were rough, but Nexxa appreciated them. The farmers walked them through a building that led them out to the field. Quinn walked her over to Pearl. He hollered over to the younger man to bring him a brush, and when he delivered it, Quinn handed it to Nexxa.

Nexxa brushed Pearl. "How are you, sweet girl?" she said, delicate in her tone. With each gentle stroke that Nexxa bestowed to Pearl, Quinn felt it in his heart and had to remind himself that he was a powerful man... that couldn't be brought down by loving a woman.

When the younger man came to help guide Pearl into the barn for eating and her nighttime routine, Nexxa casually asked Quinn about him. "He's not the old man's son. He's just a farmhand," Quinn explained. Nexxa waved goodbye to Pearl. The donkey bellowed, "Eeyore."

Quinn walked Nexxa through the farm educating her about the various livestock. Nexxa laughed, telling Quinn that she knew "pudding" came from pigs. They reached the main building and the white-haired man spoke to Quinn softly. He was gentle and sad at the same time, patting Quinn on the shoulder before turning and ushering his farmhand to follow him.

As they approached Quinn's Mercedes, Nexxa took off her boots. "I love them, but my feet hurt," she told Quinn as she walked to the boot of the car. "Can I put them in here?"

"Of course." Quinn opened the boot and placed her Wellies in.

Quinn pulled onto the road and headed in the opposite direction from which they came. Nexxa wanted to ask where they were going when suddenly Quinn had to pull over because a farmer was moving some of his sheep whose wool was marked with blue. His car was practically in a ditch, so Quinn came to Nexxa's side to help her exit. "I'm going to have to carry you out. It's just over that hill there," Quin said as he helped her.

"Wait, my boots!" Nexxa whined as she looked over the shoulder of the strong Irishman carrying her.

"You're fine. You have on socks." They laughed.

Over the hill, Nexxa insisted Quinn put her down. Rain came and, without the mercy of the most devout Catholic, pelted them. Quinn grabbed her hand, and they ran the rest of the way. Arriving at their next planned destination, he opened the door, and Nexxa dashed in and found herself in a true to character Irish country pub and inn. She held her chest catching her breath before wiping her cheeks and forehead. The men at the bar turned and had a look. Quinn ushered Nexxa past them to a room with tables and a fireplace.

"I hope you know someone here," Nexxa breathed.

"I have no idea who these are," Quinn said, guiding her into a booth before he winked. Nexxa shivered. Quinn stood holding out a hand. "Come here."

She kept her hands in her lap and looked around before reaching one out. He led her to the fireplace. "I didn't pack well. I mean for my whole trip," Nexxa explained, looking down at her cold feet. She had worn a fitted black knit scoop neck dress, a casual one for her, with the socks and Wellies that Quinn gifted her.

Quinn lifted her chin. Nexxa looked at him. She noticed the lines in his face. They shaped him well. "Take off your socks," Quinn suggested as he removed his boots and socks. Nexxa took hers off and a short older man with the look of Bogdan, the Irish version, came over and took them.

Nexxa grasped Quinn's arm and asked, "What's happening?"

Quinn imagined sliding her hand down so their fingers were interlocked, pulling her into him and kissing her. He knew if he did, he wouldn't be able to stop there. He would pull her dress off her shoulders so it could fall. His hand would be between her legs pulling aside her black lace thong. "You'll see," Quinn assured her. Nexxa turned and faced the fire, holding her hands out to it. She moved a tiny bit closer and squeezed some water from her dress. Quinn noticed, saying, "Why don't you take it off. I'll get you something to wear while it dries."

Nexxa reached up to touch her wet hair. "Okay. Okay," she responded, looking around.

A few minutes later, Nexxa sat across from Quinn, in a man's work shirt, both of them barefoot. She had refused a kind offer for a pair of men's cargo pants that the bar owner kept in the back. Nexxa had the shirt buttoned up halfway with the sleeves rolled up. It hung mid-thigh on her, just enough for Quinn to remember how it felt dancing with her in Hôtel Costes in Paris. Quinn ordered oysters and a bottle of champagne to start.

"So, who was the older man? The one at the farm," Nexxa asked with seriousness.

"That. That was a relative of Kilmer," Quinn answered as he put down his glass of champagne.

Nexxa leaned in closer to Quinn. "Was that his father?"

"No, no," Quinn assured her, shaking his head. He wanted to reach across and hold her hand before he explained further. Instead, he threw back a glass of champagne. "He's," Quinn said as he wiped his chin, "he's an uncle." What Quinn didn't say was that after Paris he had found anyone he could that was related to Kilmer and Klarin. The only living relative was this estranged uncle in Connemara with a farm, and a donkey. The farm was struggling with debt, so Quinn, being who he was, stepped in and offered to provide financial backing. He had a small ownership in the agreement: Pearl the donkey.

The local band started to play and "Irish Bogdan" delivered Nexxa's and Quinn's warmed socks in foil and her dress. "Oh!" Nexxa had a look of surprise as she opened the foil. She swiftly moved out of the booth and hugged the man. Sitting on the edge as she slipped on her socks, Nexxa thought back to when Sergei had given her wool socks when her feet were cold after she told him about her lavender. Looking pleased, Quinn put on his as well, just as his phone vibrated with a call. Nexxa pointed over to the locals dancing, Quinn nodded in acknowledgment, and she shimmied over close to the fire holding her dress. A man in dirty workman's clothes hopped off his barstool and made his way to the back room where the band and the fireplace were. Quinn answered Kieran's call. "It's been done."

"Did you send confirmation?" Quinn asked.

"It's all done. Black Eyes will be happy now," Kieran replied.

"That's good. I'll be back tomorrow." Quinn laughed to himself thinking about the code name Kieran had given one of their clients in the Middle East. They spoke a few more minutes, and Kieran told Quinn what he was craving for dinner. A burger.

Nexxa looked over her shoulder and caught Quinn's eye. She smiled and then looked around for the way to the ladies' room. Quinn watched as Nexxa left the dining area making her way to the back where the bathrooms were. A bloke promptly followed her. Still on his call, Quinn noticed and stood from their table.

The dodgy-looking man shifted around for a minute before he pushed on the bathroom door so hard the lock broke. He shoved Nexxa against the vanity. She had just changed back into her dress and the man tore at it, revealing a breast, while licking the side of her face. Quinn grabbed the man from behind with his right arm under the man's neck and the other behind his head. He kept him in the choke hold and dragged him out of the bathroom through the opening to the kitchen. The staff jumped out of his way. Quinn slowly lowered the man to the ground. "You, fuckin' shit!" Quinn shouted. The owner, Irish Bogdan—named Brian—and another man took the bloke out back.

Quinn moved swiftly back to Nexxa. He put a hand on her arm and caressed her face. She said nothing, lowering her head into his chest. "Let me get you out of here," he told her in a protective voice as he kissed the top of her head. With his hand around her waist he escorted her back to their table. He lifted her purse from the seat and his phone from the table. He motioned to the bartender. The bartender grabbed some keys hanging from the wall behind the bar and headed outside. An old pick-up truck pulled up outside and Quinn escorted Nexxa in. The bartender drove them down the road to Quinn's car.

Back at the Rosleague Manor, Quinn parked and took Nexxa's Wellies out of the boot. He brought them to her car door and knelt, helping her slip them on. "I'm sorry, Nexxa."

Quinn reached for her hand. Nexxa barely nodded.

He walked her to her room, and when Nexxa couldn't find her key in her purse, he gently took her purse and found it for her. After opening her door, he said, "I'll make sure he never hurts anyone again." In his mind he really felt: *I wish I had fucking stopped Kilmer. Fucking killed him myself.*

Nexxa took a few steps into her room before saying, "I feel gross."

"I'll only be down the hall," Quinn told her with an apologetic face.

"No, I mean, I want to shower." Nexxa tugged at her dress as if her skin was crawling with disgust.

"Sure, sure," Quinn said, and turned to leave.

"Quinn. Don't go," Nexxa blurted and immediately felt wrong. Wrong for needing someone.

"I can stay." Quinn reached, touching her arm as he held a stoic face, doing his best to hide his joy.

Nexxa lifted the black chemise that she had placed neatly across the top of her bed and went to the shower. Quinn ordered some bottled water and dessert from room service. A Scotch for himself. When Nexxa was done showering she emerged from the bathroom wearing her chemise holding a towel in front of her. "I... I can't find my robe." Quinn looked down and Nexxa looked around before realizing the robe was on the back of the bathroom door. Only a few seconds were needed to remind him of how she looked months before lying in his bed, cold and wet from the snow in upstate New York. How he had removed her chemise and covered her with a dry towel.

Nexxa came out of the bathroom and tightened the tie to the robe. She sat on the bed and Quinn sat in the chair. When room service came, Quinn opened a bottle of water for Nexxa, poured some into a glass, and took a big sip of his Scotch. "Do you want any wine?" he asked her.

"No, no. Water is fine." *Where is Sergei? He could have been here. With me*, Nexxa thought.

Quinn carried over the bowl of dessert he had ordered and placed it on the nightstand, taking off the wrapping. "Cherries help you sleep. And it can be good to have something sweet when you're in shock." Nexxa squinted her eyes. "Here." Quinn held out a cherry for her. Nexxa took the cherry and ate it. She took the pit from her mouth, and Quinn held his palm out for it. Nexxa smiled. He handed her another cherry and again took the pit from her. Nexxa drank a full glass of water and Quinn refilled it.

A knock came on the door. Nexxa looked past Quinn. He answered the door and took his overnight bag from the porter, handing the man fifty quid. Quinn casually placed his bag by the chair.

"I was going to ask you to stay the—"

Quinn interrupted her, "I thought I should stay with you."

Nexxa took a deep breath. Feeling safe, she removed her robe and got under the duvet. Quinn removed his shoes and took some clothes from his bag and changed in the bathroom. He turned off the lamps, removed the Glock from his bag, and sat back in the chair.

MOSCOW & DUBLIN

"My flight is tonight, back to Moscow."

Quinn felt his pectoral muscles tighten. He gripped the steering wheel hoping to hide his discomfort. "Quinn?" Nexxa turned, placing her hand on his arm.

He looked at her and smiled. "What time?" he asked.

"Eight."

"So time for dinner, right?"

"Uh, I guess. Sure," Nexxa said, feeling his energy matching his voice.

Back in her room in The Westbury, Quinn had walked her up and said he would pick her up at three—a little early, but she agreed—Nexxa finally listened to the voicemail she had from Sergei.

"Nexxa, my love, please call me back." She heard him sigh

before he had ended the call.

Nexxa called him. "Nexxa!" Sergei answered right away.

"It's done. I needed to be done… before I called you back," Nexxa said. She wasn't sure what reaction she would get from Sergei.

"I'm sorry. I know I was wrong to get mad," Sergei apologized before she could say more. Sergei wanted to ask why in the hell she hadn't called him back. He had been furious but told himself he wouldn't bring it up. That he could live with that, but not without her.

Nexxa felt tears swell in her eyes. The events of the past week from Moscow to Dublin rushed to her mind. "I'll be there to pick you up when you land," Sergei spoke since Nexxa hadn't. She stood looking out of the door to the terrace.

"What's wrong, Nexxa?"

If her heart spoke it would have said—I'm worried about your anger. That you'll behave like my ex-husband did.

Instead, she held her forehead. "I don't know. I don't know," she said hastily. She thought about Quinn wanting to take her to dinner. Pearl the donkey, her new shoes. Ugh, the gross guy from the pub in Connemara. The fairies and Kilmer's ashes. None of this was really about her except the shoes.

"Okay," Sergei said before taking a deep breath. He knew she was not telling him everything. He felt justified in what he had done to Kilmer—Nexxa needed to be in the present with him in Moscow.

"I need to pack. Have dinner. And get to the airport," Nexxa said quickly while thinking further: *I want you to say more than you are sorry. That I'm not crazy. That you trust me.*

Believe me over some fucking crazy housekeeper.

"Sure, sure," Sergei said just as Nexxa ended their call. She plopped her phone down on the bed. The call log screen was visible, displaying the number of times Sergei had called. He had only left one voicemail in the last few days. Looking over to her new Wellies, Nexxa decided they would need to stay in Ireland. Maybe she would keep the cozy Sweaty Betty socks.

Quinn knocked on Nexxa's door right at three p.m.

"Hi," Nexxa said as she pulled open her door. Quinn looked so good standing before her, like the mature businessman she had a crush on ten years ago. Nexxa looked down then back to him with her lovely eyes. "I just need my purse." She stepped away and Quinn took a few steps into her room. As he watched her gather up her purse and sweater he thought back to when they had stood inches apart, him caressing her arms, in Mr. Albert's library. With all of his Irish blood he craved that feeling again.

As they exited the hotel Quinn waved to a taxi. He helped Nexxa in and scooted in next to her. "The restaurant doesn't have a big car park," Quinn explained. As the driver pulled away from the hotel, Nexxa closed her eyes and remembered how she had felt being there in Dublin when she was only twenty years old, how it had a busy yet gentle rhythm. They arrived, and once inside were promptly seated by an older East Indian man. The place smelled good, like authentic Italian cuisine.

"This is one of my favorite places to eat," Quinn offered after he ordered a bottle of wine. "I hope you like Italian."

Quinn laughed.

"Yeah, of course." Nexxa looked around. The place was quaint, not that decorated, but the energy was balanced. Nexxa figured he took his ex-wife there.

"I just discovered it. After my divorce." Quinn poured her some wine. "I don't like to eat alone."

"Okay," Nexxa responded, repositioning in her seat.

"Cheers." Quinn held his glass. Nexxa tapped hers against his. She took a sip then withdrew her phone from her purse to check the time.

"I'll get you to the airport on time," Quinn assured her.

"What about my luggage?" Nexxa asked with a bit of panic.

"Kieran will bring it. He's going to drive us," Quinn explained. "To save time." Quinn motioned with his head leaning in toward Nexxa.

Nexxa couldn't imagine herself on the flight back to Moscow. Not that she didn't miss Sergei. She longed for him in ways she couldn't explain. Her responsibility and love for his niece and babushka were there. So, what let her accept Quinn's help? His dinner invitation?

"Nexxa, what do you want?" Quinn leaned back some in his chair.

"Want?" Nexxa looked over at the young waitress as she was cleaning up a table. She caught her eye and the young lady, all of sixteen, came over and asked if she needed anything. Nexxa noticed the family, the family run business, and it reminded her of having to work at a young age to help her own family. She thought of Iliada. Glancing at her phone, she said finally, "I want to have a purpose. I no longer work for my firm in

New York. So..." Nexxa flipped her hand around. "I feel a bit out of place. In life."

Quinn poured her more wine, then poured into his glass. He waved the waiter over and ordered another bottle of wine and another appetizer. He suddenly had an appetite. "I want to show you something."

"I've already seen Pearl, Quinn," Nexxa said playfully.

"I have something to show you. Something I think you'll like." Quinn's voice was just a tad seductive. Nexxa tapped her fingers on her wine glass. She repositioned in her seat, again. "Like what?" she asked boldly.

The waiter approached and served the calamari and another round of bread. Quinn plated Nexxa some calamari while he explained, "I have a business. Private jets. We buy used ones and refurbish them. Customize them, for some clients."

Nexxa thought back to the few times she had flown privately. The first time was with Quinn to Paris, and the second was—fast forward—from Moscow to Rome with baby Natina in tow after a mystery woman had smashed a flower.

"My flight is in a few hours, Quinn." Nexxa shook her head indicating that she couldn't.

Quinn abruptly stood from his seat. "Stay here," he told Nexxa. He moved over to the doorway to the kitchen and told the kitchen staff that he needed his order to go. He returned to the table with a cork and corked the wine. He lifted his phone and called Kieran to tell him that there was a change of plans; that he was to come pick them up now and take them straight to his hangar.

Quinn rode in the front with Kieran on the way to the airport.

Nexxa checked her phone once then counted the rest of the way. They hit some after-work traffic, and Quinn turned, looking back. "I won't let you miss your flight," he said in a very assuring tone.

Dublin and its sky had a red haze by the time they arrived. The emerald greenery beyond the FBO was covered with red ash—sirens and alarms could be heard in the distance. Nexxa emerged from Kieran's Range Rover and spun around seeing the cast, feeling the heat from its energy that warmed the damp Irish air. Quinn came to her and grabbed her hand, running with her into his hangar. Kieran dashed in behind them and pushed the button on the control panel to close the massive hangar door.

"What is this?" Nexxa asked as the three of them stood together watching the door close.

"Fuckin' bollocks," Kieran chuckled.

"Come on." Quinn motioned with his head and took Nexxa's hand. "My office is over here." Quinn turned on the lights and the telly. He told Nexxa to take a seat. Nexxa watched as he stared at Sky News for a few minutes before flipping around. "Bloody hell! There's nothing on the news," Quinn blurted before turning off the TV.

Nexxa looked at the photo of Quinn on the wall, the Businessman of the Year article he had framed. Kieran came into the office and told Quinn he should look at something. Nexxa continued looking around Quinn's office. There was a modern dark grey oak credenza which housed a humidor. Behind Quinn's matching desk was a butler's pantry which had a wine fridge. Nexxa bent looking through the door of the fridge. It reminded her of taking a bottle of Beaujolais from Mr. Albert's wine fridge during her Ice Queen party. She thought about the money that Quinn had left for her. Then she noticed a magazine in the trash. The cover looked familiar. She lifted it from the bin. She was holding the same Forbes Middle East magazine that Diane was in.

Quinn returned to his office looking down at his phone. "So, we just checked outside, the air quality is not good." Quinn moved over to his desk and took the wine out of the bag. "Do you want some wine?" he asked.

"No, I don't want some wine," Nexxa said with a laugh. "Quinn. I'm not flying tonight, am I?"

Quinn rubbed his jaw. "Flights are being delayed. They think it's, maybe, from a fire on Isle of Man." He stepped closer to Nexxa. "I'm sorry."

Nexxa closed her eyes and looked down. She could feel Quinn in front of her. Looking up at him, she said, "I need to see."

Nexxa walked out of his office and Quinn followed. Kieran

unlocked a door in the hangar. Nexxa emerged to a reddish sky and smoky air. She coughed. Quinn looked east. "That way is Isle of Man."

Kieran came out. "Me fuckin' car," he said with his arms out toward his car, shaking them, seeing his Range Rover was covered in reddish ash.

Nexxa darted over to a pigeon pecking at the bit of dirty grass that lined the side of the hangar. She knelt and reached her hand out, and the pigeon stopped before her. Nexxa caressed it, then she stood looking at her palm. *Is this Krasnyy? Is this what Ankica was talking about?*

Nexxa mouthed *okay* and they all went back inside. "So maybe that glass of wine now," she half-laughed, half-cried.

"Yeah, yeah," Quinn responded quickly. They made their way together into his office, and Quinn closed the door. Kieran sat in the seating area outside with a bottle of water watching his phone.

After Nexxa had a glass of wine in hand, she knew by now she was late for her flight, she asked Quinn, "So what were you going to show me?"

Quinn stood against his desk, arms folded. "My assistant is moving back to Germany." He held his hand in a fist up to his mouth as he cleared his throat. Nexxa held eye contact with him. Quinn let out a sensual chortle. "And… I will need to replace her."

Nexxa stood, and her phone buzzed. She glanced at it, seeing an update that her flight to Moscow had been canceled. "So, I guess you will replace her."

Quinn took a drink of his wine. Nexxa did the same. He placed his glass down and stepped over to her. She was looking at his framed article again. "I think you could be the person for the job," Quinn just about whispered while standing behind her.

Nexxa turned to see she was now standing inches from him. "How so?" she asked remembering being with him in his home a decade in time's past.

"For one, you are brave. You're loyal." He wished that weren't true, or at least that she would give up what he felt was beneath her, to be with a Russian. "And you are classy. That can't be learned." Quinn walked back to his desk and grabbed the wine bottle. Nexxa held out her glass, and he refilled hers, then his. "That's a yes?" he smirked.

Nexxa didn't answer. *I'm interested, but really could I work for him? I mean, I want to be with Sergei. Fuck me, I need to work though.*

Kieran knocked on the door before opening it a crack. "The weather's lookin' worse," he told them while expanding the screen he had open on his phone. "Are yous ready to go?" he asked, looking from Quinn to Nexxa.

"Give us a minute," Quinn instructed Kieran.

Nexxa swallowed the wine she had left. Quinn did the same. She reached for his glass, saying, "I'll rinse them in the sink." Quinn watched as she tidied up in the butler's pantry.

"You ready?" Quinn asked as Nexxa finished and walked over to the chair lifting her phone and purse.

"Yeah." She nodded. Quinn waited for her to walk out before he turned off the lights and locked the door behind them.

Nexxa walked over to the Lear Jet in the hangar. She stood admiring it. Quinn called out to her, "I wanted to show you.

The jet." Nexxa looked back to Quinn. Kieran opened the door, and a rush of air blew through the hangar—Nexxa turned toward the jet and inhaled. She smelled something and noticed a long black hair tangled with a strand of blonde blowing, clinging to the railing of the jet's stairs. She stepped closer, then walked up three steps where a lavender fingernail rested. She lifted the nail.

"What is it, Nexxa?" Quinn called out with his brow furrowed, walking back toward the jet.

"Nothing, nothing." Nexxa smiled, stepping down the steps. *Only I smell Crimson in your hangar.*

Kieran drove his Range Rover his expected speed: extra fast. Nexxa placed her hands on the supple black leather on each side of her seat and paused her breathing, closing her eyes. She imagined how the flamed heaters felt on her skin a decade ago when she attended Quinn's summer party when she was supposed to be "Claire." His art, cigars, the unfuckable woman, and his minders. Then they were there, Quinn's home.

Standing in the massive foyer, Nexxa saw the touch of a woman. "It's different, right?" Quinn commented as he wheeled in her suitcase behind her.

Before she spoke Nexxa imagined his wife in his home. She had dark brown hair, independent like herself, but was self-centered and spoiled. "It is, different," Nexxa remarked, looking around at the country-esque décor that struggled to look on trend. Buttercup beige curtains flanked the floor to ceiling windows. Quinn showed Nexxa to his kitchen. He had remodeled again since his divorce. A grey stone waterfall island flourished in the space. Nexxa walked to the end, where the waterfall ended, and the massive glass doors waited. The landscape, the paver patio, the Emerald of Quinn was masked in reddish ash. Nexxa turned seeing Quinn and Kieran and felt regret for deceiving them way back with Kilmer; she pushed it back. "Quinn, I can only be here for one reason," Nexxa offered.

Quinn looked to Kieran, and Kieran took his beer and left the kitchen. "Do you like cinnamon rolls?" Quinn asked, moving over to his refrigerator.

"What?" Nexxa questioned, rubbing her lips together.

"Let's see. Ah." Quinn pulled a can out of the fridge. "They just started selling these here." He looked at the can. "Some brand from Germany, Tippie Rolls." Quinn opened a drawer and pulled out a baking sheet. Nexxa watched as he pulled out parchment paper, tearing off a perfectly sized piece, and opened the can. He struggled to pull the roll apart neatly. Quinn looked over at Nexxa and winked. "This is the hardest part."

Nexxa moved over to the island and placed her purse on one of the dark grey velvet barstools, retrieved a hair tie, and pulled her hair back. Standing next to Quinn, she touched his hand. "I can help." Quinn resisted the urge to lift her onto his massive stone island and push her back with his mouth starting from the outside of her leggings between her thighs up to her breasts whilst she would breathe heavily until his mouth reached hers. Mr. Kane showed her how to turn on his oven and the rolls went in.

Quinn opened a bottle of wine, because Nexxa agreed that

red wine went with everything. It was a new wine he had selected to serve in his private club, an Italian wine from the region of Puglia. He poured and swirled the wine around. He handed her the glass. Nexxa took a sip and handed him the glass, so Quinn threw back the remainder. *Deutsche* cinnamon permeated the kitchen, and Quinn refilled Nexxa's glass then his.

Kieran made his way back. "I smell cake," he said, leaning into the doorway. "Could yous spare a bite?" he asked.

Nexxa laughed. "Come here," she said, motioning with her head. Quinn pulled the rolls from the oven while Kieran took another beer from the fridge. The three of them clanked glasses, Kieran his beer. The cinnamon rolls were eaten with little grace. Nexxa first with a drip on her chin, Quinn next with a drip on his dress shirt, and finally Kieran with a drip on his beer bottle while trying to be cheeky.

Kieran abruptly left the kitchen, and music came from the "Art Room." Quinn squinted his eyes. Nexxa shook her head laughing. She hopped off her barstool and found Kieran dancing to "Waterfall" by Vok, the Neelix remix. Kieran looked up and motioned with his hand for her to join him. *No*, she mouthed shaking her head thinking he was surprisingly good. Looking over her shoulder she saw that Quinn was standing in the doorway to the kitchen, his face the same observing her as he had ten years ago.

The grandiose staircase seemed less intimidating, and as Nexxa climbed to the top she glanced over at the loo thinking back to when one of Quinn's minders had brought her upstairs.

How she applied the new lipstick that Kilmer had bought her in the bathroom. But now, she was going to a guest room and not trying to work the "subject."

If felt good that Quinn brought her upstairs himself. He turned on the lamps, opened the ensuite, inspecting it. Nexxa heard her phone ring. It buzzed again with a text message as Quinn was telling her where she could charge her phone. "Okay, thank you." Nexxa placed her purse on the dresser. She took her phone out and said, "I have to call—"

"Yeah, I'll close the door," Quinn spoke quickly. He didn't want to hear more.

Nexxa figured Sergei knew her flight was canceled since he had called her. Normally she would prepare herself, sort out her thoughts, but she swiped on the last call.

"Are you at the airport? I was going to call my concierge service and reserve you another night at the hotel and get them to reschedule your flight." Sergei seemed, surprisingly, in a good mood.

"No. No, I'm not," Nexxa answered while standing and looking out of the window. "Sergei, I am at Quinn's home. The man you met at my friend's house." Nexxa inhaled, waiting for what was surely a lifetime for his response.

"What?" Sergei lowered the phone from his ear and made a fist with his other hand, breathing through his nostrils.

"I wanted to talk to you in per—"

"I need to call you back." Sergei hung up. Nexxa let her forehead fall against the window and teared up. If he would just let her tell him one more thing, that she sensed someone was after her.

That someone was in Dublin.

In the bathroom with the door closed, she turned on the water. Sitting on the floor against the vanity, she cried thinking about the first date they had had at the Sursock Palace in Beirut. How nervous she had been when she saw Sergei. Him putting her lace thong in his jeans' pocket and giving her money for new clothes when they arrived safely in Turkey. Then she heard a knock on her bedroom door. "Nexxa?" Quinn called lightly before cracking the door.

"Yeah, um, just a minute," Nexxa hollered from the bathroom. She blew her nose as quietly as she could and washed her hands before splashing some water on her cheeks. She dabbed her face with a hand towel and opened the bathroom door.

Quinn had let himself in the room, and he could see she had been crying. He grabbed her with his overpowering but sexy arms, lifting her against the wall. His mouth was upon her neck kissing her and breathing with all of his life. Quinn moved his mouth to hers; Nexxa resisted, lowering her face.

OSIAN'S DRAGON | 26

Quinn tossed and turned in his king size bed. He knew he wouldn't be able to tame the Osian in himself. His father, Mr. Osian Kane, had met with unfortunate Emerald Isle circumstances, leading to a disenchanted life. From 1989 to 2013, his son had been fulfilling what his father could not have in his own lifetime. Quinn didn't have remorse for almost kissing Nexxa. Everything he did was in the name of his Irish lifeblood, which lived on the edge of battle.

   Nexxa wasn't able to sleep. She kept waking and thinking about Quinn trying to kiss her. She touched her head, and it felt like her guilt was going to open up her brain and jump out. She turned on the lamp and got out of bed, going over to the phone that was charging on the desk in the room. Sergei had still not called her back.

   Nexxa showered and dressed. She packed up the few things

she used in the bathroom and brought her suitcase downstairs. Kieran was in the kitchen. "You want a cuppa?" he hollered out to her as she idled outside the doorway.

"Yeah," Nexxa answered, and Kieran motioned for her to come in. Nexxa left her suitcase and purse in the hallway, and she took a seat at the grey stone island. Kieran placed a cup of tea in front of her. "Thank you," she said with a smile that hid her remorse.

Quinn approached the doorway and stopped, seeing her suitcase in the hallway. He looked over and their eyes met. Quinn closed his eyes briefly before he made his way into the kitchen and stood across the island from Nexxa. "Do you want me to get you a flight?" Nexxa looked over at Kieran, as he smirked, shaking his head. She wondered if the guilt that had kept her up was hungover now and needed a nap. Kieran left the room, patting her on the shoulder.

Nexxa looked over to her suitcase, her purse. She still hadn't heard from Sergei. "You're dressed for work, right?" Nexxa asked Quinn.

"I need to meet with a client." Quinn walked over to his Miele machine and pushed a button.

"Right," Nexxa responded, taking a sip of her tea. "So, you or Kieran can just drop me at the airport. I'll get a flight when I'm there."

Quinn turned around saying, "Just drop you?"

"Yeah," Nexxa responded, waving a hand in the air.

"Is that really what you want?"

"I don't—"

"Nexxa." Quinn leaned with his hands on the counter. "In no

way am I just dropping you off at the airport." He continued looking at her like if she said yes he would fuck her on his cold grey island. "I wanted you to meet with my client. See what you think of the business. Then meet with my assistant. That's leaving."

Nexxa touched her forehead. Last night flashed in her mind, Quinn pressing her against the wall. The caffeine was waking up her remorse. "I don't know," she barely let out.

Quinn drove the black Mercedes SUV that he used whenever he thought he might drive a client around. Nexxa had insisted that Quinn take her back to stay in his hotel after meeting with his client. She mostly looked out of the passenger window on the way to the private FBO, but she wanted to bring up him almost kissing her last night. Logically, how could she blame him? How could she chastise him for something that they had done only months ago in New York at Mr. Albert's home. Was it wrong of him to desire her? As they pulled up to the gate and Quinn was typing in his security code, Nexxa twisted her hair into a French twist and dabbed on her subdued red lip.

Quinn drove in and parked. He turned to Nexxa. "My client, is a woman."

"Okay," Nexxa said, closing the visor mirror.

"So—"

"One thing," Nexxa began, turning to Quinn. "I had a successful career in finance. I didn't get that far not knowing how to dress for meeting with a client," Nexxa said in a matter-of-fact tone.

"I was only going to say that you look lovely," Quinn told

her, looking remorseful.

"Oh." Nexxa looked down, nodding.

"That you look professional." Quinn reached, touching her face.

Inside the hangar in his office, Quinn rummaged through his desk looking for the notes on his client. He grumbled a bit, covering up his frustration by commenting on how presentable Nexxa looked again. He walked them out of his office, and they climbed the jet and each took seats. Nexxa took a deep breath. Quinn still hadn't told her any pertinent details about his client. She assumed she and anyone accompanying her would be intimidating and that they would speak a foreign language. A brief sheet would have been nice, but perhaps that would be something she would put together for future clients since it seemed his current assistant wasn't adept—*if* she accepted a job offer from him.

DIANE'S DRAGON

Diane's eyes began to flutter. She could smell... Nexxa. A sudden thrill. Quinn's driver looked in the rearview mirror; he wished he hadn't. Diane held her head straight with her coffin-shaped nails digging into the sides of her dark hair. When that didn't stop her excitement, she drew a fingernail down the back of her neck until a mark of blood was there—just a spot, just a bit—dripped and dried.

Quinn's driver escorted Diane into the hangar. She boarded the jet and Quinn stood inadvertently blocking Nexxa and holding his hand out to welcome her. "I'm glad you could make it," Quinn told her with a professional handshake. Diane leaned around him; she saw something she had been missing.

"Diane?" Nexxa asked as she stood moving next to Quinn.

"Nexxa!" Diane squealed. "I have not seen you in so long. Since Beirut." Diane lied. But was kind of telling the truth because she had not seen "business Nexxa" since Lebanon. Quinn had a look that said *what the bloody hell* as he watched them converse.

Several thoughts went through Nexxa's mind: her abduction in Beirut, the botched private placement with Faroud, leaving Kuretz Investments, all of her disenchantments. Diane giggled, extending her hand to Nexxa. Quinn turned his head sneezing; Diane pulled her hand back, and instead she and Nexxa smiled at each other. Nexxa noticed how Quinn's eyes were watering.

"Excuse me," she apologized, stepping back to her purse. She found a few tissues and handed them to Quinn.

"It must be the red smoke," Quinn suggested, dabbing his nose and then his eyes.

"Come on." Nexxa motioned for them all to leave the plane. As they climbed down the steps, Diane swooped her hair to the side. Nexxa's head tilted. She noticed a scratch with the smallest amount of blood on Diane's neck.

The three of them settled in Quinn's office with Nexxa and Diane sitting opposite of Quinn. "So, yous know each other," Quinn said, leaning back in his chair with his arms behind his head.

"Yes," Nexxa answered stoically, looking at Quinn. He made eye contact with Nexxa before looking at Diane then back to Nexxa as if he was trying to figure out whether this was going to be bad.

"Nexxa vetted my company, China Black Road, for her client in Beirut," Diane offered, turning to Nexxa with a smile and nodding.

Quinn raised his eyebrows. "Really?" he asked as he sat

straight.

"Yes," Nexxa offered, looking directly at Quinn.

Diane practically hopped out of her chair as she twisted toward Nexxa holding out her nails. "I have a new polish. *Lavender Gliss*," she giggled, wiggling her fingers. Nexxa turned, Diane extended her hand more, and Quinn's assistant abruptly entered the office apologizing in her German accent for her tardiness. Diane pulled her hand back. Quinn stood, Nexxa stood, and he introduced her to his assistant. She towered over Nexxa but had a jolly laugh and insisted on taking her out into the hangar.

"So this is where I usually meet with clients," Tolya explained as they approached the sitting area in the back of the hangar. Nexxa looked at the furniture and nodded. "Have you been on a Lear Jet? Do you speak any other languages?" Tolya asked.

"Yes, yes, some," Nexxa answered her.

"Well," Tolya's voice became high-pitched as she removed a folder from her bag. "Here is a list of my ideas." She handed Nexxa the folder.

"Okay, thank you." Nexxa peeked in the folder. The notes looked chaotic. In English though. "By the way, I like your hair."

"Ooooh, thank you!" Tolya's theatrics started. "I did this because I've been called "sir" so many times." She laughed, caressing a few of the purple streaks in her gray hair. "Do you want a cocktail?" Nexxa thought for a moment. She heard Quinn and Diane talking as they were emerging from his office. Tolya yelled, "I thought we'd have a cocktail to celebrate," to Quinn. Nexxa and Diane locked eyes as she crossed the hangar coming closer. Tolya heavily made her way back to Quinn's office to get some champagne while continuing to shout to Quinn, "Oh this is so great! Nexxa's going to be so good for you!"

Standing alone, Nexxa calmed her breathing and silently called for protection. Faster than Kieran drove, Diane was standing before her. Crimson slithered in the air, with Nexxa catching the faintest hint, and her lavender pulsed.

CADAVER | 28

UPSTATE NEW YORK

The rain was coming, according to the weather radio in Mr. Albert's kitchen. Iliada went upstairs and looked in the back of her closet. She found an old rain jacket from when she was in high school which still fit and was black. In the city she carried an umbrella. She had always hated it. This rain jacket had a pocket that Flash could sit in too. Iliada came downstairs and stood at the door in the kitchen that led to outside. Mr. Albert emerged from wherever he had been and stood facing out of the floor to ceiling windows. Krasnyy swirled around in from the east, and rain fell coming from the west, converging on Mr. Albert's upstate New York estate.

Flash hopped up onto the kitchen island. "You want to go outside?" Iliada asked him.

"*Da.*" His voice was furry as he walked to the opposite side of the island.

"Maybe, it's not good today," Mr. Albert spoke, looking outside, grasping his chin.

Iliada was pulling on her rain boots. Those she liked, since she had needed them when walking to work in Manhattan. "What's wrong? It's just raining a little." Iliada looked up from her boots to see that the rain was coming down harder than before. "I'm still going. I need my herbs for dinner," she insisted.

Flash fluttered his wings. "Take me."

Iliada scooped him up and he jumped nicely into her pocket.

Mr. Albert withdrew his A. Lange & Söhne pocket watch and studied it for a moment, then looked back outside. His assistant came to him and held out a tablet with *The Irish Times* displaying the cover story about unconfirmed fires from the Isle of Man. He looked down at the article. "Unconfirmed." He laughed as he waved off his assistant. Looking outside, he watched Iliada inspecting her basil and parsley plants, "Determined," he said under his breath. Mr. Albert went to a hall closet and dressed in a parka and boots. Walking a landscaped pathway lined with red Hibiscus flowers, he continued until he was before his purposely erected Buddha statue. Red ash faintly covered parts of him. Mr. Albert placed his hand on the statue, removing his hood and bowing his head. The rain paused—he received his message: Crimson had dispersed her negative energy, the red ash. He pulled on his hood and dusted his hands shedding the Krasnyy-colored dust.

Flash slid down her jacket and hopped onto the floor. He fluttered his wings and said, "I'm feeling the cold." Iliada hung up her jacket on a hook by the kitchen door as Flash toddled off to the double-sided fire that was between the sitting room and the dining room. Iliada took off her boots and followed Flash. After she arranged a blanket that was on an ottoman, he hopped up. Back in the kitchen, which was open to the living and dining areas, Iliada started to prep dinner. She had been watching episodes of the *Barefoot Contessa*, Ina Garten, on TV. But because she felt conflicted over who "Jeffery" was, she switched to watching the *Naked Chef*, Jamie Oliver, and her crush on Prince William subsided. With some select choices of wine she felt confident to cook one of his recipes. Tonight was Pasta alla Ricotta.

Mr. Albert entered the kitchen when Iliada was stirring her sauce while watching *Interview with the Vampire*. "It smells good," he commented on his way out to the corridor. He pulled off his parka and noticed some red ash that had clung to the cuff of his right sleeve, so he brought the parka upstairs to his private study and hung it on his Honorific black walnut valet stand. Mr. Albert unlocked a drawer in his desk. It had been eighty-eight years since the book, *Ponce a Time*, had been consulted.

Where do I begin? Mr. Albert turned and revealed page one, black with splotchy brown trees and white marks dotted all around. Page two was covered with illuminated white tree branches. *Leave it to the end,* came to his mind. Turning to page three thousand, a silhouette of a woman's face—she had a tear in the middle pulling her apart.

There was a footnote, *Cadaver/Anima*.

A dead body and a soul. Where is the soul going? What should I understand? Mr. Albert wondered as he closed the book with his right hand weakening, as he placed it back in the suede-lined drawer.

Iliada served dinner in a large stone bowl using the parsley she had snipped from her mini herb garden to garnish the top. Sitting across from Mr. Albert, she watched for his reaction to her cooking. He slurped. They laughed. Flash fluttered over and tossed some more parsley on the serving bowl. Iliada poured some wine from the Umbria region in Italy, first in Mr. Albert's glass then hers. Iliada watched as he would take a bite, look out through the dining room windows, take a bite, look out through the dining room windows, and then take a bigger than normal gulp of wine before looking outside again. When he looked at her, she smiled, he smiled, but she felt an elephant in the room.

Since it was May and had rained again, Iliada turned on the electric fireplace in her bedroom. She changed into her "spring pajamas," which meant a silk camisole and shorts. She had a matching pillow made for Flash, and they nestled into bed. She selected Netflix and restarted *Interview with the Vampire*. Eating tortilla chips and apple slices, she would tear tiny bits of apple for Flash. She came to the part in the movie where Lestat turns the girl into a vampire. Iliada turned looking toward the fireplace. It extinguished.

"Oh," she gasped, holding a hand over her mouth as she sat up in bed.

Flash hopped off of his silk pillow and down onto the floor before making his way over to the fireplace. Looking at his reflection in the glass fireplace he said, "*Anima.*" Iliada stood up and pulled on her caramel-colored cashmere sweater and walked over to the fireplace. She leaned from one side to the other looking in the glass. The fire flamed, and she jumped back. Flash crawled up her leg and Iliada held him with her arm bent against her abdomen as she slipped on her furry wedge slippers, walking down the hall with questions in her mind.

"Mr. Albert." Frustration mixed with worry was in her voice as she knocked on his bedroom door. "Mr. Albert! Mr. Albert!" Iliada called out, knocking more.

When he failed to answer his door, she huffed and looked down at Flash. He motioned with his head, so Iliada held him closer to the door, and he looked through the lock opening. "He's not in there," Flash said as he tried to mimic shrugging his shoulders.

Iliada huffed again and turned, looking further down the corridor toward Mr. Albert's private study. She tilted her head when she saw a red light emitting from his study. Walking with a temper, Iliada made her way down the hall. She pulled on the door lever, feeling that it was locked. Flash fluttered and landed on it. "You shouldn't go in there," he warned as his eyes became big and he shook.

"Flash, no—no, I feel like something is wrong." Iliada pressed her hands on the door. She knew it was too dense to hear through. She took a deep breath, and Flash closed his eyes.

Mr. Albert stood in the middle of his study watching the lights in the wall sconces, the lamp on his desk glowing red. He had left his bedroom for his midnight snack, a bowl of Cinnamon

Toast Crunch, when he noticed his study door was ajar. With his arms he scooped up the air, crossing his face and over his head holding, trying to contain the nefarious energy—he turned, hearing Iliada pulling on the door lever—Crimson had made its way across the Atlantic.

Sergei was intrigued now. Not by Nexxa, but by an Irishman—Quinn. He had Hooli find out everything he could about him. Whatever an Irishman could hide. Money, weapons, and naughty skeletons.

Hooli finished his report on Quinn Osian Kane and boarded a flight to Dublin. The last few months he had become closer to Sergei, like a work brother/cousin since Sergei's head of security, Bogdan, had vanished and he felt the need to do some in-person recon. Hoolihane happened to like pudding. Black to be specific.

Kieran liked the waitresses, sometimes the kitchen staff, at Quinn's private club in Dublin. So when he exited the club around midnight with a mousy but willing looking Irish girl, all of twenty-five, Hoolihane started his rental car and followed them to Kieran's row house on the Northside of Dublin. Hooli looked at his phone thirty-five minutes later, just long enough for Kieran to impress her with some stale wine and a clever joke. A shag and she was out smiling, hoping he would call her as he helped her into a taxi. Hooli dipped his hand into his bag of crisps and took a gulp of Club Rock Shandy. Patiently he waited for Kieran, who most likely had a sandwich, before he pulled his front door closed, locking it, and speeding away in his Range Rover. Hooli tuned the radio in the car, finding it a welcoming companion. Pleasy 101 Night Tunes by DJ Nilz played in sync with Hooli shifting for the first time with his left hand.

Quinn had always been an ethical businessman. His connections from his days at Merchiston in Edinburgh, a boys' boarding school, and his inherited charisma afforded him opportunities that didn't mesh with his UVF affiliation. Kieran was Quinn's proxy when it came to his Loyalist activities. And, Kieran was motivated by keeping intact the ceasefire between the Loyalists and the INLA: Irish National Liberation Army. Funding the cause *or* peace took more money than the family oyster business Quinn took over right after school could provide.

Kieran was the roughneck in the pair and this year was the first time that he had convinced Quinn to stray from his ethics. He had devised a plan to put together groups of dormant UVF members and utilized them for training militia groups from Beirut to Africa. This amounted to some cash flow… but the real money was made in assassination for hire. One particular client from the Middle East wanted her husband executed. It was reported in the media as a heart attack. Nothing clever, more a cliché that was believable being that pics of an escort leaving his hotel room in London were leaked to the press from the day of his demise.

Hooli felt Kieran's operations were amusing. Kieran employed a high-school-aged computer tech, his nephew, and while he was good, he was sloppy at times. It had been too easy for Hooli to investigate Kieran. Quinn was a little bit of work. It wasn't exactly like he was on LinkedIn. He was layered well behind legitimate businesses and credentials. Hooli's intentions lay more in the respect of getting eyes on Quinn, on Nexxa.

The next morning, Hooli woke to the sound of a female *Garda* banging on his window. "You can't park here," she told him. He sat up, startled, and grabbed the gear shift. She banged again. He lowered the window. "You need to move your car," she instructed. Hooli nodded. He started the engine. The car stalled, and she turned looking over her shoulder. He nodded at her through the windshield and after two more tries, successfully started the car. He saluted her. She rolled her eyes. Hooli crept along, and she motioned with her hand. He smiled.

In his rearview mirror he saw Kieran exit the warehouse and hop into his Range Rover. Hooli did a U-turn and was quickly in fifth gear two cars behind him. He trailed Kieran to Jobstown in Tallaght—a real dodgy area, he soon discovered. After getting stuck at a red light Hooli finally found parking along the street. Approaching the run-down diner he watched a hefty bloke exit his red BMW and enter through the back door.

Hooli wasn't exactly eyed as he entered the place as much as he was noticed. He ordered the regular breakfast with black pudding. When the young waitress with stressed bleached hair and a tattoo of a Gaelic cross on each forearm served his plate he said, "Thanks, love," and she replied, "Feck off." Kieran snickered and took a bite of his white pudding. Hooli heard. The young waitress complained to the fat bastard behind the counter who happened to be her "boyfriend." He shouted expletives to Hooli, which he couldn't quite make out. When Hooli didn't respond, the fat bastard moved from behind the counter with a knife in his hand. Kieran turned in his barstool to face Hooli's direction.

Hooli pointed out to the quaint carpark saying, "Is that your BMW parked next to the Range Rover?" Before he had entered the diner, he had approached a few teens that were hanging on the street. He gave them each fifty quid and told them there would be more. They were instructed to come around in fifteen minutes and start loitering in the carpark, specifically next to the red BMW with the license plate PHAT BOI. "Phat Boi" ran outside with knife in hand shouting and Hooli ate his last piece of black pudding, wiped his mouth, and exited the diner.

Kieran was on his tail catching the door as it swung closed. He called out to Hooli as he walked toward his car, "Jobstown isn't for tourists." Hooli turned and saluted him.

Sergei turned on the shower and lowered his head. "And I love you, and I love you," he whispered, reminiscing about Nexxa. "Fuck!" He smashed his fist against the tile. He laughed and cried, slumping down on his knees looking up with the shower falling on his unshaven face.

Dried off and in tracksuit pants, Sergei packed a suitcase. He needed to be in Croatia to meet with the head of the commercial general contractor for his ongoing project to build a Croat version of Russia's Tower West, but he was able to push their meeting back a few days. So to Dublin it was. Sergei chose a hotel different from the one he had originally booked for Nexxa. There was no way he was staying in Quinn's hotel. After he checked into The Marker Hotel, he headed to the bar. While drinking a beer, he got a call from Hooli. "Yeah," Sergei answered the call.

"I'm in Galway," Hooli said through the noise of a pub.

"What? You're where?"

Hooli took his call off of speaker and continued, "I'm in Galway."

"Galway?" Sergei questioned with just a tad of irritation in his voice.

"I'm in a pub. Yeah, it's loud."

"Why the fuck are you there?" Sergei scolded.

Hooli snickered. "Well, you see. They took a road trip there. Went here."

Sergei lowered his head, grasping his forehead. *What the fuck is she doing?*

"But they are back now," Hooli offered in a tone that said *this is good news.*

"Back in Dublin? You have confirmation?" Sergei quizzed Hooli while looking around the rooftop bar. The view of Dublin was nice but nothing spectacular, he determined. He wondered what in the hell Nexxa would have gone to Galway for, with Quinn. When he pressed his mind harder, he grimaced and slammed his fist down on the table. A few patrons looked his way, and he smiled at them saying, "My team lost."

Morning came soon since Sergei woke every few hours, eventually deciding to just get up. He opened the file on his phone that had the report on Quinn. After he received his coffee from room service, he drank some and then took his phone to the bathroom. One section he wanted to look at again, the section on the UVF. The chain of events was clear now. Kilmer, Nexxa, and then Quinn.

Nexxa could have recently been recruited by Quinn. She obviously was daring, being that Sergei had met her in Beirut. What Americans, let alone women, travel there? Maybe she had worked both sides, the IRA and the UVF in the past like a double agent. Sergei thought back to last December when he, it killed him to remember, first came across Quinn. "Nexxa's friend." The one that had found the dragon eggs at Mr. Albert's home. It didn't make sense how Nexxa and Quinn reconnected at that time. Of course Hooli had found credit card charges for Quinn at Mr. Albert's cigar lounge in New York City. So that had to be the logical connection, or unfortunate reconnection, between Nexxa and Quinn.

What Sergei really needed was to establish motive. Was Quinn still connected with the UVF and using Nexxa like Kilmer had a decade ago? Or was it something entirely different? Something that was related to Nexxa disappearing with Quinn during her Ice Queen party, to when Sergei found her in a robe with Quinn's initials on it having tea in the kitchen. Either way, Sergei was prepared. His emotions were precisely intact. He wouldn't only snap Quinn's neck—he would cut off his head and take it back to Mother Russia.

Quinn received a call in the car from the head of security for The Westbury on his way in to meet Nexxa for a lunch that she barely agreed to. "I've got to go check on something, give me fifteen minutes," Quinn explained.

"I'll be fine," Nexxa assured him, ending the call quickly.

Nexxa stood on her terrace for a moment closing her eyes, inhaling she smelled Dublin's city aroma. It had an undertone of something else: Sergei. Suddenly Nexxa smelled Sergei. She grasped the railing, steadying her body as her legs went numb and she grasped her stomach feeling butterflies.

Downstairs, she shrugged off Quinn's concerned eyes, he saw the worry on her face, as he was waiting for her with the hostess of the restaurant. He told her to take care of Nexxa and that he would join her as soon as he could. Nexxa ordered smoked salmon—two orders—and some oysters. White wine. After the wine was served, Nexxa downed a glass. She then took out her phone and called Sergei.

"Nexxa," Sergei answered on the first ring. He sounded happy and relieved at the same time.

"You're here," Nexxa said as if telling him rather than asking him, relieved her wolfness was working but worried he wouldn't listen to her.

Sergei made a perplexed face, and his silence told her that he was. "Yes, I'm in Dublin. Where are *you*?"

Nexxa looked toward the entrance of the restaurant to see if Quinn was around yet. "I'm in a restaurant in The Westbury hotel," she replied.

"Right. His hotel."

"Sergei, look, I wanted to tell you. But you wouldn't—"

"Nexxa, I need to be in Croatia."

"Okay so—"

"I'm here. I want to see you." Sergei's voice sounded more direct.

Nexxa shook her head yes. She held her chest wanting so badly to explain about Crimson. "So… when?" she asked, the words just barely coming out.

Sergei lowered the phone from his ear seeing that he had a call coming in from The Minister of Physical Planning, Construction and State Assets, Ivan Jubić. He knew he had to take the call. "I'll call you back, Nexxa."

Sergei had only ended the call when Nexxa felt her eyes fill with tears. She stood from her seat and began her way out of the restaurant toward the lobby bathroom while dabbing the corners of her eyes. Quinn was walking off of the elevator when he saw her. With a sprint, he crossed the lobby, approaching her. When he grasped her arm, Nexxa turned. "Are you okay? What happened," he spoke tenderly to her.

Nexxa laughed, wiping her tears. "Let's just," she shook her head, "go back to the—"

"Shh, it's okay. It's okay," Quinn assured her, grasping her hand and walking her back to their table.

"I'm embarrassed," Nexxa announced, lifting her wine glass after the waiter refilled it. Quinn noticed her lips, her tone. He knew it was Sergei. Part of him was happy that she was sad. But he hadn't won yet. When Nexxa didn't cry over Sergei, *then* he had won.

Sergei finished his call with Ivan Jubić. He huffed. His mind hurt and his heart was fractured. When he had left Moscow, he hadn't told his babushka anything about him and Nexxa. He figured that she knew he had lost his temper. He had Hooli's report, he was in Dublin, and Nexxa had called him. Sitting on the end of his bed he realized that she had known he was in Ireland. *That's right. She can smell.* Sergei swiped on his last call with Nexxa. He tapped on his phone to end the call and put it in his pocket before heading down to the lobby.

In a taxi he gave the driver his destination: The Westbury hotel.

Sergei exited the taxi and moved fiercely through the hotel with his James Bond face which had always served him well since he didn't have "Russian" stamped on his forehead. He was there—in the restaurant—just as Quinn lifted his glass of pinot grigio to take a sip, looking at Nexxa wishing she would slip off her lace panties for him. It was then Sergei approached their table and said, "Nexxa, come with me."

In one motion Quinn stood and withdrew his Glock from the back of his pants. Nexxa had detected Sergei's scent becoming stronger but had tried to suppress smelling him by keeping pieces of smoked salmon on her plate. She pushed her chair back from the table and mentally told herself to stand. "Okay," Nexxa spoke with her heart wavering as her eyes moved from Quinn's blue eyes to her Russian's. Sergei extended his arm —Nexxa grasped his hand—Quinn moved in on Sergei.

Swiftly, with patrons gawking, Sergei led Nexxa away with Quinn following right on their heels.

The lives of Nexxa, Sergei, and Quinn converged on the steps of The Westbury. The Russian briefly let go of Nexxa's hand and turned with Quinn upon them. "She's with me!" Sergei asserted, lifting his chin and stepping into Quinn. The Irishman looked to Nexxa—her eyes told him what he knew and didn't need to be told—and he tucked his gun away in his back.

Nexxa's feet burned from running down the hotel steps and onto the streets of Dublin. "Sergei! Sergei! What, what are we doing?"

Sergei faced Nexxa, grasping her arms. "Come back to Moscow. Now!" he pleaded.

"I can't! Not yet," Nexxa explained holding her arms out, shaking her hands.

Sergei lowered his head, rubbing a hand over. This was not his plan. Not the *calm* plan that Hooli had suggested. He should have been in Ireland at least a few days to know what he was up against, but she called because she smelled him. Sergei would carry her on his back all the way across Europe to Russia if needs be—if she would allow him. A taxi came to a stop and Sergei motioned to the driver before opening the door. "Get in," he said sternly to Nexxa. She remained still, closing her eyes. "Please," he begged, reaching for her hand and her face. Nexxa looked over her shoulder as she moved into the taxi. She saw Quinn with his arms folded, standing next to a doorman. Watching.

Nexxa took two steps into Sergei's hotel room, barely leaving room for him to close the door. She grasped her chest and started to slump against the wall. Sergei turned back and caught her. She could feel his skin through his long sleeve gray t-shirt and jeans. That was how much she craved his touch—more than she had ever told him. Sergei swooped her up and carried her to his bed. He moved swiftly over to the desk and opened a bottle of still water, pouring some before he carried it to her. "Thank you," Nexxa spoke softly as she sat on the end of his mostly made bed. She held back the feeling that was intoxicating her mind, telling her to cry.

"He offered me a job in his aviation business," she blurted out.

"Why do you need to work? I can take care of you. I told you that. I told you that!"

"Why do I need to work? Really, Sergei?"

"I know. I know. I get that you, that you've worked before."

"Worked before? Like no one has ever taken care of me. I have to take care of my—"

Sergei grabbed her face and kissed her. Tears fell from her eyes into their kiss. "I don't want to make you cry," he whispered, wiping her face.

"I just, I can't depend on you."

"Why?" Sergei took a deep breath before continuing, "Why can't you?"

Nexxa reached, grasping her right shoulder. "Because I don't know anything else. I was going to ask to work remotely and to have my own clients eventually that I might meet with on my own."

Sergei heard her words. It all felt like one continuous excuse to not forgive him. Sergei sat down beside his love with his hands clasped together between his legs.

"He just offered me a job. The day of the red smoke, when I couldn't fly home."

He looked down. "He didn't just offer you a job." Sergei started. "You knew him in the past with Kilmer." Sergei looked up and turned, facing her. "He shows up at your friend's house in New York. What is this? Huh, what are you not telling me?"

Nexxa took a deep breath and exhaled. "Yeah, I was—I was caught off guard in New York. I did, I met him with Kilmer. I know you have Hooli so I'm sure you've—he's—pieced it all together by now. He did kiss me in New York. I was stupid; I let him."

Sergei hopped up and shouted, "You were stupid? He didn't offer you a job! He wants to fuck you!"

Nexxa reached her hands up, touching her temples. Shaking her head she said, "No, no, it's not like that."

Sergei grasped her hands and pulled her up. "Look at me!" Nexxa looked in his eyes. He knew he would be able to tell if she had been with him. "Did you fuck him?"

"What? No! No!" Nexxa pulled her hands away from his grasp. "I want—I want to be with you!"

"Then why are you here?" Sergei screamed.

"Because you told me to go. Go, get rid of that man's ashes! That 'this is *my* house!'" Nexxa answered with haste in her voice, raising a hand, mimicking the anger he had had in Moscow.

Sergei lowered his head, rubbing his hand over it. Looking

up, he said, "I know. I know. I'm so, so sorry for hurting you."

"Even if I didn't take the job there is something else I have to take care of. I have to take care of it here. Because it's here, in Dublin!"

Shaking his head, Sergei asked, "What is it?"

"It's hard to explain." Nexxa held her forehead.

"Why, why can't you explain?" Sergei asked with a calm voice while grasping his chin.

Nexxa bit her bottom lip. "Remember how I explained that I can smell things, people?"

Sergei nodded.

"So… someone is here that I think was also in Moscow. A woman that I met in Beirut."

"A colleague?" Sergei thought back to information he had discovered last fall. Details about a person of interest that had been in Beirut when Nexxa was there.

"No, well, a client. Who actually would be the first client I would work with, with Quinn," Nexxa explained, shifting her interlocked fingers.

Sergei scoffed, walking across the room. Just hearing her say his name disgusted him. Nexxa moved over to Sergei as he stood facing the wall leaning with one arm. Reaching her hand toward his back, she felt his warmth. She wanted him. She wanted something of her own too, though. Nexxa placed her hand on his back and slowly moved her hand up to his shoulder caressing him. Sergei spun around and lifted his love, moving her over to his bed. His mouth was on hers, then his lips were down her neck as he had a hand between her legs.

Sergei leaned up and unzipped his jeans. Nexxa pulled off

her top. Sergei tugged at her leggings, and Nexxa helped him while they kissed. "What the fuck?" he shouted, pushing himself off of her.

"What? Sergei, what's wrong?" Nexxa held her chest as she sat up.

Sergei stood up and moved away from the bed with his Russian eyes wide and piercing at the same time. "Is that for him?"

She looked down at herself. Marks & Spencer. Red lace panties and matching bra by Kiki de Montparnasse. "Get the fuck out," Sergei said with a collected demeanor.

"No! Sergei, No!" Nexxa tried to look him in the eyes. "Look at me. What's wrong?"

He motioned with his head toward the door. "I'll send your things to Dublin." Cold.

Nexxa gave him her professional face. Her red lips were more than subdued now, more like smudged. She stood, dressed, and said, "It's for me." The lingerie she had bought for her *faithful* self, not Quinn.

Nexxa had risked her life in the Russian bear's woods for Sergei, and now she was going to stay in Ireland and take a risk for her life— if Crimson was really after her in the Emerald.

FUCK KIKI | 32

Nexxa walked to the elevator looking back once toward Sergei's room and pushed the button to go down. When the elevator didn't arrive immediately, she dashed down the hallway, and entered the stairwell. Down eight flights of stairs and with just enough adrenaline left she flung open the door. Standing in the hallway that led to the lobby, she felt her side for her purse. "Fuck!" she half-screamed, half-cried.

She turned back looking at the stairwell door, and she heard the elevator ding in the lobby. *Is that Sergei? Is he coming to say he didn't mean it?*

Walking toward the concierge, Nexxa felt her forehead trying to steady herself. *I can give them Sergei's name and ask them to call his room. Tell him I need him.* Almost to the desk, and a couple approached the concierge before Nexxa.

And then—there was Diane.

"Nexxa, what are you doing here?" she asked with a cheery face as she approached her. The breath in Nexxa's body left her momentarily as Diane embraced her, moving in for a kiss on the cheeks. Nexxa gasped and subtly Diane released the breath she withdrew from her. *Just a test, not time yet. Soon*, Diane giggled in her mind.

"I don't have my purse, my phone," Nexxa told her with her eyes darting all over, counting people.

"Come, let me get you a cup of tea. You can use my phone," Diane offered, gently grasping Nexxa's hand. Nexxa felt her cold skin as she glided the two of them into the hotel bar. At a table, Diane ordered two cups of tea and a bottle of still water.

The water was served and Nexxa took a good drink. "I have to find him," she said breathless, looking around the restaurant.

Diane called the waiter over and paid, saying, "Okay, let's find him." Nexxa saw a man exiting the elevator, tall and wearing a gray shirt. She stood, and without pushing her chair back in she darted out of the bar. Diane was by her side in seconds. Nexxa spun around searching before Diane said, "There's no man here, Nexxa."

Nexxa reached, pushing her fingers against her temples. "I have to! I have to find..." Hotel guests began to stare at Nexxa. Then, lowering her hands and in a calmer tone, "Can you call Quinn?"

Diane placed her hand on Nexxa's back and said, "Okay, I will call him. Let's go outside. I'll help you." As they exited the hotel, it occurred to Nexxa that Diane didn't have any reason to be there, at The Marker Hotel. She remembered Tolya asking Diane how she liked her hotel, the Dylan. Nexxa took a few steps away as Diane had her phone out scrolling through to Quinn's name. While Diane called Quinn explaining to him that Nexxa was hurt, Nexxa's mind replayed: eating salmon, oysters, white wine, smelling Sergei, Quinn's Glock, Kiki de Montparnasse and "Get the fuck out!" all the way to feeling breathless when Diane gave her a kiss on the cheeks, a woman who again smelled of the Crimson scent.

Quinn's Mercedes barely made it into park before his conquering Irish self exited the car and wrapped his arms around Nexxa. She fell into his chest, but she only saw Sergei's face in her mind. If he were to come out of the hotel chasing after her, she would run with him—run all the way to Russia.

Quinn extended his hand out to Diane, and they shook hands. *Thank you,* he mouthed with the sincerest part of him. Quinn's car smelled good. Not only like him, but with an essence of collected control, Nexxa decided as she sat in the passenger seat. She knew she couldn't apologize. Quinn didn't expect her to. As he drove away from the hotel, slowly at first, he looked over at her and moved his hand in her direction. Just as he accelerated, Nexxa grasped his hand. He knew in that moment that she could be his.

Nexxa allowed her heart to adjust to his rhythm. She would have to be in this new normal, Ireland, while she figured out what the hell Crimson, if it turned out to be Diane, wanted from her.

Diane returned to the hotel. She adjusted her side bang, pushing it behind her ear before she opened the door to the stairwell. She followed Sergei's scent. It was like a tease because she could smell Nexxa's scent still moving around with arousal in the stairwell all the way to floor eight and to Sergei's room. She knocked on his door. He didn't answer, but she could hear him talking to someone. She opened the door and moved around watching him; he couldn't see her.

Sergei sat at the desk with his laptop. He was looking through a site for escorts. Lifting his phone, he made a call. Diane heard the voice on the other end. A female who sounded peppy and very accommodating. She resisted the urge to lift the phone out of his hand and smash it. How dare he hurt Nexxa and then call an escort! Sergei ended his call with the woman and placed his phone down. He ordered champagne from room service and then went into the bathroom. When he entered the shower, Diane hovered around his bed inhaling the scent of Nexxa. *Red, she had on red panties*, Diane detected. Lying on the comfortable queen bed, Diane felt Nexxa's pain. She wanted to kill Sergei, but she knew that would destroy a part of Nexxa, so that wouldn't work.

Sergei dressed after showering. He packed the few toiletries he had in the bathroom and kind of made the bed. Once everything was in his suitcase, he positioned the camera that Hooli had given him. The waiter from room service arrived, and Sergei had him open the champagne and pour two glasses. He tipped the server and closed the door.

Kessly arrived. Sergei let her in. Her fuchsia mini dress barely covered her bum. She smelled okay, more like a grocery store candle, Sergei determined. He handed Kessly a glass of champagne, and she giggled when he toasted to her in Russian. He liked her energy. She would be easy. Sergei sat in one of the armchairs with his glass of champagne. Kessly knelt before him and pulled the top of her dress down. Sergei adjusted in the chair and spread his legs. Kessly unzipped his jeans. When she saw that he didn't have an erection she reached into his underwear and began to pull his penis out. Sergei sat straight and moved her hand away. He explained to her that he was depressed because his wife had cheated on him. Kessly grinned before making a pouty face and telling him that she could make him forget about her.

"But what if I wanted to make him suffer? I could pay. I could pay you some now," Sergei proposed as he pushed a napkin on the side table revealing five thousand British pounds. Kessly pushed off of her knees, held her chest, and squealed. Before she could reach for the money, Sergei grabbed her arm. "Who would I need to speak to?"

"Me boyfriend," she answered with a matter-of-fact tone.

"Yeah." Sergei drew a hand along her collarbone. "Who is that?" he questioned.

"Gonna cost ya." She smirked, looking to the money.

Sergei lifted the money off of the side table, handing it to her. "His name?"

"Quinn," she squeaked with a matching perky smile.

Sergei stood and stepped back from her. He squinted his eyes. *Is she fucking with me?* "So the man is Quinn? Quinn who?"

Kessly giggled again and said, "Who cares, why don't ya shag me? You're hot," she hissed, pulling down her panties.

Sergei moved into her and put his hand under her dress. He slowly moved his hand up her thigh. She moaned before he even touched her pussy. "So the man," Sergei started, whispering into her ear. "Who would I contact if I wanted to kill the fucker that fucked my wife?"

As he reached her clitoris, massaging it, she breathed, "Quinn. Quinn Osian Kane."

"How can I know he could do the job? You're probably fucking with me?"

"No, no," she said, turning in to kiss him.

Sergei kissed her before saying, "I need to be certain."

"Hey!" She pulled away. "Are you a coppa?"

Sergei pulled her back into him and kissed her passionately and moved his fingers into her vagina. She moaned and he asked, "Now, how can I be sure?"

"He had me do a job."

"Yeah, what was that?"

"Kieran asked me to go to London with him. Some oil sheik, Drake Suleiman. I was only to take pictures leaving his room. But Kieran said that Quinn would pay more if I sucked him off first. The sheik, you know, blow him."

Sergei stopped fingering her and nodded. He pulled her into him so she was facing the camera. "So it was Quinn Osian Kane that hired you to take pictures with Drake Suleiman before Kieran killed him?"

Kessly pulled from his embrace. "Yeah, I told ya. Now are you going to shag me or not?" she complained, pushing her hand between her thighs. Sergei pulled down his jeans and his underwear, pulling them off. He pushed her over to the bed and bent her over. His phone vibrated, so he walked with his half erect penis back to the desk. Hooli had sent him a text that he had her confession on video and that all was a go. He also attached a video for Sergei to watch. The still on the video showed Nexxa.

Sergei looked over at Kessly bent over on his bed. "Come get me, come get me pussy," she told him. Sergei tapped on the video. It showed Nexxa spinning around touching her face looking distraught in the hotel lobby. There was also an Asian woman speaking to her who helped her outside. Another text came through with a second video. This one showed Nexxa outside of the hotel and stepping away from Diane before Quinn arrived. The video ended with Nexxa falling into his embrace before he helped her into his car. Sergei paused the video where the Asian woman seemed to turn and smile at the camera. He pinched the screen, enlarging it. He knew who she was. He played the rest of the clip showing Diane returning to the hotel.

Sergei laid his phone down. He moved over to Kessly.

Nexxa signed the contract Quinn presented her, drawn up by his former assistant Tolya, in his hanger. It was double what she had made working for Kuretz Investments in New York and would allow her to take care of herself and Iliada. Quinn insisted they celebrate her accepting his proposal, so he took her to a decadent restaurant that was designed after a castle in Dubrovnik. Glancing at herself in the mirror in the ladies' lounge, she wanted to be happy and dance to the electro-pop, feeling the champagne kick in, but she couldn't even enjoy how the lighting made her look. *She* could see her lavender glow. She thought about Sergei—and Crimson.

Nexxa didn't accept Quinn's offer to stay in his home. She did accept his offer to stay in his guest house under one condition: That he would provide her with a car. He countered by saying that he would need to teach her how to drive on the opposite side of the road. Touché.

"Sergei, I just need a few weeks." Nexxa stood in the living area of the guest house which consisted of an open layout with floor to ceiling windows on the side that faced the main house practicing a conversation with him. The day Nexxa moved in, Quinn had the buttercup beige drapes removed and replaced with gray ones. She huffed and plopped down on the cream-colored sofa. She looked over at the dark gray throw blanket, and Nexxa pulled it toward her. There was still a tag on it from Marks & Spencer. She imagined the night she sat on Sergei's lap by the fire outside of his bedroom when they had too much wine and some chips. Her mind flashed: looking at his thighs as he drove his Jaguar, his lips with Scotch on her vagina. Nexxa let her head fall back. A tear fell, and just as it reached her high cheekbone, she heard a knock on the door.

Irish mist fell on him and Nexxa could really see the lines on his forehead and his blue eyes. Quinn looked hella sexy when he seemed pitiful. "Here, I thought you might be hungry. I'm not sure how well they stocked the fridge for you." Quinn almost sounded timid as he held out a bag of takeaway.

"Okay. Thank you." Nexxa reached for the bag, still warm.

"So, have a good night." Quinn took a step backward. Then another before he turned walking away. Nexxa watched him before adjusting the bag in her arms.

"Oh," Quinn shouted through the rain that was coming down harder, "I got two meals. Wasn't sure what you liked."

"Quinn! Come here, come in," Nexxa hollered to him motioning with her hand. Quinn dashed back to the door.

Inside he wiped his face and stood on the rug by the entrance. Nexxa took the takeaway to the kitchen island and opened a few drawers until she found one with kitchen towels. She brought one to Quinn and reached up to his face to wipe it. "I'm sorry, I don't know. I don't know why I did that," Nexxa offered before looking away from him.

Quinn reached for her hand, taking the towel. "You don't need to apologize."

"Oh, do you want to eat?" Nexxa quickly countered, twisting her body and pointing to the food.

In the kitchen, Nexxa and Quinn discovered where the plates and silverware were and together plated food and each took a seat at the island. Quinn hopped up quickly. "Forgot the most important thing," he said as he approached the wine fridge and withdrew a bottle of white wine. "Is white okay?"

"Sure. I think wine glasses are in that cabinet," she answered, pointing. Quinn opened the bottle and poured two glasses. Nexxa ate—the food was excellent, curry shrimp with rice—and finished a glass of her pinot grigio.

"So, I thought you might," Quinn started saying before he took another sip of wine, "might need to go shopping," he finished, placing his wine glass down and turning to Nexxa.

Nexxa thought about all of her clothes that were in Sergei's closet in Sergei's house in Sergei's Moscow.

"I'll take care of it," Quinn explained, holding a hand to his chest.

"I'll pay you back," Nexxa said, flipping her hand out.

Quinn held up his hand as if to say *no need to*.

"Well you are my boss now… so I can consider it an advance."

Nexxa finally smiled. Quinn liked it when she smiled. When she cried. And when she did anything else in his presence.

They finished eating and Nexxa cleared the plates and rinsed them, looking out of the window above the sink watching the rain come down even harder. She was honestly tired and ready to fall into bed.

Standing before Quinn, she held her hands together, moving them, caressing one hand then the other. Quinn reminded her how to lock up and set the alarm. Nexxa listened, still moving her hands, now interlocking her fingers and pulling them apart. Quinn stared in her eyes and then glanced down at her hands. Nexxa rubbed her lips together.

A branch fell outside the living room windows. Quinn stepped over to the window, turned off the lamp nearby and inspected. "I should get a better look," he said to Nexxa. She waited in the doorway as Quinn walked around the branch and then the perimeter of the guest house. He returned soaking wet. "The storm might go all night. You sure you don't want to come?" he asked, motioning with his head toward his house.

"I'm okay," Nexxa assured him.

He felt like he wanted to grab her and kiss her until she succumbed to letting him carry her to the bedroom—instead he took his game and let the night end.

Nexxa counted all of the windows and doors. The alarm could fuck off. That wouldn't save her. The one thing that was going to save her, for about a fortnight, was a color that was going to cost about two and a half million—lavender.

Nexxa opened the door. Kieran stood before her sipping his

coffee. Nexxa looked past him to Quinn's home. "Should I pack a bag?"

"Nope." Kieran shook his head.

Kieran brought Nexxa to his Range Rover. He opened the passenger door for her. "Isn't Quinn coming?"

"He's already there."

"Already where? We're supposed to go shopping."

"Yous are, get in." Kieran was part-gruff, but his coffee breath smelled of vanilla—so part-sweet.

Nexxa hopped in and buckled her seat belt. Kieran drove slower than she had expected and seemed extra chatty. She thought about the Italian mafia movies she had watched with Kilmer. Was she being told she was going to be a "made man" only to be shot in the back of the head? Or was she letting in the paranoia Kilmer had once had? She sent a text to Iliada just in case, just because she loved her too. The car ride seemed so long. Nexxa noticed things she hadn't in awhile: school buses, moms and dads in cars with kids in the backseat, elderly crossing the street. When Kieran didn't take the exit for Dublin city centre, she knew.

Pulling into the FBO, Nexxa's stomach wanted to be upset, but suddenly she saw Quinn outside, and the forehead lines that gave him a hella sexy look, were relaxed. Nexxa knew that he must have a plan to take her somewhere.

"Shopping in Dublin is blah," Quinn explained with an almost comedic tone. Nexxa looked over at the jet on the tarmac.

Kieran gave him a pat on the shoulder. "I'm out."

Nexxa sat opposite Quinn and looked out of the window for

the entire flight while Quinn read the news on his phone. They landed and deplaned without saying much. A driver awaited their arrival and drove them into central London. As Nexxa looked out of the car window she thought back to when she and Iliada had had brunch at Faroud's house in Beirut and her concern that they were being followed on the way back to their hotel. Then the feeling of spotting the Beirut Mall and realizing they would get back safely.

"Nexxa?" Quinn patted her thigh.

"Oh, yeah," Nexxa answered with an out-of-it voice. The driver pulled up to Harrods and Quinn exited the car. He came to Nexxa's door and opened it, reaching for her hand. As he guided her out, the scent that Nexxa had tried to avoid encircled her. Quinn grinned. The doorman in green held open the door and inside Quinn answered a call. Moments later a short but dapper man with suave hair approached them with a huge commission smile. As he introduced himself, "Mr. Schaffer," Nexxa heard his voice and relaxed. He was like the friend she didn't know she needed.

Mr. Schaffer walked by Nexxa's side toward the women's clothing area of the department store. Designers Nexxa was familiar with were plentiful, and some that were emerging caught her eye. Quinn milled about. He had had practice with his ex-wife staying out of the way until it was time to pay. Nexxa moved her hand along a few garments. Her personal shopper observed. *Black*, he thought, as her tense shoulders succumbed to a few pieces by T by Alexander Wang. He pulled a black bootcut pant and summoned the area saleswoman over. He told her to go to the Wolford section and retrieve a black scoop neck bodysuit.

In the dressing room, Mr. Schaffer assisted Nexxa by unboxing the Wolford bodysuit. She undressed in front of him. He stood behind her and pushed her hair to the side saying, "My friends call me Johnnie."

Nexxa grasped his hand on her shoulder. "Thank you," she said with more sincerity than he expected. "How did you know—"

Johnnie shook his head. "Love, you're exquisite."

Nexxa turned and stepped out of her heels to be more his height. "Johnnie, how can I pay for this on my own?" Nexxa only had her Amex, which would require full payment each billing cycle. And until she had her first paycheck from working for Quinn, she wouldn't be able to pay for extras, like Harrods.

"Come, love." Mr. Schaffer ushered Nexxa out of the dressing room. "Just up to lingerie," he hollered over to Quinn.

Across the store Nexxa went in a lift up to Mr. Schaffer's personal office. She handed over her Amex and passport. A phone call and a few strokes on his keyboard and Nexxa had an official Harrods credit card. Her credit line would have been higher if she had disclosed her current employer as a reference, Johnnie already knew who she was with, but she had declined.

With a few rigouts, bras, panties, and chemises, Nexxa hugged Johnnie goodbye. He reminded her that his business card was in one of her shopping bags. Quinn looked up as Nexxa walked toward him, and he promptly ended his call. "Where is Mr. Schaffer?" he asked.

"Quinn, I'm done." Nexxa had a mix of confidence and professionalism in her tone. He looked at her shopping bags and quickly reached for them, and Nexxa released her grip. He resisted the urge to scold her for paying for everything. Every molecule of Quinn was committed to playing the long game. The long game was where Quinn had sacrificed the whole of his self for her, for Nexxa, to be his soulmate. Only, simply, there was another who desired her soul. Diane.

"You hungry?" Quinn asked casually while looking through the front of the car and then out of his window. Nexxa noticed how the driver remained silent but looked at Quinn in his rearview mirror.

"Okay, sure, I could eat."

Quinn gave a nod to the driver and the car suddenly changed lanes and sped up. He kept his eyes on the road and then glanced at his phone. Nexxa adjusted her legs, twisting to look out of her window. She rubbed her palms together, interlocking her fingers while counting pedestrians that looked like tourists. Twenty minutes in London traffic and they arrived.

He held the door open for Nexxa and they were promptly seated at a table that had been reserved for Quinn. He ordered for them: a bottle of white wine, shrimp cocktail, and bruschetta. "This place is lovely. It's nice to be in London," Nexxa commented, telling herself to just be in the moment.

"Yeah, it's quite nice. I've been here many times," Quinn responded while shuffling around his flatware and bread plate. The waiter served the wine, Quinn tasted, and he gave him the okay.

Nexxa sipped her wine and pulled out her phone. She tapped on the app for calls even though she could see she hadn't missed any. "I'll be right back," Nexxa announced, standing with her phone in her hand.

"Wait," Quinn said and stood in one motion.

"I'm going to the ladies' room," Nexxa explained, lifting her purse. She placed her phone on the table. Quinn moved his hand onto hers and Nexxa glanced down.

"It's that way and to the left," Quinn told her, pointing.

Quinn lifted his phone and plopped it down again. He looked to Nexxa's phone, willing it to ring. He assumed only one person would call. A Russian man. It wasn't as if he wanted to speak to Sergei. He only wanted to tell him to feck off. But like a really hard fuck off. Kieran had told Quinn that he had been followed. It only made sense that it was someone working for Sergei since Nexxa had recently entered Quinn's life.

Nexxa returned from the bathroom. They ate the appetizers and Nexxa told Quinn she was full. She also asked when they were scheduled to fly back to Dublin. Quinn reminded himself he was playing the long game.

Nexxa told Quinn she didn't need help carrying her shopping bags to the guest house. Inside she locked the door behind her and shut the drapes before sitting at the kitchen island with Tolya's notes. She reread through them. She tossed the folder. Without a laptop, hers wasn't powering on anymore, she didn't have a use for them right now. Nexxa lifted her phone and texted Dan, her former boss. He responded by calling her. After catching up, Nexxa told him she needed a favor. The favor was to borrow their security director. Dan offered up any help that he or Ezio could provide.

Nexxa texted Ezio—she felt the excitement she once had when working for Kuretz Investments. While she awaited his response, she occupied her mind by hanging up her new clothes from Harrods next to the clothes she had brought from Moscow. Ezio finally had a break in work and called Nexxa. She asked him about his family. After they chatted for a bit, she told him what she needed. Ezio told her he was more than happy to investigate Diane Soo Hoo. When Nexxa had first vetted China Black Road, including Diane, it was more of a soft due diligence: confirming credentials, where the company was domiciled, their financial rating. Now she needed to know everything.

The next morning, Nexxa wore an outfit that she had brought from Moscow. Black and sleek enough to meet Quinn's client, Diane. Nexxa had declined to have breakfast with Quinn in his home; she only had tea in the guest house. Quinn drove them to the FBO and they only spoke about the weather, but she could feel his eyes on her. They entered the gate, drove up to the hangar and parked. "You have a laptop I can use, right?" Nexxa asked before reaching for the handle.

"Yep."

"Okay, good. I'm ready." Nexxa didn't mind that he seemed cross with her. In a few moments she was going to see Diane and get started with whatever may be.

"Why didn't you wear the new clothes?" Quinn turned, reaching for Nexxa's arm.

She thought for a moment looking out of the passenger window. *Clothes, the color red. Red clothes like my bra and panties. Scents like Crimson. All the things fucking up my life.* Saying nothing, Nexxa opened her door and walked to the hangar telling herself to hold back her anger. Quinn cuffed his mouth and exhaled before he exited his Mercedes.

In Quinn's office, he opened a locked drawer and withdrew a laptop. He found a charging cable in another drawer. "You can use my desk if you want." Quinn's tone had softened as he moved some things around on his desk.

Nexxa picked up the laptop and charging cable and said, "I'd actually like to work out there," as she leaned her head toward the door. "Sure." Quinn nodded. Nexxa walked out of his office and set herself up on one of the sofas in the client meeting area. She watched the time as she, from memory, created a template for a client brief sheet. She started a more detailed version but decided to save it for later, anticipating Diane's arrival. Quickly, she emailed the Italian company that was located on the outskirts of Milan regarding the customized leather seats for the jet.

It was 10:25 a.m. when Quinn stepped out of his office and looked toward the hangar door wondering where his client was. Nexxa had already finished what she could and was walking around the perimeter of the hangar. She hadn't smelled Diane and knew she wasn't coming.

Quinn walked over to the client meeting area holding up his hands saying, "Where is she?" Nexxa walked back over to him. He glanced down at the laptop. "You made some progress?"

"Yes," she answered as they heard a noise from the front of

the hanger. Nexxa looked over out of the corner of her eye. "Ah, she's here," Quinn stated, turning and taking a few steps toward the sound.

Nexxa sat and powered off the laptop. She closed it and unplugged the cord. "She's not coming, Quinn," she spoke softly.

"What?" Quinn looked back, barely hearing her as he continued across the hanger.

Nexxa lifted her purse and laptop and walked over to him. "Quinn, she's not here," Nexxa said just as he opened the hangar door. He turned and gave Nexxa a confused look. "So, other clients I should get familiar with in the meantime?" Nexxa questioned. Quinn remained silent before grasping his chin, moving his hand along his jaw. Nexxa was disappointed. She wanted, needed, to see Diane to get some answers about why she smelled like Crimson, but she had to remain in the game while Quinn, hiding behind his blue Irish eyes, was playing his own long game.

EMBLÉMATIQUE | 34

Diane rolled onto her side in her tartan print pajamas and set the snooze on her alarm for eight minutes, for the eight floors that Nexxa ran down in Sergei's hotel, and then she cried for her love Reyhan. Up from the bed leaving her sadness, she withdrew a piece of hotel stationary. Her index fingernail screeched around the paper until an outline of a woman was visible. Diane drew in her face; she was smiling. Nexxa was going to be happy again—and then ready to play tradesy. Nexxa would receive Reyhan's soul, and Reyhan would take on Nexxa's.

With an extra apologetic text including some sad face emojis, one for fire, and one for a volcano, Diane texted Quinn expressing remorse for missing their meeting. She gave the excuse that she was tending to personal matters. Really, she was running low on energy. Releasing her frustration in the form of the red ash a few days ago had taken a lot out of her. After she texted him, she emailed her father that the plane would be finished on schedule.

Nexxa dressed, starting with a bra and a pair of panties she had brought with her from Moscow. She had buried her red bra and panty set in the bottom of a drawer, the last drawer in the dresser. She had cried so much the last few nights that she was starting to look like she had had Botox injections where her high cheekbones met her eyes. Despite how she looked, she wanted to give it another go, press forward.

Nexxa crossed the lawn and knocked on the kitchen door. Quinn hopped up from a barstool and let her in. "Good morning. Want some tea?" Quinn greeted Nexxa in a voice that said he was aware she was sad.

"Good morning, yes," Nexxa replied.

Quinn motioned for her to take a seat, and he moved over to the kettle, turning it on and taking a mug from a cabinet. He turned back to Nexxa, seeing her swollen eyes, and fought the urge to ask her what had happened the other day with Sergei. He assumed they fucked and then fought. "Milk?" he asked her instead, after handing her a cup of tea.

"Yes, that would be nice," Nexxa answered, feeling like her mouth was swollen too.

"So, I got a text from Diane, our client," Quinn explained, lifting his phone to show Nexxa.

"And?" Nexxa's eyes showed she was intrigued.

"Well, she apologized for missing our meeting yesterday. Some strange emojis."

"Set it up," Nexxa spoke with determination.

"You feel up to it?"

"Yes, yes of course." Nexxa's spoke, swiftly moving off of the barstool and over to the other side of the island. Quinn looked confident, but inside his Irish soul was yearning for her. "You know, I want to meet with her alone. You can take me, but I'm ready and have gone over some of, all of, the notes. I might have been out of sorts yesterday, but I'm ready for this."

Quinn nodded. "Sure. Sure."

Nexxa reached up feeling her forehead and Quinn suddenly moved in, putting a hand to her head. Nexxa laughed. "I'm okay."

Quinn pulled his hand away saying, "Sorry, sorry, I don't know what I was thinking." He shifted, leaning against the counter, and rubbed his hand along his chin.

Nexxa faced him and grasped the hand by his side. "Quinn, thank you. I don't know how to thank you enough."

"You don't need to thank me," he said with a remorseful face.

"I do. You've given me the opportunity to have my dignity again." Nexxa's mind flashed to Sergei telling her to get the fuck out of his hotel room.

"I'm happy to do that for you."

Nexxa walked away, looking out of the glass door. "He was so angry and told me to come here. And then he told me to get the fuck out of his hotel room." Nexxa sounded like she had taken her last breath. Quinn had a look of disbelief. "I, we didn't have sex. He was just so angry. I want to work, and I explained that to him."

Quinn leaned on the kitchen island with his hands and lowered his head. "I hate seeing you cry," he explained before taking a deep breath. If he didn't calm down, he knew he would either try to kiss Nexxa again or send for Kieran to drive him to kill the Russian. Nexxa turned, seeing him, and in that moment, he reminded her of when he seemed vulnerable in Mr. Albert's library. She walked over and placed her hand on his back, and he twisted, grabbing her, kissing her.

"We have to stop," she breathed, abruptly pulling away.

Quinn stood inches away from her catching his breath. "I'm sorry, I'm sorry," he told her.

Nexxa reached, touching his chest, and he grasped her hand she held to him. "Quinn, I can't be with you." He briefly closed his eyes. Nexxa teared up. "I wanted to… ten years ago," she confessed, putting a hand on her heart.

Hearing that she didn't fuck the Russian and tasting her, Quinn caught his Irish soul. It was the best thing he had ever heard, that she had wanted to fuck him a decade ago. He wanted to fuck her until his last breath.

"St. Audoen's Church," Nexxa had told Quinn. She could have told him they were going to meet Diane at the deli counter in a Spar and he would have agreed. While Quinn was a Protestant, he found it sexy that Nexxa was Catholic. His mother was a Catholic, but she had died when he was young, so he was raised by his father as a Protestant.

There had been a nagging image of her rosary, so Nexxa packed it when she traveled from Russia, and the scar on her breast remained even with new lingerie from Marks & Spencer, so she brought the rosary with her to mass. She kneeled before she entered the pew; Quinn didn't. Nexxa went down on her knees, withdrew her rosary, and said the Hail Mary prayer, thinking back to when she was a child. How she always felt the power within the walls of a Catholic church. "Okay, we can go now." Nexxa stood; Quinn stood, and he followed her out of the church. "Wait here." Nexxa smiled at Quinn and turned, going back into the church. She found the door that led to the stairs for the tower. When the senior citizen church volunteer walked away to direct a tourist, Nexxa pushed open the door and dashed up the century-old staircase.

Nexxa emerged from the stairs seeing Diane across the tower. She calmed her thoughts, then said, "You're Crimson. You always smell of Crimson."

"I do," Diane agreed with her eyes showing she was proud. "I do smell of Crimson," Diane said, smoothing her hand along a pleat in her tartan print skirt.

Nexxa imagined a woman that wanted something from her. Maybe to be like her. Maybe she was like her. Like in the movie *"Single White Female"*. Then, Nexxa calmed her breathing before she blew out a breath. Diane closed her eyes and inhaled with her chest vividly moving. And, instantly Diane was before her. Nexxa struggled to breathe but managed to open her hand, allowing her rosary to dangle. Diane's body slammed against the stair railing. Nexxa moved closer, standing in her personal space, and held the rosary she had acquired in Rome closer to her, then said, "You're like me."

"Yes. I have the wolfness like you," Diane confessed with a

weakened voice.

Nexxa felt excitement in her body, and relief in the hand that held the religious symbol. Diane smiled, her search for a woman born in the Year of the Dragon had ended

Quinn quickly put his phone in his jeans' pocket when Nexxa walked down the path from the church. She handed him her rosary. He looked in his hand then back to her. "It went well. Diane will meet me later," Nexxa offered as she started toward his car, turning and smiling with her hidden wolfness but red lips.

When they returned to his house, Nexxa had a cup of tea with Quinn. She noticed how he kept stalling by offering her biscuits and random items from his pantry. "So, I will need wine and some takeaway."

"That can be arranged," Quinn said, motioning for Nexxa to follow him. In his wine cellar he started describing wines by their varietals and regions.

Nexxa walked over to a rack and pulled out a bottle. "This will do," she said.

Quinn approached her and pulled out another bottle. "This one first, and then have this."

"Then that will do." Nexxa flashed a cheeky, slightly seductive face. Quinn grinned, and Nexxa realized what she had done. She quickly asked, "Would it be possible to order from the Italian place you took me to?" as she began walking up the cellar stairs.

"Yeah, I can arrange that," Quinn answered, thinking about what he would order for himself.

In his kitchen, Nexxa said, "Good," before moving over to his commercial-size refrigerator. She opened the massive stainless-steel door and quickly shut it. "Quinn, so, I say this nicely. You have nothing but cinnamon rolls and beer." She walked over to his pantry and opened it. "You actually have biscuits. And some random, looks like it's old, container of flour," Nexxa hollered from inside the walk-in pantry while opening a container that held stale baking flour.

She stepped out and could see Quinn leaning against the side of the kitchen island that was by the pantry. He wanted to pull her into him and tell her that she could be what he ate for dinner. He imagined her lying atop his island; he had never fucked anyone in there. It was a new kitchen, and time would make that happen, he told himself. "I'll ask the restaurant for an antipasto platter." He always had a good answer, it seemed.

After the food was delivered and Quinn brought it to the guest house for her, Nexxa opened the wine and had a glass before Diane was due to arrive. She sent Quinn away, and he told her he would show Diane the way. Nexxa knew from the client notes that Diane had requested to have custom seats in a specific shade of lavender. She thought about how she had spotted a lavender fingernail on the steps of the jet. The video of a blonde ponytail clad woman in Sergei's home and all the Crimson she smelled in Moscow. It all added up to Diane. Nexxa drank her glass of wine and poured another. *Is this all just about the wolfness?*

Diane arrived on time and was professional when Quinn greeted her. He walked her through his house, and in his kitchen, she conspicuously dragged a fingernail along his stone island. Her eyes widened. *Mmm, Quinn wants to fuck Nexxa here.* Through the glass door to the garden they walked, and she passed him on the grass waving him off. He stopped aghast and watched as she approached the guest house where Nexxa was waiting with the door ajar. She waved to Quinn smiling when Diane entered the doorway. Quinn held his position for a moment before turning to walk back, looking over his shoulder.

Nexxa offered Diane a glass of wine. "This is a red blend from Portugal."

Diane took a sip, then giggled. "We should cheers first." Nexxa held up her glass and Diane clanked it. Nexxa felt the reverberation go through her hand and up her arm. She had a flashback of being in Bogdan's izba in the woods behind Sergei's house the night she heard something on the roof. Diane gushed, "Oh, cheese! Can I have some?"

"Of course, yeah," Nexxa answered, moving to the kitchen island. She plated them each some cheese, olives, prosciutto, and crackers. They each took a seat and started eating. Nexxa poured them more wine. In a short while, the first bottle was empty, so after a few more bites she got up and opened the second bottle. "Quinn said to have this bottle after the one we just drank."

"So what is it? With you and Quinn?" Diane asked, reaching for more crackers.

Nexxa looked up with her eyes, then back to Diane. "Well, I met him about ten years ago." Diane's eyes widened. "Yeah, that would be a long story to get into," Nexxa explained before she grabbed fresh wine glasses from the cabinet and poured from the bottle she had just opened.

"And what happened with the other guy? The one you were expecting to see in the hotel?" Diane was careful not to let on that she knew who Sergei was.

Nexxa shook her head. "I can't, I can't talk about him. About what happened."

Without warning rain came down hard, pelting the guest house. The curtains in the living room were blowing in the wind and water was coming in from all sides of the house through the open windows. Nexxa rushed to the living room windows, and while she was shutting them, Diane—with her lightning speed—closed the kitchen, bathroom, and bedroom windows, returning before Nexxa noticed. The lights flickered, and Nexxa wondered if this was Diane's work.

Diane grabbed the bottle of wine and their glasses and brought it to the coffee table in the living room. "Hey, let's camp out here."

Nexxa watched as the lights went out, and yet lights could be seen on in Quinn's house. He called almost immediately; Nexxa answered her phone. "Hi."

"I'm coming over, just pulling on my jacket," Quinn insisted.

Nexxa looked, seeing Diane holding up some taper candles and candlestick holders. "I, I think we are..." she responded. Diane made a silly face and placed the candles in the holders on the coffee table. *Matches?* Nexxa mouthed to Diane. She twisted around and walked over to the kitchen. After pulling open a few drawers, Diane found a lighter.

"Nexxa. Nexxa?" Quinn said.

"Yeah, yeah, we have candles and found a lighter. It's raining, Quinn. Don't come out," Nexxa told him as thunder started making the early evening even more dramatic. Diane lit the candles, took off her Dr. Martens, and plopped down on the couch with crisscrossed legs. Nexxa laughed. "I have to go now."

"Right, okay." Quinn sounded disappointed, like his chivalry wasn't needed. Nexxa ended the call and put her phone on silent. She had made her first adult "friend" with the wolfness, and if it took her life, she knew that at least she had met someone else in this lifetime that she loved that could see her lavender—Sergei—even though he had told her to fuck off.

Nexxa sat on the couch facing Diane with one leg bent and one hanging off, and she took a deep breath. "Tell me, what do you know about our wolfness?" Nexxa asked with a slight shoulder shrug.

Diane smiled and her Chinese characteristics shaped her face effortlessly. She was prepared to tell Nexxa *something*, for she was playing the long game just like Quinn. Looking into Nexxa's almond eyes, she would prefer to focus on their current work relationship: a jet with lavender leather seats.

Nexxa lifted her full glass and took a sip. Thunder boomed, and she spilled some wine on her leg. Diane quickly grabbed a napkin and started dabbing at Nexxa's leg. Nexxa reached for the tissue and Diane let go of it. She pulled up her legging where it was wet from wine. Diane saw her scar and instinctively reached to touch the wound. "Oh, I got this in Moscow running in Sergei's woods." Nexxa pulled at her top, intentionally revealing her other scar. Diane showed her best intrigued face. "And this is the other scar I acquired in Moscow."

Diane laughed, "Well, Russians can be dangerous."

Nexxa tilted her head with a half-smile, and the lights came on just a wee bit. Music started emitting, a song by Lipless, "Cimmerian," though it hadn't been released yet. Diane lifted her phone from the coffee table and adjusted the volume up. Nexxa knew what Diane wasn't divulging, stalking her in Moscow, but the song was intoxicating… and if Diane wanted her dead, she didn't want that; there was something else she desired. As much as it had hurt in the last week—should death come before she might desire in this incarnation—she had to take with her these lessons.

When the lights came back on, Nexxa said, "About the jet, I think we will be able to see one of the seats tomorrow. The custom seat in lavender."

"Oh! I'm so excited." Diane adjusted her crossed legs.

Nexxa hoped she wasn't promising something that wasn't going to happen. She had seen the date of delivery for the first sample chair in the notes from Tolya. She just hadn't checked her email for a response from the Italian company that was customizing the seats.

"When did you *know*?" Nexxa was direct, changing the subject.

Diane thought for a moment. Nexxa felt a little afraid to know the truth. "I was young, my mom told me," Diane offered, sounding blasé. *Yucky, the human that preferred my pathetic, weak, normal brother.*

"Oh. Similar to me. Not my mom, but someone else helped me understand."

"It's kind of weird," Diane started saying, flashing exaggerated eyes, thinking, *Hmm, you're eyes are a different shape than Reyhan's. I'll get used to them. But... I'm working hard on making you happy again. Just need you to fall in love with Quinn.* "I mean, who else has this? Who is just going around like us?" Diane knew of others, like the woman on the train to Serbia.

"Well, for me, I don't think of it as being weird. Do you think we are weird?" Nexxa probed.

"Kind of," Diane laughed, seeming so young in her disposition.

Nexxa slid her interlocked fingers back and forth thinking of what to ask. She knew all about how their supernatural ability worked, but she didn't know how people were chosen for it other than what Thomas had told her. His version of humans being selected by the head wolf in the territory that you were born in based on your astral chart made sense when he had told her when she was a young girl. She had never questioned him.

"Are there wolves in China?" Nexxa asked with a face that expressed, *don't laugh at my dumb question.*

Diane laughed and she reminded Nexxa of Mr. Albert when she had a genuine giggle. They heard a knock on the door, and both looked saying, "Quinn!"

Nexxa got up and let him in. "I brought you another bottle of wine," he announced, holding up a bottle. "Did you eat yet?" he asked, and Nexxa walked with him over to the kitchen. He looked full, like he had eaten *his* order from the takeaway. "I can stay and open the wine for you," he continued, glancing at the food on the counter. Quinn looked desirable when he seemed desperate.

"We're having a good time. We can open it when we finish this bottle," Diane piped up. Quinn nodded, looking again at the unopened food containers. Nexxa was sort of relieved when Diane spoke up. If Quinn lingered, it would only prevent her from getting answers.

Nexxa opened the wine when Quinn left, knowing they were probably ready for another bottle. It was a gamble: Diane would either continue to hold her alcohol well, or she would not and Nexxa would regret doing what she always did—making friends with the wicked.

Nexxa sat down on the sofa. Diane had been scrolling on her phone, a dating app. She plopped her phone on the coffee table with a thud. "What is it?" Nexxa asked. Diane exhaled. She had seen a dating profile for Sergei on the Dubliner's Love dating app. She wanted to tell Nexxa. But what she needed to do was see that Nexxa could move on and be happy with a Dubliner, Quinn.

DUBLINER'S HEART | 36

Crimson had left. Quinn had Kieran come around and drive Diane back to her hotel. It was his way of ensuring he could check on Nexxa for the evening. He lingered in the kitchen after he helped Nexxa clean up. "I'm just going to get changed and brush my teeth," Nexxa said as she walked into her bedroom. Quinn stared out of the window over the kitchen sink, but he couldn't see anything in the dark after the rain. He poured the last bit of wine. Ready, he walked down the hallway and knocked on the bedroom door as he pushed it open, seeing Nexxa with her back to him standing by the nightstand in her bra and leggings looking at her phone. She had typed out a message to Sergei asking about babushka and baby Natina.

Quinn walked over to her, and she could feel him moving closer. He reached around her and placed a glass of water on the nightstand. She turned and looked up at him. Quinn looked a mix of a man that could hold his alcohol and a man who would never stop wanting her. "I need to go to sleep, Quinn."

He kissed her on the forehead. "I'll check on you in the morning."

She closed her eyes and the last thought she gave breath to was Natina. *How, how will I make it back to her?*

Nexxa had only slept because of the wine. She stepped out of the shower and heard her phone ping. She had a text from Sergei. He wanted to meet her at his hotel at nine p.m. Nexxa laid her phone down and sat on the bed in her towel. Tears came down her face. A second text came through. It said to come alone. *Is he fucking with me?* She knew Sergei would not be the man to back down. He didn't need her to come alone. But what if he really wanted to see her? She tapped on the button to call him and at the same time a text came through from Ezio saying that he had emailed her. Nexxa ended the call.

After she dressed, she sat at the kitchen island and opened her email on her work laptop. She clicked on the link Ezio attached, opening the documents directly in her Dropbox account. Skipping the first few pages, she read where Diane had taken monthly flights from Shanghai to Ürümqi for several years. There were details showing chartered flights through a jet share under her father's company to Moscow and to NYC with dates that aligned with Nexxa being in both locations. Diane's name was absent from the manifest for those flights.

Nexxa stood from the barstool. She walked over, looking out of the living room windows. *If someone were to meet me now,*

I would be hiding that I was heartbroken. I would hide behind, what? Everyone is hiding from something or is hurt. What is she not telling me?

Nexxa walked back over to her laptop. She continued looking through the report on Diane. A medical record in Diane's name at a clinic in Ürümqi. The patient's description listed auburn hair. Same height and age. But auburn hair, even listed as the color of the pubic hair. The reason for the visit was listed as unexplained abdominal pain and a procedure for a vaginal examination. *Why would a medical report list the color of pubic hair? Oh, I wonder if this was a friend using her identity card.*

Nexxa's phone rang with a call from Quinn. "Pelle Italia emailed me a tracking link. It's en route to be delivered by eleven a.m. today," Nexxa informed him.

"Let's go for breakfast," Quinn suggested before they were to meet Diane at the FBO in Quinn's hangar to show her the custom leather seat.

"I'd actually like to go for a run," Nexxa countered.

"I could order us smoothies while you're out."

"Sure." Nexxa quickly changed and put her hair in a ponytail.

She made her way around the side of Quinn's house and out of the main gate. The road that led to his house was secluded. They had driven down it many times in the last week, yet it looked different when on foot. She noticed the smell of Ireland more now that she was there for more than just to release ashes.

There wasn't much room to run on the side of the road, so as she picked up her speed, she moved in between the lanes. *Hmm, in that article in Forbes, Diane stated she liked to wear wigs and dress up for cosplay.* Nexxa's mind was bouncing around. A dog ran along the inside of its fence barking in stride with Nexxa. She wanted to stop, but then she would lose her rhythm and her thoughts. *Whatever Diane is hiding... is it a game? Infatuation?* Nexxa ran until the road had a curve. She abruptly stopped and held a hand to her chest. She felt out of shape not running the last few weeks and panted while looking around the neighboring properties.

Back at Quinn's house Nexxa walked up to the kitchen door, and Quinn was waiting for her. "I wish you had a trail around the back of your house," Nexxa said without thinking.

"I could do that," Quinn offered immediately with enthusiasm, handing her a smoothie as green as the luck of the Irish.

"Thank you." Nexxa reached for the drink. "I mean, that didn't come out right."

"What's that?" Quinn looked confused but smiled.

Nexxa took a sip through the straw and said, "It's beautiful around here. I appreciate everything."

"Would you like a treadmill?" Quinn asked. Nexxa tilted her head thinking. "A running trail it is," Quinn announced. He lifted his phone and made a call as he walked out of the kitchen. Nexxa could hear him. He was asking whomever he called to get someone around to see about clearing some trees. She wanted to tell him that whatever he was planning wasn't necessary, but her leg started throbbing where she had cut it. She sat at the kitchen table and took off her sneaker, pulling her legging up, touching her scar.

Quinn walked back into the kitchen as he ended his call. "What's that? When did you do that?"

"Oh, this. It happened in Moscow." Nexxa looked up to Quinn. Quinn crouched down and gently touched her wound. Nexxa flinched. "I don't know why it hurts now."

"It could be infected." Quinn had a scrunched forehead.

"I'm sure it's fine. Probably just that I haven't run in a while." Nexxa started to move her leg but stopped when it continued hurting.

"You should have it looked at." Quinn was insistent with his tone.

"Well, I think it will be okay. Besides, I don't have health insurance here. Or anywhere." Nexxa let out a laugh. She attempted to stand. Quinn moved back, and tears came down her face.

"Hey, hey, shh," Quinn said, pulling her to embrace him. Nexxa let her head fall into his chest. She hated that he smelled good. She hated that it wasn't Sergei holding her. Quinn grasped her face. "You actually," he chuckled, "do have health insurance." Nexxa knew that her offer of employment included benefits such as health insurance. It would take thirty days to become effective though. She was always thinking of how to be independent. And how to make it without any help from Sergei. "I'm taking you to my doctor. He'll take care of you. You don't need to worry about a thing."

"No, I'm fine. We have to meet with Diane," Nexxa asserted. She maneuvered her foot into her sneaker, taking a silent deep breath as the pain shot up her leg. "I'm going to get ready, and I'll be back in about twenty minutes."

"She should open it with me," Nexxa suggested to Quinn as

they stood in the hangar next to the delivery that contained the lavender leather seat.

"What?" Quinn scoffed. "That's absurd. I've managed many businesses, my private club, oyster harvesting, the hotel."

"Yes, but women love to get something in the mail. Take the plywood off. Leave the inner box," Nexxa countered, moving next to Quinn. She looked over and popped her shoulder up as she smiled at him. "Now, I just need a box cutter."

Diane arrived with one minute to spare. She used that minute to stand outside of the hangar and inhale something new. The air was swaying, and Diane held her hair out of her face. She detected the aroma of a heart that was mending... just a tad.

Quinn watched as Nexxa greeted Diane as if they had just met. Her ability to maintain her professionalism was remarkable. This also worried him. But then as she embraced Diane whispering in her ear while handing her the box cutter, Diane gushed, and he realized how brilliant she was. He envisioned her working with extraordinary clients, the oil sheiks of the reformed Middle East.

The first slice was successful. Diane inhaled. Nexxa nodded lightly. Quinn stood back watching them. In unison the ones with the wolfness looked back at Quinn. Nexxa stepped forward, the pain in her leg was there, and she pulled one side of the box down revealing the padding. She held her hand out, Diane handed her the box cutter, and Nexxa gently sliced through more tape and foam. When the seat was revealed, Diane came closer. Her eyes widened. She looked from Nexxa to Quinn. "Try it," Nexxa urged, motioning for Diane to sit. Quinn stood with his arms folded, a pleased look on his face.

Nexxa had Diane sign a document giving her approval of the sample leather chair in lavender. After she had "one more *whiff* for the road," an Irish phrase Diane changed to suit her, she informed them that she would be checking out of her hotel in Dublin and would go sightseeing around Ireland until the delivery date of the jet. Nexxa envisioned Diane whiffing her way amongst locals and donkeys. She told her to text her pictures of her travels and walked her out of the hangar.

"In my car," Quinn directed, motioning with his head. Nexxa lifted her purse, and Quinn grasped her hand. Nexxa looked down at their hands before he led her out of the hangar to his Mercedes. On the drive back into the city centre to Quinn's primary care doctor's office, they spoke very little.

"I'm Dr. Murphy. Nice to meet you, Ms. Davoren," he said, walking into the room. Nexxa sat on the exam table with her legs lowered. He politely asked her to push back so her legs would be upright. With her permission he pushed her legging up to examine her scar. At his gentle touch, Nexxa flinched. Dr. Murphy looked to Quinn before excusing himself. He returned with a nurse and asked Nexxa to change into a gown.

"I'll just step out," Quinn said.

"No. Quinn, stay," Nexxa spoke abruptly. The doctor and nurse left the room while she changed. Quinn turned while Nexxa removed her clothes and dressed in the gown.

"When was the last time you saw your primary care doctor?" asked Dr. Murphy once he returned.

"Well in Moscow I saw a doctor for my leg."

"And now, when was the last time you saw a gynecologist?"

continued Dr. Murphy.

Nexxa looked from the doctor to Quinn. "So, at this point, it's been about a year," she replied just as she felt a cramp and grasped her abdomen.

"Ms. Davoren," the doctor began speaking, "Nexxa, if I may, I insist in my care you should have a vaginal examination and then we will take a blood and urine sample." Nexxa looked over at Quinn, and she felt her eyes becoming heavy. He stepped over to her and took ahold of her hand before leaving the room.

The doctor, with the nurse present, began her gynecological examination, and Nexxa winced when he touched her breast with the scar. "What is the scar from?" he inquired.

"Oh it's just a scratch." She brushed off his question. He told her to relax her legs and continued with her vaginal examination.

"Is there any chance you could be pregnant?" inquired the doctor.

"No. No. Definitely not," Nexxa answered, feeling certain since she had had her period recently. The doctor left and the nurse prepared her supplies for a blood sample. With the needle just inserted in Nexxa's arm, she asked looking at Nexxa, "So how do you know Mr. Kane?"

Watching the tube start to fill with blood, Nexxa saw her blood coming out less than red and more like lavender. She yanked the needle out and said, "You know, I'm feeling lightheaded. I should just give a urine sample today."

"Oh, okay, Ms. Davoren," the nurse replied and when the lights flickered distracting the nurse, Nexxa took the opportunity to toss the needle and vial into the nearby medical waste bin. Standing she said, "I'll just use the bathroom now." Nexxa used the toilet and left the sample on the counter in the examination room. As she left, the young woman at the front desk said, "Ms. Davoren, we'll be calling you with the results of your pregnancy test."

Quinn drove with one arm propped against the window all the way to his home, only once looking over at Nexxa. He kept hearing, "Results of your pregnancy test."

"I think you should stay in the house, here with me," Quinn finally spoke as they stood in his driveway.

"I'm exhausted and I don't know why," Nexxa told him like she was turning down a date.

"Exactly. All the more reason that you should stay. Stay here and let me take care of you."

Nexxa stalled, grasping her forehead. "Quinn, there is something I need to do tonight."

"No, no, not this guy again." Quinn shook his head, allowing his face to show his disgust. "This guy left you. Told you to fu—" Quinn stopped himself and moved closer to Nexxa, touching her cheek. "Whatever you need to do. But I'm taking you."

"I'm… I need to go alone."

"Me fuckin' bollocks you're going alone," Quinn huffed.

Nexxa closed her eyes. She could smell the faintest of Crimson. She sensed Diane leaving the area. Part of her, the senseless part, wished Diane was staying in Dublin and would go with her to meet with Sergei.

"I don't belong to anyone," Nexxa finally responded when Quinn huffed again. "I don't belong to him but… But I need to know something. I'm not with anyone. So where does that leave me? Where the fuck do I live from now on?" Nexxa never imagined she'd be so unsettled and wishing to be around another with the wolfness, even if that person had wanted to harm her.

"Here," Quinn answered and motioned with his hand toward his house.

Nexxa shook her head. "I can't, I… I don't know."

Quinn grasped her hand and squeezed it lightly. "What time?"

"His message said nine p.m."

On the drive into the city centre, Nexxa felt flutters in her stomach. These weren't white butterflies, she decided as she looked out over the city lights while second guessing her decision to let Quinn drive her. Her phone pinged with a text from Sergei. Before she could read the message Quinn asked, "What does it say?"

"You're not alone. Change of plans. Spar on Chatham Street," Nexxa read aloud to Quinn.

"That's near my club," Quinn responded, looking over at Nexxa before he changed lanes. "What is this?"

"I don't know." Nexxa lowered her head holding her forehead. She knew this wasn't Sergei. She felt stupid. She felt angry and wasn't detecting his scent. "I think this is his tech guy." Quinn pulled up to the Spar and double parked. A guy with a smaller ego and vehicle than Quinn's started shouting for Quinn to move his Mercedes SUV. Quinn stepped out of the car and explained to him that he had a Glock.

Nexxa entered Spar. She looked at the East Indian man behind the counter and he smiled. She saw a dude down the way in aisle one looking at feminine products. *Hooli?* she thought. She walked down aisle one; he turned and quickly looked away. Nexxa stood beside him and lifted a box of tampons. Her hand trembled. He reached, touching her hand and easing the box back onto the shelf. He pulled his hood down and faced her. "Sergei," he spoke before clearing his throat, "he is..."

Nexxa grasped her abdomen. "Sergei's what?" Hooli shifted his shoulders and looked back at the products on the shelf. Nexxa touched his shoulder. "He's what? Sergei's what?"

Hooli repositioned taking an awkward step closer. "He, he wants to take Quinn down. Expose him." Hooli shifted his shoulders again and turned, smiling at a woman coming down the lane. Nexxa calmed her breathing. Images of a fetus, of an injured body, flying souls, all scrambled her mind.

She put a hand to her face. "Wait, so what does that mean? Is he still here in Dublin? His scent isn't. I mean, is he coming back?"

Hooli grabbed her shoulder. "No, but come with me." Nexxa looked back toward the front of the store. She saw Quinn standing outside in front of the door. She mouthed, *just a minute,* holding up one finger. Nexxa ran along with Hooli to the back of the store. They stopped in an aisle that had pet food. Nexxa thought about the kittens she had found in the bathroom in Sergei's house. She looked back down the lane thinking about the feminine care products, and how she had needed Sergei to go get her tampons. Now she was standing in a convenience store with bad lighting, a hacker in a hoodie, and her ride home was outside brandishing a Glock.

"Do you have a cat?" asked Hooli.

"Hooli!" Nexxa exhaled. "Look at me," she said, touching his arm.

He turned and without taking a breath blurted, "He will take Quinn down and you should get away from him, not be with him, like away."

"I'm not *with* him!" Nexxa lightly shouted, holding out her hands.

Hooli huffed.

"What? What? Tell me!"

"He knows you're *with* him. You know." Hooli tried to make an eye gesture.

"No. No. I don't know." Nexxa tried to lower her tone. "I'm not with anyone."

"I know," Hooli offered, looking sympathetic.

"You do? Then tell him," Nexxa spoke and then looked at a bag of organic feline food. It reminded her of Vlasta. "Tell Sergei I didn't fuck anybody!" Nexxa asserted. A woman in a hijab passed by her. She turned and actually gave a smirk. Nexxa huffed and gave the young woman a nod. "I have to go," she breathed, touching Hooli on his shoulder. "Be well. And tell him. I'm not done yet."

Nexxa pushed open the door and exited Spar. Quinn was standing with the bloke he had blocked in. They were both eating sandwiches. Quinn promptly wiped his face. He handed the bloke his sandwich and escorted Nexxa to the passenger door. She got in and buckled her seat belt. Quinn was swift getting in the car and driving off. He looked over at her a few times. She kept her gaze looking out of the passenger window. Hooli's words went round and round in her head.

"I need to go to bed. I need to think," Nexxa explained, pulling open the passenger side door once they were back at Quinn's.

"I really think you should stay with me," Quinn said with confusion on his face. She could feel the pain in her leg, and as if they were communicating, the scar on her breast began pulsing. Nexxa grasped her chest. She knew the pain needed to continue because it would help her sort through things.

"I'll be fine," she promised as she turned and started to walk around the side of Quinn's house to the guest house.

"Nexxa," Quinn called out.

"Let me be alone tonight!" she hollered.

For fuck sakes! Quinn yelled in his mind as he let her go.

Nexxa closed the door to the guest house and collapsed to her knees. She screamed, "Fuck! Fuck!" then she locked the door even though she knew Quinn could access the house if he wanted and that Diane could most likely scale the roof. Nexxa rolled her neck around. *What the fuck was Hooli talking about? I have to talk to Mr. Albert and Ezio.* She plugged her phone in to charge, undressed, and got into the shower. When she got out and saw herself in the mirror she couldn't tell if she looked defeated or enraged.

Her phone pinged. Nexxa stood with the towel around her as she lifted it. Her banking app showed that she had an alert.

She signed in and saw that a new deposit of three thousand was there. Nexxa could see the transaction was from Sergei's account. Since she had lived with him, monthly he would transfer over a few thousand and also gave her use of his credit card. She had barely needed any of his money, taking as little as possible to pay for the basics and help Iliada.

Lying back on the bed, her towel fell open, and Nexxa stared at the banking app. She enlarged the screen touching the space that showed his account reference. Tears of love breached the surface of her eyes when a text from Diane came through. Nexxa abruptly sat upright. Diane sent a selfie in front of Ashford Castle. She wrote: *Hi Nexxa! The castle is old. Lol. It smells like burnt croutons here.* Nexxa squinted her eyes, leaning her head to the side looking at the text. *What does a burnt crouton smell like?* She looked back in the banking app at the funds transfer. *What does this mean? If I called him, would he even talk to me?* Nexxa thought back to him telling her calmly, coldly, to get the fuck out of his hotel room. *Could I even forgive him?*

Nexxa walked to the kitchen and turned on the kettle, thinking about why Diane was being so nice to her. *I'm just going to call*, Nexxa thought as she held her cup of tea, feeling the steam against her face.

Sitting on the couch, Nexxa held her phone with Sergei's number visible. She blew out a small breath. She dialed. It rang a few times and she heard his voicemail, "You've reached Sergei Kozlov, leave a message." Nexxa stood and held her chest.

"Sergei, I want to talk to you. I have since the day in your hotel room. I want Natina and Ankica to know I love them. If you could *just* call me back." Nexxa caught her breath. "I have more I want to tell you." Nexxa heard the beep ending the recording and she let her phone drop to the floor.

Quinn had Kieran come around to his house late morning. He smelled of cigarettes and late-night debauchery as he made his way to Quinn's fridge. "Any of those Tippie Rolls?" he asked with his head moving around.

"I ordered breakfast. Here, have a cuppa," Quinn said in a subdued voice, pushing a cup of tea he had just made for himself over to Kieran.

"Right, so what is it?" Kieran slurped up a bit of tea.

Quinn stood facing Kieran, who sat at the kitchen island. He sighed, "Nexxa. I took her to meet with that fuckin' Russian blo—"

"What?" Kieran made a face that looked like he was more in pain from drinking the night before than shocked.

"She insisted to go alone. No fucking way was I letting her go alone! It wasn't this Sergei guy. It was his fuckin' hacker that showed up."

"His hacker?"

"Yeah," Quinn huffed.

"Why the fuck you didn't take me?"

Quinn's voice became more professional. "I need to find out what this guy wanted. What the hell is going on."

"What did he look like?"

"Like all hackers. Shifty white bloke in a hoodie." Quinn made an impression of someone hunched over, looking down.

Kieran thought back to the "tourist" he saw in the diner in Jobstown.

"Where's me food?" Kieran drummed his hands on the island.

Quinn shook his head. "So you'll get with it today, right?"

Kieran nodded his head. "Yes, boss, after I take me a leak."

Quinn's phone buzzed. He lifted it and saw a text from an unknown number. It contained a link to an audio and one for a video. Quinn tapped on it and listened, hearing:

"So it was Quinn Osian Kane that hired you to take pictures with Drake Suleiman before Kieran killed him?"

"Yeah, I told ya. Now are you going to shag me or not?"

When Kieran returned from taking a leak Quinn placed his phone down in front of him. He tapped on the link again and the recording started. Kieran stood back and folded his arms. "It's him. He sent it to ya."

"Him? Who? And how the bloody hell is Kessly involved?"

Kieran huffed. "The fuckin', man, the fuckin' bloke from Jobstown."

"Jobstown?" Quinn furrowed his brow.

"I told ya."

"Yeah, yeah. Right." Quinn nodded, remembering.

Kieran shook his head looking disgusted. "Your girl Nexxa. Kilmer, Paris. She's trouble. She's trouble."

"You better take care of this. Kessly," Quinn demanded, rubbing a hand over his head while looking out toward the guest house.

GRIM HEART | 37

Every question she asked, her pendulum refused to answer. Time and time again she had had white butterflies—now she felt like she needed Pepto-Bismol—all because of a Russian. Nexxa lifted her phone and, again, let her fingers call Sergei. The call went to voicemail. She heard his voice with each syllable carrying, caressing the dire feeling of the dark reaper in her abdomen.

Nexxa turned off her phone and plopped it down on the sofa. Her mobile buzzed anyway. She looked down at it. *That's Mr. Albert.*

"Hi, Mr. Albert," Nexxa answered.

"I see that you should come back to New York," Mr. Albert spoke with certainty. Nexxa could hear the early morning birds in the background. She imagined him walking the grounds of his estate in the dawn.

"I have accepted a job offer here in Ireland."

"There is red that has traveled across the sea," Mr. Albert responded, without alarming her, not mentioning page three thousand, a silhouette of a woman's face that had a tear in the middle pulling her apart, nor the footnote, *Cadaver/Anima*.

Nexxa had assumed her situation was under control in Ireland. "This is Diane," she spoke as if admitting guilt.

"The Crimson is bad. Not what you think, Nexxa."

She nodded her head even though he couldn't see her reaction. "She's also a client of Quinn's."

"Sergei. I see he is—"

"What? You see he's what?" Nexxa asked, her body becoming tense.

"Nexxa, you need to come back to here. To my home." Mr. Albert's voice was calm yet direct.

"What do you see? I can't see anything with him. My pendulum, nothing is working," Nexxa said, waving a hand in the air.

"What I see, you will see."

Nexxa closed her eyes. She could only see murk. No Crimson. No Russian. She turned and through the living room windows saw Quinn walking toward the guest house. "I have to go, Mr. Albert."

Quinn knocked on the door; Nexxa briskly made her way and unlocked it. She still had her phone in her hand. Quinn looked to her phone. Nexxa smiled with her eyes but simultaneously sensed he was unhappy. "You want tea?" she asked.

"No. How did your night go?" he probed, distracting himself from what he was concerned with.

"Good. I really just went to sleep. I did get a text from Diane. She is at Ashford Castle," Nexxa said in one breath, trying to divert herself from what she was thinking. Quinn remained silent. He looked around and then back to Nexxa as she started saying, "It looks beautiful. I would actually like to see—"

"What did he tell you?" Quinn questioned.

Nexxa thought about what Mr. Albert had just told her. But then as Quinn stepped closer to her, she knew he meant Hoolihane. Nexxa looked down at the rug and then Quinn was in her face. He pushed her hair behind her shoulder and grasped her hand. Nexxa released her grip on her phone, and he took ahold of it. He tossed it over to the couch. Nexxa rubbed her lips together. Her phone buzzed. Nexxa and Quinn looked over to the sofa. She wondered if it was Mr. Albert or Diane. "He's Sergei's hacker. So it's apparent he had something important to tell you."

Nexxa had no idea where her loyalty should lie. Sergei had told her to fuck off. Quinn had been there for her, but what Hooli told her was worrisome. So she had to be loyal to herself.

"He told me to get away from you and that Sergei had left Ireland."

Quinn grasped his jaw. Nexxa looked over to the kitchen. She thought about being in Rome with Kilmer and the knife he had used to cut cheese. "What's in the kitchen?" Quinn looked over, seeing her laptop on the counter. Nexxa knew she had a browser open and her personal email, as she was contemplating sending Ezio a message, to ask if he could continue helping her. Was Quinn going to insist on seeing her laptop, which was the one he had given her?

"Oh, I just thought that a cup of tea might be good right now."

"You've got some luggage to use?"

Nexxa thought for a moment. *Why is he asking this?* Before she answered, Quinn was walking down the hall to the bedroom. "So, yeah, I have the suitcase that I brought with me," Nexxa called out, taking a step and stopping before she walked toward the bedroom. She found Quinn standing in the middle of the room.

"How did you like this bed?" he asked, pushing down on the mattress.

"It is, was nice. Comfortable," Nexxa responded, looking over her shoulder. *Will Kieran be coming to drive me away? I guess I was a fool for thinking I had a job.*

"Pack your gear. I'm taking you to Ashford Castle," Quinn announced, stepping over to Nexxa and kissing her on the cheek.

Quinn offered Nexxa a mint in the car. "I'm okay," Nexxa told him without a hint of happiness.

"C'mon, what's wrong?" he asked, reaching and touching her arm.

"I'm fine."

"It's not like the mints are poison," he said, and laughed. Nexxa repositioned, looking out of the passenger window. Quinn swerved and took the next exit off of the M6. He pulled over on the side of the road and put his Mercedes in park. Turning to face her, he asked, "Nexxa, what's wrong?"

Nexxa closed her eyes before looking straight ahead and

saying, "Quinn, whatever could happen, I don't want to be in the middle of it or cause any problems."

Quinn sat back in his seat with his arm resting on the window grasping his chin. He knew he could cut her loose and deal with what was an impending problem. Not one that he couldn't sort out. Or the second choice: keep his heart alive. Quinn merged back onto the highway, and they remained silent for most of the trip.

About two hours into the ride, Nexxa asked him to stop so she could go to the bathroom. Quinn walked her into the petrol station and then waited outside by his car. Nexxa wrote out a text to Ezio while she stood at the mostly clean bathroom vanity. A woman entered, holding the door open while her toddler followed; Nexxa looked out but didn't see Quinn. She sent the text and waited, shifting her interlocked fingers together, for a free stall.

"You right?" Quinn asked as he put his car in drive, and they merged back onto the M6.

"Yeah, I think I'm just tired. I could use a run."

"That's a good idea. If you feel good enough. Your leg." Nexxa smiled at Quinn and leaned back, closing her eyes for the rest of the drive.

When they arrived, Nexxa grasped her chest. "Oh wow."

Quinn looked over at her with an almost accomplished grin before pulling up to the valet. They were greeted at the entrance with a glass of champagne and a bellhop promptly retrieved their bags, wheeling them inside. Quinn checked in and that's when Nexxa realized he had only arranged for one room. Part of her wanted to protest, and then she heard Sergei saying he would send her things to Dublin.

In the room Nexxa saw there was a king size bed with a red velvet bench at the end, dark blue velvet drapes and a separate living room. Quinn tipped the bellhop, and he left. "I'll sleep on the sofa," Quinn told Nexxa.

She walked over to the desk and placed her purse. Next, she pulled out some clothes, and said, "I'm going to change." Quinn shook his head in acknowledgment.

Quinn left the room and walked the grounds. He called Kieran. "We're still workin' on it. We've found him. It will take some time," Kieran said, before shushing someone in the background. The connection became spotty. "She's no good, though, that I can tell ya," Kieran spat off.

"Oh yeah, and what makes you certain?"

"Are ya jokin' me? Quinn, c'mon."

"For fuck's sake. This isn't about some fuckin' whore you're gettin' your rocks off with!" Quinn raised his voice.

"Oh like you never took a ride on Kessly."

"No. No. Never in me life did I touch that skank!" Quinn made a fist and the lines on his forehead strained. He heard Kieran talking to someone, most likely his hacker nephew. Quinn ended the call.

Nexxa had heard Quinn shout to her that he was going to go out for a walk and would be back in about an hour. She undressed in the bathroom and looked at herself in the mirror twisting, thinking she needed a tan or to start working out more, tone some. With only her panties on she crossed the bedroom to her luggage to retrieve her other bra, the one she used when not running but doing Pilates. She could hear chatter from guests out in the garden, so she walked through to the living room and peeked out of the window. A couple were seated at a table having drinks. When the woman took a call and left the table, Nexxa observed the man lightly bang his fist on the table. He sipped his drink, fidgeting with his cocktail glass. *Oh I wonder if she's having an affair*, Nexxa giggled a little in her mind.

Quinn returned to the room; Nexxa was unaware, captivated—watching, wanting to know what would happen when the elegantly dressed mature woman would return to the table. "Nexxa," Quinn called out. She let the curtain fall closed and cupped her breasts turning around. There was no time left to grab the sweater that was across the room or to dash back to the bathroom. "Oh sorry," Quinn remarked with a shocked face.

"I was only going to," Nexxa said, pointing toward the bedroom, thinking about changing from one workout bra to the other. Quinn chuckled, smirking. "Oh, shit!" Nexxa realized she had let go of covering her right breast so she could point.

She took a few steps toward the bedroom when Quinn said, "Wait a minute." She froze, feeling her breathing pause. *What is he doing?* she thought as he stepped over to her and touched her shoulder. "You have a ladybug on you," he said, lifting the bug and showing it to her. "They're good luck, like you." Quinn caressed her cheek. "Something I've always wanted," he told her. Quinn had been here before. The wanting, the almost kissing, to the sweetest taste when he finally had kissed her. She turned from him and walked away to the bathroom. As Quinn watched her tight bum walk away, he made a fist with both hands, grimacing. He would never force her to do something that she didn't want, that would push her forever away. *Long game, man*, he reminded himself.

"I thought we would go for a walk before dinner," Quinn hollered.

"A walk?" she called out from the bedroom as her mind went to Sergei. She and Sergei walking to his parents' cemetery and his crypt. "Quinn, like why are we here?"

Quinn exhaled. "I also got a text from Diane. She said she really liked you and was worried about you."

Nexxa grasped her forehead thinking, *She told Quinn she's worried about me? That's pretty personal, strange.*

"Nexxa?"

"Shouldn't we be working leads, retaining new clients?" Nexxa said sternly from the bedroom, accidentally letting her frustration out as she dressed.

"Look, let's have a bite to eat. Some more champagne?"

"Yeah, I guess," Nexxa conceded, half-plopping her sneakers down. "Don't worry, I'll keep my clothes on," she spoke with a self-deprecating tone, walking back to the bedroom and back to the closet. She pulled a black dress off of a hanger and slipped it on. "Okay, let's go," she said as she entered the front room.

Diane arrived at the next hotel on her list for sightseeing. As she walked through the lobby, she could see a wedding party taking photos out on the back garden terrace. She took a mental picture of the happy bride. Her silhouette. The groom's pride. In her room, Diane decided to order room service so she could continue working on her artistic project.

Her order arrived, lobster tails and fries. The waiter began explaining her dish, how it was prepared and her condiments. Diane grabbed a lobster tail, cracked the shell and took a large bite. His eyes bulged. She motioned to some cash on the dresser; he took a step, then moved over to it. Diane nodded. He took the cash, wished her a lovely evening, and left with his brain boggling.

After she stuffed her mouth with too many fries, some with mayo and some with ketchup, Diane wheeled her room service cart out into the hallway and onto the elevator; she pushed the button for the ground floor and hopped off with a wee second to spare before the doors closed. Back in her room she ran exceptionally hot water over her hands before drying them with the hair dryer. Sitting with her back straight, shoulders back, she laid flat the rendering she had started of Nexxa.

This first image she had drawn was *happy*. Tilting her head to the right then the left examining the drawing, she decided to make an adjustment. *No, draw in a series.* Diane moved that drawing to the side and removed the stationary from the hotel desk's drawer. Her index fingernail screeched around the paper again. This image had the same lovely woman's face and full body. Lovely perky breasts and shaved between her thighs. Now, the woman had the look of *bliss*. The third image, Diane drew with her fingernail a woman with a white veil covering her face. Beside her she drew a man. The woman was blonde. The woman was Nexxa. The man was Irish. The man was Quinn.

When they stepped out of the room Quinn grasped Nexxa's hand. "Is this okay?"

She looked to him and squeezed his hand just enough to let him know, and then he led them to the castle's cellar for dinner.

They were seated next to an older couple. The woman had fashionable grandmother hair, brown and above the shoulders. The husband had a typical head of gray hair and a slender face which matched the large hands that held his glass of white wine. The woman promptly introduced herself. "I'm Mary Ann."

Nexxa turned in her seat. "Hi, I'm Nexxa. This is Quinn." Nexxa held a hand out toward him. "Are you here for a special occasion?" Nexxa followed with a poised tone.

"Why yes, my dear." Mary Ann's eyes twinkled with the thoughtful question. "Today is our fiftieth wedding anniversary." She grasped the long necklace she wore that had a piece of jade on the end. Nexxa focused on her aging hand fidgeting with the stone. Quinn struck up a conversation with Mary Ann's husband, George. They both learned they were Irish, Quinn more so, and that they were both entrepreneurs. Nexxa heard Quinn's refined Irish voice intertwining with George's mature American accent while she listened to Mary Ann tell her how her legs hurt from flying even though they flew business class with fully reclined seats. Mary Ann continued on about the Delta Club—Delta Sky Club, she corrected herself, making eye contact with her husband—which they were members of. The seating was awful where they waited before their flight.

"So you're here for your anniversary. Is this your first time to Ireland, to Ashford Castle?"

"Oh no dear, our eldest daughter married a man from Dublin and our youngest daughter has decided to go to *university* here for her masters," she explained with her tone emphasizing university.

Nexxa looked over to Quinn. He winked at her. The waiter came around and refilled their glasses. George lifted his glass and proposed a toast to new friends and the four clanked glasses.

As the men continued conversing between bites of bread, Mary Ann leaned into Nexxa and whispered, "Now, is this attractive man your husband?"

Nexxa thought with her eyes looking up, seeing the cellar's graceful age. "Well, what I can tell you is that this is my first time here at Ashford Castle, and I don't think the pictures online do it justice." Mary Ann made an empathetic face and reached for her glass of wine, taking a long sip.

"Dear," she motioned for Nexxa to lean in and said, "when I met George, he hemmed and hawed and I said no, no, no. If you want Mary Ann, then you have to marry Mary Ann." She finished with a hand gesture that meant *no, no, not good enough*. Nexxa laughed and out of the corner of her eye she saw Quinn. Quinn, not Sergei.

Their appetizers were served and the four struggled to take breaks in their conversations to eat. The main courses were ordered, and while the men did good to eat, Nexxa and Mary Ann mostly pushed their food around. Mary Ann told Nexxa about her daughters. "My eldest, Nessa, is forty-five and has lived in Ireland for the past five years when her husband got a job transfer back to Dublin. Now, my youngest, Riona, well, she's a spitfire," Mary Ann explained, shaking her head before taking a sip of wine. George heard Mary Ann talking about Riona and summoned the waiter over, ordering another bottle of wine and some Midleton Very Rare Whiskey.

Nexxa leaned into Mary Ann. "So any grandchildren?"

Mary Ann shook her head. "Nessa is trying all sorts of IVF and whatever they do now, I don't think much of it. And my Riona, she wants a sperm donor!" she finished with a high tone, her face exaggerated. "And the worst part is that Nessa wants me here for her treatments. Monthly treatments!"

"What about a Lear Jet? You could have a customizable flight schedule." Nexxa gently rubbed one of Mary Ann's knees. "I hear that George is selling his share in Time Warner, and I bet if he doesn't make his annual donation to his preferred political candidate that would cover the cost of fuel. You might have to stay with your daughter; make her buy a good mattress for you." Nexxa looked Mary Ann in her eyes and smiled. When the waiter came around again, Mary Ann asked for a pen and paper. Nexxa thought back to asking for a pen and using a napkin in order to give Quinn's minder her number in his private club over ten years ago. Mary Ann wrote her full name and address along with her phone number. Nexxa asked for her fax number; she guessed that neither was using email.

When they parted ways, Nexxa hugged Mary Ann. She shook George's hand, feeling his handshake was firm, sincere, and kind all at the same time as he placed his other hand over theirs.

Leaving, Nexxa reached for Quinn's hand. She felt their past spark with his warm-blooded touch. When they were on their floor walking down the corridor with flickering wall sconces, Quinn stopped her before they reached the room. Alone, he whispered in her ear, "In any time, you are the one." Nexxa could smell the whiskey on his breath. She liked it.

LAVENDER LANE | 38

Nexxa ran on the treadmill that Quinn had waiting for her when they returned from Ashford Castle. She thought about how she told him it was "grand and gorgeous" as he laughed at how she mimicked an Irish accent. She tapped on the display seeing she had run three miles and stepped off. Drinking from her water bottle, she looked out of the kitchen window seeing that the trail for her to run on was almost cleared. *Am I supposed to be in Ireland or Moscow?* she wondered as she went outside to have a look. When her iPod began playing another song, she started to jog on the unfinished trail hearing Quinn say: *In any time, you are the one.*

In the shower Nexxa used a body wash she had just bought. It stung when she used some on her vagina. It honestly felt good, she decided. She heard Quinn's words again and it was as if something was blowing the smell of whisky and his cologne around her. She turned off the shower, barely drying herself, and positioned herself on her back on the bed. Nexxa let her thighs fall open and slowly moved her hand down her abdomen to between her legs. Her phone buzzed and simultaneously someone was knocking on the door to the guest house. Nexxa scrambled to find something, so she yanked the first black dress she saw in her closet and slipped it over her head.

"Hi," she answered the door with a breathy voice.

Quinn stood there for a moment before speaking. "Going somewhere?" he asked.

"No, no, I was just, you know," Nexxa replied as she twisted her wet hair into a low bun, pulling a piece through to hold it together. Quinn could see she wasn't wearing a bra. Nexxa took a few steps toward the kitchen. "I'm not going to have tea, but I'll make you a cup." She really wanted a glass of wine and to go back to the bedroom.

"No, I'm good. Don't make tea for me."

"So I was going to review the proposal and, in a few hours, fax it to Mary Ann," Nexxa explained as she stood on the opposite side of the island placing her hands on the counter. When Quinn didn't respond Nexxa said, "Because of the time difference." Quinn nodded.

"So… what are your plans for today? Did you try out the treadmill?" Quinn inquired, walking over to it in the living room. Nexxa nodded then realized he had his back to her. "Yes, I did. And I even ran on the trail outside."

Quinn spun around. "You did? It's not safe yet. Nexxa, you could get hurt." He moved over to her in the kitchen. Nexxa shivered. Quinn stepped closer and rubbed his hands along her arms. The left strap of Nexxa's black tank dress fell off her shoulder, and Quinn gently pushed it back up. Nexxa closed her eyes, and whisky with his cologne encircled her again. He caressed her face.

"I'm uh, Quinn, I'm…" Nexxa practically panted.

Quinn leaned in saying, "How about a glass of wine." Nexxa heard herself agree like someone was speaking for her.

He opened the wine fridge and removed a bottle of pinot grigio. Nexxa reached for two wine glasses and Quinn noticed her dress raise up in the back. *Behave. Control yourself, man*, he told himself.

Nexxa placed the glasses down on the island saying, "I'll be right back." In the bedroom, she left the door ajar. She took off her dress and she heard Quinn open the wine. Panties on, she slipped on a bra, then quickly found a tank top and her comfy leggings. Nexxa caught a glimpse of herself in the mirror over the dresser. She lifted a lipstick and dabbed some on. She shifted her shoulders contemplating spraying on perfume. She lifted the bottle. It was the perfume Sergei had bought her, so she placed it back down. Quinn's cologne wafted down the hallway and through the bedroom door. *Fuck, fuck me. I want to be fucked.* Nexxa blew her cheeks wide, making a silly face in the mirror. *Okay, just have a glass of wine. Talk about Mary Ann and then he will leave. Yeah, uh-huh, leave all the way back to his house.*

Quinn was holding a glass of wine and pressing buttons on her treadmill, *beep, beep*, annoying and all. Nexxa walked into the living room. "Quinn, should we talk about Mary Ann?"

He faced her and chuckled, "What's that?" before taking a big gulp of wine. Nexxa bit her bottom lip and looked to the kitchen island. Her laptop was as she had left it. A glass of wine was waiting for her. Quinn took a brisk step forward.

"I can get it," Nexxa told him as she grabbed her glass and made her way to the couch. "Sit with me." She patted the space beside her. Quinn sat at the end of the sofa. Nexxa put her legs up, bending one knee and letting her other leg reach to him. He grasped one of her feet and started to caress it. "Take off your shoes," she instructed.

"I might need a Scotch to do that." He laughed.

Nexxa shook her head saying, "Off." Quinn pulled off his suede loafers and socks, placing them neatly under the coffee table. He looked over at Nexxa.

Nexxa pushed up on her knees and motioned for Quinn to lie back on the sofa. He obliged and Nexxa grasped his left foot and started massaging it. "What do you know about me?" Nexxa asked.

"I know what you're comfortable telling me," Quinn responded. "I would love to know everything about you, my dear."

"I met Kilmer only in Dublin. It was a man named Patrick, older man, that I met in Canada that encouraged me to move to Ireland," Nexxa said without taking a breath before she let go of Quinn's foot and lifted the other. As she continued to massage, he closed his eyes, listening. Nexxa thought about her lavender glow and how her sister knew about it, Mr. Albert of course, and now Sergei. She wondered if it pulsed whether Quinn would be able to see it. Nexxa sighed.

"What is it, Nexxa?"

"I miss my sister. Part of the reason I need to work again is because I'm responsible for her."

Quinn sat up questioning, "She doesn't work?" Nexxa let go of his foot. He bent down and slipped on his socks and shoes before looking over at her smiling, continuing, "The best foot rub in my life."

"Well, it didn't work. I didn't think it was safe for us to be in the city. So we relocated to Mr. Albert's estate." Nexxa grinned before continuing, "And, that's when I met you again."

Quinn smirked. He finished his wine and stood, going to the kitchen and bringing the bottle back to refill their glasses. "Why weren't you safe?" he asked.

"I… honestly thought Kilmer was there. I mean, he lived in the city." Nexxa bit her bottom lip. She stood and walked looking out of the living room windows. She realized she could see Quinn's house; out of the kitchen window she saw where trees had been cleared for her, and in the living room she saw the treadmill Quinn had bought for her.

"Kilmer is dead. You're safe here with me." As Quinn spoke, he received a call. Nexxa looked back and could see Kieran's name on Quinn's phone. Quinn swiftly lifted his phone and answered, telling Kieran he would call him back. Something about how the phone rang and the timing told Nexxa that maybe she wasn't safe.

"I should check what I'm sending Mary Ann. You should call Kieran back. It might be important," Nexxa said grimly.

"Kieran can wait," Quinn responded, sounding irritated.

Nexxa huffed, "I just need to work."

"What is wrong? Huh? What is wrong?" Quinn asked, the lines on his forehead becoming intense.

"You tell me. You show up here the other day asking what Sergei's hacker told me. What should he have told me? You tell me I'm safe. Am I though?" Nexxa had raised her voice and could feel her lavender about to pulse. She lowered her head grasping her forehead. Quinn grabbed her and lifted her chin. He kissed her forehead and moved his full warm lips down the side of her neck. He pulled her top down and moved his lips down to kissing her chest where it met her breasts. "Quinn, Quinn," Nexxa breathed.

"I know. I know," he said, stopping and adjusting her top back. Nexxa moved his hand off of her. "I have some things I have to take care of. I'll let you start working," Quinn said with a half-hurt face before leaving. Only a few steps outside and he promptly called Kieran.

Nexxa watched as he crossed the lawn and entered his house through his kitchen.

It was approximately five a.m. in New York, but Nexxa called Ezio anyway. The call went straight to voicemail and she didn't leave a message.

Nexxa pulled up the proposal she had typed up the day before for George and Mary Ann. The jet she was recommending was more than she expected George would pay, but she knew Mary Ann could make a good case for the Lear 60, which was in excellent condition with a mid-size cabin and had been based in the Midwest. Nexxa was a fast learner, already able to compare jets for their engine times and engine maintenance programs. She didn't just want a sale. This would be personal, unlike Diane's purchase which had been established before Quinn had hired her. Nexxa included some aircraft operating cost reports; she knew that George could most likely look this up himself, but being that Nexxa had access to the app Quinn used, she wanted to be thorough from the start. After another glass of wine, Nexxa finally faxed the proposal to George and Mary Ann. From the kitchen she heard her phone ping several times. She had forgotten to check it earlier when Quinn had come over.

Diane had texted a few more selfies. One was with a donkey. Nexxa enlarged the picture wondering if it could be the farm Quinn had taken her to. Was it Pearl? Nexxa held a hand to her chest, and thinking about Pearl caused her to think about Natina. If only Ankica had a cell phone she could call. Check on the two of them. Explain why she was gone and that she wanted to—hoped to—be back. Nexxa sent a heart emoji to Diane's text with the donkey. Diane promptly messaged back.

Diane: *How are you?*

Nexxa: *I'm good. How's your sightseeing?*

Diane: *Quinn took you to Ashford??*

Nexxa: *Yes. How did you know?*

Diane: *I think he likes you* ☺

Nexxa: *I don't know what to do. Sergei said he was going to mail my things to Dublin.*

Diane: *He hurt you! NO! Bad man. Lol*

Nexxa: *Yeah. I know.*

Diane: *Quinn is a good man. You should be with him.*

Nexxa: *I'm still in shock over what happened with Sergei. Maybe I should call him one more time.*

Diane: *If a man wants to be with a woman. He moves a mountain.*

Nexxa: *I'll message you when I have an update on your jet!*

Diane: *Ok.*

Nexxa turned her phone off and went back to the kitchen. She filled up the kettle and turned it on. She leaned with her back against the sink and closed her eyes, rubbing her temples wondering why, why was Diane being so nice over Sergei. *Is she just trying to mess with me because we both have the wolfness?* When the kettle bubbled and clicked off, she jumped. She turned, looking out of the kitchen window. There, she saw a mountain, a metaphorical one which Quinn had moved for her. The trail that would be completed in a few weeks.

Diane withdrew her final drawing of Nexxa and drew in a diamond—a glimmering diamond from a downhearted Irishman.

MOUNTAIN | 39

The next day Nexxa awoke to workmen and machinery as work on the trail had resumed after a bank holiday. The guest house seemed unusually cold, so she pulled on a sweater over her chemise. Nexxa brushed her teeth and washed her face, noticing how she looked glamorous in the mirror. Her lips looked plump, and she had a glow. She pulled her hair tie out and tousled her hair.

Looking out of the kitchen window as she prepared tea, she saw workmen walking around the other side of the guest house. Nexxa walked over to the living room windows and saw that they were starting a walkway from the entrance of the guest house to the trail. Nexxa opened the door and inquired. They confirmed that the job was to build a walkway from the doorstep to the start of the trail. Nexxa looked to Quinn's house and then over to the start of the pathway and dashed toward his house. She could see him in his kitchen on the phone. As she approached the kitchen door, he started walking out of his kitchen toward the foyer. Nexxa pulled on the door handle, feeling it was locked. "Quinn. Quinn!" Nexxa shouted. When he didn't hear her, she turned and ran around to the front of his house. Quinn was in his Mercedes SUV pulling out of the driveway. Nexxa sprinted and managed to reach the back and hit the SUV. Quinn abruptly stopped and, still on the phone, hopped out walking to the front of his vehicle, inspecting.

"Quinn!" Nexxa yelled out of breath.

He lowered his phone. "Nexxa?" He walked to the back of his Mercedes. "Are you okay?" he asked, concerned.

"I'm okay." Nexxa twisted, pointing. "The men. They are…"

Quinn looked confused. "They are what, Nexxa? Did one of them do something?" he asked before ending his call.

"The walkway, the guest house," Nexxa spoke, her lungs tired.

Quinn embraced her and looked past her toward the side of his house. He could hear the machinery and men. "Are you okay?" he persisted, now rubbing his hands along her arms.

"You moved a mountain. For me," she told him, reaching to touch his face. Quinn leaned in kissing her. Nexxa pushed her body into his and allowed him to move his lips wherever he wanted.

Nexxa shivered and Quinn said, "You're cold. You're only in this. Let's get you back inside." Quinn dashed over to the driver's side of his SUV and turned off the engine and shut the door. Then, he dashed over to Nexxa, taking her by the hand, and walked her back to the guest house.

On his drive into Dublin, Quinn Osian Kane smiled.

SUAVE VODKA | 40

The dire of Dublin was ending. Sergei had sent Kessly home; she left *without* Sergei "come get me pussy" and he was now heading to the airport.

Vodka slid down his throat on the flight to Zagreb. He lifted the magazine from the seat pocket and flipped through, landing on an advertisement for a luxury resort in Switzerland featuring a woman in a red bra and panties and a suave-looking man with salt and pepper hair. The air hostess came around to the passengers in business class one last time before landing. Sergei ordered another vodka, and with strong hands he stuffed the magazine back in the pocket.

When he landed in Zagreb, he had his driver and friend Srđan pick him up and drive straight to the job site for the Croatian Federation Tower. It was dark and he could only stand outside of the eight-foot-high chain link fence. Tomorrow he was to resume meetings with the Minister of Physical Planning, Construction and State Assets, Ivan Jubić, and the general contractor. Srđan stepped out of the car and lit a cigarette, moving over to Sergei. He wasn't formally educated beyond communist era high school other than race car driving school, but it didn't take an Ivy League degree to see that Sergei wasn't bothered by the project; it was a woman behind those weary eyes.

He blew from his cigarette and put his arm around his friend. Sergei reached for his cigarette and took a drag. "It's bad?" Srđan asked. Sergei nodded. "C'mon, let's go. We have some drinkin' to do!"

Sergei sat in the passenger seat looking out at Zagreb's lights thinking how they were different from Dublin's or even Moscow's. They had an ambiance that if he were there with Nexxa he could enjoy. Srđan shifted into fourth gear and then patted Sergei on the shoulder saying, "It's gonna be okay, man."

"What, are we fucking boyfriends now?" Sergei groaned.

"Nah, man, it's just, you wanna be sad, okay."

"Yeah, I know." Sergei sounded remorseful as he turned to Srđan. "Sorry, man, I don't know what the fuck I'm doing."

Srđan parked and Sergei peered out through the windshield of the beat-up Opal. "A gentleman's club?"

"Hey, they have good food. The old lady in the kitchen is good cook." Srđan held his arms out mimicking a big woman's hips while laughing.

"Well I guess it's better than a men's spa with sausages everywhere," Sergei huffed, opening the car door. Inside they were seated slowly by a young, unenthused, and unimpressive-looking woman. They grinned at each other with wide eyes before trying to contain their laughter. At the table they ordered drinks and the only option for the night, which was the "special." Surprisingly, the drinks came quickly, and they turned to watch the show. A woman dressed in lingerie and thigh-high tights sauntered around on the tiny stage in a hopeful way. It was a sad attempt at a burlesque performance. A couple of minutes passed and the food, a chicken dish with dumplings, was served. They both started and the table fell silent as they forgot about the woman on the stage. Sergei slopped up the sauce with bread like a savage and once finished sat back feeling good. Not as good as he would feel if he were back in time, back to when Nexxa was on his lap by the fire pit though.

While he was in a meeting on the job site with the general contractor, Sergei mostly paid attention but looked at the calendar on his phone. The month was still June. His babushka called and he pushed the button to silence the call. He placed his phone down with "Babushka" flashing on the screen. He had gotten her a cell phone before he left to seek out Nexxa in Ireland and was surprised by how well she adapted to using it. Natina was excited too, so he had downloaded some apps for babies on the phone for her.

When the meeting was over, he called her back as he walked around looking at the foundation that had just been started. "Babushka, how are you? How is the baby?"

"Ah, my Sergei. We are okay."

"I'll need to be here at least a few more weeks," he said, avoiding what he felt as he rubbed his hand over his head.

"Krasnyy." Ankica's voice was cracking and her hand trembled holding the phone.

"What? Babushka, what is Krasnyy?" Sergei had hired a woman temporarily while Vlasta was out with her injury to help his grandmother and the baby. She came over to Ankica and took the phone from her hand, placed it on the table, and tapped on the speaker button. She told her in Russian to just speak and that he would be able to hear her.

"Nexxa. The Krasnyy wants her. Eh, Sergei, you need to go to her."

Sergei lowered the phone shaking his head. "Babushka, I… I'll try." Sergei ended the call and then with his hands in fists he screamed like the Hulk. A construction worker looked over, and Sergei made eye contact with him before charging his way. The guy's eyes widened, and Sergei asked for a cigarette. Luckily, the man had a pack in his pocket. He lit Sergei's cigarette, and Sergei thanked him before motioning to a folding chair. The guy nodded and Sergei sat down. He took another drag and then went into the last text message he had from Nexxa. The one he had ignored where she asked about his family.

He typed out a text: *I need to talk to you. Call me.*

He sent it, and when he finished his smoke, he listened to her voicemail.

Nexxa listened to a message that resurrected her ego. Mary Ann had called and left Nexxa a very kind response to her proposal. Promptly, Nexxa emailed George's wealth manager a copy of the proposal and wiring instructions for Quinn's business bank account. She had made Quinn a couple hundred thousand profit from one night of being her gorgeous, irresistible soul.

  Nexxa packed her clothes and stripped the sheets from the bed. She watched as Quinn collected the trash from the bathroom and the kitchen and then came to her bedroom to take her suitcase. It was one of the more heartwarming things he had done for her. He closed the door behind them and locked it with the keypad. They entered Quinn's house through his kitchen, and he wheeled her suitcase toward his stairs. Nexxa paused in the kitchen looking toward the pantry.

There wasn't any food. She continued walking toward the staircase. The buttercup curtains were gone from the front room. She looked to Quinn, who was standing before the first step. She saw the man who had caught her in Howth. The man who had introduced her to Pearl. The man that had given her back her pride.

Quinn brought Nexxa along with him to his private club. He was selling it and needed to meet the man who was taking over. Nexxa waited for him at the bar while he met with the prospective buyer in his office. Quinn was ready to focus on his aircraft broker company, Q. Osian K. LTD., and his partnership in The Westbury hotel. She declined the bartender's offer of a white wine spritzer, and then as she ran her hand along the bar she felt her younger self and reimagined the night Kilmer had brought her there. "Yes, I'll have it," she said, succumbing to alcohol at ten in the morning. After a few friendly exchanges with the bartender, Nexxa took the last sip of her drink and decided to leave. She asked him to let Quinn know she would be waiting outside when Quinn left his office.

Nexxa walked down the street from Quinn's club. She liked the feeling of being in an overstimulating environment. Alone, yet not. She could hear the difference in footsteps and detect the varying Irish brogues. A Brit here or there, someone from Northern Ireland and the occasional tourist. She continued until she saw a corner shop. Nexxa thought she had walked in the direction of the Spar, but she hadn't. This shop was a bit run-down and looked to have been taken over by Pakistanis. She pulled open the door, and as she stepped in smelled the sweetest yet most overwhelming incense. Her head felt heavy as the man behind the counter greeted her. Nexxa smiled and approached the counter, lifting some mints and placing them by the register. She quickly paid, thankfully she had some cash, and waved him off when he tried to give her change, exiting before her heavy head turned into a headache. Nexxa opened the mints, white Tic Tacs, and they smelled like incense, so she tossed them in a rubbish bin on the sidewalk.

Quinn finished his meeting, and when he stepped out of his office, he looked around at the empty bar area. The bartender was on the phone, and he motioned with his head toward the door. Quinn felt heaviness in his chest as he dashed outside. He looked both directions and didn't see Nexxa. Nexxa looked both directions and crossed the street walking up behind him. "Quinn," she said with a happy voice, touching his back. He spun around and wrapped his arms around her. Nexxa closed her eyes and inhaled him. "I bought some mints."

"You're okay?" Quinn questioned, kissing her on the forehead.

"Yeah, but my mints aren't. Weren't," she responded, looking up at him.

"I thought you were going to wait at the bar."

"Well, yeah. But, I thought about Kilmer and—"

"Next time *tell me*. Tell me where you're going."

"Quinn, I told the bartender." Quinn exhaled. "Hey, it's okay. I'm fine," Nexxa offered, tugging at Quinn's hand. "I'm with you."

As Nexxa spoke, Quinn thought about her words. How could he ever feel like she was truly "with him." Truly his. His worry showed in his eyes, and then something, like someone encouraging her, tugged at her. "I'm not going anywhere," Nexxa added as she took his hand and interlocked their fingers. "Besides, behind every successful man is a woman. Isn't that the correct answer on Jeopardy?" Nexxa remarked with her fuckable brown eyes.

Quinn grinned and patted her bum. "Yes, you are correct," he said right before he pushed her against the building and kissed her like he was making her his. "C'mon." Quinn grasped her hand. "Let's go celebrate."

When they exited the car, Nexxa saw a few restaurants. Quinn took her hand and led her toward a shop, a local jeweler. *Okay, I guess he's picking up a watch he had repaired.* Nexxa noticed how the man in a suit and the woman with plumped lips seemed to be waiting for their arrival. While the atelier was nondescript from the outside, the inside was equally unimpressive. Nexxa anticipated the watch that had been repaired as Quinn made small talk with the man whom Nexxa presumed was the owner.

Quinn turned to Nexxa. "I have something I want you to see." The suited man led them to a door that when it was opened revealed a narrow hallway. Nexxa closed her eyes and clenched Quinn's hand. "We're only going to the back," Quinn whispered in her ear. A much better-looking room, quaint and a little musty, with an old monarchy feel awaited them. The lady with the lips sauntered in behind them, closing the door and locking it from the inside. Quinn moved over to the velvet loveseat and sat down. Nexxa stood in the middle of the room spanning it with her eyes. The ceiling was wallpapered with a gothic pattern, and the original fireplace and mantle had been painted black. Quinn motioned for her to sit beside him. *So it's either a sex room, human trafficking, or off with me head*, Nexxa laughed in her mind.

With a giggle still in her hesitant mind, Nexxa sat her bum next to Quinn, crossed her legs and held her shoulders back. Before she could adjust her mindset from gothic horror film to everything a girl could dream of, a display of diamond jewelry was presented on the gold and glass coffee table before them. Quinn leaned forward and touched a few pieces. He held up a necklace. Nexxa followed the beam from the diamond around the room as Quinn dangled it on one finger. Before she could calibrate her eyes, he was standing over her and undoing the clasp and closing it around her neck. She felt the diamond that was so immense that it begged to burn into her heart etching, *Quinn Osian Kane*.

Sitting at the quaint table in the same Italian restaurant that Quinn had taken her to, Nexxa couldn't resist touching her diamond necklace. Quinn stared at her while they were supposed to be perusing the menu. He couldn't resist imagining her with a diamond ring on, and maybe a baby bump. Nexxa looked up from her menu. "What, what is it?" she asked.

Quinn looked to his menu and cleared his throat. "I think we should order some mussels."

"Okay," Nexxa agreed.

The wine was served, and Quinn held up his glass. Nexxa raised hers. "To a lovely day with you." Quinn grinned as they clanked wine glasses.

Nexxa took a sip. "Thank you for sharing red wine with me tonight," she said, twisting the bottle while looking at the label. "This is much better than the Tic Tacs I had earlier." Quinn chuckled, but in his bold mind he was still making plans for their future, even more so since he had received a call from Dr. Murphy. Nexxa wasn't pregnant with a Russian bastard.

Quinn answered his phone. "Fuck me," he said to Kieran as he lay next to Nexxa, who was asleep. He jumped out of bed and pulled on his lounge pants. Looking back at Nexxa he whispered into his phone, "I'll be down."

Downstairs in his kitchen he drank a glass of water while waiting for Kieran. He walked around in the dark of the front rooms of his home, finally seeing the lights of Kieran's Range Rover pulling up to his house.

"Why ya whisperin'," Kieran asked as Quinn let him in.

"Nexxa's upstairs," Quinn replied motioning with his head. Kieran made an unpleasant face, showing he was shocked and displeased before he made his way to the kitchen and opened the fridge, ducking his head in looking for whatever. "So you finally got into her knickers, huh," he said with a snicker.

"No, it's not like that. I'm taking it slow."

"Takin' it slow? Ya not gettin' your hole?" Kieran let out a bellow as he pushed aside some milk finding the last beer. Quinn stood with his arms folded on the opposite side of the kitchen. "What's up with the buyer for the club?" Kieran asked when Quinn remained silent.

"I should close the deal by the end of the week."

"Why are you doin' this? I saw Kessly." Kieran started

mimicking fucking a woman from behind. "She's ready for the next job."

Quinn nodded with a disinterested face to what Kieran had to say.

"You know, she told me about that Russian arse," Kieran quipped as he took a gulp from his beer. "I thought we were going to keep the club to run the money through. Now you're gonna mess with that, selling it," Kieran mumbled, pointing his beer bottle at Quinn.

Quinn's dedication to keeping the peace, between a Loyalist like himself and the INLA, was waning. He felt it was time to pass the torch and remove himself from the cause. What he hadn't told Kieran yet was that he was planning to give most of the money from the sale of the club to him. For Kieran to do as he pleased. Fuck all the Spanish women he could in the Costa del Sol. Or he could choose to put the money back into the cause for maintaining peace in Ireland. Quinn admired the part of Kieran that had started clubs for young teen boys in dodgy neighborhoods—Jobstown, in particular. To show them the right way and that all could exist, Loyalists, Catholics, and the INLA.

Quinn grasped his chin, rubbing it before he spoke. "It's time I step back."

Kieran took a sloppy sip of his beer and squawked, "What the bleedin' hell?"

Quinn nodded slowly. "My priorities have changed. I have the hotel and the jets," he offered as he shrugged his shoulders, standing with his arms folded.

"We have the new job lined up. Kessly, me nephew, the

boys!" Kieran's voice became louder. Quinn remained still, offering nothing else. Kieran poured the backwash from his beer in the sink and let the bottle drop rolling around. Quinn watched as Kieran groaned and walked out of his kitchen and out of the front door before speeding off.

Quinn made his way back to his bedroom and got back into bed, turning on his side and putting an arm over Nexxa. The truth was his priorities were aligning before he had seen her in his hotel. Now that she was here, she was his ultimate conquest. He had moved a mountain for her without even realizing it. She had a diamond on from him and was in his bed. Quinn closed his eyes. *Take it slow*, he told himself suppressing his erection before he managed to drift off to sleep.

Nexxa walked around Quinn's entire house in the daylight without anyone else there. He had gone to the hotel and left her after they had tea together. She liked that the house seemed empty, almost barren. Nexxa decided to start with the neglected pantry. As she wiped off all the shelves, she sensed a woman before her that was disenchanted. Not necessarily unhappy with Quinn, but with herself. *How could you not want to be with Quinn?* she thought. She opened a kitchen drawer, finding a scrap of paper and a pen. She saw a key on a key chain with the initial R. Nexxa lifted the key chain, feeling its weight. She heard laughs and then silence. She felt wisps of air going and coming out of the front door and the kitchen door.

It felt too quiet, so she wandered into the den and found a remote, getting lucky finding the right button and turning on the TV. Sky News blared, so she flipped through finding the adult channels. She stopped, intrigued by an Italian porn with a laughable plot. Nexxa sat on the cold dark burgundy leather sofa and started making a list for the kitchen. When the plot thickened and Nexxa decided to change it, she fumbled with the remote and it plopped on the floor. Nexxa bent down to get it and noticed that the immense wood coffee table had drawers. She opened one and saw some magazines. They were old issues, from about ten years ago, she saw as she pulled a few out. She flipped through a bridal magazine noticing a few markings and some pages that had been turned down in the corner. The dresses they donned looked like something Nexxa would have liked, albeit ten years ago to be consistent with the trend at the time. Nexxa ripped a page out with a dress she liked, thinking that she and Quinn's ex-wife had similar styles.

Later around lunchtime Quinn returned and found Nexxa at the kitchen island checking her email and sipping a cup of tea, since that's all there was besides bottled water. He kissed her on the cheek. "How are you? Should we order takeaway?"

"I'm good. I cleaned the pantry," she answered, closing her laptop and standing from the barstool. "Want to see?" She smiled.

"Yeah, yeah." Quinn nodded, smiling.

Nexxa pointed to the back shelves. "Here I can put things I won't use as much. And on this side, I was thinking dry goods like pasta. And on this side, I don't know, some cleaning supplies."

Quinn looked around using his imagination since it was

empty and had never really had anything for the shelves to hold. He grasped her face with two hands and kissed her saying, "Thank you."

"I made a list of some things I will need for when we go shopping," she said when Quinn took a breath, releasing her lips.

"Okay. Sure, we can go back to London," he responded with enthusiasm.

Nexxa laughed, explaining, "No, I mean to the store for food. Like a supermarket."

Quinn thought with his eyes looking up, "I can drive you."

In the supermarket Quinn pushed the cart and found himself looking around more than steering in the right direction. "Why don't you stay right here," Nexxa suggested, pointing to the end of a lane. Quinn stopped and pulled out his phone. A few minutes later Nexxa returned plopping in a variety of meat, cheese, olives, bread, and some condiments. Quinn quickly lowered his phone, showing he was present. "You can keep looking at your phone. I'm not done," Nexxa joked and left again.

Quinn scrolled through the news, switching back and forth to his email. Nexxa returned with pasta and some items from produce. At checkout as Quinn unloaded the cart, Nexxa zoned in on a bridal magazine. She lifted it and ran a finger over the white lace veil the woman was wearing. As the items moved along the belt, Nexxa laid the magazine down and flipped to page fifty-two. "It's the same. The same dress," she spoke to herself. The clerk had finished ringing up the items and asked if she wanted the magazine. Nexxa flipped to another page that contained the featured lace veil.

Quinn stepped over to Nexxa and put his arm on her shoulder. "Nexxa, do you want me to get the magazine?" He looked down, realizing the model was wearing a wedding dress and veil.

Nexxa looked at him. "I don't know. It just looks so pretty," she explained with distraught yet excited eyes. Quinn gently closed the magazine and handed it to the woman, who by then seemed irritated.

In the house Nexxa arranged items in the fridge and the pantry. "I'm so tired. I don't know why," she spoke softly as she walked over to the tea kettle, reaching to turn it on.

"I'll make you some tea. Why don't you go lie down?"

Nexxa agreed and Quinn watched, making sure she climbed the staircase safely. The kettle boiled and he prepared her a cup of tea. He lifted the magazine from the kitchen counter and carried both upstairs. Nexxa was lying in her tank top and panties on his bed. Quinn placed the cup of tea and magazine on the nightstand. He pulled the duvet over her.

Downstairs, he grabbed a beer and went to his den. Sitting on the couch, he noticed a piece of paper on the coffee table. Lifting it, he realized it was a picture of a bride torn from a women's magazine. He laid it back down and lifted the remote to turn on the telly. Italian porn was on. Nexxa had never changed it, only turning off the TV. Quinn chuckled. *Italians are shagging and this Irish bloke wants to get married again.*

NEXXA KATE REYHAN | 42

Quinn closed the deal on his club. He bought a black Mercedes GLA SUV for Nexxa. He hadn't forgotten her requirement to have her own car. Quinn picked her up and drove them further out of the Dublin area. They swapped seats, and Nexxa started down the road, on "not really the right side," as she had told him. A mile, then a left turn, and continuing on, Nexxa drove—even managing to look over at Quinn without straying to the wrong side of the roadway.

Nexxa pulled off of the road and into the parking lot of a restaurant. She parked with ease over on the side that bordered an empty lot and took off her seat belt. Quinn unlatched his and reached for the door handle. Nexxa reached, touching his thigh and moving her hand along, so he pulled his hand back. Nexxa slithered her fingers over his crotch and started to undo his jeans. Then, they heard a loud bam. A lorry had parked next to them and the driver exited, slamming the back door shut after removing some boxes for delivery. Nexxa laughed and Quinn said, "Bleedin' hell."

Quinn drove on the way home, stopping at a Thai restaurant for takeaway. Nexxa didn't care what they ordered, and only asked Quinn for some wine to go. He told her to hold tight and walked next door to the shop while their food order was being prepared. With the food and Nexxa's car wine, they continued to his house.

Back home, Quinn placed the food on the kitchen island and started to open the bag. Nexxa stood on the opposite side watching him. She had almost tasted Quinn and that desire mixed well with the taste of car wine. As Quinn rattled off what he had ordered while he pulled containers from the takeaway bag, Nexxa came up behind him and placed her arms around him, moving a hand slowly to his groin. Quinn moaned and spun around grasping her, pushing her hair back and kissing down her neck to her breasts.

With his help, Nexxa hopped up on the island and Quinn removed her leggings and she laughed as he shimmied down her panties, finally getting them off.

As Quinn started with his clothes, Nexxa looked to the panties he had dropped on the floor. "Quinn, Quinn," Nexxa breathed. "I, I can't. I'm sorry," she said.

"I know. I don't want to rush you."

"No, it's just that..." Nexxa pushed his face saying, "Look." Blood. She had started her period.

"It's okay," he said, turning back and kissing her.

"Quinn, I'm so sorry," Nexxa whispered, caressing his face

just as a helicopter flying over his neighborhood, his home was heard. A vision of being in a helicopter with Sergei rushed her mind causing the feeling that her time of the month was a perfectly timed blessing.

Quinn kissed her forehead and then lifted her panties from the floor saying, "In any time, you are the one."

A few days had passed and Nexxa worked diligently making the walk-in pantry into something more than a room with bare feelings. She insisted on cooking dinner and Quinn rushed home through Dublin traffic each night to be there on time. He had had the treadmill moved from the guest house into his house, pushed for the trail behind his home to be finished and put pressure on the crew to complete Diane's jet that was being outfitted with custom lavender seats.

When the customization was done and the jet scheduled for a final walk-through with Diane, Nexxa received an email from the Italian designer that the manufacturer needed to recall the mechanism in the custom leather seats that was used to recline them. Nexxa called Quinn to give him the update. "Have you already informed Diane?"

"No, no," she told him. "It would be better to plan an excursion. A girls' trip, to divide and conquer the circumstances!" Nexxa said playfully. She didn't mention that in Rome, where she had once detected Crimson, would be a good destination to settle her "wolfness business" with Diane.

"And that's why, in any time, you are the one," Quinn replied with a smile across his heart.

Nexxa called Diane. She was in the middle of fantasizing,

watching a younger version of Kate Moss behind the bar in the pub she was in. Nexxa caught her up on moving into Quinn's home and her new trail. Diane did a few Kegels as they spoke. Another pint was served, and as she sipped listening to Nexxa, she lost track of her story about a trip to Rome thinking about fucking wannabe *wish you could be Kate.*

Quinn's Irish blue eyes swelled more than his hostage-held heart could pound. Nexxa let him push her hair back and stroke her cheek before reaching to touch a tear on her face. Quinn kissed her and Nexxa made her way through security.

Rome felt—to one with the wolfness—like a wine cellar to a lush. Nexxa let her head roll before looking straight, pulling up her black hood and making her way to her driver. "Est prosecco retro," the driver told her. Nexxa let out a wolf's breath hearing his Italian accent speak Latin. She drank just the right amount to have courage to coddle a client—another with the wolfness… but to not forget about Quinn.

Nexxa checked in to her hotel, Hotel dei Barbieri, which was known for its exquisite stone and for being hypoallergenic. She showered and dressed without perfume or panties and then took the elevator down to the lobby and out to the driver, the one that Quinn had arranged for her stay in Rome. She texted Diane and she responded that she had eyes on Nexxa and was about to exit the hotel as well.

The drive was eloquently quiet and stimulating at the same time. Roman lights and wafts of passed souls permeated the Maserati Levante on the journey to a private event, where Quinn had added Nexxa's name last minute to the guest list, along with Diane's. Standing at the foot of the steps Nexxa smiled, holding her hand out for Diane. The first step steadied them, and then each century-old step incurred a hairline fracture until they reached the man who looked like a *vampire model*. He scanned Nexxa's Brit e*Post* invite and with a slithering smile turned looking toward the entrance signaling their clearance to enter.

Diane trailed Nexxa, as Nexxa took long sensual strides, inhaling the lilac between her legs. A server approached her in the space between them; Diane pushed the woman aside, barely declining the glass of champagne. She followed Nexxa as she weaved one leg at a time through the pulsating music and scantily clad Eurotrash. There were people dancing, a DJ flanked by seductive women in cages, and further through a lounge, masked men and women who were engaged in outercourse. Nexxa approached the bar and once again held her phone out to be scanned. She knew Diane liked top-shelf liquor and velvety wine. A tall male with icy blonde hair and piercing emerald eyes, another *vampire* model, emerged from the back and directed them to an opulent seating arrangement. Nexxa placed her bum down and crossed her legs. Diane moved in and sat opposite her in a regal royal blue and gold chair. She moved her hands along the arms. The sparkling red vino was opened and the vodka was mixed with something that smelled like resurrected angels. Nexxa held up her wine glass and winked at Diane. The song changed, a man behind them moaned in pleasure, and before Nexxa could calm her breathing Diane had moved, sitting next to her. She glanced down at the gold settee. It was strong enough to absorb Diane's vibration. The steps outside hadn't been. Nexxa realized the settee was the same as an antique she had known growing up with her grandmother. Familiar, comforting.

"I see Quinn has been treating you," Diane commented while leaning close enough for her hair to graze Nexxa's arm as she lifted the diamond that dangled in between Nexxa's breasts, twisting it with her fingers.

"He's the reason why we're here." Nexxa flipped out her hand as if presenting the party. Quinn used the event to recruit clients. Women mostly, that wanted to be seduced, wished their affluent husbands offed. He couldn't have Kieran attend; he wasn't refined, only had experience fucking skanks. But Nexxa, she would attract the wealthy from both sides of doomed marriages… or at least those that were looking for a new Lear Jet.

"You love him?" Diane questioned with a giddy face.

Nexxa touched her diamond and said, "I think… yeah I—"

"Excuse me," a man approached them. "Is this area neutrally?" he asked with a look that said *I'm down to fuck if you ladies are.*

Nexxa and Diane laughed at him. At his broken English. Their personal waiter came around, the icy blonde *vampire* model, and when his emerald eyes bore into the Indian man, he turned on his heel and was off. Their drinks were replenished and an offer was presented by an invitation. Nexxa took a large swallow of her wine and opened the envelope. The note addressed her by her first and last name, Ms. Nexxa Davoren. Diane wasn't included on the invitation. She glided a finger along her bottom lip as she read the card. The invite was to join a couple in a private room. Nexxa looked around. In every corner there was a masked woman fondling a man. They each seemed to make eye contact with her. "Maybe we'll go after this drink," Nexxa suggested to Diane.

"Why? What does it say?" Diane reached for the invite.

Nexxa tossed the invite and it effortlessly landed on a candelabra, igniting.

"You love Quinn, don't you?" Diane pressed again.

Nexxa tilted her head. "I guess we'll see."

Diane stood holding a hand out for Nexxa. "Let's go."

"I don't know, maybe I will join them," Nexxa suggested with a tad wicked, tad joking smirk, dancing in her seat.

Diane grasped her head. "Oh, I just feel so tired. Too much vodka," she giggled.

Nexxa sighed. "Sure, sure, we can go. I'll text the driver."

In the car, Nexxa held up Diane's head on her shoulder using a hand to compensate whenever her head rolled down. Without warning their route changed and the driver swerved to take an exit off the highway. He pulled into a petrol station and fled the driver's seat giving no explanation. Nexxa looked through the windshield and then through her window which was dimmed for protection, so she saw nothing. With awkward maneuvering, she positioned Diane's head on the headrest of the seat next to her and adjusted the seat belt to support her head. Nexxa unlocked her door and stepped out, closing it. A few steps in her heels, she shivered as she scanned the parking lot. She saw cars at the pumps with mostly men and one waved at her. Nexxa pulled at her hem and started walking to the convenience store.

A man in an older gray Peugeot pulled out of a parking spot and rolled up to her as she continued walking. With his window down, he asked her how she was doing. Nexxa ignored him and he persisted, finally stopping his car and stepping out. His hand grazed the back of her Alexander McQueen black lace bustier and was just taking ahold of her arm when Diane appeared in front of them. Nexxa twisted out of his grasp, and he froze in Diane's gaze. His friend hopped out of the passenger seat and at the same time their personal driver emerged from the convenience store shouting *fuck off* in Italian.

The ride back to the hotel was not filled with all of the Vampy feelings that it consisted of on the ride to the private party. The driver apologized profusely in English explaining that he had to go to the toilet and that was the reason for the sudden diversion. Nexxa told him to apologize in Latin and that only then would she forgive him and then she winked.

Back in their hotel, Nexxa walked Diane to her room and in return she insisted on walking Nexxa back to hers. Nexxa gave Diane a kiss on the cheeks and sensed something she had yet to understand.

Her phone vibrated, and Nexxa saw it was Quinn. She hurried to wipe and flush, answering as she was washing her hands. "Hi," she said with a soft voice.

"I wanted to see how you were this morning," Quinn spoke with a calm, direct voice.

"Okay, I'm okay." Nexxa put her hand to her mouth.

"How was the event?"

"Good, good." Nexxa lifted her toothbrush. She hurriedly brushed her teeth silently, doing her best not to push the button on her electric toothbrush.

"How is our client?" Quinn really wanted to ask how many men, or women, hit on her at the party. And did she forge any new friendships. He knew if he asked he would sound jealous. The truth: He wasn't jealous, but it could be lucrative if she had made some acquaintances. But, for the first time in his life his ego was worried about losing someone.

"She's okay," Nexxa answered as she swooshed her mouth with water. "Sorry, I wanted to brush my teeth."

Quinn laughed, "You needn't do that to talk to me."

"No, even if I talk to you on the phone, I need to be clean. I mean, I miss you," she explained walking back to the bedroom looking at her black bustier and skirt on the chair wishing Quinn had removed them from her body the night before.

"You've got enough money?"

"I think so." Nexxa moved over to her purse, and before she looked in, she received a text from Diane.

Diane: *Brunch? My treat?*

Nexxa: *Okay, need to shower.*

"I'll call you later. When should I call?" Quinn was quick.

Nexxa thought for a minute. *Should I wash my hair or use dry shampoo?* She walked over to the armoire and opened it. Her black was lacking.

Diane: *Shopping after?*

Nexxa: *Ok.*

"Nexxa?"

"Oh, yeah, so we can go. I have enough money," Nexxa answered Quinn.

"I'll call you around eight," Quinn said confidently. He ended the call and braced himself with his elbows on his kitchen island, clasping his hands together and lowering his head.

Nexxa tasted the freshness of a recently cracked egg, then the hatch of what could have been. The prosecco went down her throat like a first love, but then breaking her heart… intense, leaving her wanting more. But, when a waiter began lighting candles, even though it was only eleven and the light was annoying the outside, Nexxa moved her hair over one shoulder and flashed Rome her inner happiness.

Diane flirted with the waiter as she settled the bill and Nexxa assessed her mannerisms and inhaled wisps of her breath trying to discern if she was tipsy or faking. Leaving the restaurant, she offered her a piggyback ride being silly, and Diane accepted. Nexxa had core strength and had always told herself if she had to, she could carry someone away from danger—or an enemy to the grave. So along a strip of Italian ateliers Nexxa carried Diane on her back, and right about as she approached a bridal shop Nexxa realized that her wolf friend was weightless.

Diane hopped down and said, "We should go in." Nexxa watched the women in the shop attending to a bride-to-be. When she didn't answer, Diane persisted, "You would look lovely in that dress." She motioned with her hand donning coffin-shaped nails with the colors of the Irish flag. Diane held open the door and Nexxa walked in. Within minutes she was in the dress from the window, the body-hugging sweetheart dress in a powdery white mesh and lace material. The dress had a cape that ensconced the body from the waist down and was by a Croatian designer, she was informed.

As the sales attendant stepped away to retrieve prosecco, Diane approached Nexxa, putting a hand on her back and whispering, "You love Quinn, don't you?" Nexxa nodded and her eyes filled with tears. She looked down reaching for the tissue box and missed Diane's eyes eerily flutter before she dug a fingernail into her left temple.

Nexxa thanked the kind Italian shop owner and the woman gave her a business card. She patted Nexxa's hand and told her that when she had chosen her love they would be there to customize a dress for her. "Oh, I'm in love," Nexxa reassured the woman. The shop owner looked to her sales associate, who slightly shook her head no. They both smiled at Nexxa and Diane hurried them out explaining to Nexxa that she needed to get back to their hotel and check her email, call her dad, and rest up before dinner.

Srđan pick up Sergei from the job site and in the car, Sergei complained about the seat and the way the car shifted. "Where do you go to buy a car in Zagreb?"

"I don't know, man," Srđan chuckled before taking a drag from his cigarette.

"Drive there, now." Sergei motioned with a hand up to the windshield.

In evening traffic it was thirty-seven minutes of Sergei deprecating his car before they arrived. On the lot Sergei said,

"Choose one."

Srđan walked over to another Opal. In the back a black Audi A8 glimmered just a bit amongst the rest of the subpar vehicles. Sergei walked over, looking in the window. The salesman that had greeted them trotted over to him, and Sergei waved over Srđan.

He was less of a prick on the ride to dinner. Srđan couldn't stop thanking him, but Sergei was still annoyed that Srđan hadn't told him about his "not fit for anything" car before he had arrived in Croatia. Srđan took him back to the gentlemen's club for dinner. Sergei joked that that's all he could afford after dropping thirty-five thousand euros for an Audi.

When Srđan was occupied by flirting with the dancer during her break, Sergei decided to call Hooli. "Where are you?" He was short. Hooli was used to it by now.

"I'm in Berlin," he told him.

"I don't speak German so don't, don't annoy me."

Hooli lowered his phone; he was afraid Sergei would hear him smile, laugh a little. "What's up, man? What's next?"

"I need to know where she is."

"Now?"

"Yes, I want to know now and where she's been in the last few days."

"Okay man, I'm on it." Sergei could hear Hooli typing, and Hooli could hear Sergei eating. "Are you going to wait on the phone?"

"Yeah," Sergei answered.

"Look man, I'll call you back."

Sergei finished his meal and was not really enjoying watching his friend try really hard to get a girl's number. Sipping his cocktail, he thought about Nexxa. The first time he tasted her. Showing her his parents' grave site. The way she took care of his baby niece and babushka. The intimate dinner where he saw the general, the helicopter ride. Then seeing her in new red lingerie in Dublin.

He abruptly stood, and almost dropped his phone while answering his call. "So what? What is it?"

Hooli spoke, "She's in... well, she was. She was in Dublin, and now—"

"Now, where?"

"Calm down, man! I mean. Calm, I'll tell you," Hooli responded. Sergei walked outside and exhaled. "She was at Ashford Castle, then a jewelry store on the high street," Hooli began rattling off locations that Nexxa's phone had sent out pings from. "The rest of them are from on his property in Dublin."

Sergei breathed anger out through his nose and asked, "Is that it?"

"No, no. Uh, well. Now it seems she's in Rome."

"Rome?" Sergei questioned, pulling his chin back furrowing his brow. "So, she's there with him, right?"

"No, not exactly," Hooli replied.

"No?" Sergei turned facing the wall of the restaurant, leaning his head back. "Well? Hooli!"

"Okay, so there was a woman. She and her, Nexxa and this woman, texted a few times. So, yeah, her phone pinged in Rome too."

"So Quinn is not there with her?" Sergei sounded like he

might be happy with the information.

"No, she's mainly been shopping. A ping from a wedding dress shop," Hooli spoke then made a face after hearing himself.

Sergei slammed his fist against the wall. He looked out over the parking lot, and screamed. Two guys walking in asked if there was a problem, but Sergei waved them off and lifted his phone saying, "And then, after the dress shop?"

"They went back to the hotel."

"Who is this woman?" Sergei asked, parlaying his irritation once again to Hoolihane.

"So it seems she is the woman she worked with in Beirut who is from China and has also been in Ireland to buy a jet," Hooli reported in one breath.

Sergei grasped his jaw. The video of the woman who had invaded his home flashed in his mind. "I'll call you back, and make sure you answer your phone," Sergei demanded before returning inside and ushering Srđan to pull himself together. "Let's go," he half-ordered, motioning with his head toward the front of the restaurant. Srđan shook his head, showing he was confused. "I'll explain outside, but you're driving me to Rome."

They never made it. At the border of Slovenia they were turned away even though they presented the correct papers for Srđan's new car and their passports. Sergei wasn't even sure if Nexxa needed saving again. He had saved her once and now he was unsure if she was marrying that Irish prick. Hooli called Sergei before Sergei could call him. He explained how he could help while crunching on some hard candy. Sergei blocked out the sound of Hooli's chomping—he could only envision the Asian man he saw in the villa in Rome before Kilmer said, "Crimson is coming for her soul."

Her eyes opened to a dark room but Nexxa knew she was in her hotel in Rome. She saw wisps of red like ribbons flowing and fading all around the room. Diane emerged from the side of the bed and held up her phone showing an app. "Jupiter is out of retrograde." And then after she kissed Nexxa on her forehead, she continued, "Are you ready?"

"Retro... Retrograde?" Nexxa barely spoke before Diane started withdrawing her breath, simultaneously mimicking tai chi movements. She was able to command the most beautiful shimmering cloth in the air over Nexxa's body. Nexxa became drowsy and the cloth gently ensconced her.

With her body completely covered, Diane placed a white lace veil over Nexxa's face. She lifted her body and carried her out of her hotel room and through the lobby. The few night staff admired Nexxa, applauding her and Diane believing they were playing parts in the festivities. This evening was the celebration of the June solstice, and the Chinese observed this as a celebration of femininity.

Outside Diane walked the street until she made a turn and joined the crowd parading down Via Arenula celebrating the solstice. There were men in white cloaks and *lumini* in glass candle holders lining the streets. Italians in historical costume danced along to music emanating from all around. She approached the Fiume Tevere, and down a steep set of fourteen steps she made her way with Nexxa's listless body. A man was waiting by a small speed boat she had hired for a tour. He asked her if the woman she was carrying was okay. Diane smiled and said that she had drank too much, and into the boat she went with one effortless step. The man stepped in after her and started the engine. At about forty-eight kilometers per hour, Diane was upon him and he gave her a look that said, *What the fuck are you doing?* So she tossed him over. With her hands on the wheel she weaved the small speed boat south toward the Tyrrhenian Sea.

Not long down the river she saw the Ponte Palatino was blocked with the Italian Guardia Costiera, Italian coast guard, for the celebration. Diane pulled the boat over on the north side of the Pons Aemilius. She saw the shimmering cloth around Nexxa withering in the Roman air. She knelt beside her, and her black hair blew in the wind as the boat rocked from the waves. "In any time, you are the one," she breathed Quinn's words into Nexxa's mouth. She grasped Nexxa's right hand and bore her eyes into her until she could see her beloved redhead Reyhan alive waiting for her in another dimension. She was ready to prepare Nexxa's body for Reyhan's soul, willing to accept a blonde, but thrilled to once again share the memories she and Reyhan had in the past.

When Diane first met Nexxa she had the finest anno Domini mind fuck when she discovered that she also had the wolfness. And with all the work, time stalking her, time nudging her to believe she loved Mr. Kane, she had finally come to the right spot. A secluded historic site surrounded by water, a symbol of life and renewal. Diane could finally feel her work, emotional desirous drawings, coming to fruition. A blonde who was once heartbroken, but now, like a rescue animal, was in supposed love ready for transition.

She lifted Nexxa, her blonde head dangling, and carried her out of the boat up the steps of the dilapidated bridge and onto a square portion of stone, then finally into an arched opening in the bridge. She placed Nexxa's body down, adjusted the veil on her face and pulled out her pocketknife.

She needed to harm her only a tad, only then to prove she could protect her. She positioned Nexxa's right arm across her stomach and turned her palm up. Diane cut, tracing the lifeline on Nexxa's palm. Next, she pulled her phone out of her bag and tapped on a video. It was of Reyhan. She was smiling and saying, "No, don't video me. I don't look pretty today." Diane could hear her giggling as the video continued to play. Lastly, she pulled a white pillar candle, a symbol for purity, from her bag and struck a match.

The ancient air stirred through the space they weren't invited into, and Diane stepped away trying to light the candle. Nexxa lay still but now able to hear. Hear Reyhan saying, "Isn't this beautiful? Look at the flowers and the trees." And Diane saying, "Stand there. I'll take your picture. I *love* you."

Nexxa lifted her left hand, and with a frail gesture pulled the white veil from her face and moved her shaky fingers over her lips.

KRASNYY = CRIMSON

Nexxa pushed herself up. Nexxa Davoren maneuvered her body to the stance of a woman who only had sex with kings while her creamy skin had lavender blood dripping from her lifeline.

"What's… happening?" Nexxa asked just as a swirl of wind came through and Diane's candle extinguished. Diane hurriedly struck another match and the candle flamed. Nexxa looked to the phone, a new video had started to play. She saw a redhead. She heard Diane's voice speaking in the video. Diane stepped toward Nexxa, as Nexxa lifted her hand seeing her blood was now not red at all, but lavender. "Is this some sort of ritual?" Nexxa asked with what little strength she had as she held her chest. "Like an induction into a wolf… coven?" Diane moved her tongue across her teeth, pushing herself closer to Nexxa. Nexxa held her wounded hand out to push her away and in went a drop of blood into Diane's mouth. Diane fell to her knees, her deceitful personage slumping at the edge of Nexxa's feet. Nexxa looked at the blood on her hand then back to Diane, seeing the power it held. "She's dead. Isn't she?" Nexxa's words competed with her breath as she braced herself against the wall, looking at the video of Reyhan. "You want me. Or you want me to be her?"

Diane reached and dug a coffin-shaped nail into Nexxa's wounded leg saying, "You're going to do. Do what I want. Now!" Nexxa lost her balance, falling onto the stone pedestal below the opening. Then, Diane pulled herself to the edge and her eyes bulged, seeing Nexxa lying with her head dangling off of the pedestal—her hair looked to be glowing red.

Diane flopped out of the bridge's opening, landing next to the woman she wanted to love. Nexxa lay with her eyes closed and her mind flashing between images of Reyhan's life memories and her own. She heard the giggle of baby Natina right as Diane managed enough eternal selfish desire to grab Nexxa's legs, pulling her back up into the ancient covered space.

Nexxa's heart pumped and moved more lavender blood down her arm to her right hand, as Diane reached for her phone swiping vigorously to restart a video of Reyhan. Nexxa saw the knife—she reached, grabbing it with sudden strength, and sliced her wound deeper. Diane turned seeing a tear fall from Nexxa's lovely brown eyes.

Nexxa held her left hand out, and Diane took hold, letting her head fall back and roll to only see Reyhan's red hair. Nexxa yanked her down and twisted atop of her hammering her right fist into Diane's face, blood seeping over her mouth. Her might came from herself—her survival came from Kilmer—and now she had venomous lavender.

Nexxa stood over her with her bare breasts and a shaven vagina. She pushed Diane's body down and positioned her on the rocks at the water's edge. She stepped into the boat and started the engine. Her hands on the wheel, she put the boat in forward and pushed the throttle, ramming, crushing Diane's body. Nexxa put the boat in reverse, backing up and then putting it back in forward as she looked over, seeing a smashed Crimson before she pushed the throttle forward, and away she went up the river.

Seeing familiar territory, she docked the boat unnoticed and stepped out. A conglomerate of people celebrating passed along, Nexxa pulled a cloak from a man's shoulders as he stumbled and draped her bare body. She sprinted up the steps, and with drunks all around her, Nexxa found a mask on the ground and covered her face. She approached her hotel and after taking a glance inside she saw the night staff, tipsy, cavorting, so through the lobby of Hotel dei Barbieri she made her way.

Monday morning, in black leggings and with a secret, Nexxa donned her light gray sweater coat, and attended breakfast in the hotel. As she sipped a Bloody Mary, she watched a tourist read the local newspaper. The article had an image of an unknown Asian woman found on the Pons Aemilius. Nexxa took a long taste of her cocktail. Standing, she adjusted the tie belt to her sweater, and a few breaths later she was leaning over the shoulder of the tourist. The man flinched at Nexxa's touch. He leaned back from her; he saw her eyes, her intense beauty. He offered her the seat across from him.

Nexxa maneuvered her hand along his thigh, starting from his knee to his unimpressive crotch. "No, thank you. I've got some cock in Ireland."

APRÈS | 44

Nexxa watched as a gypsy woman and her daughter begged outside of the airport passenger pickup terminal in Dublin. Nexxa walked over and knelt, reaching for the girl's hand, giving her some money. "You are pretty," the girl, who was all of six, said with only a hint of an Irish accent. Nexxa smiled. The girl twisted Nexxa's hand and ran her dirty finger along Nexxa's palm saying, "You have a hurtie," while Quinn put Nexxa's suitcase in the boot of his car.

  On the ride to his home he looked over at her, noticing how the rush hour sun was illuminating her profile. Nexxa crossed her left leg over her right, pushing up in her seat when Quinn came to a slow in traffic. She reached into his lap and massaged his crotch. When she felt he was hard she rested back into her seat and maneuvered her hand into her panties. Quinn came close to rear-ending a lorry. After that he switched lanes and sped up, cutting off a driver who then proceeded to honk endlessly. Nexxa pressed the button to open the sunroof. She took off her seat belt and before Quinn could ask what in the bloody hell she was doing she had kicked off her sneakers and was standing in her seat. Traffic had slowed, but she could have handled herself at a faster speed.

Nexxa raised her left hand as if to say hi and the driver of the dark green BMW made an ugly face. She made the horns gesture, the devil's horns which are said to drive away curses, commonly used in traffic in Italy, and she added a sign she picked up from one of the *vampire* models at the party in Rome, holding his eyes in her gaze. Back in her seat, she re-buckled her seat belt. Traffic began to move freely, and after about ten minutes they were finally pulling into Quinn's driveway. Quinn wanted to ask what the hell she did to quell the driver, but he really really needed to have Nexxa in his bed.

Nexxa was only halfway up the staircase when she stopped and turned around to take a step down next to him. She took off her top and then pulled the rest of her clothes off. Quinn watched as she stood before him with nothing on. He gently ran his hand along her abdomen. He looked at her with worried eyes, thinking she looked too thin. His mobile buzzed. "Fuck me, I'm not answering that," he said.

"No, no, you should answer it. I'll be waiting upstairs." Nexxa winked and turned, going up the rest of the stairs. Quinn took the call, it lasted an hour, and when he found Nexxa she was asleep. *Damn, at least she's in my bed*, he thought as he turned off the lamps.

In the kitchen, Nexxa started the kettle and made some toast. Quinn had actually slept in and Nexxa liked that she could be there waiting for him when he came downstairs. After eight, he came down, and seeing Nexxa he grinned a boyish grin.

"What is it, Mr. Kane?" Nexxa asked, walking over to him.

Mr. Kane wrapped his arms around her. "I love you being here in my home. In my kitchen. Using my kettle," he breathed, before kissing her on the forehead.

"Do you want tea?"

"Yeah, yeah, sure," Quinn answered, moving over to a barstool. He pulled out his phone and started reading his email. Nexxa poured hot water from the kettle; a spot of hot water splashed onto her wounded hand. She flinched, placing the mug down a bit hard. Quinn looked up from reading his emails. "You okay?" Nexxa looked at her hand realizing that it actually did *not* hurt. So far, she had been careful to not let Quinn see the wound on her right hand. Nexxa handed Quinn his mug and went into the pantry. She felt like she needed to bake.

Pulling items from the shelves and bringing them to the kitchen island, she heard Quinn as he was walking out of the kitchen. She looked to his mug still steaming with tea. Nexxa was back in the pantry looking for an ingredient she had bought when they went to the supermarket when Quinn approached her from behind with a hammer. "So how did Rome go?" he inquired with a tone that Nexxa thought was serious. She stared at an empty storage container and paused her breathing, preparing for something bad. Nexxa heard the force of the hammer.

"That's been bothering me," Quinn said as he placed the hammer down on a shelf.

Nexxa reached, feeling her head before looking at her fingers expecting to see blood, thinking that he must have hit her. "What happened to your hand?" Quinn reached for it, questioning as she faced him.

"Why did you do that?" Nexxa asked with a tightened chest.

"Nexxa, what happened in Rome?"

"I, I danced," Nexxa answered, looking over at the hammer. Quinn ran a finger along her newly formed scar.

"I knocked over a wine glass," Nexxa said as an excuse.

Quinn grasped her face, kissing her. Then looking in the corner, he said, "That bleedin' nail was loose for so long." Quinn heard his phone ring and left the pantry to answer it. Nexxa moved over to the place on the wall, moving her hand over the nail that had been hammered in flush with the plasterboard.

Nexxa followed the sound of Quinn's voice to his den. He ended his call and asked, "Where is Diane, did she fly back yet?"

Nexxa grinned. "Not yet. She met a lady. Said something about being really eager to show her something new in lavender. That she would be back to Dublin in a few days."

Quinn grasped his chin saying, "Oh. I didn't know she liked women."

"Yeah, I'm not her type though," Nexxa assured him with a wink.

Quinn embraced her and kissed along her neck. Nexxa winced and slumped a bit in his arms. "You feel hot." Quinn felt her chest and then her forehead. "You should lie down," he said, pulling her over to the leather sofa. He covered her with a blanket and handed her the remote. "I have to go out. Do you want a cup of tea before I leave?"

"No. I'm fine." She hadn't realized her weakness or her new strength, mostly thriving from her venomous lavender blood. "No watching that Italian porn while I'm gone," Quinn teased before he kissed her hand.

Kieran was standing in the street in front of his house smoking, reserving a parking spot for Quinn when he pulled around. Quinn turned, seeing through his window that Kessly was standing in the doorway of Kieran's house. His face showed he was fucking angry.

"You gettin' out?" Kieran asked, knocking on Quinn's window.

He stepped out. "What is she doing here?" Quinn's nostrils flared.

"Easy, easy." Kieran held up a hand. "You've only gotta hear her out." Quinn looked past Kieran; Kessly flashed her slutty smile before turning and walking into the small row house. Quinn followed Kieran in. He stood in the kitchen with his arms folded. Kessly sat in the living room on the sofa smoking. Kieran pulled up an article on his phone and handed it to Quinn.

"What the fuck is this?" Quinn handed the phone back, giving him a look and holding his hand up to match his words.

Kieran snapped his fingers for Kessly to come over to them. She blew out from her cigarette and smashed it out in the ashtray. Quinn stared at Kieran as she walked over. "It says, some Asian woman was found dead in Rome," she snarled before turning to Kieran smirking. He slapped her on the bum and told her to go sit down.

"Yeah, so. A tourist died in Rome. It's full of Chinese there. All the Italian brands are made in Chinese sweatshops." He leaned around looking over to Kessly. "And how the fuck do you speak Italian? Aren't you—"

"Relax, she googled it," Kieran offered, holding his arm out to discourage Quinn's aggressive attitude. "Look, look at the picture." Kieran handed his phone back to Quinn.

Quinn reluctantly took the phone. He zoomed in on the picture. He couldn't tell who the woman was. The body was partly blurred out with a warning that the images were graphic. "Weren't you expecting Nexxa *and* Diane, your client, at the airport?" Kieran pushed, sounding like he was a detective.

"What are you suggesting?" Quinn plopped the phone down on the shabby counter. Kieran reached, swooping up his phone. Quinn had been so ecstatic to see Nexxa that he hadn't checked the news as he usually did. The article wasn't in the mainstream media outlets yet.

"This girl is fuckin' with your mind." Kieran leaned into him. "She's gonna fuck with your business too." Quinn met him with a stare down. He thought about what Nexxa had told him about Diane taking a later flight, then meeting a woman and delaying her trip back to Dublin.

"Did ya think about the job? The new customer," Kieran changed the subject, pairing it with a cheery voice. Kessly started rattling off in her mangled Jobstown accent details about a woman from America that wanted her cheating husband dead. Some politician's wife. Kessly continued spewing crap about going to The Big Apple.

"Give us a fag," Quinn commanded, and Kieran motioned to Kessly for a cigarette before snapping his fingers. Kieran leaned in and lit the cigarette for him. Quinn took a drag—then left.

He sped through Dublin thinking about the video that had been sent to him with Kessly stupidly confessing to working for him in a murder for hire plot. He knew she would never be believed being that she had a history of misdemeanors, one being stalking him. The funds had cleared from the sale of his private club while Nexxa was in Rome. His partnership in The Westbury hotel was well established, and now all he wanted was to sell jets with Nexxa as his assistant. But then, his mind went to Nexxa meeting with the Russian's hacker. How she just happened to come to Dublin to spread Kilmer's ashes, a man that had wanted to infiltrate his life and financial streams.

Nexxa had fallen asleep, and when she awoke, she remembered she had planned to bake something. In the kitchen she mixed ingredients in the large bowl she had found earlier. On a baking sheet she arranged plops of cookie dough, sneaking a lick on the spoon, and in the oven the cookies went. She checked the time on her phone and saw it was now early afternoon. She hoped Quinn would be home when the cookies were fresh from the oven.

Standing in the pantry, she heard her phone ping with an alert. Looking at her phone, she saw it was a notification for

Quinn's business email she used. She powered on her laptop, rolling her neck around while she waited. She opened her mail app and clicked on the email. Her eyes widened. Nexxa braced herself, hands on her laptop. She reread the email looking for signs that it was fraudulent. Hooli came to mind. Then, she heard Quinn opening the front door. The timer on the oven went off. Nexxa dashed over and put on an oven mitt.

"When was the last time you spoke to Diane?" Quinn spoke with a bluntness that felt like a whack to her head. Nexxa turned from pulling out the cookies, holding the tray, and Quinn furrowed his brow. Before she could answer, he pointed to her saying, "Your hand."

Nexxa looked down at the cookies, then to her left hand in the oven mitt, and finally to her right hand that was bare. "Oh, ow!" Nexxa flinched and plopped the cooking sheet down. Quinn dashed over and turned on the water and Nexxa moved over to the sink. She winced as the water ran over her scarred hand. "I should take you to the doctor."

"I'm fine. Really," Nexxa assured him, smiling, searching his blue eyes for the reason why he was suddenly concerned with Diane's whereabouts.

Quinn's mind raced thinking about when Nexxa had cut her hand in Mr. Albert's home. It was the reason they were brought together in the private loo of his bedroom, him bandaging her hand, using the iodine he had in his toiletry bag, before kissing her. Quinn went to the powder room and came back with iodine and a burn cream. Nexxa played the part, holding her injured hand with her left hand so he could tend to it.

Nexxa's phone pinged with a text message. Quinn looked

over to her phone on the other end of the massive stone island. It was possible that she was still in communication with Sergei. That she had orchestrated the Rome trip to do something sordid. Quinn was always in love with *his* ways whether they were by the books or unethical and self-serving… lustful or backed by genuine love.

He handed Nexxa her phone. From the time it took him to walk over to it and back to her she had prepared herself for any possible outcome. Perhaps it was only Iliada texting her. Nexxa saw that it was a text from Diane.

Hi, just chillin with my girl in Rome. We're heading to Venice for a few days. XO ♥. What the fuck? She's dead. Is this infatuation from the other side? she worried, managing to elicit no emotion while reading the text aloud.

Nexxa typed back: *Oh that's great! I'm happy for you.* ☺, and placed her phone on the counter with the screen down, thinking, *This better be Hooli, or some other fucking hacker and not still "Single White Female."* Quinn lifted her phone and read the texts himself.

Nexxa moved in closer to him. "I made cookies," she said, touching his chest. Quinn breathed out through his nose and pulled her hand away from him.

"Why are you upset?" Nexxa asked, looking at him as he avoided eye contact.

Quinn walked outside through the kitchen door. Nexxa watched as he lowered his head and rubbed a hand over it. Nexxa lifted a cookie from the tray and took a bite. It was edible, maybe a tad good for a novice baker, so she picked up another one and carried it outside. "Quinn," she called out. He didn't turn around. "Quinn!" she hollered as she walked over to him.

He spun around. "What? What is it, Nexxa?"

"I have a cookie for you."

He looked down shaking his head saying, "I don't want a bleedin' cookie."

Nexxa lifted his face. "Quinn, what is it? What happened today?"

"Are you telling me the truth?" Quinn asked, scratching the side of his nose with a face that matched his thoughts: *I'm angry but I want you to tell me something that will make me not.*

"About what? Rome?"

"Yeah. Rome." He stepped back shaking his head.

"I told you, she met a woman. I…" Nexxa said, holding a hand to her chest. "—Didn't do anything that would jeopardize what I have, she continued, "*You.*" Nexxa looked at him with daring yet adoring eyes. When Quinn crossed his arms and exhaled looking down again, saying nothing, Nexxa blurted, "Quinn, she paid. She paid the balance for the jet! I got the email today regarding the wire transfer to your bank account." Nexxa wondered if the balance payment had been automatic.

Quinn leaned his head back blowing out a slow breath saying, "That fucking prick!"

"Who's a prick?" Nexxa moved closer with her hands up, questioning.

"I don't want—" he started struggling, choking on his emotions.

"What? What don't you want?" Nexxa pleaded, tearing up.

"I don't want a cookie. I want you." He laughed and cried at the same time.

Nexxa moved her lips to him. Quinn grasped her face, inhaling her with his tongue in her mouth. Nexxa breathed heavily, and he held onto her—tightly, while she wondered again if the balance payment had been automatic.

Hooli sat on the toilet with his laptop typing from one application to another. His foot bumped a bowl on the ground, which had the remnants of vanilla ice cream crusting inside, turning yellow. "I sent a text from Diane's phone."

Sergei zipped his suit pants and said, "Yeah, okay," as he washed his hands.

"So I see that she read it already. I see she opened the email too."

"Did the wire go through?" asked Sergei.

Hooli nodded yes.

"Hooli? If you're nodding, I can't see you," Sergei remarked.

"Yeah, yeah." Hooli was typing, which sounded like banging to Sergei. "Yeah, so five hundred seventy-five k. Cleared!"

Sergei exhaled. He thought about her voicemail saying something about there being more she needed to tell him. And he knew how things played out. He had seen it in Beirut, was putting the pieces all together now. Nexxa's dismay may have started with Kilmer, but it was coming full circle with Diane. He knew that working for Quinn could end up bad for Nexxa if she didn't produce. He wasn't doubting her talent or charisma; he just knew that the Asian woman found in Rome was Diane. That Nexxa had ended Krasnyy.

MACABRE | 45

It wasn't that Quinn's bed wasn't comfortable or that his sheets weren't a high enough thread count or that his duvet wasn't the perfect plush of down. Quinn only mildly snored, and that was only if he had had whisky. It was only the macabre that was lurking.

Nexxa leapt from the bed. Moving with anxious precision across the high pile rug that carried her to the open window, she flung aside a drape. All that Drakos from Rome would tell her as he blew onto her so that her blonde strands froze in the chilly Irish air was that he was enthralled by her lavender blood and continuing to blow, that there in the Russian land was a woman who vied for her. A Russki who liked to break the bones of the frail.

The next morning the sky hid behind the heavy drapes, and

Nexxa kidded herself with the thought that they also hid the looming feeling that was blown onto her—while Quinn had slept—from Drakos, the same man in the gray hooded cloak that had given her a warning outside of the Vatican walls, "*Tua lavandula a lupo desideratur.*"

Quinn entered his ensuite as Nexxa was showering and said, "Come here." Nexxa stepped out of the rainfall and shivered just as he grasped her bum and kissed her.

"I'll see you at the hangar at one," Quinn confirmed. Nexxa stepped back into the water. "Wait," Quinn walked back.

Nexxa already had conditioner in her hand. "Yeah." She looked to him and moved the product through her hair. "Do you want to come in?" She smirked.

"Mmm, I would love to," he told her thinking that his virtue of patience—they hadn't been intimate yet—was going to get him into Heaven. "Are you sure you are okay driving?"

"I'll be fine," Nexxa assured him, stepping back into the water and leaning her head back. Quinn stood for a moment and watched her. *Get it together, man*, he told himself.

After maneuvering around the annoyance of traffic and blocked streets, Quinn finally made it to his hotel. A table in the lounge had been cleared of tableware, ready for him and his guest. His jeweler arrived with a minder and he took a seat. He withdrew his case and rolled it out on the table. There were only three rings presented. The jeweler pushed one forward. Quinn lifted the five-carat ring with a bloom of diamonds surrounding the stone in a cathedral setting. "You knew I would like this one," Quinn quipped, looking through the loupe.

Even though she was going to "work," Nexxa dressed in her black Wolford Fatal dress. The intent was to be workplace chic. She let her hair dry naturally, pulling it up in a half ponytail. Twisting in the mirror, she could see her panty line. She shimmied off her panties and walked to the closet, pulled out her suitcase and laid it flat on the floor. She unzipped the main zipper and felt around in one of the interior compartments searching for her seamless thong. Hearing a clank, she unzipped another section and felt her tweezers inside. She changed panties and put the tweezers in her purse before looking around the room, seeing a framed photo of Quinn with his mom. She thought of the photo in Sergei's office he had with his mom. With her heels on, holding the handrail tight as she maneuvered down Quinn's massive staircase—an element vibrated her lavender, whispering to her the warning she received the night before.

Nexxa drove out of Quinn's driveway and onto the path that led to Ballycorus Road. Successfully, she merged onto the M50. A few times she withdrew her right hand from the steering wheel to flex it. The satellite radio emitted a radio station from the Netherlands; the beat was steady with just the right Euro enthusiasm. It wasn't until she reached the entrance to the FBO and typed in the code that she felt her hand throb. Nexxa pulled through the gate and glanced in the rearview mirror as it rolled across the ground, closing.

Kieran pulled up and almost butted the gate with his Range Rover.

Mr. Kane had chosen the diamond that was to be placed on

a petite bone of a blonde that had the surname of a deceased enemy. As discussed, they were given the details on how to access the private FBO, and his jeweler escorted by security would deliver the ring to Quinn's hangar. Quinn passed an envelope with twenty thousand across the table. The remaining he would wire. They parted ways and Quinn walked through the lobby greeting staff, with the women and men in their proper attire, donning their hospitality smiles with mostly bad teeth and sorrowful hearts.

Before Quinn visited his office to wire the rest of the money, he noticed a little girl standing by the entrance holding a tattered shopping bag. Her golden hair reminded him of Nexxa. Made him think of a daughter they could have. She had the attention of the doormen and the guests that entered—she had Quinn's beating heart. The day manager approached him, he wanted to go over the weekly numbers, and the girl waved at Quinn before dashing out. He ignored the manager, pushing through the doors and exiting to see her being yanked away by her mum. The girl looked back flashing "help me" eyes.

"Gypsies," the doorman explained. Quinn looked to him shaking his head.

The girl screamed out; Quinn dashed after them. They crossed the street and Quinn turned, rubbing his hand over his head laughing. "What the bloody hell." A city bus pulled to a stop. The door opened. No one exited. Then, the bus driver jumped out just before the door closed and ran.

A loud boom erupted as the bus exploded. Glass scattered the street and the sidewalk. Fire raged from the metal structure of the bus.

Nexxa walked through the hangar and greeted the crew that had been detailing Diane's jet after the installation of the new mechanisms in the seats. The pilot flying her and Quinn to London was at the flight desk reviewing the weather. She waved to him. One of the ladies cleaning the jet popped her head out. "Any chance you have a bandage, ma'am?" Nexxa climbed the steps of the plane. She rummaged through her purse and in the interior pocket she felt her ring and then a bandage. Her face said nothing as she held up the bandage before plopping down to her knees holding the ring, remembering when Sergei had given it to her telling her it was his mother's.

One of the ladies gushed. "What a lovely ruby ring, ma'am. Did your boyfriend give that to ya?" Nexxa slipped the ring on, holding her hand out, staring at it. "Lovely, ma'am," the woman spoke again.

"Ye… yeah," Nexxa looked up to the woman with her thoughts competing for an emotion.

The ring changed to a pale rose—Nexxa smelled tobacco—she smiled as she stood in her Wolford.

Down the jet's steps she went, seeing Kieran with just enough light shining on his face to reveal the delicate benefits of a never-ending pack of fags. "Ya havin' a look?" His voice pierced the hangar. Nexxa inconspicuously exhaled. Quinn hadn't mentioned Kieran coming to the FBO. She looked across, seeing the pilot still at the flight desk. Behind her she heard the chatter of the cleaning ladies on the jet.

Kieran embraced Nexxa. She felt the cold Irish summer on his black leather jacket. She smelled feminine malevolence on his facial stubble. "Quinn should be here soon," Nexxa informed him with a tinge of attitude in her voice.

"So I understand that his client Diane didn't come back with ya from Rome," Kieran said, scratching the side of his chin.

"Yep, that's right." Nexxa stood tall, looking him in the eyes.

"So what, she didn't want to come get her plane?" Kieran lifted his chin, motioning to the jet behind Nexxa.

The cleaning ladies had finished and started coming down the steps of the jet. "Bye ma'am," they each said warmly. The last one to leave turned looking back at Nexxa, then to Kieran.

"Oh, thank you, loves!" Nexxa hollered to them smiling, showing she was fine.

Kieran turned to watch until the last one had left. "C'mon, I need to show you something." He grabbed Nexxa's arm, pulling her to Quinn's office. He unlocked the door and motioned with his head for Nexxa to enter. She looked to the back of the hanger; the pilot only had eyes for the screen that displayed weather and news.

Kieran lifted the remote to the television and turned it on. He plugged something into the side of the TV and connected it to his phone. He started a video and cast it to the flat screen mounted on the wall. Nexxa watched as Sergei stood with Kessly in his arms and his fingers in her vagina, kissing her on the mouth. The left side of her heart hurt. The right side believed it loved Quinn. "So, she's Irish. Bit of a muddled accent I hear," Nexxa commented looking straight on at the telly before her.

Kieran sat on the dark grey credenza beneath the TV with his arms folded. "So tell me, what's the plan? Huh, what are you planning?"

Nexxa thought about Quinn grabbing her bum in the shower earlier that morning. Him telling her the night before that he didn't want a cookie, that he only wanted her. She looked over at his desk; the office was dark except for the light from the TV and she heard, *In any time, you are the one.*

Kieran stood and stepped closer to her. He ran a finger across her collarbone and down her décolletage. Nexxa calmed her breathing. Kieran leaned into her face and whispered, "I should have fucked ya ten years ago."

Detective Framisi had managed to sneak away one particular thing of interest from Diane Soo Hoo's belongings that were in her hotel room in Rome: Renderings of a woman. Her face was delicately chiseled with soft looking plumpish lips, almond eyes. She donned a wedding veil that draped just the right amount, framing her gorgeous cheekbones. He had been the first one in Diane's room being that his partner had called in *"nauseato"* the first day of the investigation. Detective Framisi had also requested video footage from the hotel. He matched Nexxa's face, the lovely blonde, to the sketch of the woman.

He played the footage several times of Diane carrying Nexxa's body out of the hotel. He knew what Diane was, one with the wolfness but with sinister longings. Detective Framisi had a fortunate upbringing that consisted of a wise Italian *nonno*. One that had used a cane. So he knew that until the renderings were gone, they still held power.

He ignited the drawings of Nexxa and tossed them into his fireplace, watching the flame burning from the veil, the blissful bride, the groom, the diamond.

Kieran yanked on Nexxa's right arm. His eyes bulged when she forcefully pulled her arm from his grasp, causing him to lose his balance taking a step backward. "We're off." He gruffed, reaching for her again, saying, "You're just a whore to him. Nah, now yous gonna work for me, like Kessly. She can show ya the ropes. You've already learned to have a Russian dick in your hole."

The video had stopped, and the news started playing. "Local renowned businessman Quinn Osian Kane believed to have been killed in the bombing of a city bus." Kieran turned away from Nexxa. She fell to her knees. Her eyes read the scrolling caption as she watched the news anchor standing on a sidewalk a few blocks from The Westbury hotel. She heard him say, "We now have confirmation that Mr. Kane has definitely, unfortunately, perished in the terrorist bombing attack."

Kieran hovered over her, blocking her view of the TV. "C'mon, get up. We're goin'," he said with haste in every syllable. Nexxa extended her fingers on her left hand, seeing her ring turn almost transparent like a withering opal. Kieran yanked off her diamond necklace, the gift from Quinn that tried to win her heart. She smelled the flames from a "blissful bride" burning in Rome and with her right hand she held the part of her heart that should have ached for Quinn.

"Would you have had the balls to fuck me in Paris? Or would you had rather tasted me in Dublin?" Nexxa taunted before she jabbed him up his chin with her palm, causing her hand to graze his canines and slice a part of her wound open. Kieran reached into his jacket in his holster for his gun, but as

Nexxa stood forcing her hand over his mouth and just the right amount of her lavender blood trickled in, he struggled.

Kieran managed to pull his gun—Nexxa hammered him in the face with her right fist. "Now, I'll be on me way," she breathed, leaning down to him as he lay on the floor of Quinn's office. Nexxa lifted the gun and exited Quinn's office, closing the door behind her. She looked over to the pilot, and his face showed his shock and condolences as he stood almost at attention while she walked across the hangar to him. Nexxa plopped the gun down on the stand, holding it with her left hand. Her ring was gradually turning back to rose, and the right side of her heart realized that she had never loved anyone but Sergei. "Change your flight plan. You're flying me to Moscow."

NEXXA HEART MOSCOW

An older man with a mustache donning mid-century military attire and a woman with long gray hair and lavender lips stood guard behind Nexxa the entire flight from Dublin to Moscow. When they landed, Nexxa saw red fill her ruby ring. She thanked the couple, the spirit guides sent as a courtesy by Drakos, the man from Rome who had deliberately, chillingly, summoned her to the window the night before.

Nexxa landed at the same FBO that Sergei used when he flew with his jet share. Inside the flight operations building she went to the front desk and asked for a driver. She was silent on the drive to Sergei's house. When they arrived, Nexxa exited the vehicle, looking through the gate to Sergei's home. She pushed the call button. "I need to see Sergei." The new housekeeper answered and said that he was still away in Croatia. "Okay, open the gate. I need to speak with Ankica."

The woman said she needed to check with her. A few minutes later the gate opened, and the housekeeper was waiting to greet Nexxa at the front entrance. After Nexxa stepped inside, she told her that she had just helped Ankica upstairs to the sitting room.

Nexxa dashed up the stairs, and when she turned the corner she saw Ankica sitting, sipping her cherry brandy. She moved to push herself up, but Nexxa rushed to her side and knelt at her lap, grasping her hand. "Krasnyy. Krasnyy," Ankica repeated in her life-lived sounding voice.

"I'm okay. It's over," Nexxa assured her. And when Ankica gripped her hand as best as her Russian bones could, Nexxa teared up. "Natina?" Nexxa asked with a face of regret. Ankica nodded. Nexxa kissed her hand and stood.

She pushed Natina's bedroom door open. She could see two eyes looking at her. Nexxa moved over to her bed and knelt. Natina giggled, pulling at the hair that had fallen out of Nexxa's ponytail. Then she started to cry and thrash around in her bed. Nexxa stood and pulled off her heels and then lifted Natina out of bed. She bounced her as she struggled in Nexxa's arms crying. "Shh." Nexxa tried to soothe her over her own tears. Natina resisted and Nexxa did her best to hold on to her. On the floor, Natina clung to Nexxa's leg screaming. Nexxa managed to lift her up again and sat down on her bed. She cradled Natina and soothed her to sleep. When she felt she could leave her bedroom, Nexxa tiptoed out and sat with Ankica. She motioned for her to take some brandy from the bottle. Nexxa obliged but really wanted to stay awake, alert, all night and every night.

After Ankica went to bed, with Nexxa's help, Nexxa found the housekeeper in the kitchen and asked her to retrieve some of her clothes from Sergei's room. In the hallway between Natina's room, the housekeeper's room, and Ankica's, Nexxa slept.

Nexxa only stood sipping her tea while acknowledging Ankica's insistence that she sit at the kitchen table. Nexxa allowed her shattered eyes to glimmer while looking at Natina. The housekeeper spoke very little English but motioned for Nexxa to eat. On the range, soup wasn't boiling over, and the bread on the table was fresh from that day. The tile floor looked a shade lighter as the sun shone in through the kitchen window.

Nexxa rinsed her mug and lost her grip when she tried to dry it, dropping it on the counter. The housekeeper jumped from her seat and lifted the cracked mug, placing it back in the sink. She noticed Nexxa's cut on her right hand and pulled her gently over to the pantry. Inside there was a first aid kit, but all Nexxa could see was the tidiness. Her hand had already started to scar, but the housekeeper could see Nexxa was in pain. She told her to sit on the stool in the pantry and she gently stretched out each of Nexxa's fingers, relaxing her hand.

That night after Nexxa bathed Natina and played with her until she closed her eyes, she retired to the sitting room with Ankica. She could see the blush in her skin instead of the gray that had taken over when Vlasta was there. "Sergei was worried. Eh, for you," Ankica muttered while moving her hand along her cloth. Nexxa thought back to when she had called him after money had once again been transferred into her account. Telling herself it was the last time. Quinn was dead, but that wasn't why she was there. Even if Sergei had been home and told her to go the fuck away, she would have remained with her guides and slept outside of his gate.

Sergei's trees looked pleased to see her, carrying from one to the next the scent of feelings Nexxa had suppressed while in Ireland. Nexxa did a head bow, acknowledging them, as she took a walk the next morning. Looking down the path she used to run, she remembered how not long ago she was in Bogdan's house with Crimson trotting on the roof. Spotting a good branch, Nexxa stepped off of the path and lifted it to use as a walking stick. An owl hooted—the aroma of her love for Sergei swirled the tops of the trees. She smiled, curtsying the forest, knowing that now was the time to call him.

About one hundred feet from the perimeter of Sergei's house, her walking stick grabbed the ground, stopping Nexxa, and there was the scent of horror secreting from a woman with dirty layers of skin.

Nexxa entered the house through the kitchen door, the same as she had left. The housekeeper was there at the stove preparing dinner, and Nexxa looked to her, giving her a smile. Ankica was sitting watching the TV. Natina was upstairs in her room. Nexxa darted upstairs, and the horrific scent was by her side in every room in Sergei's house. Natina was busy playing, gabbing to her toys when Nexxa peeked in her room. Nexxa turned looking down the hall toward Sergei's bedroom. She walked by the sitting room and took a step toward his door, placing her right hand on it. Her hand throbbed. Not from pain—from longing.

That night she slept on the loveseat in the sitting room, closer to Sergei's room, closer to the place her heart had always wanted to be but couldn't admit and in a position in his house where she could still guard Natina and Ankica.

In the darkest of the night, again, Drakos awoke Nexxa summoning her to the window. Nexxa stepped over to him, and as he spoke, warning her, she turned back, seeing that Vlasta was standing there. She watched as Vlasta lifted the blanket Nexxa had slept under and snarled in it. When she tossed it down and stepped toward the bedrooms, Nexxa dashed over and grabbed her with her right hand. Vlasta was strong, but her fatty body smelling like it did was more of a hindrance than her hysterical strength. She tossed Nexxa and she landed crashing into the sideboard that housed Ankica's brandy. The bottle toppled over and broke, shattering glass on Nexxa.

Nexxa pushed herself up, and with a jagged piece of the cherry brandy bottle slit her wounded hand. With a fractured rib, she moved after Vlasta, reaching her just as she had opened Natina's door and took a few steps in. Nexxa crouched down crawling on her knees. When Vlasta turned with terrifying eyes that were illuminated by Natina's nightlight, Nexxa used her right hand to grasp Vlasta's still-healing broken leg. Her incision from surgery was split open from the weight of her table-heavy legs, and Nexxa's lavender blood seeped all over the opening. Vlasta struggled and Nexxa twisted onto her back just as she fell with a plop. Vlasta landed on Nexxa with her weight punishing Nexxa's abdomen. Nexxa gasped for air trying to push her off.

Natina woke and crawled out of her toddler bed. She bent, and Nexxa heard her diaper crunch, as she leaned over Nexxa's face. The faint light of the nightlight that held three illuminated plastic balls was all that Nexxa could use. She managed to point to the light, and Natina toddled over and grasped a ball. She brought it to Vlasta, and when she reached for it Natina backed away giggling.

"NO! That's not nice. Give it to me!" Vlasta demanded, slumping off of Nexxa onto her knees trying to get to a staggering stance while reaching further for the glowing ball.

When she finally stood and was able to chase after Natina, Nexxa saw the man with mid-century military attire in front of her. He told her, "Get up and be a general! Command this room!" Nexxa reached her hand out; he took hold and she rose.

Vlasta had Natina in her arms as she squirmed and screamed like death had her in its grip. Nexxa moved over to the dresser and turned on the lamp. Vlasta grunted and dropped the baby then stammered over to Nexxa. Natina cried with her arms out, reaching toward Nexxa. Vlasta pushed Nexxa's head back with her palm on her chin and then let her go. Nexxa breathed heavily, looking over to Natina as she lay on the floor hiding her head in some toys. Vlasta stammered out of the room muttering, "Old lady bones. Old lady has bones."

The door creaked a little when Vlasta pushed it open, and Nexxa knew she was going into Ankica's room. She rushed to

Natina and picked her up, putting her in her tent and covering her with a blanket. Nexxa held her finger up to her mouth saying, "Shh."

Nexxa followed Vlasta and found her already accosting Ankica to get out of bed. "Let's go to the kitchen to make something to eat. You want some soup?" Vlasta's tone sounded as if she was normal. Nexxa watched as Vlasta held tightly onto Ankica's arm, not allowing her the use of her cane. Ankica inconspicuously looked to Nexxa as they passed by her in the hallway. The housekeeper had woken and opened her bedroom door. Seeing all of them in the hallway, her eyes bulged. She asked in Russian what was happening. "We're making soup! I just need a bone to make it tasty," Vlasta announced cheerfully. The housekeeper looked to Nexxa frantically. Nexxa held up a hand, telling her to stand down.

Nexxa watched as Vlasta walked Ankica toward the stairs, so she motioned with her hand for the housekeeper to go into Natina's room. Natina peeked her head out from under a blanket and looked out of her tepee tent. The housekeeper lifted her up and followed Nexxa down the hallway. Nexxa tried to step around Vlasta before they made it down the first few steps. Vlasta winced, saying, "No, I'm okay," as she started down the stairs and almost lost her grip on Ankica. "You want some bread?" she asked Ankica kindly. Each step, two feet at a time, they all descended Sergei's staircase with Nexxa reaching out for Ankica whenever she saw Vlasta wobble.

Sitting at the kitchen table, Ankica played along with Vlasta. She sat still while Vlasta hummed and brought bowls to the table. Nexxa stood in the entryway watching, and the housekeeper handed Natina to her and took a step, then another toward the kitchen island. Vlasta slid a plate in front of Ankica. "Now, you can be good. You can eat." Ankica's voice was low as she thanked her. Vlasta bent and took a pot from a lower cabinet and filled it. She plopped it on the stove and huffed, leaning with her arms stretched out to hold her balance. Nexxa watched her, noticing how she was gradually losing her strength. It was like witnessing a bull after being given a tranquilizer. Vlasta garbled to herself as she managed to pull a few items from the fridge and drop them on the counter.

The housekeeper looked at Nexxa and motioned toward Ankica; Nexxa shook her head no. Ignoring Nexxa, she moved with soft steps over to Ankica. "Hey!" Vlasta shouted, burning her eyes into the housekeeper. The woman froze and began to tremble. "Uba, huba, uba," Vlasta mocked her, making a troubled face.

Nexxa put Natina down and bent to her saying, "Can you be my brave little girl?" Natina reached and touched her sweet little hand to Nexxa's cheek. Nexxa thought back to when she tried to protect her from Kilmer in Rome.

Vlasta lifted the pot, the flame still on high, and carried it to the table. As she dropped it, water sloshed out. Ankica jerked her head back as some boiling water splashed her face. "Now! Eat!" Vlasta demanded. The housekeeper and Nexxa with Natina swiftly moved over to the table pulling out chairs and sitting. Vlasta stood at the head of the table and motioned with a hefty open arm. "The feast is ready!" She smiled big, then winced with her wounded leg giving way, causing her to slump onto the chair. Nexxa leaned over the pot and spooned some water into the bowls on the table. As they all sat eating boiled water, Nexxa looked to the cellar door. She hoped she could will a sound to emit from the cellar, perhaps that radio Vlasta had down there. Anything—anything that would spur her interest.

"Eat more! Eat more!" Vlasta demanded, doing her best to shake the table and regain her balance. "How does it taste?" Vlasta asked as she dipped her finger in and tasted it. "Oh, this needs a bone," she announced sternly, looking over at Ankica before Ankica slumped in her seat toward the housekeeper. Leaning on the table, Vlasta grabbed the bread knife and pulled the cutting board toward her. She held onto the board with one hand and reached toward Ankica, losing her balance. Then, she sliced back and forth even though there wasn't any bread to slice. The knife struggled back and forth, going into the wood. Vlasta screamed, and bracing herself on the table, she started moving to the side where Nexxa was seated.

Nexxa pushed Natina down and under the table and stood just as Vlasta was upon her with the knife. Behind Vlasta, Nexxa saw the woman with long flowing gray hair who smiled with her lavender lips looking toward the cellar door. Suddenly, sirens could be heard and paramedics conversing. Vlasta turned her head with raging curious eyes. Nexxa reached for the bread knife, and just as she grasped it Vlasta yanked the hand holding the knife slashing across Nexxa's chest cutting the scar, the one from Diane. Blood soaked through her tank top and Nexxa gasped as she held her chest. Vlasta looked back to the sound of sirens emitting from her CB radio in the cellar. Nexxa grabbed her by the back of her head and pushed her face into her chest. Vlasta snarled before licking the blood. "Open the cellar door," Nexxa said in a determined voice in Russian, and the housekeeper jumped from her seat unlocking the door. Nexxa stepped sideways toward the door with Vlasta attached to her chest. She turned so that Vlasta had her back to the opening and then she pushed her down. Nexxa fell back on her butt and the housekeeper shut the door. Trying to turn the lock, the housekeeper felt the brunt of a body slam against it. Nexxa saw the woman with gray hair before her again. She wiped her lavender lips and swayed her hand to her. Nexxa rose to her knees and pushed on the door with her wounded hand while locking it. Blood dripped from both of her scars, seeping under the door where Vlasta was slouched, lapping.

The housekeeper ran to the pantry and came back with the first aid kit. Nexxa twisted with her back against the door, and she pushed up Nexxa's top and applied pressure with a gauze. "I need to explain, but it won't make sense," Nexxa said, looking over to Ankica at the table. "My body, my blood has changed, and I can use it to save us." The housekeeper looked over to Ankica. Babushka lifted her hand motioning to Nexxa and translated, telling her to trust Nexxa.

Nexxa felt her eyes become heavy. Ankica managed to stand and, holding on to the edge of the table, moved around to the other side and coaxed Natina out. "I'm going to need my sister," Nexxa said before she closed her eyes, letting her head fall back against the door.

ILIADA HEARS THE LOUD | 47

Nexxa opened her eyes and the sexy nurse was there. She knew if that were the case she was okay. For now.

She didn't remember until Natina said, "You say sit." She pointed to the cellar door behind Nexxa.

"Oh baby, you're so cute," Nexxa spoke softly as she held out her right hand, seeing it was bandaged before she reached for Natina and pulled her into her lap. A bang came on the door and Natina jumped, leaning and looking closer, giving in to her curiosity. Nexxa called out for the housekeeper, who was at the sink; she was more resilient than Nexxa expected, and she ran to collect Natina.

Ankica was such a great asset explaining to the doctor and nurse what Nexxa could, though she most likely wouldn't be believed given that she wasn't Russian. She told them there had been a breach in the security and that Nexxa thwarted the threat. And that they had summoned Sergei to return from Croatia. The housekeeper told Nexxa in the little English she knew that she was glad she had returned.

Iliada called Nexxa before Nexxa could call her. "I'm on the next flight out of JFK," she spoke, before placing the call on speaker as she was shoving more clothes than she would need into her suitcase. "I knew Mr. Albert was right about the Crimson," she scolded.

"It's not Crimson… I didn't have time to explain. I'm in Moscow."

"Oh, then I guess I'm flying to Russia. Who is it then? I heard banging," Iliada asked, waving a hand up around her head indicating that she had physically felt the noise.

"It's—"

"The fucking housekeeper, right," Iliada scolded again, rolling her eyes.

When Iliada arrived at Sergei's house the next morning she found Nexxa sitting by the cellar door. Her hair was starting to look oily and her lips looked chapped. Iliada knelt to hug her and when Nexxa leaned away from the door, a loud thud was heard. Vlasta made a huge dent on the right side of the steel door. Iliada jumped before shouting, "NO!" slamming her hand on the door. Nexxa started unraveling her bandage and the housekeeper ran over to her to help. She handed Nexxa a paring knife and Nexxa slit her hand. Iliada's eyes widened. Nexxa flipped over on her knees and put her hand close to the opening under the door. The sound of a rabid animal ensued and then snoring.

"Nexxa, what the fuck?" Iliada stood shaking her hands.

Nexxa turned around. "Yeah, my hair is dirty. I look unfuckable," she said with an exhausted breath.

"Oh, I'm sorry. I love you." Iliada knelt and started fixing Nexxa's stray hairs.

"I can't leave. She's getting weaker."

"Weaker? She just fucking, like, put a dent in a steel door," Iliada said as if she was shocked but mad at the same time. "Why are you cutting your hand?" Iliada asked, trying to rewrap the bandage. "Can we call a doctor?" Nexxa laughed and Iliada shook her head. "What? And why is your blood, like, lavender?"

Nexxa let out a small breath. "Nexxa! What is going on?" Iliada almost breathed fire as she stood with her hands on her hips.

The housekeeper called the doctor again, and within one hour he arrived with the sexy nurse. Nexxa explained in Russian that she needed a blood drip. He sent his nurse out to his car, and she came back in with a pack of blood. "No, I need to give blood," she started to explain in her exhausted state. Ankica stood by Nexxa with her cane and nodded, assuring the doctor. The snoring from Vlasta subsided—Nexxa stood holding out her arm and pointing to her vein—a needle went in, and blood filled the bag.

A tube connected to the first full blood pack was placed at the slight opening under the door. Iliada helped Nexxa upstairs and to the bathroom that was adjacent to the sitting room. The housekeeper trotted up the staircase after them and tapped on the bathroom door, insisting that Nexxa should use Sergei's room. Nexxa fell to her knees and lifted the toilet seat, throwing up. Iliada held onto her, holding her hair back. "Just put some blankets in the sitting room," Iliada told her.

After she helped her shower, they sat together on the sofa in the sitting room while Ankica sat across from them. Nexxa told her what had happened in Rome, how she had added Kilmer's ashes to a small cut she had made on her hand, while Ankica sipped her cherry brandy. The housekeeper took care of Natina, and when it was time, she helped Ankica to bed. Iliada sat with her legs crisscrossed while Nexxa rested her head in her lap.

Nexxa was the first to wake, hearing an unpleasant sound coming from the kitchen. She woke Iliada and they ran down the staircase. Nexxa took a deep breath, blowing out her relief when she saw the cellar door still closed.

"What's that smell? Eww." Iliada held her hand over her mouth and nose.

"I think it's Vlasta." Nexxa dashed over to the cellar door. She put her hand on it and leaned, listening.

"I'm jealous," Vlasta said in an uncharacteristically soft voice. Nexxa pulled back.

Iliada widened her eyes. "What? What is it?"

"I'm going to need more blood," Nexxa announced, opening the fridge and looking in. Then she turned on the kettle.

"Nexxa! You can't be serious! Like, how much blood can you lose?" Iliada walked over to the cellar door and sniffed, making a face before going over to a cabinet and looking for mugs.

"I don't have a choice. She's still fucking talking!" Nexxa motioned toward the door before stretching out her arm and looking at the bandage from the needle. Iliada took over making tea, and within a few minutes the housekeeper was downstairs. She offered to make breakfast, and Nexxa translated for Iliada as they sat at the kitchen island. When they heard Natina on the baby monitor, Nexxa jumped from her seat and went up to her bedroom.

After she checked in on Ankica, she was still sleeping, Nexxa and Natina brushed their teeth together and then Nexxa held her hand as they descended the stairs. In the kitchen, Iliada was helping, since she couldn't help but make breakfast. They all chose to sit at the kitchen island, each glancing over at the cellar door. Natina giggled watching *Masha and the Bear* on the kitchen TV. For a moment it seemed as if this was a normal Thursday morning.

Then—a loud boom.

The force against the cellar door rocked the whole kitchen. Nexxa jumped from her barstool, wincing from her fractured rib. From the side counter she grabbed a blood collection bag and ripped open a package with a needle. Iliada jumped up. "Here, let me help."

With the assistance of the housekeeper and Iliada, Nexxa sat with a needle in her arm watching her lavender blood stream into a bag. "See, I blood," Natina said, standing at Nexxa's side and pinching her little finger so the tip looked red. Nexxa reached, touching her finger to Natina's.

"You have the family I always wanted!" Vlasta barked with

her face at the bottom of the door. When the bag was full, Nexxa hurried over to the door and placed it with the tube at the crack. They all watched as the tube was yanked, pulling the bag against the door.

"It's like you're breastfeeding," Iliada huffed.

Nexxa watched the blood bag, seeing how quickly it was emptying. "I have to do more. This won't be enough," she announced before bracing herself on the kitchen table. The housekeeper quickly withdrew some juice from the fridge, filling a glass and ushering Nexxa over to a barstool.

Iliada looked through the pantry saying, "There must be some vitamins or something that can help with her energy."

"I can't." Nexxa pushed the juice away. "I feel worse."

Iliada popped her head out of the pantry. "Wine?" she asked with a strained grin, slowly holding up a bottle.

"You're brilliant," Nexxa said, holding her forehead. The housekeeper looked from Iliada to Nexxa confused and worried.

Iliada opened the wine and poured Nexxa a glass. She drank it and placed the empty glass down saying, "Ahhh."

"Fuck it, I'm having a glass too." Iliada fetched a second wine glass and filled them both.

The housekeeper approached Nexxa and told her that she needed to talk to Sergei. That she was afraid of being fired if she didn't tell him what had happened, and that she was supposed to give weekly progress reports to her agency.

"I will tell him. I will call him now, now that things are under control," Nexxa assured her just as Ankica entered the kitchen while on the phone with Sergei. Nexxa closed her eyes hearing his voice since Ankica had him on speakerphone.

She understood that Ankica said, "I am safe. But we had a problem. Eh, Vlasta came back."

"What's the problem? Let me talk to the housekeeper."

The housekeeper shook her head no with her eyes showing she was nervous. Nexxa held her hand out to Ankica, and she gave Nexxa the phone.

"Sergei," Nexxa spoke while looking to Ankica.

"Nexxa? What are you doing in my house?" Sergei demanded.

"Sergei, I needed to come back. I needed to protect babushka and baby Natina."

"Protect them from what? Give the phone back to my babushka." His tone moved from irritated to angry.

Nexxa took the call off of speaker and started her way out of the kitchen saying, "I won't do that. They're my responsibility now." She made her way up the stairs taking the steps exceptionally fast. "Now, I'm at your bedroom door. What is the code?" Sergei had added the electronic lock before he left for Croatia. There was silence on the phone. "Sergei, I just want to get my clothes from your closet." She could hear him breathing. "I can get the housekeeper to, but I want to get them myself. Unless you already mailed them off to Dublin."

"What the fuck is this about Vlasta?"

"Oh, that. Yeah, she's locked in the cellar. She tried to fucking—Ah! She tried to kill me. Then, she woke up your grandmother in the middle of the night talking about needing bones to make soup!"

Sergei stood looking out over the sea on a pier outside of a restaurant. "I can get new security." His voice expressed his masculinity.

"Security! Where's Bogdan? Huh? I was in his house before I went to Dublin. All of the sudden he is gone and Vlasta is here. I don't care what you think, Sergei, but I'm staying here with them until she fucking dies!" Nexxa leaned her head back and blew out a breath. She looked back to his bedroom door. "My sister Iliada is here to help me."

"Six seven nine nine three."

Nexxa typed in the code and pushed on the handle, stepping in. Seeing his bed, his room, the organ that pumped her blood hurt more than her fractured rib. Nexxa needed her armor—all her black. If someone were going to be jealous of what she had, then she should be properly dressed each day for battle. "Are you in?" Sergei finally asked, sounding curious.

Nexxa looked through her clothes in his closet, noticed some empty hangars.

"Nexxa?"

"Oh, yes, I'm in. My clothes. I missed them," she responded as she pulled a strappy black tank off of a hanger and found a pair of black leggings that were appropriate for the impending occasion.

Sergei lowered his head, rubbing a hand over it before smiling at some tourists who walked by. A family of three: Tata, mama, and a young girl. The thought of Nexxa wedding dress shopping in Rome flashed in his mind and he heard Kilmer's voice, *Crimson is coming for her soul.* Sergei grasped his jaw. He wondered where her heart was.

"Do you love him?"

Nexxa sat on the pouf in Sergei's closet. She could smell him everywhere in the house but mostly, and in the kind of intimate way she wanted to smell him, in his room. "No, I never loved him." That was partly a lie. She loved Quinn for taking care of her, but she believed she loved him more because Diane had commanded that it be so.

Iliada came into the bedroom. "Nexxa, I think we need to get ready." Nexxa held the phone away and said, "Just a sec." They were going to try to summon help.

"Sergei, I have to go. I have to stay focused."

"There's a gun in my safe. In the closet."

Nexxa pushed some of Sergei's hanging clothes around until she saw the safe. "I see the safe. But that won't help," Nexxa replied, shrugging her shoulders.

"Open the safe, thirty-two, nineteen, seven."

"Sergei, you should have known. You should have trusted me."

"Nexxa, I—"

"What? What, Sergei?" Nexxa held up a finger to Iliada. Iliada mouthed *okay*.

"I know I should have done things differently."

"It doesn't matter now. I took care of the woman with the wolfness like me that wanted my soul. I killed her in Rome. I take care of myself, and I'll always take care of the people that I love."

Sergei heard her and wanted to tell her that from the moment he had seen her at the horse racetrack in Beirut that he knew he wanted her and would do anything for her. He secured her release from Hezbollah, he ended Kilmer in Rome, and did what it took to keep her safe around Quinn by paying the balance for Diane's jet.

Crimson had been her battle, something that even Hooli couldn't have helped Sergei save her from.

"Nexxa." Sergei looked out over the blue water of the Adriatic Sea. "I miss you," he said, sounding like he would need her to pick up where he finished speaking.

Nexxa closed her eyes. She missed him.

Nexxa slipped on a pair of sneakers she had in Sergei's closet. Looking down at them, she said to Iliada, "They're dirty, but I might get blood on them." She handed Iliada the gun.

"I don't know what to do with this," Iliada remarked as she huffed bigger than she ever had.

"Well, we shall see." Nexxa shrugged a shoulder before tightening her ponytail. She didn't tell Iliada yet, but this thing with Vlasta needed to end today however that might be.

Downstairs, Nexxa gave babushka a hug. She looked into her wise Russian eyes and Ankica said, "You will, eh, be okay."

Nexxa lifted Natina and gave her a kiss. She held out her finger, pinching it again. Nexxa kissed her finger saying, "Go with babushka now. I love you, baby." Natina looked back at Nexxa as she held the housekeeper's hand leaving the kitchen.

Iliada removed the gun from under her top and placed it on the kitchen island. Nexxa looked at the gun before taking the white sheets she had carried down and making a circle on the kitchen floor. They stepped into the circle and held hands as Nexxa commanded, "I call for protection around this property." The kitchen became cold, and the sheets forming the circle began to billow in the sudden draft. Nexxa and

Iliada looked into each other's lovely eyes. The back door in the kitchen rattled and the barstools moved away from the island, stopping and blocking the entrance from the foyer. The cold illuminated Nexxa's skin, showing her hidden armor of lavender blood.

"Stay in the circle! I'll open the cellar door," Iliada said confidently. "No! I'll do it," Nexxa shouted, as the air became louder. "Your power is stronger than mine!" Iliada argued before looking over to the gun.

Nexxa looked to the back door and it flew open. Iliada stepped out of the circle, lifted the gun, and walked over to the cellar door. The bag of blood was empty, and a whirl of Russian cold swirled by the cellar door.

Iliada turned the lock and the door gave in from the weight of Vlasta, pulling away from the door hinges as she fell out on the kitchen tile. Nexxa took a step forward in the circle; Iliada held out her hand to dissuade her. She knelt and felt the aging flesh on Vlasta's neck for a pulse. Iliada mouthed *no*. Nexxa leapt from the white circle and grabbed Vlasta by her wrists and pulled her. Iliada placed the gun down and pushed on her legs, slipping. They laughed. She got herself back up, and once Nexxa was able to get a better grip, they dragged her to the back door. Nexxa stepped down the two steps and then the weight of Vlasta's body pushed her down. "Shit!" Iliada blurted out, stepping out of the doorway.

Half-covered by Vlasta's sinister smelling body, Nexxa looked up to the sky. A cloud in the shape of the older man in mid-century military attire was positioned overhead. She heard, *Get up and command this!* Nexxa rolled and twisted out from under Vlasta. She looked over to the second-floor window, and she saw the woman with long gray hair and lavender lips. Nexxa sat up with her arms bracing her on the ground, and Vlasta managed to pull herself to a crouch. Nexxa looked around the earth beneath her for something to cut her hand with.

Then—the sound of brass sliding into a steel chamber.

Iliada shot and the bullet entered through Vlasta and exited, grazing Nexxa's shoulder, knocking her back to the ground.

Nexxa's lovely eyes closed; she could hear the aging flesh of Vlasta rustling against the ground as she charged forward and licked at Nexxa's open wound, followed by Iliada screaming. The older man with a mustache donning mid-century military attire shouted and the woman with long gray hair and lavender lips slowly fell like Nexxa had. Iliada pulled on Vlasta—she stood and staggered off into the woods with lavender blood dripping from her saggy skin—Nexxa opened her eyes…

She saw Natina in the upstairs window.

He played with karma so that he could execute her freedom. He committed a deadly sin in Rome to avenge her pain. He showed her his parents' grave, the Kozlovs, then his crypt. He placed a family heirloom, his mother's ruby ring, on her finger. The hardest Sergei had pushed himself to do was to throw money to his adversary so that she wouldn't be under suspicion.

Sergei called Ankica's phone. The housekeeper answered with a tremble in her voice. With a shaking hand she put the call on speaker and placed the phone down next to Ankica.

"Eh, Sergei, she's okay. The sister shot the gun."

"Babushka, can you put Nexxa on the phone?"

"Eh, we called the doctor again."

"Why? What happened? Is she hurt?" Sergei's worry was as intense as his tone.

"Vlasta eh, fell on Nexxa," Ankica explained, shaking her head.

"Put me back on with the housekeeper." The housekeeper lifted the phone, already nodding her head before he spoke. "I'll call back. Keep the phone by you."

Sergei called Hooli and told him to activate the drone. He made another call to his investor, the one whom he had met in the woods, the one whose daughter he shot, and asked him to send one of his men over. Within enough time Hooli called Sergei and sent a link to access live footage from the drone. They both watched as the drone surveilled the area behind Sergei's home. One person was visible running through a sparse area of the woods. Sergei immediately tried to call Nexxa while still on with Hooli. "Fuuuck!" he shouted when her phone went straight to voicemail.

Sergei ended his call with Hooli and called his babushka's phone. The housekeeper answered the call and told Sergei that she would go downstairs to see if Nexxa and her sister were back in the house yet.

Downstairs, Iliada stood by Nexxa cleaning the spot where the bullet had grazed her arm. The housekeeper ran and checked that the kitchen door was locked. Iliada looked to her, managing to smile. Nexxa mouthed *spasiba*.

"Sergei." The housekeeper held the phone out for Nexxa.

Iliada motioned with her head for her to put the phone down. She dropped it on the island with her hand shaking. Iliada lifted the phone and gave the housekeeper a pat on the arm smiling. "She's fine. We'll call you back."

Later that night as Nexxa lay in Sergei's bed after being treated by the doctor, she called him. "Hi," Sergei answered on the first ring.

"It's good to hear your voice again," Nexxa told him as she moved her hand across his sheets inhaling his scent.

"How do you feel now? I should be there."

"I'm okay," she explained with a little laugh. "Your doctor and sexy nurse gave me some pain pills."

"That's good, that's good," Sergei said.

"But. I didn't take any."

"Why? You should. Yeah, Nexxa, you need to rest."

"Sergei, I know. It's just that—"

"You have orders to rest and heal. I have someone watching the house now." Nexxa remained silent. "I should have had someone after Bogdan," Sergei continued, sitting on the bed in his hotel room. "I don't know how. But it's over now and she's gone. Yeah, I was wrong for—"

"Sergei," Nexxa spoke with all her courage in her throat.

"Yeah?"

"I kissed him." Hearing her own voice made her grasp her abdomen. Before the silence could gnaw her to death, she continued, "I, I never would have. Then something changed. You told me to fuck off and then Diane was there to help me."

Sergei thought back to when he had told her to *get the fuck out,* leave his hotel room, the part about sending her clothes to Dublin.

Nexxa thought about how she had handled herself when he told her to "fuck off." How she didn't feel like she owed him an explanation of how she had been faithful, in the moment of his haste. She wished she had stayed and tried to fix things. Nexxa could hear his contempt as he did mundane things in the background like taking a long piss. In the present, she believed he had fucked Kessly. It hurt. But nothing would hurt like never being with him again. Nexxa heard the toilet flush, the faucet, and his electric toothbrush. She looked to the pain meds prescribed to her on the nightstand. She now only heard the Croatian news on the TV and other ambient noises from his hotel room.

Sergei lifted his phone again and said, "I have to go. I have another meeting."

"Ser—"

He ended the call.

Nexxa pushed herself up in bed. She stared at the call on her screen that had just ended. "White, white glow!" she yelled. Then, she texted: *I love you! I have always loved you!*

Sergei was just stepping off the elevator into the lobby when he heard his phone ping and withdrew it, reading her text. His face grinned without taking into consideration Nexxa's sins while his hand gave in and called her. "Nexxa," he spoke looking out over the lobby.

She stood and breathed, "Sergei," through her pain.

The ground rumbled beneath Sergei with windows shattering in the hotel. Nexxa heard loud voices with a commotion that sounded like an invasion with gunfire. She then listened as Sergei must have dropped his phone while shouting in English, "Get down!" before firing his gun.

"Sergei!" Nexxa screamed. The connection ended. She pounded the wall with her fist, crying, and then dialed his number. "Fuuuck!" she screamed so loud that Iliada heard her from the sitting room. Within moments she rushed into the bedroom asking her sister what had happened as she frantically looked around the room before running over to the glass doors that led to the terrace and checking that they were locked. Nexxa clutched her side with one hand and held out the other saying, "I—I don't know what happened. I heard him shout and fire his gun!" She grasped her side with the fractured rib with both hands, lowering her head.

"Who? Sergei?" Iliada asked loudly.

A few minutes later, Nexxa's phone rang, and they both looked in the direction of it. Nexxa's mind saw Sergei with the white glow, replaying when she had stood with Mr. Albert on his dais watching the Winter Tag game. Iliada lifted her phone, answering, "Hello. Who is this?"

"Uh, this is Hooli. I need to speak to Nexxa," he said with a tone that was both rattled and direct.

"Yeah. Just tell me," Iliada demanded before putting the call on speaker.

"There's been an explosion in the port," he said before clearing his throat. "Um, I was monitoring live chats in the area, stuff that well—"

"Hooli! Listen to me. Something else happened!" Nexxa cried, cupping her mouth.

"Yeah. Yeah, I think I know."

Nexxa lifted the phone to her ear and said, "I'm going to Croatia. I'm going to find Sergei."

Nexxa looked toward the black that was approaching her outside of the airport in the quaint Slavic city. Even though the airport was newly built, she could still smell the story of the former communist Yugoslavia as she looked out at the fields beyond the parking lot.

"Hi," Srđan said with a solemn face as he emerged energetically from his black Audi A8 with his petite self that bore a shaved head and a dusting of dirty look.

On the ride to the coast he started, "You know that Croatia was communist country, Yugoslavia, until nineties, then terrible war, lots of genocide happen." She knew the history of Croatia, she had been to Zagreb in the past to see a fashion designer, so she nodded thinking back to when Sergei was telling her the history of Beirut when they were there together.

The highway was busy with work trucks and semis heading

toward the coast. The explosion had affected some smaller boats and yachts, leaving cruise ships untouched. The hotels along the coast suffered the most damage. Nexxa hadn't had time to read or watch the news. She mostly cried, getting little sleep lying with Iliada in Sergei's bed. Hooli had been busy looking through all of Sergei's messages, emails, and associates.

Nexxa pulled out her pain pills; she hadn't taken any yet. "I have brandy," Srđan piped up, motioning to the back of the car.

Nexxa put the pills back into her purse. "Yeah, I'll have that," she agreed, feeling in the center compartment and pulling out the bottle and a small glass.

"Help the pain," Srđan added.

Nexxa nodded before she took her sip.

"What happened? I get this call from Sergei's business partner, Hooey."

Nexxa laughed, saying, "Hooli," as she poured more brandy. "And he's his hacker."

"Yeah, yeah." Srđan waved his hand. "So he say something has happened to you and to Sergei. I was in Zagreb for one night," he continued, holding up one finger and shaking his head. "Now, I call him and no answer. Phone doesn't have the voicemail, anything."

Nexxa leaned her head to the side. She winced when she twisted her legs trying to find a comfortable position. "You are hurt, yeah?" Srđan asked when she winced.

"Yeah," Nexxa answered.

"What?" Srđan scrunched his face.

"I took care of a problem that was in Russia. The housekeeper. She needed to go."

"The housekeeper, huh?"

"Not the current one. The one that can drag a deer all by herself. The one that wanted to make soup with old lady bones."

Srđan's eyes widened, and he quickly shifted to a lower gear as traffic started to slow down. "It will be one more hour in this traffic," he informed her, lowering his window and hanging his head out as if he would be able to see around the big trucks ahead of them. Nexxa lifted her nose trying to get a whiff, as something from outside smelled familiar. "I can smoke?" Srđan asked, holding up a pack of cigarettes. Nexxa nodded. She didn't care if he drove while naked as long as he got her closer to Sergei.

When they arrived in Rijeka, the street leading to the coast was blocked off, so Srđan was forced to pull over at a petrol station. He got out of the car and walked around to the side of the station, attempting to get a view. Nexxa exited the car, ran past him, and started to step over the wall that formed the perimeter on the back side. She was just over when Srđan turned and saw her. She slid, landing on her butt and he ran to help her. "You crazy?" Srđan asked, grasping her under her arms and helping her to stand.

"I have to get to the hotel."

Nexxa looked past Srđan, seeing a truck driver walk over to his truck. She darted after him. "Sir, hey!" she called out. Srđan shook his head, holding his hands up wondering what she was doing. "Please, please, I need to get down there to a hotel," Nexxa pleaded while walking next to him.

The driver explained to Nexxa that he was headed down another road and told her to leave him alone before Srđan ran over, reaching them saying, "Hey. Hey, I can pay you!"

The three of them hopped into his cab and made it to the first *policija* checkpoint. The driver presented his ID and then they were denied passage. Srđan withdrew his phone and called his cousin, Ivan Jubić, Minister of Physical Planning, Construction and State Assets. Nexxa looked to him holding back tears of gratitude for him and pain for Sergei.

They were waved off after speaking to his cousin and around the barricade they went. Nexxa scanned out of the window looking around at the tourists receiving aid roadside under white tents. They reached the strip the hotel Sergei had been staying in was on, and the driver stopped, telling them they had to get out there. Srđan helped Nexxa out and he put his arm around her waist to help her walk. The front of the Hotel Continental was blocked off and crowded with emergency personnel and *policija*.

"Can you help me?" Nexxa called out. "I'm trying to…" she continued. "I'm looking for Sergei Kozlov," she tried to shout, collapsing into Srđan's grasp.

A *policija* caught view of her and came closer toward them asking in Croatian if they needed help. Srđan indicated no and said, "Come, come. We have to go."

"Why, Srđan?" Nexxa cried, wiping tears while facing him and holding onto his arms.

"You are sick. Hurt. You should rest," he told her, looking

around at the chaos wondering where they should go next.

Nexxa woke and thought she saw babushka. She reached to touch her head and closed her eyes again. The accents weren't Russian, she determined, and then she opened her eyes. "Who is there and where are we?" Nexxa asked with a mildly agitated tone.

"This my cousin, Andrea. She was taking care of you," Srđan explained.

Nexxa pushed herself up on the sofa. "Has Hooli called?" she asked, and he shook his head no.

"We're wasting time. And, why was Sergei here anyway?"

Srđan looked down and rubbed his hand over his bald head. He looked up and took a cigarette out and lit it. "He was going to party on the yacht," he said, shrugging his shoulders and blowing from his cigarette. "They blow it up." Nexxa covered her mouth. She threw up and stood running to the kitchen, and Andrea ran after her, giving her some paper towels.

Nexxa wiped her face and used water from the faucet to rinse her mouth. Andrea poured her a glass of water. Nexxa drank and thanked her. "Is that a terrace?" she asked before darting across the room. Srđan moved quickly, putting his cig in his mouth, and helped her open the glass door. Nexxa stepped out and moved to the railing. She could see smoke billowing in the harbor and could hear sirens. "I don't smell him," Nexxa announced.

"What?" Srđan asked, and when she didn't answer he looked around her toward the port.

"Not here," she finally said, turning to face Srđan.

"What's not here?" he asked.

"Sergei," Nexxa asserted. "In the car, before you started to smoke." Nexxa started moving closer, sniffing Srđan.

"Hey." He leaned back as he was taking a drag.

"I thought maybe it was just you. The cigarettes. The Croatian air," Nexxa explained, waving her hand around. Srđan chuckled and stopped when Nexxa grasped her side with her fractured rib. He helped her steady herself. Looking down at her side, Nexxa asked, "When was it when you started smoking?"

"I was fourteen, maybe younger."

Nexxa laughed. "Ouch. Don't make me laugh. No, I meant where were we? On the road."

"Oh." Srđan thought for a few seconds. "Karlovac."

"Then that's where we are going."

Srđan's cousin Andrea drove them around the side streets back to the petrol station where he had parked his car. Nexxa gave her a slight embrace and thanked her. She rode in the front this time, keeping her phone in her lap and the window cracked. She thought about Kieran and how he had shown her a video of Sergei. *Ick, don't think about him fucking her*, she told herself.

Hooli called. Nexxa jumped and the phone slid off of her lap. "Hi Hooli," Nexxa answered as she winced, bending to retrieve her phone.

"Am I on speaker?"

"Yes."

"Call me back when you get to Vukova Gorica," Hooli

instructed.

"Why? And... oh, right. You're tracking me," Nexxa huffed, ending the call. She looked over at Srđan and he made a confused face, shrugging his shoulders. Nexxa looked straight on, then back to Srđan and then out of the passenger window. He asked her if he could turn on music and Nexxa lifted a hand indicating she couldn't care less. The electronic music permeated the Audi and Nexxa's mind.

When they reached the next town, Srđan pulled over at the McDonald's. He went inside and got in line and Nexxa stood outside by the car and called Hooli.

"It took me some time." Hooli said.

"Some time? It's only been a day," Nexxa countered.

"You won't like what I've found."

Nexxa braced her mind, and she closed her eyes.

"So—"

"No, no, I can smell him," Nexxa blurted out, hoping to cover whatever despair Hooli was about to give to her.

"What? Are you talking to Srđan, about McDonald's?"

"No. No, I'm not talking to anyone. I mean, I'm talking to you." Nexxa shook in agitation. "Forget it. But whatever you have to say, I know Sergei is alive."

"Yeah, yeah, I'm sure." Hooli's tone was positive, lending to agreeable. "So, I found some guys that are connected to Ivan."

Nexxa thought, remembering Sergei mentioning Ivan. Hooli started talking again as Nexxa walked away from the car to get eyes on Srđan; he had stepped out of line and went to the men's room. "What? Say that again," she asked.

"So, right. I have calls between these guys and Ivan right up until the explosion."

"Were they there? In Rijeka?" Nexxa asked right as Srđan walked over to the car.

"One of them made a slip." Hooli chuckled with pride. "Yeah, so this chick posted on Instagram a pic with this guy, she's the kind you pay for."

Nexxa thought with her professional face looking at the man across from the Audi that, unbeknownst to her, Sergei had bought, as Srđan popped a fry in his mouth holding up the container suggesting she have some. While still on the phone, Nexxa walked around, took the fries and mouthed, *Can you go get more?*

"Okay, so how do you know?" Nexxa asked.

Hooli huffed, sounding like a teenager.

"Well I suppose you work for me now. I'm Sergei's proxy," Nexxa explained, looking at herself in the reflection of the passenger window before glancing back into McDonald's.

"Have you ever heard of Six Degrees of Kevin Bacon?"

"Uh, yeah." Nexxa nodded.

"So this guy, he is the son of an old ass tractor repair man, who they used to call Mr. Fixit back in the eighties and his wife is a local salon owner on the outskirts of Zagreb whose cousin has a daughter who is friends with a girl who works the port area, well you know, for those things."

"And you used facial recognition?"

"Nexxa, I know. I know because I found a photo from a local newspaper from about twenty-five years ago that, well, glorified Mr. Fixit for other reasons, and his son with the same birthmark on his face was pictured with him. Now for Ivan, his father and Mr. Fixit were from the same town as kids. Look, do what you can on the ground. Let me know what I can do to support you."

"Hooli," Nexxa said quickly before she lost him. "Tell me something. Tell me. I'm not crazy, right?" Nexxa held her forehead thinking about Sergei, but images of Kevin Bacon and French fries kept popping in.

"He's alive. I mean, these guys are probably just doing a shakedown."

"Yeah," Nexxa exhaled, letting her tense shoulders fall.

"Hey, he—Sergei got you out of Beirut."

"I figured that was partly, mostly, you."

"You were worth it. He—he loves you."

Nexxa closed her eyes hearing Hooli's words. She wanted to thank him. Then Srđan returned with more fries than they could both eat, and she remembered he was Ivan's cousin as they both got into the car.

"So what did Hooey say?" Srđan asked after shoving some fries in his mouth and wiping his hand on his pants as he drove on the highway.

"Not much that was helpful," Nexxa fibbed, looking down at her ruby ring, seeing it was still a perfect shade of red. "Let's see once we get closer," Nexxa continued as she adjusted her hair, smelling Sergei's scent again just as the town of Karlovac was coming up. Srđan took the exit for the town and drove them down the main street. The village, although it was early summer, had a haze that could be called Commi Era Gray if you were naming a color for Behr paint.

Nexxa directed Srđan to an area where the Korana and Kupa

rivers converged. He pulled over on the narrow roadway and Nexxa stepped out of the car. She peered into a window in a vine-covered building on the river. "He was here," Nexxa said with an excited face but with a heart that didn't match.

"Why? Why he's here?" Srđan asked with squinted eyes.

"Ivan. Your cousin."

Srđan, Sergei's friend—good friend—lowered his head, shaking it. "I didn't know this. Sergei is my friend. He's my good friend. I'll call him, Ivan. I can fix it, this problem," Srđan assured as he pulled his phone out of his jeans' pocket and called his cousin.

Nexxa walked up to him and put her hand on his, pushing it down. "Hang up," she whispered as he lowered his phone. They heard Ivan answer. Nexxa took the phone and tossed it into the river.

BLACK CAST WHITE GLOW | 50

Mr. Albert only sipped bottled water on his flight to Croatia, but Flash ate all the snacks that business class offered. Standing outside in The Land of Slavia, he stood in his all-grey ensemble and looked to the sky that still held the desire for submission. Mr. Albert's black leather Tumi carry-on jumped and he smiled while declining the offer from his driver to take his bag.

Srđan drove them back to the center of Karlovac and Nexxa bought a map. From there they went to Dubovac Castle. Nexxa headed to the tower and Srđan stood at the entryway telling tourists the tower was closed. She spread the map on the floor and, kneeling, withdrew her pendulum. "Where is Sergei?" Nexxa asked in a strained voice that matched the way she kept smoothing out the map. Srđan told a few more tourists the tower was closed and then looked over, making eye contact with Nexxa. She closed her eyes and lowered the hand holding her pendulum. He darted over to her and knelt, placing an arm around her shoulders. Nexxa looked up and whispered, "Thank you." Srđan hopped up and returned to manning his post.

Finally, the pendulum swung and indicated Zagreb. Nexxa folded—mostly crumpled—the map and tucked away her pendulum in her bra. When Srđan told another couple that they couldn't enter, Nexxa stood saying, "Zagreb, our next stop on our vacation." Srđan lifted his head in acknowledgment and motioned with his hand, which yearned to hold a cigarette, for the accumulating tourists to enter the tower. Nexxa grabbed ahold of his arm and smiled, kissing him on the cheek just as the castle manager approached them. "Honeymoon," Nexxa offered, laughing and pulling a giddy Srđan.

On the way to Zagreb, Nexxa called Hooli. "Any news?" Hooli asked while assessing three monitors in front of him.

"No. But I know we need to be in Zagreb. We need a place that is private. A house to rent. I don't have time to look. Can—"

"I'm on it," he told her, already typing away.

"Thank you. Really, thank you," Nexxa said, before looking over to her driver and grasping his cigarette.

Nexxa stepped out of the car and looked, seeing lights on inside and a man in the living room. She exhaled. "I don't want to have to answer questions and listen to him explain how the house works," she expressed with exhausted eyes.

"I can listen," Srđan told her, shutting his door and opening the back to remove her suitcase. Nexxa stood in the living room hearing the voice of the man that was renting them the house while she tried to assess the different smells. She knew that upstairs in a bathroom there was a feminine hygiene product in the trash that had not been disposed of and that in the cellar there was a towel that never made it out of the washing machine.

The man smiled at Nexxa as he walked past her out of the living room to leave, and Srđan locked the door behind him. "Nice house," Srđan commented as he looked around before going to the kitchen and opening the fridge. "I could get something to eat," he continued, shutting the refrigerator and removing a cigarette as he then opened the back door.

"Yeah, sure. I mean I feel like we should drive around," Nexxa responded, looking out of the kitchen window and seeing a children's playground in the backyard. She thought about Natina. *How could I ever forgive myself if I don't find him?*

In the car on the way to a restaurant, Nexxa smelled Sergei everywhere. After about fifteen minutes, they pulled into the gentlemen's club parking lot. "A strip club?" Nexxa said before opening the car door.

"We can go somewhere else," Srđan explained just as Nexxa exited the car.

"No, this will do," she told him, knowing Sergei's scent was really strong there.

Inside, after they were seated and Nexxa chuckled looking

around at the other patrons and the lazy sauntering hostess, Srđan said, "I bring Sergei here."

"Yeah, yeah I know," Nexxa told him, and he made a puzzled face.

After they were served drinks and some food, Nexxa watched the dancer on the lonely stage. She thought about what Hooli had said about the girl that had posted on Instagram with the man that was partly responsible for ambushing Sergei. "When we leave here, let's get you a new phone, drive by the construction site, and then have you show me the places your cousin Ivan frequents."

"Okay." Srđan looked up from his plate.

"What did I just say?" Nexxa asked, turning her head slightly and squinting an eye.

"That you want to get phone, see the construction, and find my cousin."

"Yes, in that order."

After they stopped at a VIP store and Nexxa bought Srđan a new phone he drove them to the site where the Croatian Federation Tower was being built. Nexxa stepped out of the car and once again smelled Sergei. Back in the car the radio was on, and just as Srđan went to tune to another channel an advertisement for the State Ballet Theatre of Ukraine came on. "Don't change it," Nexxa said abruptly before the announcer could finish his list of the state officials that would be in attendance for the performance the next evening. "I need shoes and a dress."

"I have something you can borrow, size for woman," Srđan

laughed, toggling his head.

"I need to make a call. Can you pull over?" Nexxa called her contact for the designer she had used for her Ice Queen party dresses and explained what she needed. She gave her a name of another designer, Matija Vuica.

Srđan drove her to the atelier. "I just need about half an hour, and then I'll need to go to a drugstore," she told him as she exited the car. After a drink and a smoke, Nexxa's new friend in fashion showed Nexxa her new collection. A dress was chosen, and a pair of heels were borrowed.

Back at the house they had rented, Nexxa called Hooli. "Is he, Ivan, still communicating with the guy you found?"

"Yeah, you were right to go back to Zagreb. The calls between them are now pinging from the area."

Nexxa looked to the dress she had borrowed, which laid across the bed. She reached, feeling the soft viscose fabric. "I'm going to see him tomorrow."

"Who?"

"Ivan."

"Why? Nexxa, that isn't a good idea."

"Well, I have to. I have to see what he is. And I need you to get me VIP entry to the State Ballet Theatre of Ukraine. They are performing here tomorrow."

"Got it. And, uh, he likes men."

"Fuck. I didn't expect that." Nexxa exhaled. "Well, top or bottom?"

"Uh, uh," Hooli said, fumbling his mouse and pulling up a picture of Ivan. "Top. He's definitely a top."

Nexxa wore a column dress with one shoulder ruched and the other with a strap bearing a gold emblem, finished with a thigh-high slit. It was reminiscent of Gucci's current resort collection, and the pale blue complemented Nexxa's lavender blood. The steps to the theatre looked like they would be challenging in four-inch heels without an escort, it wasn't exactly like Srđan could walk in with her, until she reached them and with minimal effort she sprung to the top.

A Croatian *vampire* model was there confirming the VIP guest list. Nexxa spoke with poise when he asked for her name. He looked down at his iPad. "Ah yes, Ms. Davoren." Nexxa let a smile form, and when he waved his arm directing her in, she told him in Croatian to come find her in order to make one thousand euros.

Inside the theatre, Nexxa observed Ivan with a glass of prosecco mingling. When the *vampire* model left his post, once all the guests were accounted for, he found Nexxa lingering by the open bar. She slipped two hundred euros in his pocket and asked him if he knew which of the gentlemen congregating was the Minister of Physical Planning, Construction and State Assets, Ivan Jubić. He nodded. Then she told him before intermission that he needed to come into Ivan's view and then leave the hall and go to the men's room. But first, to turn around, and once she walked away, wink at him.

After Nexxa had quickly positioned a frame on the vanity of the men's room that contained a camera like the popular nanny cams, she took her seat, which allowed her a view of Ivan. She didn't need to make eye contact to see that he was enjoying some of the dancers, especially Alexander Litnov. According to the program guide, he was from Moldova. According to his tights, he was blessed. Approximately thirty-five minutes later as scene two started, Ivan stood and quietly excused himself. Once he exited the hall, Nexxa did the same. In the lobby she saw the *vampire* model walking with a slow enticing pace toward the men's room with Ivan not far behind. When he paused before pushing on the door, turning to smile at Ivan, Nexxa knew that it was a go.

The men's room was chilly but dimly lit with wall sconces and burgundy tapestries flanking the windows. Nexxa entered and saw the model adjusting his fortunate hair in the mirror above the sink. Ivan stood by the floor length mirror adjusting his bow tie. Staying out of their view she watched as Ivan approached the model, drawing his hand along his back. The model spun around, and Ivan drew his hand along his cheek. As their faces came closer, the model began to undo his pants. Ivan did the same.

"Minister, I believe you have a call from Mr. Fixit," Nexxa announced as she stepped further into the presence of their debauchery.

The model turned his face and zipped up his pants before giving a farewell caress to Ivan. Nexxa held her hand out with the remaining euros. The Minister spun around saying, "What is this about?"

"Mostly Catholic after the ethnic cleansing of the nineties," Nexxa started with a voice that exuded confidence, complementing a body that emanated elegance, as she moved over to the bathroom vanity. "Correct, no?"

"Who are you?"

"You are on camera," Nexxa continued, motioning to the obscure-looking wooden picture frame. Ivan swatted at the frame, almost missing it. The frame wobbled and Nexxa stabilized it.

"What do you want?" He raised his voice to match his height of six foot three.

Nexxa saw herself out of the corner of her eye in the floor length mirror and was reminded of herself in Paris with Quinn. How she was supposed to get information from him but failed before time ran out and Kilmer dragged her out of Hôtel Costes. This time, she was not going to let time run out. Not for Sergei.

"Are you familiar with the phrase *impotentia sexualis*?"

"I don't have time for this," Ivan huffed with the face of a pissed off gay man with extra icy blue balls as he moved toward the door.

"Sergei," Nexxa said, exuding the most confidence she had ever had.

Ivan turned, charging her and pushing her against the vanity as she withdrew a syringe and jabbed him in the hand. His eyes bulged.

"If I push it in further," Nexxa spoke as he grabbed her wrist, "diseased swine blood. You can buy it on the dark net. Just a trickle more and no more sexy time." Ivan slapped her face. Nexxa used her right hand to push her hair back from her cheek saying, "Be careful. You're on camera."

His phone rang, and Nexxa kept her thumb on the end of the syringe saying, "Answer it."

He shimmied the phone from his pocket and said, "Hello."

"Mr. Fixit and your dad grew up in Slatina. Like she said, mostly Catholic. That's a no-no for boys fucking boys. And now you are working with Mr. Fixit's son. I get it, running drugs is a faster way to your own jet share where you can fuck all the beautiful men from Eastern Europe to Rahm Emanuel," Hooli let out in one cocky breath.

Ivan let go of her wrist and reached beside her, lifting the frame and flipping it around to inspect it. "You're crazy," he snarled in an extra thick and less looking-for-sex Croatian accent. Nexxa took the opportunity to withdraw another syringe. This one had her lavender blood, and this time she jabbed it in his thigh and pushed the liquid all the way in. Ivan fell to his knees, lowering his head.

Nexxa lifted his chin saying, "Where is he?"

"How? How did you know?"

"Sergei. Tell me where he is!"

"Swine. Pigs in Gradec."

Nexxa removed both of the syringes and tucked them away in her clutch then grabbed the frame. Leaving the theatre, she called Srđan and tossed the frame into a trash bin.

"You have something in the dress," Srđan told her as they stood in the kitchen.

Nexxa stepped out of her heels, placing them on a kitchen chair, and said, "It's wine." Really, it was a spot of her lavender blood. "So we need..." Nexxa said, reaching for Srđan's smoke, taking a drag, "to go to a pig farm."

"Why a pig farm?" Srđan asked, removing another cigarette from his pack and lighting it.

"Sergei should be in Gradec. I looked on my phone, and there is a pig farm there."

After Nexxa went upstairs and undressed, she unfolded her map of Croatia. "Is Sergei in this area?" She held her pendulum over a section of the map that was east of Zagreb. Her pendulum idled. "Fuck!" Nexxa shouted.

Srđan hollered up the stairs, "You okay?"

"Yeah," she said, before he climbed the stairs to see her standing over her map.

"Maybe there is other way," he suggested, holding out his hands.

"I don't know. Fuck, that fucking prick!"

Nexxa plopped down on the bed and kicked the map. It shifted on the floor. She closed her eyes, saying in her mind, *Iliada. Iliada, what am I going to do?*

"Hey look!" Srđan said in a voice that sounded like he had just made a major scientific discovery.

Nexxa opened her eyes and saw him holding her pendulum. "What are you—" Nexxa stopped herself when she saw how fast the pendulum was moving.

Srđan knelt holding the pendulum closer to the map. "Here." He pointed, looking back to Nexxa.

"What is there? In that town?" Nexxa asked.

"I don't know. It was always small town."

"Take me now."

"It's dark."

"Srđan, whatever you need, more money. More money, I can get it," Nexxa expressed to him as she moved closer, looking him in the eyes.

"Okay. I drive you," he agreed, giving a single nod.

In the car Nexxa was quiet as she looked out at the landscape, seeing as much as she could take in as the dark was setting in. When the exit for the town of Gradec came up, Nexxa held her abdomen with her left hand and stretched out her fingers on her right hand, looking at her palm. *How long will I have this lavender blood?* she wondered.

Following the GPS, Srđan drove to the road that was the entrance to the Gradec Farm and pulled over. There were bright security lights and they saw armed men outside. Nexxa opened her car door a crack. "I just need to get a better look."

"Are you crazy?" Srđan turned off the car and the lights.

"Srđan, what else am I here for?" Nexxa stepped out of the car and started toward the edge of the gravel road that led to the farm. She stopped, Srđan exhaled in relief, and then she turned saying, "I, I can't smell him anymore."

"Okay, we can go. Come." Srđan waved her over to the car.

Back in the car, Nexxa looked at their location on her phone. She saw another farm pop up that she hadn't seen before. It was also in Gradec, in Zagreb County. "Okay, let's go to this farm," she said, holding her phone so he could see it.

"I can drive there, but what can we do?"

"I don't care. Just drive there."

The farm was a few miles away, and once again they noticed that this farm had security lights outside with armed guards. "Why are all of these farms heavily guarded?" Nexxa asked, looking to Srđan.

"We need some help. Maybe you ask Hooey," he suggested.

Nexxa exhaled, leaning her head back. "I—I don't know anymore." Once again, she got out of the car and walked, detecting Sergei. Then a gust of farm air blew, pieces of her hair fell from her ponytail, and she sniffed, struggling to smell a morsel of him. "Something's off," Nexxa announced as she sat back in the car and fastened her seat belt.

"So, we go back?" Srđan asked, taking a puff.

"Yeah, I guess for now."

Srđan turned around and they started their way back toward the main highway. "Wait!" Nexxa shouted as he approached the ramp to enter the highway.

He swerved to the shoulder and abruptly stopped. "You give me heart attack," he said, holding his chest, allowing a little laugh out.

Nexxa opened her passenger door and got out. She screamed and started crying tears of frustration. When she collected herself, she got back in and said nothing as they merged onto the highway and headed back to Zagreb.

He knocked on the front door and stood patiently for someone to answer. Srđan flushed the downstairs toilet and stepped out waving his hand to shush the smell and saw a figure through the glass pane by the front door. He tiptoed, looking out of the living room windows, morning sun in his eyes, before he answered the door and stood with a confused face. "I don't think we order Chinese food."

"I am here for Nexxa."

In her room, Nexxa's eyes widened as she heard them talking. She dropped her stones on the bed and dashed down the staircase. "Mr. Albert. You're here!" she said and then saw his bag bulge. "Flash!" She held both hands to her chest. Srđan shook his head, shrugging his shoulders. She escorted them in, taking ahold of the carry-on that Flash was in. "Oh... Iliada," Nexxa said, realizing that connecting with her sister was the reason Mr. Albert came to Croatia. She unzipped the bag and Flash hopped out.

Srđan jumped back. "You have a squirrel?" he asked.

"I will help you find the one with the white glow," Mr. Albert said stoically as he inspected the living room before looking over to the kitchen.

Nexxa held her face, lowering her head. When she looked up as tears came down her cheeks, she saw Flash fluttering around on the furniture before resting on a throw pillow. She laughed.

Wiping her face, Srđan handed her a paper towel. She said, "Thank you, Mr. Albert. I can't believe you came all this way." He held a hand up and gave a nod.

"How, uh, how you know him?" Srđan asked her.

"He's, my friend. My Teacher," Nexxa said affectionately.

"We can go now," he stated, and Flash hopped up and scurried over to the bag.

"Oh." Nexxa looked from him to Srđan. "Okay." Nexxa continued. Mr. Albert remained still and she ran upstairs and grabbed her purse. She opened the wardrobe and retrieved Sergei's gun, which she had managed to bring from Moscow. It turned out that using Sergei's concierge to book her flight awarded her Preclearance access at the airport and she breezed past the security line.

Nexxa rode in the back and filled in Mr. Albert. He listened without verbally acknowledging anything she said. Flash told her not to worry. Nexxa had Srđan drive them to the middle point between the two farms. They pulled over and all exited the car but Flash.

Mr. Albert positioned himself on the side of the road that had trees for a backdrop. Nexxa took her place beside him. Mr. Albert raised his arms open to the sky, and dark ascended from the mountains in the distance to the flat farmlands before them. Nexxa's heart pumped her lavender blood in sync with her breathing.

In the distance there was a speck of white. Nexxa and Mr. Albert crossed the street and got back into the car. Nexxa cracked her door and Flash said, "Srđan get back into the car." He took slow steps from his stone-frozen stance and returned to the driver's seat.

After a few moments, Nexxa leaned forward saying, "Srđan, start the car and we will guide you."

Not far, only a few turns, and they arrived outside of a place with a sign that read: Dalina Apartment. It had two stars. Nexxa got out of the car and her hair blew. She smelled Sergei. Nexxa tucked Sergei's gun into the back of her leggings. She told Srđan to wait with Flash and then she walked toward the home. Right away she saw a man standing outside of a smaller building smoking. He looked rugged and was probably in his forties; he looked to be the guard. As she approached him, he tossed his cigarette and shouted in Croatian, "Get out of here, this is private property!" She kept walking, gripping the syringe with her lavender blood she had hidden in her hand.

He pulled his gun, aiming and shouting. Nexxa smiled and her blonde locks blew in the convenient wind. She knew as soon as she spoke he would know she wasn't from around there. She ran her hand along her décolletage and pulled her top down, exposing a breast. He lowered his gun—she took a few more steps toward him—he reached with his dirty hand. Nexxa jabbed him with her syringe. She pushed the blood in. The guard dropped to his knees and Nexxa stepped past him to the small apartment that was across from the main home. She withdrew the gun and pushed open the unlocked door.

Nexxa froze. She saw photos of her covering the wall in front of her, some stabbed with knives. Then, she heard moaning and turned to see Sergei with his head lowered sitting tied to a chair. "Sergei!" she screamed, running over to him, placing the gun down, and kneeling before him. She lifted his head, seeing he was covered in blood and one eye was almost swollen shut. She ran over to a picture of herself and pulled the knife out. She cut his arms loose and he fell to his knees on the floor. Nexxa hovered over him, trying to pull him up. "Go... they threatened me. They will kill you," Sergei managed to say.

Suddenly, she was yanked and pulled by her legs across the room. Sergei breathed heavily, pushing himself up as he heard Nexxa scream. Mr. Fixit, with his old rough hands and a face that wore both sides of the Yugoslavian war, had a tight grip on her legs—dragging her out of the apartment and over to the back where he chopped wood.

Sergei saw his gun on the ground and reached for it with his shaky hand. Nexxa thrust on the ground screaming, trying to cut her wounded hand on anything—a rock, a stick. With her head up on a stump and an ax overhead, Mr. Albert appeared and raised the vibration, shifting the terrain. Mr. Fixit stumbled, falling to the ground, but still managed to hold onto his ax. Nexxa heard an explosion, followed by another one. Sergei, the greatest man from Russia, shot one of the worst men from the former Yugoslavia. Mr. Fixit slumped over; his brains were scattered, and blood was everywhere, his ax falling to Mother Earth.

Epilogue
Sacre Cour

The TV in the bedroom had an unremitting commercial of a desirable male model: Ibiza-tanned, dark hair, and just the right mix of pretty boy and ruggedness. "It's something for the man to aspire to," Flash informed her in his usual raspy voice. Nexxa turned, seeing him in the doorway as he fluttered in and landed on the dresser next to the TV. Nexxa lifted the remote and changed the television to another channel. "When he is ready to be the attractive man again," Flash continued with his creature chuckle. Nexxa looked to Sergei lying in bed, and she couldn't have been more attracted to a man who had subjected himself to torture for the sake of a woman with the wolfness, and unbeknownst to him—lavender blood.

Mr. Albert had been able to place Sergei in a spiritual coma until a private doctor could be retained. He had a swollen eye, broken ribs, a concussion, a stab wound in his shoulder, and was on the verge of more had Nexxa not found him when she did. For a few hours, he was asleep and feeling no pain. Hooli worked with Srđan on security for the home they were staying in, and Mr. Albert insisted on staying ready to raise the ground as a backup for Nexxa.

Outside, the dark seemed to come faster in the evenings even though it was early summer, perhaps because Nexxa was with a heart pumping, commanding, colorful blood. Standing with Srđan, she shared a cigarette, too tired to man one all by herself. "A year ago, I was shopping. In a cigar bar," Nexxa said as she began crying. "Flashing my fuckability," she continued, laughing through tears. Srđan did a shimmy dance, a mix of a Hawaiian and Gypsy dancer with the cigarette in his mouth. Nexxa laughed so hard she had to grasp her abdomen. "Fuck, Srđan, I just peed myself."

Mr. Albert opened the back door and stepped out. "I had a cigarette once," he announced as he slipped one from the pack on the table. Nexxa and Srđan burst into laughter. When they collected themselves, they saw him blowing smoke rings. "See, I can smoke too." A Croatian, a Canadian with wolfness, and a Chinese man with inexplicable power, all laughed understanding, feeling, seeing the humor.

"Where is my gun?" Sergei asked as he awoke, sounding like an old man. Nexxa was standing at the end of the bed folding some washcloths she had used to clean his face.

"Sergei," she said softly, moving over and caressing his face. He used one arm, the other too weak, to push himself up in the bed. She grabbed another pillow, and he leaned as best he could so she could prop him up. "I have your gun. It's in the nightstand," she told him. He attempted to clear his throat, and she started to leave, saying, "I'll get you some water."

Nexxa returned with a bottle of water, poured some into a glass, and handed it to him. He consumed it all in one gulp. She refilled the glass and he drank that. "We're still in Croatia," he commented.

"Yes." Nexxa lightly nodded her head. "Two days here in this house. And Srđan and I were here for two days before that."

"How did you find me?"

"Well, Hooli."

"Yeah," Sergei responded with a heavy face.

"I... I heard the gunshots," Nexxa explained, grasping her forehead. "And then, I came here. Hooli arranged for Srđan to pick me up and drive me to Rijeka." Nexxa swallowed, trying to hold back from crying. Sergei reached for her hand. Nexxa lowered her face and used her other hand to hide the emotions she had accumulated from Russia to Dublin to Croatia. When Flash fluttered into the room, Nexxa dabbed under her eyes and introduced them. Sergei almost smiled.

They heard Srđan downstairs; he was trying to explain what Ajvar, a Croatian condiment, was. They could hear him say, "For meat, like ketchup." Then Mr. Albert, "Ahh, yes."

Flash asked, "Will your human man friend be joining us for dinner in the dining area?"

"No, no, I'll be bringing up food for him," Nexxa explained. Flash fluttered up to her, and she held out her palm; he rested in her hand before giving a respectful nod and fluttering away downstairs.

Nexxa lifted Sergei's antibiotic. "This was prescribed for you to take once you woke up. The doctor had given you an antibiotic intravenously." Sergei lightly nodded as Nexxa placed a pill in his hand and handed him his glass of water. "No sexy nurse, though," she said, twisting her head with a smirk.

Sergei laughed with his eyes and then swallowed the pill. "You're *my* sexy nurse," he joked through his wounded face.

There was a feeling in the house that couldn't be described, and no scent could be used to convey the mood. Sergei mostly slept, and Mr. Albert had left with Flash. He had received an invitation to Vespers de the Illumed in Rome. Although he had no obligation to The Grāz, he liked to keep friendly with the organization. Nexxa tried to rest when Sergei slept, but she was having unfriendly dreams—the kind that begged to send messages. Srđan chain-smoked and had taken on the responsibility of watching the app for the temporary security cameras that were set up around the exterior of the house.

Hooli communicated hourly with Srđan, but this time asked to speak to Nexxa.

"I think it's time to return to Moscow," he said, sounding like he was defeated.

"Why? Besides the obvious?"

Hooli cleared his throat. "I can protect you, Sergei, better there."

"I can protect him too," Nexxa responded with a defensive voice. She took a much-needed hard breath and let her head fall forward. "Sorry, I'm not sleeping well. Or sleeping."

"Yeah, so the security there will only alert you of an intruder, not, well, prevent someone from getting in. Sergei's house has better doors, everything."

Nexxa thought back to the woman who had made her way into Sergei's house, to Diane perching on the roof of Bogdan's izba. "Yeah, I know." But she didn't. Where were they safe?

Before Nexxa said more, Hooli rattled off, "So, I'm seeing a report of Ivan, the minister, being found unresponsive at the ballet. On the floor of the men's room."

Nexxa's breathing competed with her heavy and tired head. She lowered the phone and held a hand to her chest. Srđan jumped up from the kitchen table, saying, "What's problem? You okay?" Nexxa nodded yes. He took the phone from her and said, "Okay, what's going on, Hooey?"

"Yeah, just the local news about Ivan."

"Is he dead, something?" asked Srđan.

"No, I don't think that's the case. He's being treated in the hospital. Might release him to be with family. She did good though," Hooli explained, and after they talked about the security for the house, they ended the call.

Nexxa thought she heard Sergei calling out for her. She entered his room upstairs; he was asleep but sweaty when she felt his forehead. After she wet a washcloth, placing it on his head, Nexxa sat beside him and lifted his phone. She tapped on the app for photos and swiped through them. She stopped on a photo that looked like the picture that Sergei's captors had used and stabbed with knives. Nexxa turned with the thought of asking him when he took that photo. Then, when enlarging the picture, she discovered that he must have taken it when she was sitting with his babushka after she had hidden eggs for Natina. Easter.

Srđan stayed awake, mixing coffee, cigarettes, and vodka. He kept watch from his phone and routinely checked the windows around the house. He read the news that Ivan had been released from the hospital. Once awake, he wouldn't want to be interviewed. How could he? What would he say? That a beautiful American woman assaulted him? From what Srđan could determine, the killing of Mr. Fixit wasn't being talked about in the local news or the underground.

Nexxa awoke from another dream and turned over, checking on Sergei, seeing he had awoken. She gave him a pain pill, and when he fell back asleep, she needed to see something else besides the constant image of herself with a knife.

"Have you been awake this whole time?" she asked Srđan as she entered the kitchen.

"Oh, I can smoke outside," he replied, fanning smoke from his cigarette before tossing it and stepping a foot outside to smash it out.

Nexxa held up a hand. "So, you know that Ivan is in the hospital. I'm worried about the guys he hired to take Sergei."

Srđan shook his head in acknowledgment, rubbing a hand over his head. He had never asked her what she did to Ivan. He didn't need to know. Something told him she had some sort of specialized training, military. "Hooey said Sergei should go back to Moscow, right? I… I can come. I can help."

Nexxa let out a breath and moved closer, hugging him.

"Thank you for everything," she said, resisting the urge for a cigarette. After she made a cup of tea and asked Srđan about his parents, she told him good night—late night, since it was three a.m.

Srđan placed his cigarettes on the kitchen table and removed one, slipping it into a pocket in the front of his leather jacket. He threw back a shot of vodka and took one more look out of the kitchen window before turning off the lamps in the living room and pulling the front door closed, locking it.

"I'm here for Ivan," Srđan said into the intercom.

"No visitors," the man spoke harshly through the speaker.

Srđan stepped back from the building; he could see the apartment on the fourth floor. No balcony. He had only visited his cousin at his apartment twice, and the second time, he was so drunk from champagne that he only remembered one of Ivan's entourage coaxing him to take off his shirt. An older woman approached the entrance with her dog and narrowly let herself in the building, looking back to ensure the front entrance door closed behind her. *Always with the small dogs. Fuck, diarrhea!* Srđan thought as he looked down to a trail of dog poop on the sidewalk. With his only easy port of entry out, he trotted to the street behind the building.

The door was easy to open. He used a building stone from some construction on the structure next door to break the door lock open. Inside, he scaled the stairs. He knocked on 4Q. "Hello," he heard before he jammed the door with the stone block. The man at the door wrestled him to the floor, and Srđan used the stone to push against his neck, managing to maneuver himself up, pinning the man against the wall and crushing his throat. The man slumped. Srđan stepped back, shaking. He dropped the block and looked down, seeing blood and remnants from the stone scattered on the parquet floor. Breathing heavily, he looked down the hall toward the bedrooms before he picked up his weapon.

Ivan was covered up under a fluffy white duvet. Shrunken face, which surrendered to the few twigs of hair left. "You. Have. Cancer?" Srđan questioned, scrunching his face. Then he shook his head, realizing what a stupid thought that was. *Nexxa* had been able to do this. He thought about how Sergei looked. What Ivan's men, Mr. Fixit would have done to Sergei, to Nexxa.

Ivan's eyes were closed—he smashed the stone down.

Srđan spun around, seeing the closet and opening it. *What the fuck?* A poster of Rahm Emanuel hung, framed on the back wall. *Hmm, he is good-looking man.* A mobile phone rang. Srđan jumped, and then he saw a purple bag among the hanging suits. It had "Amsterdam" imprinted on it. In went the block. Walking down the hall, he caught a glimpse of himself in the mirror of the open bathroom. He grabbed some toilet paper, wiping his forehead and mouth, feeling like he might throw up. Careful, he flushed the paper and then lifted a bottle of cologne, spraying some on.

Nexxa was downstairs and on the phone with Hooli when she heard Srđan open the front door. "Hold on, he's back," she said to Hooli and stood. "Where were you?" her voice sounded like a scorned woman.

"I have something I take care of," Srđan managed to say, wiping the perspiration from his face.

Nexxa took a step away from the sofa, then looked down at the gun on the coffee table—Sergei's gun. Srđan walked into the living room, and Nexxa reached for the gun. "What? Something happen?" Srđan spit out.

Nexxa lifted the pistol and aimed. "Answer the question," she demanded.

"I—"

"You fuck with me, I'll kill you."

"Nexxa. Nexxa. Calm down! I tracked him. He was at Ivan's."

Nexxa kept her eyes on Srđan and lowered herself so she could lift her phone. "What is that, Hooli? Where was he?"

"He was at Ivan's apartment. It's over."

"What's over?"

"I did for Sergei," Srđan offered, holding up a hand while the other held the Amsterdam bag.

Nexxa plopped the phone down, and it landed on the floor. Srđan stepped closer, a hand still up, and slowly leaned down, lifted her phone and placed it back on the coffee table.

"Hooli! It's just me. No one else is here to help me protect Sergei," Nexxa pleaded, holding back tears.

"Ivan is dead. When the nurse came, she called the police. I heard the report come in." Hooli said. "It's okay, Nexxa. You are safe." Nexxa counted at least three more people who had been working with Ivan, but she lowered the gun.

"And how do you know?" she asked as Srđan put the purple bag down in an armchair. "How?" she persisted, looking down at the phone. Srđan moved an open hand slowly toward the bag. "Open it," Nexxa directed. Srđan pulled out the bloody stone.

She felt her lavender glow pulse, and her lavender blood moved from her toes to her toned legs, daring abdomen, and in-love heart. Her coveted breasts, then her throat.

Nexxa raised the gun. She shot.

A man working for Mr. Fixit who had followed Srđan back to the house fell against the entryway wall, screaming, grasping his leg.

"Nexxa!" Sergei called out.

Nexxa took a step forward. He started crying, pushing himself up. Dragging his leg, he staggered out of the front door. Nexxa followed him, watching as he made it across the street to his car and dropped his keys.

Nexxa returned, and Srđan was there with eyes bigger than his bald head. "It's over," she said, closing and *locking* the front door. They both looked toward the staircase, hearing Sergei. Nexxa handed Srđan the gun and ran upstairs.

Nexxa lay next to Sergei. She said nothing—she would need him to heal before explaining her lavender blood.

Stalk Smeared Vampire

If you liked *Wolf's Gliss* please leave a review!

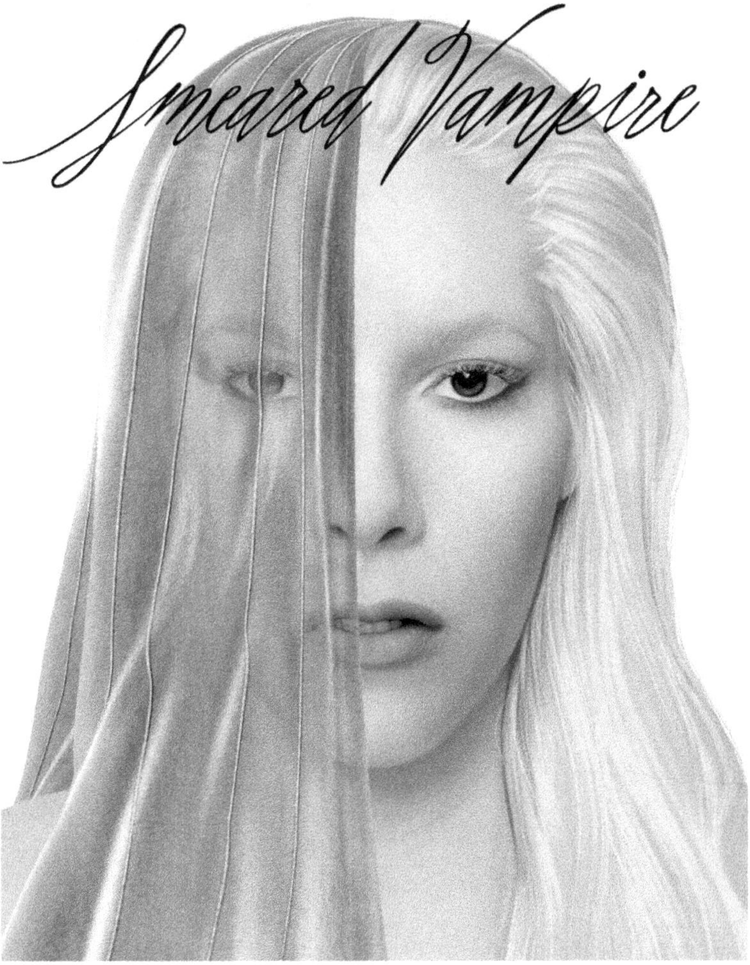

www.ingramcontent.com/pod-product-compliance
Lightning Source LLC
LaVergne TN
LVHW010306070526
838199LV00065B/5455